LIGHT TOUCH

STEPHEN LEATHER
LIGHT TOUCH

HODDER &
STOUGHTON

First published in Great Britain in 2017 by Hodder & Stoughton
An Hachette UK company

1

Copyright © Stephen Leather 2017

The right of Stephen Leather to be identified as the Author of the Work has been
asserted by him in accordance with the Copyright, Designs and Patents Act 1988.

A CIP catalogue record for this title is available from the British Library

Hardback ISBN 978 1 473 60412 4
Trade Paperback ISBN 978 1 473 60413 1
eBook ISBN 978 1 473 60411 7

Typeset in Plantin Light by Palimpsest Book Production Limited,
Falkirk, Stirlingshire

Printed and bound by Clays Ltd, St Ives plc

Hodder & Stoughton policy is to use papers that are natural, renewable
and recyclable products and made from wood grown in sustainable forests.
The logging and manufacturing processes are expected to conform to the
environmental regulations of the country of origin.

Hodder & Stoughton Ltd
Carmelite House
50 Victoria Embankment
London EC4Y 0DZ

www.hodder.co.uk

For Sharan

Matt Standing wasn't a great fan of defecating into plastic bags, but when you were five days into an operation that would hopefully lead to the death of one of the world's most wanted terrorists, there wasn't much choice.

Sergeant Standing was on the top floor of a half-destroyed building on the outskirts of a town called Idlib in the north-west of Syria. The house had been hit by a missile a year earlier and all the occupants had been killed. Satellite surveillance photographs had identified it as being the ideal choice for the mission – it was on a hill overlooking the town and had easy access from the rear. The nearest neighbour was several hundred yards away and, other than the occasional browsing goat, no one went near the place. And it had a perfect view of the target house, almost a mile away.

There was no mains water and no electricity. They had brought water in plastic bottles and used night-vision goggles when they needed to see in the dark. Food consisted mainly of dry rations, though they had some fruit and hard-boiled eggs too.

There were three SAS troopers with Standing. Karl Williams was the group's medic, a strapping six-footer from Bristol, a farmer's son who had decided that a military career might be more fulfilling than milking cows. Grant Parker was an explosive expert. As a kid he'd loved blowing things up – everything from tree stumps to live frogs – and the

SAS had turned him into the demolition expert he'd always wanted to be. He was also a trained sniper and a black belt in Shotokan karate. The third member of the unit was John Cox, the oldest of the group with two decades of SAS service under his belt. Cox was a big man with thinning red hair, a linguist, fluent in Arabic and near-fluent in Kurdish, with a smattering of European languages. He was also a signals specialist, in charge of the unit's radio and satphone.

They had set up the observation point in the bedroom overlooking the target house. The staircase had been made of wood and had pretty much been destroyed. They had piled rubble against a wall so that they could reach the upper floor. They slept in the rear bedroom, where most of the ceiling had been destroyed, and used the roof to carry out their bodily functions. At night they peed off the terrace and onto the rear garden. They stored the faeces-filled bags in a pile against the wall and would take them away when the operation was over.

They had reached the house on quad bikes that they had hidden in a ravine some ten miles away, then walked under cover of darkness wearing night-vision goggles to find their way. Nowhere in Syria was safe, but Idlib was under the control of Islamic State and one of the most dangerous places in the world for Westerners. When Syria's civil uprising had burst into life in 2011, Idlib had been a focal point of the protests and fighting, and ownership of the city kept passing between the rebels and the Syrian Army. The area had once been a source of olives, cotton and wheat, and the cherries produced there were said to be the best in the region. Small factories pressed the olives and the oil was sold around the country. No longer. In recent years the main export had been refugees, and families from the area could now be found scattered across Europe in their thousands. The town's most successful football club was Omaya Sport but in 2015 it had had to withdraw from the Syrian professional league after an airstrike had destroyed its headquarters. Normal life had stopped in Idlib and there were no signs of it returning in the near future. Life meant survival, day-to-day getting by in a war zone.

Standing went back into the front room and took up his position again, lying prone and studying the building in the distance. The house they were watching was a simple two-storey sandstone building, no different from hundreds of others in the town and a match to the one they were holed up in: small windows, a roof terrace from which laundry fluttered, metal bars on the ground-floor windows. The building wasn't the least bit special, but its occupants were. Specifically one occupant, a man of seventy-nine, who was, that very day, turning eighty. Like most Muslims, Houman Ahmadi did not celebrate his birthday, the birthdays of his children or of their children. Birthdays were *haram*. Forbidden. Like bacon and alcohol.

Houman lived quietly in the house. He was still active, despite his years, and each evening would sit on the roof terrace smoking hand-rolled cigarettes and drinking hot mint tea prepared by one of the two women who took care of him. One was his daughter-in-law, the widow of his third son, the other a distant cousin, whose family had died in a suicide bombing in the town's market: a young man had detonated a truck full of fertiliser explosives as a convoy of police vehicles drove by. Eight police officers and two dozen civilians had died that day and dozens more were injured. Houman's cousin had lost her husband and two children, most of her left arm and the sight in her left eye.

Houman had six children, fifteen grandchildren and twenty great-grandchildren. Most of his family had left the town soon after the fighting had started but he had refused to go. Three of his children had crossed the border to the north with their families and were in the main refugee camp in the south-eastern border town of Suruç. More than forty thousand refugees lived in the sprawling tent city with two hospitals, a dozen clinics and classrooms for more than ten thousand children. Two of his sons had taken their families to the Kilis Öncüpınar Accommodation Facility, a hundred miles to the west of Suruç, a makeshift town built from more than twenty thousand shipping containers where more than fifteen thousand refugees had sought sanctuary. Ten of Houman's grandchildren – all fit young men – had set out on the long walk to Europe in the hope of getting asylum there. The families had given them whatever they had, knowing they were a lifeline. If one was granted the Holy Grail of citizenship in a European country, they would all be able to follow.

Houman had one more son, his youngest, soon to turn forty. His name was Abdul-Karim and he was one of the most wanted terrorists in the world. He was why Standing and his colleagues were defecating into plastic bags and eating ration packs that tasted of cardboard. Abdul-Karim Ahmadi – known by the men hunting him as AKA – was one of the top bombmakers and strategists for the Khorasan group, made up of hardline al-Qaeda terrorists who were determined to take the fight to the United States and Europe. He had been in America's Top 10 Most Wanted list for more than a year, and there had been several failed attempts to assassinate him. The CIA had kept Houman Ahmadi under observation for more than a year, hoping that Abdul-Karim would get in touch. Houman had no phone or internet connection, and the only visitors he had were an imam from his local mosque and a shopkeeper who delivered provisions several times a week. He was just an old man getting to the end of his life. But in recent weeks his watchers had noticed a change in him. During his evening visits to the roof terrace, he was clearly finding it difficult to walk and needed the assistance of one of his carers to get up the stairs. Then one evening he was connected to a drip and both carers were needed to get him onto the roof so that he could smoke his cigarettes and drink his tea. Houman was dying, the CIA analysts at Langley, Virginia, had decided. And before he died, there was a good chance that his son, Abdul-Karim, would visit to pay his respects.

The equipment they would use to bring about the demise of Abdul-Karim, should he ever turn up at his father's house, was at Standing's side. It was about the same size and shape as an old-fashioned slide projector but it had nothing to do with entertainment and everything to do with destruction. It was a laser target designator, manufactured by US defence giant Northrop Grumman. Those who used it referred to it as a SOFLAM, which stood for Special Operations Forces Laser Acquisition Marker. The technique of using lasers to guide in missiles had been used to great effect in Afghanistan and Iraq, and the Americans were determined to make full use of it in Syria. The SOFLAM that Standing had been given was the PEQ-1C, which used only one battery rather than the five that were needed to power the earlier versions: the new model had replaced the flashlamp-pumped laser with a diode-pumped laser, using passive cooling. The P meant man-portable. The E designated it as equipment that used a laser. And the Q meant special. That was what Standing had been told by the Navy SEAL who had given it to him. Standing didn't know the technical details but he did know that if he pointed it at a building less than ten kilometres away and pressed the magic button, the target would be bathed in a pulsing laser that was invisible to the naked eye but could clearly be seen by a drone fifty thousand feet in the air. The drone would release a Hellfire missile, and sensors in its nose would take it to the target with pinpoint accuracy.

Dan 'Spider' Shepherd was not a fan of defecating into plastic bags, though he had done his fair share of it during his years with the SAS. But working long hours on surveillance operations for MI5 meant that toilet breaks couldn't be pre-planned. Among the equipment packed into the back of the Openreach van, there was a pack of self-sealing plastic sandwich bags. The van was the perfect choice for a surveillance vehicle: it was fairly roomy in the back and there were hundreds on the streets of London every day, many parked by the roadside as their technicians went about their business, maintaining the fibres, wires and cables that kept the country connected. On the off-chance that a member of the public got a look inside, the racks of surveillance and recording equipment wouldn't seem out of place.

Shepherd was in his early forties and his two colleagues were almost a decade younger, but he was clearly the fittest of the three. MI5 generally wasn't concerned about fitness levels: the organisation regarded the fight against terrorism as a cerebral one and brought in physical expertise when it was needed. There were three Armed-Response Vehicles close by, each with three highly trained firearms officers on board. It was a big operation: the intel supplied by Shepherd's boss – Jeremy Willoughby-Brown, presently ensconced in an operation room in Thames House – was that the object of the surveillance was planning to carry out a major terrorist incident, sooner rather than later.

Janet Rayner, a pretty no-nonsense brunette, her shoulder-length hair tied up with a scrunchie, was manning the comms. She had a cut-glass accent but had grown up on a rough council estate in north Manchester and had spent three years as an electrical engineer on cargo ships, running back and forth to the Far East, before joining MI5. She was in her early thirties but was still asked for ID in pubs and bars.

The youngest member of the surveillance team was handling the video feeds. Perversely, Paul Brennan looked a good ten years older than his true age, mainly because of his receding hair and bad posture, which he blamed on a childhood spent bent over a laptop. Brennan had a personal-hygiene problem, but that hadn't become apparent until they'd been stuck in the back of the van. Body odour was always a problem on stakeouts, but the van had little in the way of ventilation and Brennan clearly wasn't a fan of anti-perspirants.

All three of the team were wearing Openreach overalls and headsets. Shepherd was the only one who had drawn a firearm – a SIG-Sauer P226, the 9mm model and, in Shepherd's opinion, one of the best-balanced handguns available. It had no external safety but had three safety controls – the slide stop, the magazine release and the de-cocker – which meant that it could safely be carried with ten rounds in the magazine and one in the chamber. It nestled under his left armpit in a nylon holster.

Further along the road a black cab was parked with its light off and two passengers in the back. The driver was a middle-aged MI5 surveillance officer. His passengers were Counter-terrorist Specialist Firearms Officers. They had replaced their wolf-grey fire-proof uniforms with plainclothes jackets and jeans, and while they usually went about their business with AR-15 CQB carbines, for this operation they were carrying Glock 17 handguns in underarm holsters. If more firearms support was needed, the three ARVs would be on the scene in seconds, BMW SUVs each with three uniformed officers on board.

At either end of the street MI5 surveillance experts were kitted out as motorbike couriers, and Shepherd had another surveillance vehicle – a driving instructor's car in British School of Motoring livery. The driver was an MI5 surveillance officer, and his female passenger, holding a clipboard, was a CTSFO. She had a Glock in the door compartment next to her.

'Tango One is on the move,' said Brennan.

Tango One was a second-generation Somalian, who had spent his whole life in north London. His parents had fled war-torn Somalia in the early nineties, selling all their belongings to pay for their passage to the UK. The father was a doctor, the mother a teacher, and they had made new lives for themselves in their adopted country, raising four children. Dr and Mrs Daar did everything they could do to fit in. Mrs Daar always wore a traditional Somalian *shash* headscarf when she went out, but she teamed it with Western clothing. Dr Daar wore a suit most of the time, even when he wasn't working at the local hospital. They had given their children Western names and didn't object when their two daughters opted not to cover their hair. The girls had both gone on to study medicine, one at Edinburgh University, the other in Manchester. Their elder son was a computer programmer, working for Sony in their video-games division. The younger was the only member of the Daar family who had not inte-grated into British life. In fact, he held his parents and siblings in contempt and had moved out of the family home when he was sixteen. He had rejected the name his parents had given him – Alan – and now called himself Ali Mohammed. He had also rejected Western clothing in favour of the ankle-length dress known as a *kameez*, had grown a long, bushy beard, and had moved into a shared house with half a dozen young Muslim men in Stoke Newington.

Ali Mohammed did not have a driving licence. He either travelled by public transport or had a friend drive him. Over the last week it had been the same man who had picked him up, a British-born Pakistani by the name of Tariq Tareen, designated as Tango Two, who attended the same mosque as Daar. Tareen had been placed on MI5's watch list not long after he had returned from a six-month visit to Pakistan three years earlier, ostensibly to attend a cousin's wedding but almost certainly because he had been invited to an ISIS training camp on the Pakistan–Afghanistan border. At the time Tareen had slipped in and out of the country without anyone noticing, but an informer at the mosque had supplied a list of young men he claimed had attended the training camp. As a result, Five had put Tareen under surveillance. He ran a pro-jihadist website from his bedroom in his parents' terraced house in Southall, and was a regular at anti-Israel demonstrations in the city.

Like Daar, Tareen had an unkempt beard, but he favoured more Western clothes, usually a quilted jacket with baggy trousers and a black-and-white checked scarf tied loosely around his neck. He drove a red Nissan Juke. During the month that Shepherd and his team had been watching the two men, they had made frequent visits to a storage facility in Hammersmith. Daar had rented a large storage unit and, over the past two weeks, had been stocking it with everything he would need to construct small but powerful bombs. After his second visit to the storage facility, MI5 technicians had installed a tiny CCTV camera in the ceiling and had kept the unit under twenty-four-hour surveillance. Daar and Tareen had visited several electronics supply firms, purchasing wiring and soldering irons, and chemicals that could be used to produce explosives, including acetone, hydrogen peroxide, sulphuric acid and more than a dozen bags of ammonium nitrate fertiliser. Twice the men had driven up north and parked at the London Gateway service station between junctions two and four on the M1. There they had been met by two British-born Pakistanis from Leeds and transferred a number of bags to the Nissan. Shepherd's team had identified the men from Leeds – both were on MI5 watch lists.

'Victor One is pulling up now,' said Rayner. That was the Nissan Juke. Tariq Tareen was at the wheel and had been followed from his house in Kilburn, north-west London.

'Tango Three is on the move,' said a voice over the radio. It was Steve Turner, one of MI5's top surveillance experts. He was sitting inside a second Openreach van, stationed outside a house in Ealing, in charge of a second team that was ready and waiting to follow Tango Three – an Iraqi who had arrived in the UK two years earlier. The Security Service knew that Abdul Hakim Khalid was an Iraqi but the Home Office had granted him asylum as a Syrian refugee based on fake papers he had obtained in Turkey. Khalid was one of tens of thousands of migrants who had walked across Europe and arrived in France, claiming to be a child. In fact, he was already twenty-three years old and had been shaving for seven years. A shopkeeper in Bristol – a genuine Syrian refugee, who had been in the country for five years – had agreed to claim that the new arrival was his cousin and Khalid had been brought into the country in the autumn of 2016. After a brief photo opportunity with his 'cousin', Khalid moved to London where he stayed with a group of former ISIS fighters who had all, one way or another, lied their way into the United

Kingdom. MI5 had the house under constant surveillance and had obtained warrants to tap the phones of all the men who lived there.

Khalid had visited the storage unit with Daar several times, sometimes just the two of them, sometimes with other occupants of the house in Ealing.

'Tango Four is with him,' said Turner, over the radio. 'They're getting into Victor Two.'

Victor Two was a white van owned by one of the men in the house, though they all took turns to drive it. It was taxed and insured and had never been issued with a speeding ticket or parking fine. Tango Four was a British-born Pakistani. His parents had lived in the unforgiving border area where Pakistan butted against Afghanistan and had fled when their home had been destroyed by a Russian missile in 1987, killing their three children as they lay in their beds.

It had taken the parents two years to reach England, and another five passed before they were granted citizenship. Their son Mahnoor was born shortly after Mr and Mrs Bhutta had received their British passports. They were committed Muslims and had brought up their son to follow the ways of Islam: they made sure he prayed five times a day and attended religious lessons at their local mosque. It was at the mosque that Mahnoor was taught that Muslims were at war, that the West wanted them dead, and that it was the duty of every Muslim to fight back. A young imam at the mosque had opened Mahnoor's eyes and shown him the true meaning of the Koran. Once Mahnoor reached his teens he spent more time at the Finsbury Park mosque, where he studied under Abu Hamza, the Egyptian cleric who preached Islamic fundamentalism and militant Islamism before his extradition to the United States. There, he was sentenced to life imprisonment for terrorism offences.

Abu Hamza's imprisonment further radicalised Mahnoor, and he was sent for intensive training in Afghanistan, co-incidentally less than fifty miles from the house where the Bhuttas had once lived. On his return to the United Kingdom he had moved into the house where Ali Mohammed lived. It was the Americans who told MI5 that Mahnoor had attended the ISIS training camp and provided details of how he had entered and left Afghanistan, but by then he was already on the Security Service's watch list.

For the next thirty minutes the teams kept the two vehicles under surveillance as they drove through the early-morning traffic. It soon became clear that both vehicles were heading for the storage facility in Hammersmith but they didn't relax for a second. Shepherd knew that counter-surveillance techniques often played on the tendency for watchers to get bored by predictability and took advantage of lapses in concentration, so he kept his group on their toes by constantly changing lead vehicles and routes. Turner did the same with his.

Victor One arrived at the storage facility first and parked close to the main building. It was open twenty-four hours a day, though security was more reliant on CCTV than staff walking around. All visitors had to report to Reception where they showed ID, then walked through into the main building, which housed hundreds of individual units, from small ones not much bigger than a safety deposit box to spaces capable of holding a houseful of furniture or a car.

The larger units were equipped with fluorescent lights but none had its own power supply. That lack suggested the chemicals would be moved elsewhere to be processed.

'Victor Two is stopping,' said Turner, over the radio.

Shepherd stiffened, wondering what was happening. 'What is Victor Two's location?'

'On the main road, close to Hammersmith Tube station,' said Turner.

'I have eyeball,' said a courier on Turner's team. 'Looks like he's picking someone up. IC4 male, mid-thirties, beard, white skullcap, long black coat and Nike trainers.'

'Right. He's designated Alpha One,' said Turner.

'Alpha One is getting into Victor Two,' said the courier. 'Victor Two is now mobile again.'

Rayner called up footage from a camera at the front of the storage facility. MI5's technicians had arranged to take all CCTV feeds from the facility when they had put the hidden camera into the unit's ceiling. 'Tango One and Tango Two are waiting,' she said.

'That's unusual,' said Shepherd. 'Normally they meet inside.'

'Picking someone up is a new one too,' said Brennan. 'Maybe they need more manpower.'

'Here they come,' said Rayner, her eyes on the CCTV footage. The white van pulled up next to the Nissan. Abdul Hakim Khalid and Mahnoor Bhutta climbed out of the van and Alpha One joined them. Ali Mohammed and Tariq Tareen got out of the Nissan and all five men embraced each other.

Shepherd watched the screen as the five Asians walked to the entrance and went inside. Rayner flicked through to another feed, this one showing the reception area. Abdul Hakim Khalid and Alpha One were talking to the woman handling the comms. Alpha One took out his wallet and showed her his ID, then signed a form on a clipboard.

'Are you seeing this, Jeremy? Alpha One is signing in, not Ali Mohammed.'

Willoughby-Brown swore. Alpha One wasn't known to them, which meant that if there was a storage unit in his name it wouldn't have come to their attention.

The five men pushed through double doors to the main storage area. Rayner flicked through the various CCTV feeds from the facility. She flicked on to one camera just as the men walked out of its field of vision. 'There they are,' said Shepherd, then put up his hands when Rayner threw him a withering look. 'Sorry.'

She clicked on another feed. And another. 'I can't get a view of the area they're in,' she said.

'Are there blind spots?' asked Shepherd.

'There shouldn't be,' she said. Views flicked by on her main screen. 'But I can't find them.'

'Jeremy, this is a totally different scenario we've got here. Did we know there was another storage unit?'

'If I'd known I'd have told you, obviously,' said Willoughby-Brown.

Shepherd wasn't sure that was true because, more often than not, Willoughby-Brown operated on the need-to-know principle. 'We've no idea what they've got in there,' said Shepherd.

'Can you get a body to walk by for a visual?' asked Willoughby-Brown. 'We need to know which container it is and what's in it.'

'We have a watcher wearing a company uniform, but there aren't many people wandering around so we have to be careful,' said Shepherd. 'But, yes, I'm getting eyes on now. He'll drop by Reception first to find out the unit number.'

'I wasn't meaning to teach you to suck eggs,' said Willoughby-Brown.

'And I wasn't taking offence,' said Shepherd. 'I'm always grateful for your input.' He tried to keep the sarcasm out of his voice, but from the way that Rayner was grinning he knew he'd failed. He looked over at Brennan. 'Get Lofty on the case, will you?'

Brennan flashed him a thumbs-up.

Willoughby-Brown's voice faded and Shepherd realised he was talking to someone else at his end. After a few seconds he was back. 'Sorry, Daniel, we're checking the feeds from the storage company and they've disappeared.'

Rayner was clicking though the various CCTV feeds from the storage company, frowning intently.

'Any joy, Janet?' asked Shepherd.

'I think they've disabled the cameras where they are.'

'Did you hear that, Jeremy?'

'I did,' said Willoughby-Brown. 'We need to know for sure if this is a technical problem or if the targets have done this themselves. Because if they've blocked the feed that means it could be time-sensitive.'

'I'm on it,' said Shepherd.

Brennan twisted around on his stool. 'Lofty's going to Reception and then he'll do a walk-by.'

David 'Lofty' Loftus was unusually tall for a watcher, closer to seven feet than six. Most MI5 surveillance experts were genuine grey men or women, with no unusual features that would be remembered, no unusual hair colours, neither too ugly nor too handsome. Average. That way they could blend more easily into their environment. The blander they were, the more they blended. But Loftus was so tall that he attracted attention wherever he went, and several times a day he'd hear a whispered 'How tall do you think he is?' behind him. Because of his height, Loftus usually did his surveillance from a vehicle, ideally one with plenty of legroom, but on this occasion he'd been assigned to the storage company and was wearing one of their security uniforms. The only spare uniform to hand had been extra-large and Loftus was the only one it fitted. It was dark brown with the name of the company on the shoulders and came with a black belt and a transceiver in a holster. He decided to remove the MI5 comms in case he got up close and personal with any of the Tangos: it wasn't the sort of equipment used by run-of-the-mill security staff. He'd tuned the transceiver to a frequency the team was using, then put it back into its holster. The girl in Reception had given him the number of the unit. The customer's name was Mahnoor Bhutta and he had shown a UK driving licence as identification. He was a relatively new client and had booked the unit just two weeks earlier. She had happily answered Loftus's questions – she had been told that the company was cooperating with the police on a drugs case and that from time to time officers would be wearing company uniforms.

Loftus walked away from the desk and radioed in the details to Rayner, using the company transceiver, then pushed open the double doors that led to a corridor with bright yellow doors, left and right. They had keypad locks but many of the owners had also installed padlocks as an extra security measure. He went left, then pushed through another set of doors. There was a CCTV camera in a black plastic dome at either end of the corridor, but neither had a blinking red light to show they were working.

'I'm in the corridor. The CCTV cameras look like they're out of commission,' he said.

He walked slowly along. The unit Bhutta used was number 432. The door was closed and the padlock had been removed. Loftus walked past it, then out of the double doors at the far end and used the transceiver again to call Rayner. 'The door's shut and there's no padlock,' he said. 'I'm guessing they're inside.'

'Give me a second, Lofty.'

Loftus kept watch through the glass panel in one of the

doors until she came back on. 'Any chance of you listening in at the door?'

'I can try,' said Loftus.

'Give it a go,' she said. 'You can always say you were checking to see why it was unlocked.'

'I'm on it,' said Loftus. He slid the transceiver back into its holster and pushed through the doors. His boots squeaked on the linoleum as he walked down the corridor. He slowed as he reached door 432. He put his hands either side of it and placed his ear close to the wood. He could hear a voice. Accented but speaking English. He heard the words 'Downing Street', then guttural laughter.

There was more talking, this time a different voice, but it was so muffled Loftus couldn't even tell what language it was. He pressed his ear harder against the wood and the door creaked. He held his breath, then pushed himself back. As he straightened the door was yanked open. Daar was there, with Tareen at his side. Loftus opened his mouth to speak but Daar grabbed him by the jacket and pulled him in. Loftus stumbled, off-balance, and before he could steady himself his legs were kicked out from under him and he hit the concrete floor, hard.

'For fuck's sake!' he shouted. He rolled onto his back and pushed himself away from the men. Daar slammed the door. 'Who are you?' he barked.

Loftus fought to control his breathing. He'd hurt his knee in the fall and scraped the skin off his right hand. He scanned the angry faces, recognising four from that morning's briefing. Ali Mohammed. Tariq Tareen. Abdul Hakim Khalid. Mahnoor Bhutta.

'I work here, mate,' said Loftus. He pointed to his name-badge. 'Maintenance.' He pushed himself to his feet. 'Where do you get off attacking me like that? I'm going to call the

cops, that's what I'm going to do.' He reached for his transceiver but Khalid and Bhutta rushed him and grabbed his
arm. He tried to fight them off but they pushed him against
the wall. Khalid had his forearm tight against Loftus's throat,
making it hard for him to breathe, while the other man twisted
the transceiver out of his grasp.

'You were spying on us,' said Ali Mohammed.

'The door was unlocked so I was checking that everything
was okay.' He pointed at the transceiver. 'Let me talk to my
boss. He can tell you I work here. But the uniform is a
fucking clue, right.'

Khalid pressed his arm harder and Loftus began to choke.
Ali Mohammed started to talk to Tareen in a language Loftus
didn't recognise but which he figured was either Arabic or
Somalian. Khalid released his grip and stood back, breathing
heavily. The other two were standing by the door, blocking
any escape. Loftus was suddenly aware of how much danger
he was in. He was in a room with five jihadists planning a
terrorist attack and out of direct contact with the team. There
were a number of large black kitbags scattered around the
storage unit. Loftus counted them. Ten.

Ali Mohammed continued to talk and Loftus got the feeling
he was telling them what they had to do. He kept jabbing
his finger at Loftus and his tone was definitely hostile.

'I'm just checking that everything is secure, mate,' Loftus
said. 'So if everything is okay, I'll leave you to it, yeah?' He
took a step towards the door.

Ali Mohammed pointed at his face. 'Stay the fuck where
you are!' he said.

Loftus held up his hands. 'Hey, there's no need for language
like that, mate,' he said, playing the aggrieved employee. 'I'm
just doing my job.' Loftus didn't know if they were buying
his 'I only work here' story, but even if they did he doubted

that it would make any difference to the outcome. He was a witness, no matter who he worked for, and the discussion they were having was about what they should do with him. 'Let me radio in, yeah? And we can get this misunderstanding sorted.'

He held out his hand for the transceiver but Ali Mohammed shook his head and switched the unit off. Loftus realised he wasn't going to be able to talk his way out of the situation, and unless he could use the transceiver he wasn't going to be able to call for help. He took a step back. One of the bags was open and when he glanced down he saw a gun inside – an Uzi machine pistol or an Ingram – and a handful of magazines.

When he looked up, Ali Mohammed was staring at him. Ali Mohammed glanced at the open bag, then back at Loftus. His eyes hardened. Loftus roared and kicked out at him, catching him in the groin with his foot. Ali Mohammed staggered back, his hands between his legs.

Tareen pulled a knife from inside his jacket and lunged at Loftus. He blocked the blow and punched the man in the face, feeling a satisfying crunch as the cartilage snapped in his nose. The man screamed in pain. Ali Mohammed was bent double, yelling in Urdu. Loftus didn't speak the language but the meaning was clear. He knew he was now fighting for his life.

The one man Loftus didn't recognise also had a knife and as Loftus turned he lashed out with it, catching him on the upper arm. Blood blossomed on the sleeve and pain ripped through the arm but Loftus was in full fighting mode now and barely felt it. He kicked out at the man but missed, then the knife slashed again, this time cutting his other arm. Loftus roared as he aimed a punch at the man's face but the man rocked back and the punch went wide. Loftus was gasping for breath now. He was a watcher, not a fighter. Many years ago he'd gone on an MI5 self-defence course but he'd barely passed and remembered next to nothing from it, other than that his odds were better the longer he stayed on his feet.

Ali Mohammed had dropped the transceiver and Loftus bent down and picked it up. He put it to his mouth and pressed send, then remembered that Ali Mohammed had switched it off. He fumbled with the on-off switch but Tareen had a large knife in his hand and he slashed it across his throat. Blood sprayed across the floor. There was surprisingly little pain. Just numbness. The transceiver fell from his hand and clattered on the floor, the strength went from his legs and they buckled. He pitched forward but felt nothing as he hit the ground. His eyes were still open and he saw his blood pooling around his body. The more the pool spread, the calmer he became. His last thought was that there were probably much worse ways to die, and that having your throat cut wasn't that bad, not in the grand scheme of things.

'They're on the move,' said Rayner. She pointed at a screen where the five Asians were walking quickly along the corridor towards Reception, each carrying two bulky kitbags.

'Any sign of Lofty?' asked Shepherd.

'Negative,' said Rayner.

'Jeremy, are you seeing this?'

'We've got it,' said Willoughby-Brown.

'Do we move in?' asked Shepherd.

'Negative,' said Willoughby-Brown. 'Let's see what they're up to.'

'Are you serious?'

'They've not touched the explosives, which means some-thing else is going on. I'm thinking they've got weapons of some sort in those bags and if that's the case there could be more jihadists involved. So keep them under surveillance. Let's see where they go and who they meet.'

'What about Lofty?'

'Whether we pick them up now or later isn't going to influence what happens to him,' said Willoughby-Brown. 'As soon as they're off the premises, I'll send people in. Right now, I need you focused on surveillance. Understood?'

'Understood,' said Shepherd. He twisted around to look at the screen in front of Rayner. The five men had reached the entrance to the facility. 'Give Lofty a call, Janet. Okay, everyone else, on your toes. We don't know what they've got in those bags, but I'm damn sure it's not their laundry.'

'There's another vehicle pulling up outside,' said Brennan. 'Blue Transit van driven by an IC4 male. Another IC4 male in the front passenger seat.'

'Terrific,' said Shepherd. He swivelled towards the screen that Brennan was watching. The Identity Code 4 meant the driver was Asian, from the Indian subcontinent. IC1 was north European white, IC2 was Mediterranean, and IC3 was Afro-Caribbean. Ali Mohammed was IC6, Arabic or North African, as was Abdul Hakim Khalid.

'Right, the blue Transit is Victor Three. The driver is Alpha Two, the passenger Alpha Three.'

The driver of the blue Transit parked next to Tareen's Nissan and climbed out. He was joined by Alpha Three. Both men were in their early twenties. Alpha Two was bearded and wearing a skullcap. Alpha Three was clean-shaven with wraparound sunglasses and wearing a faded denim jacket.

Ali Mohammed and the four other jihadists pushed open the door and walked into the car park. Alpha Two waved at them while Alpha Three hurried over and took one of the bags from Ali Mohammed.

Alpha Two opened the rear door of the Transit.

Khalid and Alpha Three crossed to the white van and loaded their four bags into the back.

Tareen went to the Nissan Juke and put his two bags into the back, Ali Mohammed did the same with the bag he was carrying, then slammed the door.

The remaining three bags went into the Transit. Alpha Two closed the rear door, then went over to Ali Mohammed, hugged him, and kissed him on both cheeks.

'Have you seen Tango Two's face?' asked Rayner. 'His nose is bleeding.'

'Any news from Lofty?' asked Shepherd.

'He's not responding,' said Rayner.

'Right. This is going to get complicated,' said Shepherd. 'We now have three vehicles and seven targets. Jeremy, I would recommend we move in now.'

'I understand your concern, Daniel, but we still don't know what's in those bags. We'd look pretty darn stupid if all they've got is training manuals and prayer mats.'

'There's more going on here than that,' said Shepherd.

'I don't doubt it, but until we know for sure what it is, we're not moving in.'

Shepherd gritted his teeth in frustration but Willoughby-Brown was running the operation so it was his call. 'Okay, so my team will stay with Victor One,' Shepherd said into the radio. 'Steve, are you able to handle Victor Two and the new arrival, designated Victor Three?'

'It'll be a stretch,' said Turner.

'I'll give you one of our bike riders, our driving-school vehicle, and we'll switch two of our ARVs over to you,' said Shepherd. 'Give it your best shot.' He nodded at Rayner. 'Fix that up, Janet.'

'I'm on it.' She turned in her seat. 'Lofty's still not responding,' she said, concern written over her face.

'Shit,' said Shepherd.

'We should send someone in to check on him.'

Willoughby-Brown broke in: 'No, wait until the Tangos have gone.'

'He could be in trouble,' said Rayner.

'I understand that, but whatever happened has happened,' said Willoughby-Brown. 'I don't think waiting an extra thirty seconds is going to make any difference.'

Rayner opened her mouth to argue but Shepherd silenced her with a shake of his head. He knew from experience that there was nothing to be gained from arguing with Willoughby-Brown.

Ali Mohammed had finished embracing Alpha Two and walked to the Nissan, waving at Tareen to follow him. They both got into the car.

'Right, here we go,' said Shepherd. 'Victor One is about to go mobile with Tango One and Tango Two on board.'

The rest of the Asians got back into the vehicles. The blue Transit was first to leave, the driver beeping his horn and waving at Ali Mohammed as he drove out of the car park.

'Victor Three is mobile and leaving,' said Turner, over the radio. 'Alpha Two and Alpha Three on board. Heading east.'

The Nissan drove to the exit. 'Right, here we go,' said Shepherd. 'Don't get too close, but on no account are we to lose them. Steve, keep the ARVs close, this could all kick off with very little notice.'

'Roger that,' said Turner.

Rayner switched off her mic and leaned towards Shepherd. 'Are you happy with the way Willoughby-Brown is running this?' she asked.

'It's not the way I'd do it, but it's his operation.'

'It just seems to me that whatever is in those bags should

be enough to put them away for a long time,' said Rayner. 'Plus we have video of them with the explosives.'

'With the precursor to explosives,' corrected Shepherd. 'But I hear what you're saying and I wouldn't disagree with you.'

Rayner nodded and switched on her mic. They watched on the screen as the Nissan drove out of the storage company and onto the main road, heading east.

'Victor One is heading east,' said Brennan.

'I have eyeball on Victor One,' said one of the courier bikers.

'We're following,' said Brennan. The Openreach van moved off. Rayner began calling out routes for the watchers.

'Jeremy, we're going to need an eye in the sky,' said Shepherd. 'Three, if we can get them.'

'I've already been on to the Met and there's a chopper on the way. We'll patch through a feed once they're in the area. I've requested more. And we're bringing more ARVs into the area.'

'Any news on Lofty?'

'They're going in now,' said Willoughby-Brown.

For the next ten minutes they followed the Nissan through west London, letting the bikes do most of the tailing. There were so many black-clad motorbike couriers in London that they were the perfect vehicle for the job, especially as they could weave through traffic and, if necessary, take to the pavements and use short-cuts that weren't available to cars.

Shepherd listened to the commentary from Steve Turner. Victor Two had headed south, towards the river, and Victor Three was still heading east. Turner was one of MI5's most experienced surveillance experts, but Shepherd knew he'd be stretched following the two vehicles.

'Chopper's overhead,' said Willoughby-Brown. 'You should

be getting the feed now. I've put them onto Victor One. Let me know if you think we need to review that.'

'I've got it,' said Rayner. An overhead shot of London filled one of the screens. Rayner scanned it and pointed at the Nissan. 'There it is,' she said. Almost immediately the screen centred on the vehicle and a small square sight on the roof. It was the Nissan.

'Steve, would the chopper help you out?'

'Are bears Catholic?' said Turner.

'Victor Two or Victor Three?'

'They put four bags in Victor Two and three in Victor Three, so let's go for Victor Two.'

'Did you hear that, Jeremy? Can you put the chopper on Victor Two? We have eyeball on Victor One.'

'Your call,' said Willoughby-Brown. 'I'll get that done.'

A few seconds later the sight moved off the roof of the Nissan and started to move east as the police helicopter went in search of the white van.

'What about Lofty?' asked Shepherd. When Willoughby-Brown didn't reply, Shepherd repeated the question.

'I'm afraid Loftus didn't make it,' said Willoughby-Brown. 'They cut his throat. He would have died instantly. There's nothing anyone could have done.'

Shepherd closed his eyes and took a deep breath. He wanted to vent his anger and frustration but there was no point in attacking Willoughby-Brown. Sending in a watcher had been the right thing to do. Loftus must have done something to attract attention to himself.

'Bastard,' said Rayner.

Shepherd wasn't sure if she was referring to the man who had killed Lofty or Willoughby-Brown. 'Let's stay focused, guys,' said Shepherd. 'The fact that they killed Lofty is a sign that whatever they're up to is going down today.'

'Bastard,' repeated Rayner, in a quiet whisper.

The radio chatter was constant over the next fifteen minutes, as the watchers called out their positions. Following the Nissan had become that much harder with the reduced resources, and again the courier bikers were invaluable.

The white van went over Battersea Bridge and turned east to drive past Battersea Park, the river to its left. The Met helicopter had the van in its sights so Turner was able to pull his watchers back. There were three ARVs shadowing the van, driving along parallel streets but never more than a minute or so away.

The blue Transit continued to head east, as did the Nissan, though they had taken different routes.

Shepherd let Rayner do all the radio work and Brennan calculated the best routes for the team to take. Shepherd popped open a can of Red Bull and sipped. He wasn't a big fan of the energy drink – it was far too sweet for his taste – but his system needed the caffeine kick. Rayner motioned for him to give her a can, so he opened another and handed it to her.

'Victor Three is parking,' said Steve Turner, over the radio. 'South side of Trafalgar Square, near Whitehall.'

'It's all double yellow lines there, isn't it?' queried Shepherd.

'Yeah, they've got the hazard lights flashing. Oh, shit!'

'I need you to be more specific, Steve.'

'There are four IC4 males walking up to the van. Shit, shit, shit. I really don't have the manpower for this.'

Shepherd twisted around in his seat. 'Can you get me a feed, Janet?'

'Working on it,' she said.

Rayner flicked through several CCTV camera feeds and stopped when she got one showing the Transit van at the side of the road. It was a view from one of Westminster City

Council's cameras. The van was to the far left of the screen. The back door was open and Alpha Three was passing out backpacks of different colours to the new arrivals. As each man was given a backpack, he walked away. They all moved in the same direction – towards Trafalgar Square.

'I see four new arrivals,' said Shepherd. 'Designated Alpha Four, Alpha Five, Alpha Six and Alpha Seven. Alpha Four has a brown bomber jacket, Alpha Five is wearing a parka, Alpha Six has a blue jacket, Alpha Seven is wearing a black reefer. All are wearing sunglasses.'

'Confirm we have Alpha Four, Alpha Five, Alpha Six and Alpha Seven in sight,' said Turner. 'All are now walking north.'

'Jeremy, are you getting this?' asked Shepherd. 'We need to move in now.'

'I'm already on it,' said Willoughby-Brown.

'It's got to be guns, right?' said Shepherd. 'There were guns in the kitbags and they've transferred them to back-packs.'

'Possibly,' said Willoughby-Brown. 'They could be small explosive devices, they could be anthrax. Or it could be bloody housebricks and this is just a rehearsal.'

'You need to intercept them now, Jeremy,' said Shepherd.

'If it's a rehearsal, we could blow everything we've worked for,' said Willoughby-Brown.

'And if it's not, a lot of people are going to die,' said Shepherd. 'Look, they wouldn't have killed Lofty over a rehearsal. This is going down now.'

There was a clock on the side of the van and Shepherd watched the seconds tick by.

'Steve, get your CTSFOs to intercept the nearest Alpha,' said Willoughby-Brown eventually. 'Show his ID and do a stop and search. And get your ARVs ready to make contact with Victor Three. As soon as we have confirmation there are weapons, they are green-lit to move in.'

'I'm on it,' said Turner.

'What do we do about Victor One and Victor Two, Jeremy?' asked Shepherd.

'Just keep them under observation,' said Willoughby-Brown. 'They're still mobile.'

'Victor One is heading towards the underground car park,' said Brennan.

'Which one?' asked Shepherd.

'The main one. Park Lane.'

Shepherd grimaced. It was underneath Hyde Park and was one of the largest underground car parks in Europe with spaces for almost a thousand vehicles. He shouted through to their driver, 'Ronnie, get us closer to Victor One. I've got a nasty feeling the shit is about to hit the fan.'

'What's happening, Daniel?' asked Willoughby-Brown.

'Victor One appears to be heading to the Hyde Park underground car park,' said Shepherd. 'It's going to be tough to follow them down there.'

'I'll try to get a feed from the car-park owners,' said Rayner.

'Let's get at least one ARV down in the car park,' Shepherd told Brennan. 'And as many SFOs as we can.'

'I'm on it.'

'Jeremy, we should take them out before they go down into the car park,' said Shepherd.

'Actually, underground would be better,' said Willoughby-Brown. 'Fewer spectators. And fewer possible casualties.'

'There he is,' said Mark Robinson, nodding towards the Asian man striding purposefully towards Trafalgar Square. Robinson was a veteran senior firearms officer, with more than twenty years' service under his belt. He had done another two years in Royal Protection but hadn't enjoyed babysitting minor royals. In 2015 he had transferred back to SCO19, just as the CTSFOs were being introduced in the wake of the ISIS attacks in Paris that had killed 130 people and injured more than 350. Extra training included fast-roping from helicopters, storming buildings and hostage rescue, much of it done with the SAS.

'How do you want to handle it?' asked his colleague, Simon Pridmore. A relative newcomer to armed policing, he had only recently completed his CTSFO training. Both men were carrying Glock 17s in underarm holsters.

'I'll get ahead of him, stop him and ask for ID. You come up behind him.'

'Roger that,' said Pridmore.

'I don't see any sort of trigger mechanism but that doesn't mean there aren't explosives in there,' said Robinson. 'Any sign that he's got a bomb and you drop him, like a stone. If he puts the bag down and cooperates, you plasticuff him from behind. Let's try not to pull out weapons unless we have to.'

Pridmore nodded. Robinson winked, then started walking quickly. The target was about twenty feet ahead, and after just a few seconds Robinson caught up with him. Two seconds later, he was ahead of the man, and then he turned sharply and held out his hands to block the man's way. 'Armed police,' he said, quietly but firmly. 'Please put the bag on the ground.'

The man frowned, as if he hadn't heard.

'The bag. On the ground. Now.'

Pridmore came up behind the man. 'Do as you're told,' he growled.

The Asian looked left and right, as if wondering which way to run. Pridmore grabbed his left arm, just above the

elbow. Robinson stepped forward and took the bag off the
man. He unzipped it and looked inside. There was an Uzi
submachine pistol, with a magazine in place. 'Gun,' said
Robinson. 'Alpha Four has an Uzi and ammunition. Repeat,
Alpha Four is armed.'

Pridmore kicked the man's legs from under him and threw
him to the ground. He put his knee in the middle of the
man's back and used plasticuffs to bind his wrists.

Robinson turned and looked north, towards Trafalgar
Square. He saw Alpha Three getting onto an open-topped
tour bus. 'Alpha Three is getting onto a tour bus,' he said.
'Am I green-lit to approach?'

'It's the tour buses,' said Shepherd. 'Trafalgar Square is one
of the waiting areas. So is Hyde Park Corner. Victor Three
is getting close to the South Bank and there's a tour-bus stop
near the London Eye.'

'You think they're going to shoot up tourist buses?' said
Rayner. 'They're out to kill tourists?'

'They're sightseeing tours,' said Shepherd. 'They drive
past all the prime targets. Downing Street for one. St Paul's
Cathedral. The Houses of Parliament. All they have to do is
sit tight and they'll get taken straight to whatever target they
want. No one ever gets searched getting onto a tour bus.'

'All units move in now,' said Willoughby-Brown.

'Victor Two has just gone down into the underground car
park,' said Brennan.

'Do we still have visual?' asked Shepherd.

'One of the black cabs has gone in after them,' said Rayner.
'But no visual as yet. I'm still working on a CCTV feed.'

'Did we get an ARV down there?'

'They're heading in now, but there's a queue,' said Brennan.

'Tell them to be careful. There are probably other jihadists down there, waiting for the guns.' The van stopped and Shepherd called through to the driver, 'What's holding us up, Ronnie?'

'Traffic's bad,' said the driver. 'We'll be stuck here for a minute or two.'

The radio was full of chatter, with all the ARVs and SFOs calling out their positions around Victor Two and Victor Three and announcing that they were moving in.

'I'm going out,' said Shepherd. He stripped off his overalls and grabbed a blue Puffa jacket with a Canadian maple leaf flag on each shoulder. It would hide his SIG-Sauer and mark him out as just another tourist. He was wearing his headset and had a transceiver clipped to his belt so he could still hear what was going on as he jogged towards the entrance to the car park. He recognised one of MI5's motorcycle couriers waiting for the barrier to rise before driving in. It was going to be a nightmare finding the Nissan among all the vehicles. As he walked towards the pedestrian entrance, an Asian man in his twenties, clean-shaven and wearing a denim jacket and black cargo pants, emerged from the car park. He was staring fixedly ahead and seemed to be muttering to himself. He had a red backpack over one shoulder and Shepherd realised it was an exact match to one he'd seen being handed out of the back of Victor Three.

Shepherd ripped off his headset as he stopped and turned to watch the man go. He was walking purposefully towards Hyde Park Corner where half a dozen double-decker tourist buses waited, their engines running. They were operated by several companies and their uniformed representatives were walking up and down the pavement, waving brochures. He looked back at the entrance to the car park. A second Asian emerged carrying a similar backpack, this one dark blue.

Shepherd put his hands into his pockets and kept his head down as the man walked by. As soon as he was out of earshot he pulled out his headset and spoke into the mic. 'I have two targets walking from the car park down Park Lane,' he said. 'Both IC4 males with backpacks. I think Ali Mohammed has already handed over the weapons. They're en route to the tour buses in Park Lane.'

'The ARV has Victor One in sight and is ready to move in,' said Brennan.

'I'm following the two targets now,' said Shepherd. 'But I need back-up, SFOs or ARVs, I don't much care which so long as they've got guns.' He looked over his shoulder. Another Asian man was about fifty yards behind him. Mid-twenties, a neatly trimmed beard and dark glasses. And he was carrying a black backpack. Shepherd turned around. 'I'll call you on my mobile,' he said, and stuffed the headset into his pocket.

He pulled out his phone and called Rayner's number. She answered immediately. 'I have three IC4 males now, all heading to the tour buses,' he said, keeping his voice low. 'Alpha Eight, Alpha Nine and Alpha Ten.'

'There's an ARV en route,' said Rayner. 'But they're in traffic. Okay to use blues and twos?'

'Negative on that,' said Shepherd. 'If they panic they might pull out their guns and start firing. There are too many people around.' He began walking after the three men. The first had reached the line of tour buses and got onto the front one. He showed a ticket to the driver, who waved him on. 'Alpha Eight has got onto the first bus,' Shepherd said. 'What's happening in the car park?'

'Shots fired,' said Rayner. 'I'm waiting for details.'

'And the South Bank?'

'Victor Two is still mobile. The ARVs are in position to

move in as soon as they stop. And there are four plainclothes SFOs in the vicinity.'

'What about getting SFOs to my location?'

'On their way,' said Rayner. 'Two in a black cab, just coming up Park Lane now.'

Shepherd hurried towards the buses. All three men had got onto the same one.

'I'm getting ready to board the bus. Where's my back-up?' asked Shepherd.

'On the way.'

As Shepherd boarded the bus, an Italian father was buying tickets for his family using his credit card. It seemed to take for ever but Shepherd had to wait patiently. Announcing who he was and why he was on the bus would at the very least cause a commotion that might tip off the terrorists. It had to be done softly-softly, so he paid for a daily ticket and accepted the cheap pair of red earphones that could be used to listen to the tour commentary in any of eight languages and climbed the stairs. He paused at the top. The Italian kids – two girls and a boy – were fighting to get window seats at the front and the mother was hissing at them to be quiet.

'I'm upstairs,' said Shepherd.

'Be careful, Spider,' said Rayner.

Shepherd put his phone away into his pocket and stepped onto the upper deck. There was a roof over the first six rows and the jihadists had moved to the rear. Two were right at the back, one on each side, their bags on the seats next to them. Shepherd heard the doors rattle closed below. The third jihadist was sitting on the left behind a young couple, staring out over Hyde Park. The man in front of him was showing the woman how to change the language of the commentary.

There were four Chinese couples to Shepherd's right, chattering away in Cantonese.

The jihadist in the far right corner was staring at Shepherd, who twirled the earphones around as if he didn't have a care in the world and was deciding where to sit. The jihadist's hand was on top of his bag, toying with its zip. Shepherd smiled easily and headed for the back row. He flopped down in the centre seat and stretched his legs down the aisle.

'You can't sit there,' said the jihadist to his right.

Shepherd frowned and looked around. 'The driver said we could sit anywhere.'

'We're waiting for our friend.' He swallowed nervously. He was bearded and wearing tinted glasses.

'They've just shut the doors,' said Shepherd. 'I don't think your friend's going to make it.' He looked around, feigning interest in what was going on in the square. 'Hyde Park, how awesome is that?'

The two jihadists looked at each other. The one to his right started speaking in Urdu. The other replied, clearly annoyed. Whatever plans they'd made, Shepherd was obviously interfering with them. The jihadi sitting ahead of them was turning in his seat to see what was going on.

'Please, leave us alone,' said the man on Shepherd's right. 'Find somewhere else to sit.'

'So where are you from?' asked Shepherd. He tapped the maple leaf flag on his shoulder. 'I'm Canadian.'

The man on Shepherd's left glared at him. There were marks on his cheeks that looked like fragmentation scars, and old burns on his hands. 'Get the fuck away from us,' he muttered.

'Whoa, that's no way to talk to a tourist,' said Shepherd. He looked across to the man on his right. 'Did you hear that? Did you hear what he just said to me? What's wrong with him?'

Shepherd knew he was going to have to make his move soon. It was the way they were spread out that was the problem. One against three wasn't too much of a challenge if the three were grouped together. But the jihadists had spread themselves out and unless he fired first he stood no chance of taking them all out. But he wasn't able to fire first, not when there were no weapons in sight. There were more than a dozen witnesses on the top deck of the bus so he had to be sure that any action he took was justified. Shooting unarmed men never went down well with the press, even when the unarmed men were terrorists planning to maim and kill.

The man closer to the front shouted something in Urdu. The one to Shepherd's right yelled back. An ARV was coming down Park Lane towards them. The man to Shepherd's left pointed at it. The man at the front stood up and bent down to unzip his bag.

Across the road, one of MI5's black cabs came to a halt. The two CTSFO passengers got out and started jogging towards the bus. As they ran they pulled out their Glocks. The man to Shepherd's left spotted the guns and shouted. The jihadist at the front glanced out to see what he was shouting about and he, too, spotted the men with the Glocks. He stood up, bellowing at the top of his voice. The couple in front of him turned, and the Chinese tourists huddled together like startled sheep.

Without his radio, Shepherd had no way of knowing who was doing what, but clearly the CTSFOs were running towards the bus waving their guns, presumably to get the driver to stop. The ARV was still heading their way. Still no sirens or flashing lights.

The man at the front of the bus unzipped his backpack. He pulled out something black and metallic. An Uzi. He dropped the bag onto the seat and reached into it again, pulling out an extended magazine. Shepherd reached for his gun as he stood up. The man slapped the magazine into the Uzi. Shepherd took two steps down the aisle. 'Armed police!' he shouted. Not strictly true but he knew there was no point in shouting, 'MI5 officer with permission to carry a weapon!' He could quibble about semantics if it became an issue later.

The man swung the gun up. His finger wasn't on the trigger but that didn't make any difference. Shepherd fired twice in quick succession and both rounds slammed into the man's heart.

The Chinese tourists screamed. The Italian mother grabbed one of her daughters and shielded her. Her husband was rooted to his seat, his mouth open wide.

As the man started to fall, Shepherd turned. The man in the left-hand corner had pulled an AK-47 with a foldable stock from his backpack and was getting to his feet. Shepherd shot him in the chest but the round sparked off the gun and ripped through the man's shoulder. The man didn't seem to notice, he was probably pumped up on adrenalin and endorphins. His lips curled back in a snarl and he pointed the barrel at Shepherd, but Shepherd was already pulling the trigger again. He aimed higher this time and the bullet tore into the man's throat. He spun around and the next shot hit him in the side. Then he fell forward, bent double over the side of the bus. His weapon clattered to the ground.

There was screaming behind Shepherd and pedestrians stopped in their tracks as they tried to work out where the shots were coming from. Shepherd heard the Italian father yelling at his children and the sound of feet running down the stairs. The Chinese girls were screaming now, their men shouting.

Shepherd blocked out the sounds as he pointed his SIG-Sauer at the last remaining terrorist. He had one hand in his bag but from the way he was standing Shepherd was sure he didn't have his finger on the trigger. The first jihadist he'd shot had had to slot in his magazine but Shepherd had no way of knowing if the man facing him had a loaded weapon or not. It didn't matter. As soon as he saw a gun he was going to fire. 'It's your call, pal,' said Shepherd. 'You can drop the bag on the floor and put your hands on your head, or I'll put two rounds in your chest. As you can see I'm on a roll – it doesn't worry me either way.' His finger tightened on the trigger as he stared at the man, waiting to see how he would react. Anything short of full surrender would result in his death. Shepherd saw confusion in his eyes but there was determination also and the man gritted his teeth. 'Drop the bag!' shouted Shepherd, but he could tell from the man's body language that it wasn't going to happen.

The man began to move, plunging his hand deeper into the bag, his face contorted with anger and hatred. 'Allahu—' he screamed, but 'Akbar' was cut off by the first bullet, which slammed into his heart. He staggered backwards but his hand was still in the bag so Shepherd fired again and the second shot hit him in the throat. He continued to stagger backwards. The bag fell to the floor and the jihadist tumbled over the side of the bus and hit the road with a thump. A woman screamed further along the pavement. Shepherd peered over the side. The driver had opened the doors and tourists were flooding out into the street.

He saw one of the CTSFOs running towards the door. The other was at the front of the bus, looking up. Shepherd held his gun above his head. 'All clear!' he shouted.

The only tourists still on the upper deck were the Chinese, who had stopped screaming and shouting and were now staring open-mouthed at him. Shepherd put his gun back into its holster and smiled, though he knew it was going to take more than that to put them at ease. 'Ladies and gentlemen, I'm not great at languages so this will have to be in English, I'm afraid,' he said. 'Obviously this brings our tour to an end. If you could make your way downstairs and off the bus, there should be police officers ready to give you any assistance you require. I'm sorry for the inconvenience caused.'

They continued to stare at him in shock. Shepherd pointed at the stairs. 'Go!' he said. They finally got the message, stood up and hurried down. As they scrambled off the bus, one of the CTSFOs came up the stairs, Glock at the ready. Shepherd held his gun above his head until he was sure that the cop wasn't in shooting mode. 'The area is secure,' he said.

The CTSFO nodded and put his gun back in its holster. Shepherd did the same. The cop went over to the nearest jihadist and looked down at the gun. 'An Uzi? That's a nasty weapon to be using against civilians. With the thirty-round magazine, too.' He shook his head. 'They meant business, all right.'

'What's happened with Victor Two and Victor Three?'

The CTSFO walked to the rear of the bus. 'Both neutralised,' he said.

'Anyone hurt?'

'Among the good guys?' He grinned. 'No. But plenty of casualties on their side.' He looked down at the AK-47. 'A bloody Kalashnikov. Where the fuck do they get their guns from?'

'That's a good question,' said Shepherd. He took out his headset and pulled it on. 'This is Spider, back on the net,' he said. 'The bus is secure, three IC4s down.'

'You had us worried there,' said Rayner.

'No need,' said Willoughby-Brown. He chuckled. 'Three against one, they didn't stand a chance.'

It was day six in the observation post and there were more than forty faeces-filled plastic bags on the roof when Williams saw the black four-wheel drive heading up the road towards Houman Ahmadi's home. 'Sarge, we've got movement. Black Landcruiser.'

Standing was sitting with his back to the wall. He shuffled over to the mat next to the window, grabbed a pair of binoculars and focused on the target house, then back along the road. The Landcruiser was moving slowly. The windows were tinted so it was impossible to see who was inside, but it was the first time they'd seen an SUV in the area. Generally vehicles were military, police, or pick-up trucks.

'John, talk to base, tell them we might be up and running.'

'There's a four-door pick-up truck behind it,' said Williams. 'Could be security.'

Cox grabbed the radio and called Captain Waters. It was late afternoon, still uncomfortably hot but with a soft breeze blowing through the open window. The sky overhead was a clear blue, devoid of clouds. Standing knew that the Reaper drone would be at least twenty miles from the house, circling slowly to conserve fuel. The $17 million aircraft carried four thousand pounds of fuel and could stay aloft for forty hours. Whenever it began to run short a replacement would take over, providing for continuous coverage.

The pilot was on virtually the other side of the world at the Air Force Special Operations Command, Hurlburt Field in Florida. She was sitting in a dark, air-conditioned room wearing a neatly pressed flight suit, her blonde hair held away from her face with a pink scrunchie. Next to her was the sensor operator who manipulated the Reaper's TV camera, infrared camera, and other high-tech sensors. The sensor operator was the one who squeezed the trigger that would launch the missile. Like the girl, he was in his mid-twenties, sipping an iced latte through a straw as he watched the screens in front of him.

A grey-haired man in his early fifties was sitting behind them. His dark blue blazer was on a hanger on the wall to his right and he had rolled up his shirtsleeves and folded his arms as he, too, watched the screens. He was wearing a blue tie with black stripes, and expensive black leather shoes with tassels. The pilot and operator hadn't been told if he was CIA or NSA or Homeland Security, and he hadn't introduced himself when they had been assigned to the operation. All they knew was that he was in charge and he called the shots – literally.

Standing didn't know any of that, of course. He had no idea who was flying the drone or running the operation. That wasn't his concern. All he cared about was carrying out his mission: to bathe the target in the light of the laser.

The SUV had slowed almost to walking pace as it rattled along the rough track that ran by Houman's house. Standing focused on the vehicle. It was streaked with dirt and there were dark scratches above the wheel arches. The front registration plate was so splattered with mud that it was illegible.

He scanned back along the dirt track. The pick-up truck was red but covered with so much dust that it was closer to brown. The windows weren't tinted and Standing could make out the driver, a young man with a beard and a circular *qalansuwa* cap. The man in the front passenger seat was older, also bearded, and appeared to be cradling a Kalashnikov. 'I see a weapon in the pick-up truck,' said Standing.

'Yeah, got it,' said Cox. 'Looks like an AK.' He was holding a laminated photograph of the target.

Standing took a similar photograph from the pocket of his tunic. Like ninety per cent of the male population, Abdul-Karim Ahmadi was dark-skinned, brown-eyed and bearded, but he did have a distinguishing mole on the left side of his nose and a rash of old acne scars across his cheeks. The SUV came to a halt and the pick-up truck pulled up behind it.

'Here we go,' said Standing.

Williams was kneeling by the window. He was holding a rifle with a sniperscope and using it to check out the vehicles. The pick-up truck's doors opened and four men got out. The two at the rear were wearing long white one-piece *didashah* robes and sandals. The two in the front were in more traditional fatigues and boots. All were carrying Kalashnikovs. They were wary, checking out the surrounding buildings as they walked to the SUV.

The offside rear door of the Landcruiser opened and the four bodyguards stood around it, facing outwards. A man got out.

'Is it him?' asked Parker, but everyone ignored him.

Standing took another look at the laminated photograph, then peered through the high-powered binoculars. The man looked left and right, then said something to the bodyguards around him. He was wearing sunglasses but he took them off, dabbed his forehead with a white cloth and replaced them. Standing saw the telltale mole on the man's nose. He was wearing Western clothes, a shapeless linen jacket over a grey shirt and khaki cargo pants. 'It's him,' he said, placing the binoculars on the ground. 'Tell them target confirmed.'

'We have the target in sight,' said Cox into his radio.

'Positive ID?' asked Captain Walters, at the other end of

the radio. He was back at their base where he was in radio contact with the operators of the Reaper in Florida. Standing figured it would have been much more efficient for the SAS team to talk to the operators direct, but then there wouldn't have been anything for the officers to do.

Standing looked at Williams, who lowered his binoculars and nodded. 'Affirmative,' said Standing.

'Affirmative,' repeated Cox.

'As soon as the target is inside, light the building up,' said Walters. 'The drone is moving into position. As soon as the laser's on they'll be firing.'

'Roger that,' said Cox. He looked down at Standing. 'Ready when you are, Sarge.'

Standing put his eye to the viewfinder on the right-hand side of the SOFLAM. It was pre-focused on the building and he saw the four bodyguards clasping their weapons as they hustled Ahmadi towards the door to the house, so close to the man that there was no chance of a sniper getting anything like a clean shot. But a Hellfire missile was a whole different ball game and all the bodyguards in the world wouldn't change the outcome. The AGM-114 Hellfire missile got its name from the original purpose of the weapon – Helicopter Launched Fire And Forget Missile – which had been designed as a tank killer. The missile was a 100-pound precision weapon that could be launched from a variety of air, sea and ground platforms. But it was when it was used to target high-profile individuals – more often than not fired from a Predator or Reaper drone – that it came into its own. The Americans had used Hellfire-equipped drones to take out some of the world's most wanted terrorists, including Anwar al-Awlaki, the American-born Islamic cleric who had led al-Qaeda in the Arabian Peninsula, and Moktar Ali Zubeyr, the leader of the al-Shabaab terrorist group.

'I have another vehicle,' said Williams. 'Another pick-up truck.' He grimaced. 'Sarge, you're going to want to look at this.'

Standing used the SOFLAM viewfinder to check out what Williams was referring to. A second pick-up truck was heading towards the house, this one white with eight children sitting in the back. The girls were wearing black headscarves, the boys white skullcaps. They had small backpacks in their laps as the truck bounced and bucked along the trail. 'You are fucking joking,' said Standing. He squinted through the viewfinder and tracked back to the SUV. The four bodyguards stayed on the doorstep as Ahmadi went inside. They looked across at the approaching pick-up truck and, as one, pointed their guns towards it.

'We have to fire now,' said the captain. 'The drone is reaching the limits of its fuel.'

'Tell him there are kids outside,' said Standing.

As Cox relayed the message, Standing tracked back to the white pick-up truck. There was steam coming from under the bonnet and it had slowed to a crawl. As he watched, it jerked to a halt next to the SUV and the driver got out. It was a woman in a black burka. She walked around to the front of the pick-up truck and opened the bonnet. Clouds of steam billowed out and she stepped back, waving her arms. The bodyguards were all pointing their guns at her.

'The captain says to ignore the kids and paint the building,' said Cox.

'Tell Captain Waters to go fuck himself,' said Standing.

The woman went over to remonstrate with the bodyguards, obviously asking them for help. The ones in *didashahs* moved towards her, their weapons hanging on slings as they waved their hands at her to go away. The other two bodyguards stood at the entrance to the house, cradling their Kalashnikovs.

'He says he's ordering you to turn on the laser,' said Cox.

'Give me the radio,' snapped Standing, putting down the SOFLAM. Cox gave it to him, then picked up the binoculars and focused them on the vehicles in the distance. One of the girls was drinking from a plastic bottle. She wiped her mouth and handed it to the boy sitting next to her. He shook his head and passed the bottle to the girl on his left. He said something to the boys and they all laughed. Cox smiled to himself, remembering the days when girls had cooties and he had wanted nothing to do with them.

'Look, there's a truck filled with kids next to the target building,' said Standing. 'We have to wait for them to go.'

'There isn't time,' said the captain.

'The radiator's overheated by the look of it.'

'I don't care. We're on a tight time frame here. We need that laser, now.'

'Captain, these kids are in the line of fire.'

'Sergeant Standing, I am giving you a direct order. Do you understand?'

'I understand, boss. But if they fire now they'll kill half a dozen kids.'

'And if they don't, AKA will kill God knows how many more. Get the laser on the building.'

Standing cursed under his breath. 'Yes, boss,' he said. He gave the radio back to Cox.

Williams lowered his binoculars and glanced at Standing but didn't say anything. Cox and Parker were staring at him, waiting to see what he would do. 'Fucking arsehole,' said Standing. He picked up the SOFLAM and put his eye to the viewfinder, his finger reaching for the trigger.

Six thousand miles away in Florida, the sensor operator twisted around in his seat. 'Target acquired, sir. Are we green-lit?'

'Damn right you are, son,' said the man. He was fiddling

with a chunky class ring as he stared at the main screen. Usually it showed the visual feed from the nose of the drone but the sensor operator had switched over to the feed from the camera that was searching for the pulsed laser light from the SOFLAM.

One of the sandstone buildings was now glowing green on the screen. The laser light could be seen only by the sensors on the drone: nobody in the vicinity would notice anything untoward. 'Let's blow that bastard into the next world so he can find out for himself if there really are seventy-two sloe-eyed virgins waiting for him,' said the man.

'Roger that, sir,' said the sensor operator. He turned back and put his hand on the joystick.

The pilot had taken the drone out of its holding circle and put it into a slow descent, heading for the optimum operational height of thirty thousand feet. She counted off the descent in thousands of feet. On the main screen, the building remained bathed in the green light.

The pilot called out thirty thousand feet. The drone was now just eight thousand yards from its target. At its speed of Mach 1.3, close to a thousand miles per hour, the missile would reach its target in about eighteen seconds.

The sensor operator pressed the trigger. 'Missile launched,' he said, his voice a dull monotone.

They all stared at the main screen, showing the target building getting closer and closer. The seconds ticked by but time had slowed to a crawl. The trajectory seemed to be perfectly smooth and the target building stayed fixed in the centre of the screen. Suddenly the green-lit building filled the screen, which went blank.

'Target destroyed,' said the sensor operator.

The man sat back in his seat and pumped his right hand in the air. 'Yes,' he said. 'Finally.'

'Sir, I have a question,' said the pilot, turning in her seat.

'Go ahead,' said the man.

'You said sloe-eyed virgins. What does that mean? Like, virgins with lazy eyes?'

The man chuckled softly. 'That's sloe with an *e*,' he said. 'A sloe is a dark-skinned plum-style fruit. So black-eyed virgins. The best sort, apparently.' He stood up and patted the pilot on her shoulder. 'Nice job,' he said.

'Sir, you want to look at this,' said the sensor operator, pointing at the centre screen. 'There's something not right here.' He had replaced the blank screen with the view from the drone, still some seven thousand metres from the burning building.

'What's the problem, son?' asked the man.

The sensor operator pointed at the burning building. The missile had ripped into it and blown it apart from the inside. None of the top floor remained and what was left of the ground floor was a little more than a pile of smouldering rubble. 'That's not the target,' he said. He pointed several buildings to the left. The SUV and the two pick-up trucks were still there. 'That's the target,' he said. 'We hit the wrong building.'

The man leaned forward, putting his hands on their high-backed seats as he stared at the screen. 'How the fuck did that happen?' he asked.

'We hit the building that was lit, sir,' said the pilot. 'There's no question of that. The missile went where it was supposed to go.'

'But clearly that's not the case,' said the man. 'The missile took out the house to the right of our target. So I ask you again, what happened? System failure?'

The pilot shook her head as she studied the information on her screens. 'The system's fine.'

'It has to be human error,' said the systems operator. 'Somebody fucked up.'

Standing had to admit that the Hellfire was one hell of a weapon. It had streaked through the air, with a faint trail behind it, and slammed into the building with a flash of light, the sound of the explosion reaching them a second or two later. Chunks of masonry and wood erupted from the centre of the fiery explosion and rained down on the surrounding buildings.

The woman in the black burka had been a hundred feet or so from the explosion but it had still knocked her off her feet. The four bodyguards fanned out into the street and stared at the cloud of black smoke rising into the air. People were coming out of the neighbouring houses to see what had happened. Standing focused on the door of Houman's house. Ahmadi appeared. He wasn't wearing his sunglasses and he was carrying his jacket. The bodyguards surrounded him and bundled him towards the SUV. Two got into the SUV with him and it roared off down the track. The other two piled into the truck, which sped after the SUV. The two vehicles left clouds of dust behind them as they accelerated away.

'Elvis has left the building,' said Williams.

The captain was on the radio, demanding to speak to Standing, who gestured at Cox. 'Kill the radio, John,' he said.

Cox did so. 'Well, that'll put the cat among the pigeons, Sarge,' he said.

Standing stood up. 'I didn't join the SAS to kill kids,' he said. He brushed the dust off the knees of his camo trousers. 'Let's get the hell out of Dodge,' he said.

The British Museum had been around a lot longer than MI5. It was founded in 1753, initially based on the collection of

Sir Hans Sloane, a society doctor who had taken care of Queen Anne, George I and George II and became very rich doing it. The museum had grown to become one of the biggest and most prestigious in the world, with more than eight million exhibits. MI5 was created in October 1909 as the Secret Service Bureau, aimed at spying on the Imperial German government, and five years later was renamed the Directorate of Military Intelligence Section 5. MI5 officers had used the museum as a venue for clandestine meetings during the First World War and continued to do so in the present day. With six million visitors a year pouring into an area of more than 800,000 square feet, no one could possibly keep track of who came and went, and as the museum was a non-departmental public body, sponsored by the Department for Culture, Media and Sport, the government was able to co-opt any offices it wanted. The one favoured by Jeremy Willoughby-Brown was some distance away from the main area, accessed through a side door marked 'EMPLOYEES ONLY'.

Shepherd paid off his black cab, then spent five minutes wandering around to reassure himself that he wasn't being followed. Eventually, he headed to a black door with an intercom on the wall next to it. He pressed the button and smiled up at the CCTV camera covering the area. The lock buzzed and he pushed the door open. There was a carpeted corridor with utilitarian walls and he walked along it, knocking on the third door to the left. There was no answer so he knocked again, then turned the handle and pushed.

Willoughby-Brown was sitting behind a large desk in a high-backed executive chair, his feet on a windowsill, talking into a mobile phone and smoking one of his favourite cigars. He waved at the two straight-backed chairs facing the desk as he listened to whoever was talking on the phone and

Shepherd sat down. 'Absolutely, sir, and thank you for letting me know.' He flicked ash into the pot of a plastic plant. 'Yes, sir, of course. *Regnum Defende*, that's what we do.' He ended the call and stared out of the open window as he blew smoke towards it.

'*Regnum Defende*?' repeated Shepherd.

'The Service's motto. "Defence of the Realm". You didn't study Latin?'

'I know what it means,' said Shepherd. 'And Six has *Semper Occultus*, which always sounds like a Harry Potter spell to me.'

Willoughby-Brown grinned. 'Always secret,' he said. 'We always keep our mottoes simple. The Yanks do it differently. The CIA's is "The Truth Shall Make You Free", which I think is a bit Orwellian.' He blew another tight plume of blue smoke at the window. 'Personally, I always prefer Mossad's motto, "By Way of Deception, Thou Shalt Do War". That's exactly what we do, when you get down to it.'

'That's a myth,' said Shepherd.

Willoughby-Brown twisted around to look at him. 'What's a myth?'

'That was never Mossad's motto. A lot of people think it is, but the real motto is "Where No Counsel Is The People Fall", which is nowhere near as sexy.'

'You're sure?' Shepherd tapped the side of his head and Willoughby-Brown grinned. 'Of course you're sure, you and your perfect memory.' He swung his feet off the windowsill and swivelled his chair around so that he was facing Shepherd. 'So, job well done,' he said. 'If MI5 handed out commendations I'm sure you'd be getting one, but we don't so you won't.' He stabbed out what was left of his cigar in a crystal ashtray, then stood up and closed the window behind him.

'The intel was spot on with regard to the names,' said

Shepherd. 'It's a pity your source didn't know about the guy with the other storage unit.'

'He can't know everything,' said Willoughby-Brown. 'But it worked out well in the end. Luckily we had Five's top man on the case.' He dropped back into his chair. 'No point in assigning our top man to a case unless we have all our ducks in a row.'

'So I'm Five's top man, am I? Good to know.'

'One of them, certainly.' He smiled. 'Come on now, no false modesty. You put together a damn fine operation there. Fourteen jihadists in custody and eight dead. A huge amount of weapons and explosives taken off the streets and a message sent to the Great British Public that the Security Service has everything under control. All's well that ends well.'

'Except we're still at a terrorism threat level of severe, last time I looked,' said Shepherd. The threat level had been set at severe since August 2014 in response to the conflicts in Syria and Iraq. Severe meant that the authorities regarded a terrorist attack as highly likely. There was only one level above severe: critical – which meant an attack was expected immi-nently.

'It's all about perception rather than reality,' said Willoughby-Brown. 'Even with a threat level of severe, you're much more likely to win the lottery or be struck by lightning than you are to be killed by a terrorist. But when we're seen to be doing our job, people feel safer.'

'And we lost David Loftus,' said Shepherd. 'He was a good guy.'

'I didn't know him. But, yes, a sad loss.'

'What exactly happened, do we know?' asked Shepherd.

'The terrorists had disabled the camera covering the area around their storage unit. We think it was done late last night, so we're checking all the footage to see if we can catch whoever did it. He must have been rumbled as he did his walk-by and they decided their best bet was to kill him.'

'Do you think they knew he was with Five?'

'I'd say almost certainly not. He was wearing company overalls with company ID. If they'd known he was Five, I'm guessing they would have aborted, or kicked off sooner. The fact that they continued to board the tour buses suggests they thought they were in the clear. Was he married?'

'Twice, but divorced twice, too. No kids.'

'That's something, I suppose.'

'How is that something?' said Shepherd. 'Single men with no kids are expendable?'

'That's not what I meant. I suppose I was just making sympathetic noises.'

'You don't have to fake sympathy for my sake,' said Shepherd.

'You sound a tad tetchy,' said Willoughby-Brown.

'And I've warned you before about psychoanalysing me,' said Shepherd. 'Yes, I shot three people yesterday, but they deserved it and I'd happily do it again. Me being tetchy is not a sign of PTSD or guilt or anything like that.'

Willoughby-Brown held up his hands. 'I didn't mean to imply that for one second,' he said. 'I'm sorry my attempt to express my sympathy for the death of a valued employee backfired. We're going to need to look at what happened to see if—'

'Lessons can be learned?' Shepherd finished for him. 'I guess with hindsight we should have kept him in radio contact. That left him vulnerable. Also we were blindsided – literally – on the CCTV front.'

'We had no reason to suspect that they had more than one unit in the facility,' said Willoughby-Brown. 'When we did the work on the unit we knew about, we ran a check on the clients and there were no red flags.' He sighed. 'Still, there'll be an inquiry. We'll see what turns up.'

Shepherd wasn't sure what the inquiry would uncover, but he was sure of one thing: if mistakes had been made and fingers of blame were pointed, they most certainly would not be levelled in the direction of Jeremy Willoughby-Brown. 'It would have been nice if your source had told us they were planning to use firearms,' he said. 'We thought we were dealing with explosives, and the stuff they had was still inert. We'd have structured things differently if we'd known they were using guns.'

'My source is a bit like Father Christmas,' said Willoughby-Brown. 'He knows who's naughty and he knows who's nice. But he doesn't know the details of what they're planning.'

'He's not part of a jihadist group, then?'

'He's just a good Muslim who isn't happy when he sees other Muslims trying to hurt this country. He knows who the jihadists are but he's not privy to their secrets. It's up to us to put the names he gives us under surveillance and find out what they're doing.'

'And how did we miss Alpha One, the guy who had the second storage unit?'

'His name is Hammad Gill. Hammy to his friends. Though not sure why a Muslim answers to the name of a pork product."

'Gill? That's a British name, surely?'

'It's a Punjabi tribal name. His parents moved from the Punjab in the eighties. They came over with three kids and had another three when they moved to Birmingham. The three they brought with them are pillars of the community. The girl's a nurse and two sons run a corner shop. The three kids born in the UK have all gone jihadist. Two of the boys are in Syria. Hammad has been over to Pakistan twice in the last three years, each time for two months. He's generally well behaved, probably told to maintain a low profile until he was needed. He lives in Birmingham and took out the contract on the storage unit two months ago. We can probably assume he acquired the weapons in Birmingham and brought them down.'

'Had he had any contact with Daar in the past?'

'It's early days but we haven't found anything yet.'

'So someone else planned this? Someone put Daar together with Gill?'

Willoughby-Brown nodded. 'This attack took a lot of planning and I don't think Daar has the brains for that. He was just a cog in the machine. Gill's involvement opens up the whole investigation, obviously.'

'And the weapons. Twenty Uzis and Kalashnikovs, all that ammunition. There aren't many dealers who can come up with that much hardware.'

'We're looking at that, obviously.'

'So, is there more intel coming from this source?' he asked.

'Hopefully,' said Willoughby-Brown.

'Your man is obviously well placed,' said Shepherd. 'How come I'm not running him?'

Willoughby-Brown grinned. 'This one's special.'

'Too special for me to know about?'

'He's not for general consumption,' said Willoughby-Brown.

'You're running him yourself?'

'I'm involved. Let's leave it at that.'

'Is there a problem?'

Willoughby-Brown shook his head. 'You're like a dog with a bone. You really won't let go, will you?'

'I just thought today's operation was such a success – Dave

Loftus notwithstanding – I'd like to do more, that's all. But if you want to keep the source to yourself, that's fine.'

'It's not about hogging the glory, I hope you don't think that. We'll be keeping our customary low profile and SCO19 will be taking the credit for today. It'll be known that Five was involved but my face isn't going to be plastered over the tabloids, obviously.' He leaned across the desk. 'I trust you, of course I do. I trust those people I've hired, and I trust the people I work with.' He grinned. 'Most of them, anyway. But I can't vouch for every single person who works at Thames House these days, and the source is too valuable to risk.'

Shepherd frowned. 'You think there could be a leak in Thames House?'

'I'm not saying that. I'm saying there's a risk, no matter how small, so we're keeping him under wraps.' He settled back in his chair and steepled his fingers under his chin. 'You moved to Five from SOCA, didn't you? The lovely Charlotte Button made the move and brought you with her.'

Shepherd nodded but didn't say anything.

'I was recruited at university. My tutor invited me around to his rooms for cigars and malt whisky. I thought it was a group thing but when I got there it was just me and him. I thought he was going to offer to suck my dick, but he had something different in mind. He suggested I join MI6. He said I was just the sort of person they needed and that I'd be a great fit. That's how I was recruited, by someone who knew me and was prepared to vouch for me. And that's what happened with you, too. Charlotte vouched for you. The problem is that since Nine Eleven and Seven Seven all that's changed. Five and Six wanted to bring in more ethnic minorities – they wanted Arabs, Somalians, Iraqis, Iranians. They wanted people who spoke the language and understood the culture. But in the rush to do that, short-cuts were taken. Same as has happened in the police and Border Force.'

'Lowering standards, you mean?'

'Partly that, though obviously we still have positive vetting. But I think there's a rush to give people the benefit of the doubt. A Muslim guy with a degree in communications says he wants to serve his country. He speaks Arabic and English and hasn't ever been in trouble. Bang, he's hired, and within a few months he's handling all sorts of confidential information. But you and I both know that post Nine Eleven and Seven Seven, the bad guys changed their strategy too. They've been doing whatever they can to infiltrate our institutions. We catch most of them but it's a matter of playing the odds. Some get through. It's happened at the airports and it's happened in the cops and in the armed forces, and I'm damn sure we've a few bad eggs in Five and Six already.'

'Sleepers, you mean?' said Shepherd.

'Some will be in it for the long haul, but others are being used for intel. They only need one cop to have access to the Police National Computer. They only need one MI5 officer to have access to our databases. We're in a very difficult position. We want to recruit more Muslims, but the very fact that we're recruiting so many puts our security at risk.' He shrugged. 'We can't ever say that, of course. But what I can do is protect my sources, wherever possible.'

He reached down and picked up a battered leather brief-case. He swung it onto the desk and opened it. 'Now, on the subject of trust, I have your next job. Have you ever come across this girl?' Willoughby-Brown passed a photograph across the desk. It was a head-and-shoulders shot of a young woman with a dirty-blonde bob, grey-blue eyes and a cheeky smile.

Shepherd shook his head. 'No.'

'I know your trick memory is pretty infallible and that you never forget a face, but this girl is different. She's something of a chameleon. She's always changing her appearance.' He slid a second photograph across the table. This time she had blue eyes and long blonde hair and was giving the camera an ice-maiden stare. It was definitely the same girl, but Shepherd had to look twice to be sure. 'I've not crossed paths with her.'

Willoughby-Brown gave him a third photograph. Short black hair cut in a fringe and green eyes. She was wearing wire-framed spectacles and had braces on her teeth.

Shepherd shook his head again.

'Okay, well, that's something, at least,' said Willoughby-Brown, taking the photographs back. 'Her name is Lisa Wilson, currently an undercover operative for the National Crime Agency. Using the name Lucy Kemp, she's been deep under cover for the past eight months, getting close to a British drugs dealer by the name of Marcus Meyer.'

Shepherd frowned. 'Meyer is a Dutch name, surely?'

'His father is Dutch and, strictly speaking, he holds dual nationality, but so far as we're concerned he's a British problem.' Willoughby-Brown passed Shepherd a surveillance photograph of a good-looking man with swept-back blond hair climbing out of a Ferrari. 'This was taken in London a few years ago. He doesn't come here often – he's usually somewhere in the Med or out in the Caribbean. He's been on our watch list for a while and the DEA would love to get their hands on him.'

'No European Arrest Warrant out for him?'

'He's a clever bugger. I'm sure you've come across his type before. Never goes near the drugs, keeps the money at arm's length. Almost impossible to catch him with the goods, which is why the NCA put Lisa on the case.'

'So if there's an undercover agent inserted already, why am I here?'

Willoughby-Brown looked down at the photographs. 'The quality of her intel has taken a dive in the last few weeks and there are worries that she might have gone over to the dark side.'

'So pull her out.'

'It's not as simple as that, is it? It could be that there isn't much happening. Or that Meyer suspects her. If she's pulled out, the whole operation has effectively been a waste of time because what she's come up with so far isn't enough to put him away. Meyer is a big fish and we need to reel him in.'

'So what's the plan?'

'We'll get you close to Meyer, and you can kill two birds with one stone. Put together a case against him, and check up on Lisa. Now, how good are you with boats?'

'I can handle a rigid inflatable well enough – in fact, anything with an engine.'

'What about real sailing? Tacking and jibing and the rest?'

'I know which is port and which is starboard but that's about it. Why do you ask?'

'I'm considering ways to get you close to Meyer. The NCA used one of their snouts to introduce Lisa to him, but I'm wary of going the same route. In fact, I'm reluctant to share any intel with them.'

'Even though they asked you for help?'

'They didn't. This is off our bat.'

'So the NCA don't know what you're doing?'

'It's a matter of trust, Daniel. Let's face it, they can't rely on their own agent, why should I trust them? If, as we suspect, Lisa has gone native, how do we know that there aren't others who've gone bad? Like I said, I need to protect my assets and the fewer people who know what you're doing, the better.'

'So you'll put me in under cover and no one else will know?'

'It works in our favour,' said Willoughby-Brown. 'We'll check with them to see what Lisa's reported back about you. They won't know you're with Five, so we'll see what she says. Now, what are you doing this weekend?'

'I was planning on heading back to Hereford.'

'Ah, yes, the lovely Ms Katra. How's that working out, you shacking up with the au pair?'

'To be fair now, Jeremy, she was an au pair when Liam was a kid. He's an adult now. And it's going fine, thanks for asking.'

'I'm just saying, she was your au pair and now she's . . . Well, how would you describe her?'

'Girlfriend is just fine, Jeremy. Not that it's any of your business.'

'Actually, personal relationships are very much our business. Getting you to admit that your relationship had changed was like pulling teeth, whereas you know full well that as an MI5 officer you're required to keep the agency informed of any and all personal contacts and any changes thereof.'

'Katra was vetted several years ago,' said Shepherd.

'And passed with flying colours,' said Willoughby-Brown. 'But that's not the point.' He held up his hands. 'Anyway, water under the bridge. I'm glad it's working out well for you both. Can you tell her you're going to be otherwise engaged this weekend?'

'Doing what, exactly?'

'I'm going to teach you the fundamentals of sailing.'

'You're what?'

'I've a thirty-five-footer moored at Brighton.'

'You're a sailor?'

'You sound as if you don't believe me.'

'I just never had you pegged at the helm of a boat, that's all.'

'There's a lot about me you don't know, Daniel,' said Willoughby-Brown.

Standing's patrol drove slowly into the camp and parked their dust-covered quad bikes behind one of the Nonstandard Tactical Vehicles used by the Navy SEALs. The Americans did love their jargon. In fact, it was a Toyota Tacoma four-door pick-up truck that had been modified with belt-fed machine-gun mounts, grenade launchers, roll bars, infrared headlights, satellite communications and tracker units. It was a monster, and as it looked like a Syrian rebel vehicle, it could often pass through high-risk areas where a military vehicle would have been fired on.

Standing climbed off his quad and unfastened the green nylon case containing the SOFLAM from the back carrier. Parker was transporting the shit-filled plastic bags. As usual the patrol had played Rock, Paper, Scissors to decide who did the dirty work. Also as usual Parker lost, and Standing figured it wouldn't be much longer before he realised the other three were colluding against him. Parker carried the bags to a disposal area while Standing, Williams and Cox walked towards the tented barracks area, their weapons slung over their shoulders. A group of four Navy SEALs walked by and grunted in unison. The three SAS soldiers grunted back.

Standing needed a shower and a shave, and then he planned to help himself to a burger or two and ideally a cold beer. Alcohol was supposedly banned in the camp but the SEALs seemed to have acquired a never-ending supply of Budweiser that they were happy to share with the Brits. Early on in the conflict the SAS had based itself in Jordan, crossing the border into Syria to help the New Syrian Army take on Islamic State. Early work had involved building defences and bunkers and organising logistics, but as the fighting intensified the SAS had taken on a more active role. When the Americans had set up a base in the Syrian desert between al-Raqqah and the Iraqi border to help support the Syrian rebel forces as part of Operation Inherent Resolve, the SAS had moved in. While the British government had never approved ground troops going to Syria, the SAS always operated independently and their missions were rarely, if ever, publicised. The special-forces camp was tiny, measured against the army cities that had been built across Iraq, but it was still luxurious compared to the facilities the SAS generally had to put up with.

'Standing, you bastard!'

Standing stopped and turned. Captain Waters was walking towards him, red-faced and breathing heavily. He was wearing desert camo fatigues and a floppy camo hat and had a smear of white sunscreen down his nose. 'What the fuck do you think you're playing at?'

'Heading for a shower and then some scoff,' said Standing.

Williams and Cox faced Waters. Standing held up his hand. 'It's okay, guys, I've got this.'

'Are you sure, Sarge?' said Cox. 'He's not a happy captain.'

'I can handle it. You guys go and get cleaned up. I'll catch up with you later.'

The two men headed off as Waters walked up to Standing. 'You disobeyed a direct order out there,' said Waters. He stopped and put his hands on his hips, his chin jutting aggressively. 'I told you to light up the target. You aimed your laser at the wrong bloody building.'

'These Syrian buildings all look the same,' said Standing, laconically. 'It's easy to make a mistake.'

'Don't fuck with me, Standing. You said you didn't want to light up the target, and the next thing is we're raining destruction down on what I'm told was an empty building. The Americans are as mad as hell and want to know who fucked up.'

'They've got plenty of missiles,' said Standing. 'They'll get another chance.'

'I gave you a fucking order.'

'There were kids. I'm not killing kids.'

'Fuck that,' said the captain. 'They use kids to set IEDs out here. They use kids as suicide bombers. You've seen the videos – kids here hack the heads off prisoners and laugh while they're doing it.'

'These weren't terrorist kids. They were regular children, minding their own business.'

The captain narrowed his eyes. 'So now you're an expert on children, are you?'

'They were coming back from school. That's what it looked like. They were carrying books.'

'I don't care if they were carrying a stack of fucking Bibles,' said the captain. 'We had one of the world's most dangerous terrorists in our sights and you let him go.'

'We'll get another chance.'

'You don't know that. For all you know he could be training jihadists to take the fight to the UK. Did you think about that? He could be sending fighters to kill our friends and families. We could have stopped him cold and now he's out there planning God knows what.'

Standing shrugged. 'Yeah, well, there's no point in crying over spilled milk, is there?'

The captain shook his head. 'It's not as simple as that. You disobeyed a direct order from a superior officer. That's a court-martial offence.'

Standing laughed. 'This is the SAS. We don't do courts martial.'

'We'll see about that,' sneered the captain.

'Keep me posted.'

Standing turned to go but the captain gripped his shoulder. 'Don't you fucking walk away from me while I'm talking to you,' he said.

'Get your hand off me,' said Standing, glaring at the officer.

The captain tightened his grip. Standing grabbed his wrist and wrenched the hand off his shoulder. The captain swore at him, then pushed him in the chest with both hands. Standing put up his own to defend himself, and immediately the captain tried to grab him by the neck. Standing twisted, pivoted on his back foot and brought his right elbow up, clipping the captain under the chin. The captain's head snapped back and Standing's hand was already moving, clenched into a fist and travelling down to smash onto the man's nose. Blood spurted down the captain's chin and he fell back, arms flailing. He tripped and hit the ground hard. 'You're fucking done for now, Standing!' he shouted, sitting up. Then he wiped his nose with the back of his hand. 'I'll fucking have your stripes for this.'

'You're welcome to them,' said Standing, as he walked towards his tent, the hot desert sun burning the back of his neck. He licked his knuckles as he considered his options, but having broken his superior officer's nose he figured he didn't have many. He hadn't planned to hit the captain – he'd reacted totally on instinct – but even the SAS didn't allow its men to go around smacking officers, even when they'd asked for it.

Standing was lying on his bunk, staring up at the roof of his tent, when he heard his name called. He stood up slowly. 'Yeah?' he replied.

'The major wants you, ASAP.' It was Dave Mearns, a young trooper from Wales who had been with the SAS for less than a year.

Standing ducked out of the tent. 'Did he say what it's about?'

'I'm a mushroom, me,' said Mearns. 'But word is that the captain is going to be eating through a straw for a few weeks.'

'Shit,' said Standing.

'If ever a Rupert deserved a punch in the mouth, it's him,' said Mearns. 'He's been a fucking liability from day one.'

'Cheers, Dave.'

'Chin up, Sarge,' said Mearns, patting him on the back.

Standing walked over to the Portakabin that Major Taggart used as the ops centre. There was a mat outside and he scraped off the worst of the dust that was coating his boots before knocking.

'Enter!' shouted the major.

Standing pushed open the door. The major was sitting behind a table piled high with files and reports. On the wall behind him a large-scale map of the country was dotted with pins of different colours and a dozen or so surveillance photographs. He stood up and folded his arms. 'No need to tell you what this is about, Standing.' He was in his forties with receding hair cut short and he was missing the bottom of his left ear, the result of a firefight with the Taliban more than a decade ago, about the time that Standing had signed up.

'No, boss.' Standing stood with his arms behind his back. Normally officers and troopers were pretty relaxed in the SAS but he knew he was about get a bollocking. He stood ramrod straight and stared at the map on the wall.

'What the fuck were you thinking?' said the major.

Standing didn't answer. He had a pretty good idea where

the conversation was going and he figured there was nothing he could say that would change the outcome.

'You can't go around hitting officers,' said the major. 'Don't we have enough bad guys out here for you?' He shook his head. 'You're a fucking liability sometimes, Standing. You know that? A fucking liability.'

He paced up and down behind his desk, then took a deep breath to compose himself. 'The captain has a broken nose and a cracked jaw. And he's not going to let this drop. You picked the wrong officer to hit, I can tell you that. He's not going to put it down to a bit of rough and tumble. He wants you out of the Regiment.'

Standing gritted his teeth.

'What's wrong with you?' said the major, but the question sounded rhetorical and Standing said nothing. The major stopped pacing and folded his arms as he gazed at him. 'That's it? You're going to give me the silent treatment?'

'I'm not sure what to say, boss,' said Standing. Officers were never referred to as 'sir' in the SAS. Nor were they saluted. But that didn't give them any less authority than they had in the regular army, and Standing knew he had to tread very carefully.

'You could try saying sorry for a start.'

Standing shrugged. 'But I'm not sorry, boss. And, given the same set of circumstances, I'd probably do it again.'

'You want to make a habit of hitting your superior officers? How is that a credible career plan?'

'He shoved me, boss.'

'What is this – the fucking playground? He shoved you so you broke his jaw?'

'I just reacted, boss. I saw red. He hit me and I hit him back.'

The major sighed. 'What the fuck are we going to do with

you?' he asked, and again it was clear the question was rhetorical. He began pacing again. 'I've got to send you back to Hereford,' he said. 'I don't have any choice.'

'Boss, I'm needed here. I'm no use to anyone back at HQ.'

The major stopped pacing. 'Matt, do you understand the trouble you're in? You could be sent back to your unit for this. Maybe worse. Guy Waters wants you on a charge. You could end up in the stockade.'

'He asked for it, boss. I'll justify my actions if I have to.'

'Yeah, well, good luck with that,' said the major. '"He pushed me so I broke his jaw." I'm not sure that will fly as defence.'

'He wanted me to kill kids, boss,' said Standing, quietly.

'What? What did you say?'

'He gave me an order that would have resulted in children dying. I refused. He pushed me. I hit him. If the captain wants me up on a charge, that's his call. But I'm fucked if I'll apologise.'

The major frowned and rubbed his chin. 'Tell me what happened.'

Standing spoke slowly and quietly, running through the mission from the moment he had his target in his sights to the destruction of the wrong building. 'I wasn't going to let children die,' said Standing. 'If I'd called the jets in on the target, kids would have been killed. When I got back to base, the captain ripped into me. That would have been fair enough, but then he pushed me and I reacted instinctively.'

'Guy knew there were children in the line of fire?'

'I told him, twice.'

'And he said what?'

'He said Ahmadi was a high-value target and that any collateral damage was immaterial. What sort of arsehole says that? We're supposed to be fighting to save this fucking country, boss. If we're not saving it for the children, then who are we saving it for?'

'I think the point the captain was making was that Ahmadi is a nasty piece of work and by taking him out we'd be saving lives down the line. A lot of lives, maybe. It's a numbers game.'

'With respect, boss, this isn't a fucking game, and if we have to kill kids to get what we want then we're worse than the terrorists. The captain gave me a direct order that would have resulted in children dying and I refused to do it.'

The major scratched the back of his neck. 'This is a bloody mess,' he said. 'But I've got no choice here. You're being sent back to Hereford. You can plead your case there.'

Standing nodded. 'No problem, boss.'

'I'm going to fill in my report saying that there was a physical altercation that got out of hand. I'll also be saying that you're a bloody good soldier, a valued member of your squadron, and that I wouldn't want to lose you.'

'Thanks, boss.'

'I'm serious, Matt. You're a fucking good soldier. One in a million. But you can't go around hitting officers, not without there being repercussions.'

'Understood, boss,' said Standing.

'There's a Herc leaving in two hours,' said the Major. 'Be on it, with all your gear.'

Shepherd arrived at Brighton Marina at nine o'clock in the morning in his BMW X5. He parked and went in search of Willoughby-Brown's boat. It was easy enough to find, halfway down one of the jetties to the left of the marina. It was called *Second Wind* and was a tidy, single-masted yacht with a teak deck that had weathered to a dull grey over the years. There didn't seem to be anyone around so Shepherd called, 'Anyone there?'

'Below decks,' yelled Willoughby-Brown. 'Come aboard.'

Shepherd climbed onto the stern. He was wearing a blue waterproof jacket over a thick black pullover and black jeans and carrying a black nylon backpack. Willoughby-Brown hadn't told him what to bring but Shepherd had checked the weather forecast and it was supposed to be a mild day with little chance of rain. Beyond the wheel there was a hatch: Shepherd ducked his head and took the stairs one by one until he was in the main saloon. Willoughby-Brown was sitting at a table with a chart and a steaming mug of coffee in front of him. He was wearing a black fleece over a green polo-neck. He raised his mug. 'Welcome aboard,' he said. He gestured at the galley. 'Kettle's just boiled. Only instant, I'm afraid.'

'Instant's fine,' said Shepherd. He made himself a coffee and squeezed onto the seat opposite Willoughby-Brown.

'So, what do you know about boats?' asked Willoughby-Brown.

'Just the basics,' said Shepherd.

Willoughby-Brown pulled three paperback books from a shelf behind him. 'This is where your trick memory will come in useful,' he said. 'These cover the basics of seaman-ship and navigation.'

Shepherd took them. His eidetic memory meant that he pretty much remembered everything he read, heard or saw, so memorising the contents of the books wouldn't be a problem. But memorising facts and acquiring physical skills were totally different, and for the latter he'd need Willoughby-Brown's help.

'So, this is a Catalina 375,' said Willoughby-Brown. 'The hull is solid fibreglass, the mast is a deck-stepped with back-stays and fore and aft lower shrouds.' He grinned as he saw confusion flash across Shepherd's face. 'Don't worry, I'll run through the terminology when we're on deck. The point is that you'll need to know the jargon. So the back of the boat is aft, also known as the stern. The front is the bow. Port is left of the bow, starboard to the right. Leeward is the direction opposite the way the wind is blowing and windward is the way the wind is blowing. The boom is the horizontal pole extending from the bottom of the mast. The rudder is the piece of fibreglass sticking into the water that steers the boat. I'll explain tacking and jibing once we're under sail.' He drained his mug. 'Okay, let's get started.'

Willoughby-Brown took Shepherd up through the hatch and went over to the wheel. 'Okay, so we call this the cockpit, and this is obviously the wheel,' he said. He pointed at a rope that ran along the side of the boat. 'This is a line. Always a line, never a rope. A line might be made of rope, but it's still a line. Every line has a role and its own name. Sometimes at sea there's a lot to do in a short space of time so everyone needs to know what they're doing. So, the ropes that adjust the sails are called lines. But the one that runs up the mast to pull up the mainsail is called the halyard, and the one that brings the mainsail down is called the downhaul.'

'Halyard, downhaul,' repeated Shepherd.

'Now, there's a particular type of downhaul called a Cunningham that you need to be aware of, and then there's the vang, also known as the kicker. The Yanks call it a vang. We Brits say kicker. Potato, tomato.'

'Cunningham. Vang. Kicker,' Shepherd repeated.

'I've had a boom vang installed on this boat,' said Willoughby-Brown. 'The vang pulls the end of the boom down and bends the mast. The more you pull on the vang, the more the sail flattens, which de-powers it. So, for instance, when you're sailing upwind in a strong wind you want the sail as flat as you can get it. That means you want the vang pulled as tight as it'll go. So, with the vang right on you can then let the mainsheet out. The sail will stay flat and therefore be de-powered.'

'You've lost me,' said Shepherd.

'I'll demonstrate when we're out to sea,' said Willoughby-Brown. 'Basically, if there's too much wind passing over the sail it can destabilise the boat. You have to make the sail less efficient. You can do that by steering, but the vang is a more efficient way of achieving it.' He pointed at a line that led to the mainsail. 'The lines that we use when we're sailing are called sheets, and the name of the sheet refers to the sail it controls. So, to trim the mainsail – that's the big one, obviously – you use the mainsheet. To trim the jib – the sail at the front – you adjust the jib sheet. The rigging that supports stationary objects, like the mast, is called the standing rigging and more often than not it's steel cables. They're not called lines. They're known as shrouds or stays.'

'Shrouds. Stays,' repeated Shepherd.

'So the line that runs from the mast to the bow is the forestay. And the lines that run from the mast to the stern are the backstays . . . I know there's a lot to learn but if you're going to pass yourself off as a mariner you'll have to have these terms on the tip of your tongue. You'll be surrounded by sailors and they'll spot a fake a mile off.'

'I'll be okay,' said Shepherd.

'I'm sure you will. The engine is a three-cylinder, forty-horsepower Yanmar diesel, which will give us more than six knots at two thousand r.p.m. We'll only be using the engine to get into and out of the marina. Once we're on the open sea we'll use the sails. This is about you getting the hang of sailing, not motorboating.'

Willoughby-Brown pressed a button to start the engine, then jerked his thumb at the lines tethering the boat to the jetty. 'The lines that tie us up are called docklines or warps. So, cast off the docklines.'

Shepherd untied them. Then Willoughby-Brown pushed the throttle and guided the yacht away from the jetty. Shepherd sat down and watched him steer. There was an iPad mounted to the right of the wheel and Willoughby-Brown flicked through various screens showing the position of the yacht. 'Navigation, these days, is all down to GPS, but any sailor worth his salt will still know his way around a sextant and have a working knowledge of the stars.'

'I'm okay on celestial navigation,' said Shepherd.

'Ah, yes, of course. Your special-forces background. What about charts? Your memory okay with them?'

'Sure. I'll need to be shown how they work but, yes, I'll have no trouble memorising them.'

'There's a local-area chart on the desk. Bring it up and I'll show you how it works. Oh, and make us both a coffee, will you?'

Shepherd threw him a mock-salute. 'Aye, aye, Captain.'

'So you're in the SAS, then?' asked the taxi driver, a man in his sixties wearing a flat cap and a corduroy shirt. He had a pair of glasses on a chain around his neck. Standing had got into the car outside Hereford station and asked for the Credenhill camp, some six miles to the west. The man had driven in silence for the first twenty minutes, but he kept looking at Standing in his rear-view mirror and was clearly itching to start a conversation.

'Nah, I'm a cleaner,' said Standing, looking out of the window.

'Like fuck you are,' chuckled the driver. 'I've lived in Hereford all my life so I know the wannabes and I know the real thing.'

'Really?'

'For start, the guys who are in the SAS will never admit to it. But the wannabes, that's all they talk about. You see them in the pubs all over, talking big and trying to pick up impressionable girls.'

'Yeah?' said Standing. The man was right. It wasn't something he would ever admit to or boast about. Not to strangers, anyway. But as soon as a group of SAS lads got together and booze flowed, all you got was war stories, and most of them were embellished beyond all recognition.

'I see you've got a bit of a tan there,' said the driver. 'Been anywhere nice?'

Standing laughed. 'Not really.'

'Iraq? Afghanistan? Syria?'

Standing laughed again. 'Or D, all of the above.'

The driver grinned into his mirror. 'I get it,' he said. 'I know you can't admit to it. I respect that. But I tell you, you guys are heroes, no question. You wouldn't get me out there in the desert fighting those mad mullahs. Not for all the tea in China. Have you seen the videos of what they do to their prisoners? Fucking animals, they are.'

'No argument here,' said Standing.

'If it was up to me, I'd nuke them all. Just drop a bomb on them. End of.'

'That's a view,' said Standing.

'You don't agree?'

'There's a lot of civilians out there who just want to get on with their lives.'

'Yeah? Looks to me like they want new lives over here. You know they were going to build a mosque in Hereford? Can you believe that? The home of the SAS and they wanted a bloody mosque. They got very short shrift, I can tell you.'

'Yeah, religion has a lot to answer for. Remember the John

Lennon song "Imagine"? If people didn't believe in Heaven, maybe they'd be nicer to each other.'

'Chance'd be a fine thing,' said the driver. 'Seems to me the best way would be to throw out anyone who doesn't want to be British. And there's nothing British about wanting to pray in a mosque and refusing to eat a bacon butty.'

'I guess not,' said Standing. Any further discussion was curtailed by their arrival at the main gates of the Credenhill barracks. 'How much?' asked Standing.

The driver shook his head. 'Your money's no good to me, mate. You're a bloody hero, you and your lot. Least I can do.'

Standing took out his wallet and gave him a ten-pound note. 'I'd rather pay.'

'Okay, suit yourself,' said the driver, taking the money and shoving it into a plastic cup next to his gearstick. 'Thanks. I appreciate it. Stay safe, yeah?'

'You too.' Standing climbed out and pulled his large canvas kitbag after him. The car drove off and he went to the gate where he handed over his ID. A uniformed security guard scrutinised it and waved him through.

Standing shouldered his backpack and walked quickly to the administrative offices. Colonel Davies was the man he was there to see, the man who had Standing's future in his hands. Standing hadn't been given an appointment: he'd just been told to report to the colonel as soon as he'd arrived in the UK. It had been a long journey. He had flown from Syria to Gibraltar in an RAF Lockheed C-130 Hercules, stayed on the Rock for twelve hours while a crew change was arranged, then flown into RAF Brize Norton in Oxfordshire, where 47 Squadron was based. The RAF had been good enough to lay on a car to get him to Charlbury station and provide him with a rail warrant for the two-hour journey to

Hereford. He hadn't shaved or showered since Gibraltar but he still looked presentable in his black leather jacket, green turtleneck sweater and blue jeans.

He knocked on the door to the admin centre and went in. Two female civilian workers sat behind computers, tapping away on their keyboards. Standing knew them both. The older of the pair was Debbie, the wife of one of the Regiment's sergeant majors, the younger was a fit young blonde called Emily, who, by all accounts, was working her way through all the captains in the Regiment. If the rumours were true, she'd already slept with three.

'I'm here to see Colonel Davies,' said Standing. He dropped his kitbag onto the floor with a thud.

Debbie looked at him over the top of her glasses. 'Take a seat, Matt,' she said. 'I'll tell him you're here.'

Standing didn't feel like sitting so he paced up and down. His heart was pounding and he was sweating. Facing the colonel was more stressful than going up against Taliban fighters. He saw Emily looking at him and flashed her a smile. 'They say you've been a naughty boy,' she said.

Standing shrugged. 'Yeah.'

'Captain Waters is an arsehole,' she whispered. 'He had it coming.'

Standing winked at her. 'Thanks.'

'He'll see you now,' said Debbie, waving at the door to the colonel's office.

'Okay if I leave my bag here?'

'Of course,' she said.

Standing took a deep breath to steady himself, knocked on the door, and went in. The colonel was standing by his window, looking out towards the camp's helicopter pad. Standing stood to attention in the centre of the office. The colonel continued to stare out of the window. He was a big man, and although he was in his early fifties, he was as fit as most soldiers half his age. Colonel Davies made it a point to complete the Fan Dance every eight weeks, usually accompanied by a couple of his senior officers. The Fan Dance was a fifteen-mile march with a 45-pound Bergen backpack and a rifle. The route went up and over Pen y Fan, an 886-metre peak in the Brecon Beacons, and the march was used during SAS Selection to weed out unfit applicants. Colonel Davies did it for fun and regularly completed it in less than four hours.

'You know why they call you Lastman Standing?' said the colonel, as he stared out of the window.

'It's a pun, sir. On my name.'

'Bollocks,' said the colonel, turning now. 'It's because you're the last man anyone wants to get into an argument with. You're a hothead, Standing. You fly off the handle. You lack discipline.' His hair was steel grey and cut close to the scalp, while his nose and cheeks were flecked with broken blood vessels, the result of years spent on active service in inhospitable climates. He was wearing green fatigues and Gore-Tex boots, and had a chunky TAG-Heuer watch on his left wrist.

'Yes, sir,' said Standing. The colonel was the only officer in the Regiment who was called 'sir', though even he was never saluted. The SAS never saluted because in the battlefield it told any watching snipers whom they should be aiming at.

The colonel frowned. 'So you're agreeing with me?'

'I'm acknowledging that I heard what you said. Sir.'

'So you're disagreeing with me? Which is it, Standing?'

'Neither, sir. I'm just listening.'

'I don't understand you. You're one of the best soldiers ever to have served with the SAS. In combat, you're second to none. I've never seen a soldier with better gut instincts than you in a firefight. Then you go and assault an officer. You have anger-management issues, Standing. Very serious anger-management issues. In combat, your short fuse is an asset, but outside combat it's a liability. A serious liability.'

'Yes, sir.'

The colonel walked across the room from the window and stood in front of Standing. 'That's all you have to say? "Yes, sir"? You're not apologising? You're not promising you won't do it again?'

'I'm not sorry, sir. And, under the same circumstances I'd probably react the same way again. I couldn't control what happened. I was protecting myself.'

'Captain Waters pushed you.'

'He shoved me, sir. Hard.'

'And you broke his nose and his jaw.'

'I was under attack and I defended myself. I wasn't thinking about what I was doing to the captain. I reacted instinctively. It was over in a second. He pushed me and I hit him with my elbow, then my fist. He went down and I stopped. It was a defensive blow, not an attack.'

'Blow? You mean blows.'

'It was one motion, sir. I elbowed him to the jaw, then brought my fist down on his nose. I wasn't attacking him.'

'You were, Standing. When you hit someone, that's an attack.'

'With respect, sir, the captain attacked me and I defended myself.'

'You said he pushed you. If that's true, he was in the wrong. But the correct response to a push is not to break a man's jaw. An equal, proportionate response would have been to push him back. You would still have been in the wrong, but you wouldn't have put the man in hospital.'

Standing said nothing.

The colonel went to his desk and sat down.

'Why did Captain Waters push you?'

'We were having an argument over an operational matter, sir.'

'What, specifically?'

Standing gritted his teeth. If he told the colonel everything that had happened in Syria, all hell would break loose. There would be an official investigation and, no matter how that worked out, it wouldn't be good for Waters or for himself. 'It was just a disagreement over tactics,' he said.

'That's funny because that was exactly the phrase Captain Waters used,' said the colonel. 'You two haven't put your heads together, have you?'

'No, sir.'

'So you disagree about tactics, the captain pushes you and you break his jaw?'

'That's pretty much what happened, sir. Yes.'

'And it's not the first time you've assaulted an officer, is it, Sergeant Standing? Last time you lost your stripes as a result. Was that a disagreement over tactics?'

'I forget, sir.'

The colonel raised his eyebrows. 'Really? You forget? It's in your file if that would help refresh your memory.'

Standing hadn't forgotten, but he was fairly sure the true details of what had happened in Afghanistan weren't in the file. The officer had been a lieutenant in the Parachute Regiment, a nasty piece of work, who seemed to think that abusing the local population was part of the job. The British forces were pulling out of Afghanistan, supposedly because the task they had been given to do had been accomplished, but in reality because the British government had realised that they were fighting a war they could never win and that the sooner they pulled out the better. Standing and three

SAS troopers had been driving to Kabul when they saw a group of Paras rounding up a group of young Afghan women. They were all wearing *niqab*s so Standing couldn't see their faces but they were obviously kids, teenagers at most.

Standing had been in the front seat of their white Toyota Landcruiser and he'd told the trooper who was driving to pull over. He had watched in the wing mirror as the Paras had circled the women, like sheepdogs rounding up a flock, except sheepdogs didn't carry automatic weapons and wear Kevlar helmets. Standing could hear the soldiers shouting at the women, who were crying and wailing. He had told the troopers to stay in the Landcruiser. He had left his weapon in the vehicle and walked over to the soldiers. He was in desert gear, his trousers and tunic covered with dust and a black-and-white checked *keffiyeh* scarf tied loosely around his neck. 'What's happening, guys?' he'd asked. His skin was sunburned and he hadn't shaved for a week, but he had no military markings on his clothes so he held his hands to his sides to show he wasn't armed.

'Who the fuck are you?' asked a soldier in his late twenties. Standing didn't know at the time but he was a university-educated lieutenant on his first – and only – tour of Afghanistan.

'Hey, mate, I'm on your side,' said Standing. 'What's the problem here?'

'We're just interrogating these locals,' said the lieutenant.

'Yeah? Well, strictly speaking, you're supposed to have a female soldier asking the questions. These girls aren't supposed to be speaking to men who aren't family members.'

'Fuck that. They'll do as they're told.'

'Well, yeah, but you're putting them on the spot. If they're seen talking to soldiers, they'll be in all sorts of trouble.'

'Who the fuck are you?' said the lieutenant again, walking towards Standing.

'Just a guy who's been here a bit longer than you and is offering you some advice.'

'When I want advice, I'll ask for it. What are you? A civilian contractor?'

'Not exactly,' said Standing. He put his hands into the air. 'Listen, I'm not looking to spoil anyone's day, but this is all about hearts and minds. We're pulling out, they know we're pulling out, and they're going to have to deal with the way things are after we've gone. So, leaving aside the whole man-woman thing, they're not going to tell you anything.'

'You need to get back in your vehicle and fuck the fuck off,' said the lieutenant. He swung up his weapon. It was an SA80, the British military's standard assault rifle. Standing wasn't a fan of the SA80, and neither was the SAS. They had tested the weapon and decided they preferred the AR-15 family of assault rifles. Early versions of the SA80 had a tendency to malfunction outside a very narrow temperature range: they jammed, the magazines had a tendency to drop out, and some of the plastic components failed under pressure. But the manufacturers had tweaked it and it was now the weapon of choice of Britain's armed forces. It took the standard NATO 5.56 x 45mm round with thirty cartridges in the magazine, and from the way the lieutenant's finger had slipped over the trigger, it looked as if he was quite prepared to give Standing a demonstration of its firepower.

Standing had a SIG-Sauer P226 strapped to his right leg but his main weapon, of course, was in the Landcruiser, an L119 assault rifle based on the Canadian-made C8 CQB, a variation of the Armalite AR-15. He kept his hands in the air because he could feel the tension pouring off the lieutenant. 'You need to get your finger off the trigger,' he said quietly. 'That's how accidents happen.'

The lieutenant's jaw tightened and he continued to swing

his weapon up. His finger was still on the trigger and Standing knew that it wouldn't take much to send a hail of bullets in his direction.

The lieutenant's eyes had narrowed to a squint, and he made no move to take his finger off the trigger. He was only six feet or so from Standing, and as the barrel centred on Standing's chest, he moved, taking two quick steps to the right and pushing the gun away with his left hand. The fingers of his right hand curled back into a claw and he thrust the palm under the officer's chin. The man let go of the gun with his left and tried to push Standing away, but Standing pulled his arm back and elbowed him in the sternum. The breath exploded from the officer's lungs and he bent over, coughing and spluttering. Standing pulled the gun from him and slammed the butt into the side of his face. The officer hit the ground hard and lay still. It had happened so quickly that the officer's men hadn't even started to react. Standing kept the barrel of the SA80 pointed at the ground to show that he wasn't a threat. For a second or two everyone seemed frozen. Then, as one, the Paras were shouting and aiming their guns at Standing. They started to shuffle towards him, kicking up sand.

He raised his left hand high in the air and kept the gun pointing down, his finger off the trigger. 'It's over, guys, no need to get excited,' he said.

The Paras fell silent but they all kept their weapons aimed at Standing as they shuffled forward. They were so busy staring at him that they didn't notice Standing's three colleagues slip out of the Landcruiser. By the time they did, they were staring down the barrels of the SAS guns. 'We're SAS, mate,' said Pete Simpson, a lanky Geordie with a full beard and impenetrable shades. 'You need to lower your weapons right now.'

The paratroopers looked at each other nervously, then slowly did as they were told. Most of them were barely out of their teens and were clearly lost without their officer.

'Good call, lads,' said Standing. 'Now we'll get into our vehicle and be on our way. As our American allies would say, you all have a nice day.' He placed the SA80 on the ground next to the unconscious officer, threw them a mock salute and turned his back on them.

'Fucking hell, Sarge, you can't go around hitting officers,' Simpson said, as they got back into the Landcruiser. He was right, of course, and forty-eight hours later Standing had been busted back to trooper.

'Well?' said the colonel now.

'I was protecting myself, sir,' said Standing.

'You assaulted a lieutenant with the Paras.'

'He was pointing a loaded weapon at me and acting aggressively. I reacted accordingly.'

'With proportionate force?'

'If he had pulled the trigger, I would have been dead, sir.'

'You seriously thought he would fire?'

'I wasn't thinking, sir. I was reacting.'

The colonel nodded thoughtfully. 'That's your problem. You know that?'

Standing didn't say anything. It was clear he wasn't going to be let off. The question was, how severe his punishment would be. He just hoped he wasn't going to be RTU'd. He doubted he would be able to go back to his unit. The SAS were the best of the best and he didn't want to serve with any other unit so that meant he'd be out of the army and his career prospects on the outside would be grim at best.

'When you're under fire, your instincts save your life. I get that,' said the colonel. 'I get that to be as good a soldier as you are you have to react quickly to situations. In a firefight you don't have time to weigh up your options. Your problem is that you react just as quickly when you're not under fire. You don't think, you act. And sometimes your actions are out of all proportion to the situation you're in.'

'Yes, sir.'

'Is that yes, sir, you agree with me, or yes, sir, you hear what I'm saying?'

'Both, sir.'

The colonel nodded. 'Okay, Standing, this is what's going to happen. You're no longer a sergeant. You're not going to lose any pay or privileges, but you're on suspension for a month. I want you to use that time to get professional help with your anger-management issues. I've arranged for a list to be drawn up of therapists who can help and I want you to avail yourself of their services. At the end of the month you'll be examined by the Regiment's medical staff to see if you're fit for duty.' He held up a hand. 'Mentally fit for duty. No one is doubting your physical fitness. But, believe me, if there are any doubts at all about your mental fitness you'll be returned to your unit. If they'll have you. Are we clear?'

'Yes, sir.'

The colonel leaned towards Standing and lowered his voice. 'Look, Standing, I know you didn't have the easiest of upbringings. I know what happened, obviously, with your father and all. But violence isn't in your DNA. It's learned behaviour, and you can unlearn it. Violence in combat is a necessary evil, but it has to stay there. You can't use violence as a way of solving your everyday issues. Hopefully, a therapist will help you grasp that.'

'Yes, sir.'

'Go home, relax, and sort yourself out. Come back here in a month's time and prove to us that you can be the sort of soldier we know you can be.'

'Yes, sir.'

'Good man.' The colonel smiled thinly. 'Dismissed.'

Standing went outside and picked up his bag.

'I'm to give you a rail warrant to wherever you want to go to,' said Debbie. 'And I have to put together a list of therapists for you.'

Standing frowned. 'I'm not going anywhere.'

Debbie shook her head sadly. 'You have to leave the camp, Matt, and hand in your pass before you go.'

'I live here,' said Standing. 'All my stuff is here. This is my home.'

'I'm sorry, Matt. The colonel was very specific. You're no longer allowed to live in the camp.'

'What about my stuff?'

'You can take it with you. Or you can leave it with me and I'll have it delivered to you.'

Standing glanced at the door to the colonel's office. He could feel his heart pounding and part of him wanted to storm in and grab the man by the throat. The colonel had said he should go home, but the SAS was his home. His only home. In fact, he hadn't had a real home since he was eleven years old. And, with his father beating the shit out of him at every opportunity, he wouldn't have described that as home, not really. He took a deep breath.

'Matt?' asked Debbie.

Standing forced a smile and turned to her.

'Where shall I make the rail warrant out for?' she asked.

Standing tilted his head to one side and thought about it for a few seconds. 'London,' he said.

Willoughby-Brown guided the yacht out of the marina, then let Shepherd take the wheel. The wind was coming from the south and the boat made good progress as it headed south-east. Willoughby-Brown pointed up at the sail where two strips of red tape about a foot long were fluttering in the wind. 'Lesson one,' he said. 'See those red things on the sail?'

Shepherd nodded.

'They're called telltales. Your old sea salts would say they're the equivalent of training wheels but they're invaluable. They tell you how to trim your sails and steer the boat. You can get the same information from studying the shape of the sails but the telltales are a short-cut.'

Shepherd frowned as he looked up at them. There were three sets, at the top of the sail, halfway down and at the bottom. They were all fluttering happily.

'Now turn away from the wind. Just a bit.'

Shepherd did as he was told. Almost immediately the strips started to drop.

'There you go,' said Willoughby-Brown. 'Now the sail is less efficient and the telltales are letting you know. Turn back into the wind.'

Shepherd turned the wheel and straight away the telltales picked up again.

'It's as easy as that,' said Willoughby-Brown. 'If you need to know how efficient the sail is, the telltales will tell you.'

'Got it,' said Shepherd.

'Now, the two basic manoeuvres are tacking and jibing. If you're sailing into the wind, as we are now, you have to tack. You can't sail directly into the wind, obviously. You need it to be off to the side to generate the thrust that moves the boat forward. So if you're sailing into the wind you may have to move the boat left and right to get to where you want to go. That's called tacking. You turn the boat through the wind so that the wind goes from one side of it to the other. That means the boom will move, often quite quickly, so watch out for it. It's easy for the boom to knock you overboard, no matter how big your boat is.' He smiled when he saw Shepherd's frown. 'It'll make more sense when I show you.'

'I hope so,' said Shepherd.

'We'll go through tacking, and jibing, which is the opposite of tacking. In jibing you turn the stern of the boat through the wind. Again, you need to watch out for the boom. You tend to jib a lot less than you tack, but you need to be familiar with both manoeuvres.'

The coastline was now far behind them. The nearest other boat was about half a mile away so they had plenty of space to practise. In the far distance, Shepherd could see oil tankers and container ships, thousands of times their size. 'Didn't I hear that we have right of way in the shipping lanes?' he asked.

'In theory, yes,' said Willoughby-Brown. 'Power has to give way to sail. That's the rule. But the problem is, a container ship has so much inertia it's a big thing for it to change direction. If the crew suddenly see a small sailboat in their path, by the time they've got their vessel moving it's too late. Also, you're dependent on them seeing you. The bridge might be twelve storeys high, the waves could be ten feet or more, and the guy on watch might be at the end of a long, boring shift. Is he going to see a thirty-footer in the dark? Or on a rainy day? No. It's all very well saying that sail has the right of way, but if you find one of those buggers bearing down on you, you really need to get out of its way. Having maritime law on your side doesn't help you if your boat's been reduced to matchwood.'

Willoughby-Brown spent the next two hours having Shepherd practise the two manoeuvres. He was soon able to perform them automatically. It wasn't difficult: all he had to do was follow the steps in order. The next hour was spent practising heaving to, using the mainsail and the jib to work against each other so that the yacht could be held steady in the sea. Heaving to was harder to master, but again Shepherd was quick to learn. While he had his hands on the wheel to keep the boat heaved to, Willoughby-Brown went down into the galley to make two mugs of coffee. He gave one to Shepherd, then lit a small cigar. 'Heaving to takes some getting used to, but it can save your life if you find yourself in really bad weather,' he said. 'Basically you ride out the storm rather than fighting your way through it.'

He sipped his coffee. 'Right. Time to teach you about reefing.'

'I'm all ears,' said Shepherd.

'Reefing is reducing the area of the sails you're using. You reef when the boat is heeling over too much. There's nothing wrong with heeling over, but it can scare a less experienced passenger or crewman so we tend to reef when we get to an angle of twenty-five degrees or so, or when the wind is up to fifteen knots.' He grinned. 'Time to test that memory of yours,' he said. 'Here's the drill. You slacken the boom vang and the mainsheet. You stabilise the boom by taking up the topping lift. You lower the main halyard until you've reefed as much as you want, then tighten and make fast the reefing tack line. You hoist the main halyard until the edge of the sail is wrinkle-free, then take in the reefing clew line and make fast. That done, you ease the main stopping lift, trim the mainsheet and tighten the boom vang.' He grinned. 'Easy-peasy.' He had another sip of his coffee.

'So you say.'

'Can you repeat that back to me?'

'Sure.' Shepherd did so, word for word.

'Impressive,' said Willoughby-Brown.

'There's just one problem,' said Shepherd.

'What's that?'

'I haven't a clue what any of it means.'

Willoughby-Brown chuckled drily. 'You're a funny guy, Daniel,' he said. 'Don't worry. You'll soon get the hang of it and the jargon will come naturally.' He put down his coffee mug and rubbed his hands together. 'Let's get started.'

The train pulled into Paddington station but Standing stayed in his seat. He hadn't thought through what he was going to do. He had no friends in London. Family, barely. His father was in prison there. And his sister lived there, but she had a new family and it had been made clear that he wasn't welcome. So clear that her new parents had taken out a restraining order against him, which, as far as he knew, was still in effect. Debbie had given him a list of London therapists. He could choose which one he wanted and the Regiment would pay for up to ten sessions. He sighed and stood up, stretched and shouldered his kitbag. It contained all his worldly goods. Debbie had offered to send anything on to him, but there was nothing to send. Other than clothes, a few books and a digital radio, he had very little else. The SAS was his life and the Regiment gave him everything he needed. He shuddered. The thought that the SAS might no longer want him was terrifying and he wasn't sure how he would deal with it.

The first rule of survival when thrown into a hostile environment was to find shelter, then food and water. He stepped off the train and walked along the platform. The station was busy: people were hurrying to and from trains, many of them staring at smartphones as they walked. There were two armed policemen on the concourse, British Transport Police officers holding LMT CQB carbines, short-barrelled semi-automatic rifles chambered for the 5.56mm x 45mm NATO cartridge and based on the AR-15 design. Standing nodded his approval as they walked by him.

He went out into Praed Street, and looked left and right. Shelter. That meant a hotel. He had money in the bank but he didn't want to throw hundreds of pounds on a luxury establishment. He needed intel. He took out his iPhone and googled 'cheap hotels in London near Paddington station'. Most seemed to be in Bayswater and he headed in that direction. Fifteen minutes later he was walking down Inverness Terrace. Most of the houses had been converted into small hotels, and many had 'VACANCY' signs in the window. They all seemed pretty much the same but then he saw one that advertised 'SERVICED APARTMENTS'. That would probably be better privacy-wise so he went into a small reception area where a young Indian girl in a black suit explained that they rented studio apartments by the day, week and month. The colonel was expecting him back in Hereford in a month but he wasn't sure how long he planned to stay in London so he opted for a month and paid with a credit card. She handed him a keycard and showed him where the stairs were. There was a lift, she said, but it was slow and always quicker to walk. Standing thanked her and headed up to the second floor.

His studio was one large room overlooking the main street with a sofa and a big-screen TV on the wall, a small table with two chairs and a kitchen area with an oven, a hotplate and a microwave. He dropped his kitbag on the table. A door opened into a small shower room. There was another door but when he opened it there was nothing but a washing machine, a stack of bed linen and two pillows. He went back into the main room, then realised that the sofa folded down into a bed. It was small, but functional, and considerably better than his accommodation had been in Syria.

He switched on the TV and tuned it to CNN, then took out his phone. It had been a month since he had last spoken to his sister, and there had been no phone coverage in Syria so he hadn't even been able to text her. He sent her a text now: I'm in London. You OK?

He put the phone on the table and went over to the kitchen area. There was a carton of milk in the fridge but it had gone off so he poured it down the sink. There was also a packet of cheese, which seemed okay, and some bacon, which didn't. He found a jar of Gold Blend coffee in a cupboard over the sink, with a bag of sugar lumps and half a dozen Pot Noodles. Standing switched on the kettle and made himself a cup of coffee with two sugars, then went to the table. There was no reply from his sister. He sat down and sipped his coffee as he watched a blonde woman with too much make-up explain why China's worsening relationship with the United States meant that more Chinese companies were doing business in Africa.

He picked up his phone but there had been no reply. He called her number but it went straight through to voicemail so he sent another text: *Lexi?*

He put his feet up on the sofa and closed his eyes. He was dog-tired and within minutes was fast asleep and snoring loudly.

Willoughby-Brown kept the yacht out at sea until the sun went down to give Shepherd the experience of sailing back to port in the dark. It was a totally different environment: the horizon disappeared as the sea blended into the sky and the land was nothing more than a dark smudge. All around there were red, green and white lights, some of them flashing, on the boats around them and on the buoys marking the entrance to the marina.

It took more than half an hour for Shepherd's night vision to kick in properly, but even then it was tough to work out where he was and what was going on around him. He wished he had a pair of night-vision goggles.

'Sailing at night is a whole different animal,' said Willoughby-Brown. 'To be honest, you'll want to avoid it as much as possible. At least, you don't want to be entering or leaving port at night.' He turned the wheel to starboard and Shepherd discovered that the dark shape ahead was a motor launch – for some reason it hadn't switched its lights on. 'I'm comfortable enough around Brighton but I've been sailing in these waters for years. I'd be a lot less confident trying to find my way into a port I'd not been to before.'

'It's all about the buoys, right?'

Willoughby-Brown nodded. He had put on a thick fleece and a floppy hat to protect himself against the cold wind blowing from the land. 'They're on the charts, and they'll guide you in. You have to keep an eye out for other boats, and you don't want to be doing it under sail at night. In fact, generally I'd use the engine to enter and leave port. You have more control.'

He motioned for Shepherd to take the wheel. He pointed at a flashing green light in the distance. 'Keep to the left of that buoy,' he said.

The flashing light was easy to focus on, but he was worried about other boats. The only clues to the direction the traffic was heading were the running lights. Each boat had a red light on its port side and a green light on its starboard side. So unless a vessel was pointed directly towards or away from him he would see a red light or a green one. If he saw a red light the other boat had right of way. If he saw green, he had right of way. Hopefully, with both boats knowing who had right of way, collisions shouldn't happen. Except, as Willoughby-Brown pointed out, some sailors just didn't care and others didn't have great eyesight. That meant he had to be on his toes all the time, and it was exhausting work.

The fact that he had memorised the chart made it easier but it still took a tremendous amount of concentration to keep on the right course and avoid other craft.

'You're doing fine,' said Willoughby-Brown, as if sensing his discomfort. 'Try to relax. You're gripping the wheel as if your life depended on it.'

'Well, it sort of does,' said Shepherd.

'Take deep breaths. And keep moving your head, not your eyes. Make use of your peripheral vision as much as you can.'

Shepherd followed Willoughby-Brown's advice, but he still felt as if they were travelling too quickly and that the boat was ever so slightly out of control. Eventually they reached the marina. Shepherd had assumed that Willoughby-Brown would take over the wheel when they got there but he seemed happy enough to talk Shepherd through it.

'I hope you're insured,' said Shepherd, as he guided the boat through a narrow strip of water, multi-million-pound yachts and power boats on either side.

'I have more faith in your ability than you do,' said Willoughby-Brown.

He let Shepherd bring the yacht into the jetty, then took over the wheel and the throttles and had Shepherd tie it up. Once it was secure, Willoughby-Brown switched off the engine and checked his knots. 'Nice work,' he said. He went through the hatchway and down into the main cabin where he switched on the lights. 'Hungry?'

'Sure,' said Shepherd, sitting down at the main table. He was surprised at how tired he was, probably because he wasn't used to being on a small boat, where his body was constantly having to adjust itself to the movement through the waves. There was a lot of running around, too, especially when tacking and jibing, and every muscle in his body ached. Willoughby-Brown had provided Marks & Spencer sandwiches and some shortbread to eat while they were sailing, but Shepherd had skipped breakfast and was ravenous.

Willoughby-Brown opened a refrigerator. 'I can offer you lasagne, a roast chicken dinner, a rather nice salmon in parsley sauce with sliced potatoes, or sausages and mash with onion gravy. It's got to be microwaved but it's good stuff.'

'I could eat anything at the moment,' said Shepherd. 'The sausages sound good.'

'Excellent choice,' said Willoughby-Brown. He pulled out the pack and took the lasagne for himself, put them into the microwave, tapped in the power setting and time, then pulled out a bottle of red wine from a rack built into the cabin wall. 'Nuits-Saint-Georges,' he said, handing it to Shepherd with a corkscrew. 'Quite a good year. Do the honours, will you?'

Shepherd opened the bottle while Willoughby-Brown took two crystal glasses from a cupboard. 'I can live with microwaved food but I refuse to scrimp on the wine,' he said, sliding onto the seat opposite Shepherd. He held out the glasses and Shepherd poured.

They clinked and drank. Shepherd had to admit it was a very good wine, rich, fruity, and so smooth that he drank almost half of his without realising. Willoughby-Brown laughed. 'Try to savour it, Daniel. It's forty quid a bottle and that's wholesale.' He continued to chuckle as he topped up Shepherd's glass.

'You haven't told me why you're so keen to get me sailing,' said Shepherd.

'It's your way of getting close to Meyer,' said Willoughby-Brown. 'He operates around the world. Heroin from

Afghanistan, marijuana from Jamaica and Nigeria, cocaine from Colombia. He usually ships in bulk. And by bulk I mean tons. The DEA has been tightening up on Colombian shipments moving by land so Meyer has been using yachts. Big catamarans, specifically. The cocaine is built into the hulls in Colombia, and he has them sailed to the Caribbean. Then the crew goes back to Colombia, and when he's sure that the shipment is safe and not being watched, he gets another crew to sail it to Europe. He uses shipbrokers to arrange a fictitious sale and often the crew have no idea what's inside the hull.'

'Lisa gave you this, did she?'

'No. This was an informant within his organisation. The DEA picked him up and turned him. The yacht connection came up during his interrogation. The DEA sent him back with a wire and he disappeared soon afterwards. The assumption is that Meyer had him killed. Either that or he's sitting on a beach somewhere, laughing his arse off. I suspect the former.'

'So the plan is to set me up as a sailor and get him to offer me a job?'

'The sailing is your way in. It's up to you then to show him you can be more of an asset.'

Shepherd frowned. 'I'm not following you.'

'We'll give you a legend with . . . attractive qualities, shall we say? Army background, a spell in prison – maybe you killed a man. We're still working on it. When he meets you, he'll think you're just a jobbing sailor, but if he digs into your background he'll discover the meaty stuff and that will intrigue him.'

The microwave pinged. Willoughby-Brown eased himself off his seat and went to retrieve their meals. They were piping hot so he used a pair of oven gloves with nautical flags on to carry the food to the table. Shepherd peeled the plastic film off his sausages and mash and steam billowed out. Willoughby-Brown took knives and forks from a drawer, bottles of Heinz ketchup and HP sauce from a cupboard, and plonked them on the table, then sat down again. 'Hope you don't mind not having plates, but it saves on washing up,' he said.

'All good,' said Shepherd, pouring HP sauce over his sausages. 'So, how do I get an introduction?'

'Again, we're working on that. It'll be something cute, something from left field. But once you get close, you'll need to be involved with Lisa, too. We want to see what she sends back about you. If Meyer takes you on board – no pun intended – it'll be a major red flag if she doesn't report you to her handler.'

'Who is her handler?' asked Shepherd. He could tell from the way Willoughby-Brown's jaw tensed that he'd struck a nerve so he smiled and tucked into his food as he waited for the answer.

Willoughby-Brown took a long drink of wine, then a deep breath. 'Sam Hargrove.'

Over the years as an undercover agent Shepherd had learned to hide his reactions – showing his true feelings could be dangerous, even life-threatening at times – but his jaw dropped and he stared at Willoughby-Brown with a mixture of contempt and distrust. 'Are you fucking serious?' he said, putting down his knife and fork.

Willoughby-Brown shrugged and looked out of the port-hole.

'Just how duplicitous are you?' hissed Shepherd. 'Are you trying to set up Sam Hargrove the way you screwed Charlie Button?'

'Now you're comparing apples and oranges,' said

Willoughby-Brown. 'Charlotte was using MI5 resources to pursue her own agenda.'

'And you're the one who forced her out.'

'If it hadn't been me, someone else would have done it. I hope you're not trying to justify what she did, Daniel, because you'd be on very shaky ground.'

'You forced her out, and you ended up with her job. That was a coincidence, was it?'

Willoughby-Brown looked Shepherd in the eyes. 'When I began investigating Button, I had no intention of doing her job. That is a fact. You might not like it, you might not believe it, but it's a fact nonetheless. I was asked to take over her role after she had left.'

Shepherd shook his head. 'No, I don't believe it. Yes, I believe you were given her job only after she'd gone, but you must have known you'd be in line to succeed her.' He was still hungry so he picked up his knife and fork and started eating again. The sausages were surprisingly good.

'I did what I did because it was in the best interests of the Service,' said Willoughby-Brown. 'She was using MI5 assets to kill the men who had murdered her husband.'

'And how is it in anyone's interests for you to undermine Sam Hargrove?'

'That's not what's happening here,' said Willoughby-Brown. 'We're mounting an operation to check the standing of an undercover agent who is supposed to be investigating one of the world's most successful – and ruthless – drug dealers.'

'Behind Sam's back.'

'If Sam Hargrove has a problem in his unit, he needs to know.'

'But you're not telling him you're checking up on him.'

'Because that's not what's happening here.'

'You're playing with words. You suspect that one of his operatives has betrayed his trust. If that's the case, why don't you tell him?'

'He seems to think everything is proceeding as normal.'

'There you go again, playing with words. Why are you doing this behind his back? That's a simple enough question.'

'And the answer is simple enough. Hargrove seems happy with the intelligence he's getting back from his operative. We aren't. So we're running a check to see how accurate Lisa's intelligence-gathering is. This started as an NCA investigation into a drug dealer but there are now other ramifications that mean Five is taking much more of an interest.'

Shepherd sighed. 'Getting information from you is like pulling teeth. What ramifications?'

'Well, for a start, Meyer is buying some of his heroin from the Taliban. Not directly, obviously, there's a middle man involved, but his money is funding the Taliban. Plus he's started using the Hawala system to move his money. You know how that works, of course.' He sipped his wine and smacked his lips in appreciation.

'Obviously.' Hawala was a method of transferring money without it actually leaving the country. You went to a hawala broker and handed over your cash. You were given a code or a note, which could be redeemed with any other broker anywhere in the world. It was all based on trust and while it was predominantly used in the Middle East, Africa and India, there were hawala brokers around the world.

'So, then, you can understand that Meyer's money is now moving around a system that is also used by Islamic State and al-Qaeda.'

'That's a stretch,' said Shepherd. 'The whole point of the hawala system is that money isn't physically moved around.'

'Nevertheless he's dealing with people who are dealing

with terrorists. That's guilt by association. The point I'm making is that this has moved well beyond the NCA's capabilities and we need to be more proactive.'

'So take the case off them and get Sam to pull Lisa out.'

'That would be counter-productive if she's still a productive asset.'

Shepherd sighed. Willoughby-Brown was going around in circles. Arguing with the man was like trying to grab mist. 'Let's suppose I discover that Lisa has turned, what then?'

Willoughby-Brown frowned. 'What do you mean?'

'I find out that she's gone over to the dark side. What happens?'

'To her? Or to Hargrove?'

'Both.'

'It depends. In Lisa's case, on whether or not she can still be useful to us. If she's gone bad, she's facing a long prison sentence. We can use that for leverage.'

'Turn her into a double agent?'

'If Meyer trusts her we can use that to our advantage.'

'And if she has gone bad, what happens to Hargrove?'

Willoughby-Brown's fork hovered over his lasagne. 'That's not up to me. That would be a police matter.'

'The NCA aren't going to be happy if one of their undercover operatives has gone over to the other side.'

'Agreed.'

'Which would put Sam in a difficult position, wouldn't it?'

'You're asking hypothetical questions, Daniel.'

'I'm trying to find out where I stand. I worked for Sam when I was an undercover cop, and when he was with the Serious Organised Crime Agency. He's one of the good guys. Now you're asking me to betray him.'

'When did I say that? Lisa Wilson is the focus of this case.

And her connection to Meyer. That's all that needs concern you.'

'It's about the consequences, Jeremy. Everything we do has consequences and I don't want to be responsible for jeopardising Sam's career.'

'You're over-thinking this. As usual.'

'You've already shafted one of my bosses. I'm not going to help you do it again.'

Willoughby-Brown's eyes narrowed. 'If you'll forgive the metaphor, you're sailing a tad too close to the wind.'

'I'm serious, Jeremy.'

'So am I. I understand that when you were a police officer, and when you were with SOCA, you got to choose your assignments. But you don't work for the police any more. You're employed by the Security Service where the arrangements are less flexible. The choice you have is to work for MI5, or not. If at any time you feel unable or unwilling to carry out the duties assigned to you, you're perfectly entitled to quit.'

Shepherd gritted his teeth but didn't say anything. Quitting wasn't something he intended to do on the spur of the moment, and if he ever left MI5 he would make sure he had another job lined up first.

'Are we clear, Daniel?' asked Willoughby-Brown. He put down his knife and fork and Shepherd realised he'd finished his lasagne while he was only halfway through his sausages and mash.

'Absolutely,' said Shepherd, his voice a dull monotone.

Willoughby-Brown took out a pack of small cigars. 'Excellent,' he said. 'Why don't you make us another cup of coffee while I smoke one of these on deck?'

'We're not driving back to London?'

Willoughby-Brown laughed. 'You need to experience a

night in a bunk, and we'll go out again at first light to check that everything I've taught you has sunk in.'

'Are you serious? Aren't there hotels nearby?'

'We're teaching you to be a sailor,' said Willoughby-Brown. 'And you'll be surprised by how comfortable it is.'

'I snore,' said Shepherd. He really didn't see the point of sleeping on a cramped boat with Willoughby-Brown when Brighton was full of perfectly good hotels.

'That's okay,' said Willoughby-Brown. 'So do I.'

Standing groaned and opened his eyes. He looked at his watch. Nine o'clock. He'd fallen asleep on the sofa. He sat up and rubbed his face, then went over to the table and picked up his phone. No missed calls and no messages. He called his sister's number but it went straight through to voicemail again. He didn't know what to say so he ended the call. Then he realised he had to say something so he hit redial. 'Lexi, hey, it's Matt. I'm in London. Give me a call, yeah?'

He was hungry so he left the apartment and went downstairs. There was a different Indian girl on Reception – she looked as if she might be the older sister of the girl who had checked him in. He headed out and walked to Queensway, the area's main shopping street. It was busy with a vibrant mix of tourists and locals, and within two minutes he had heard half a dozen languages spoken. He walked past several Chinese restaurants, with glossy roast ducks hanging by their necks in the window. He'd never been a fan of Chinese food, or Asian food generally. He'd eaten mainly army food over the past eight years, which was bland at best, so spicy dishes tended not to agree with him. He reached an Italian restaurant, sat at a table by the window and ate spaghetti carbonara, drank two bottles of Peroni beer, then had a coffee as he watched the world go by. He kept his phone on the table in front of him, but there were no calls and no texts.

He got back to his apartment at eleven, thought about folding the bed down but decided not to bother and slept fully clothed with the television on.

Shepherd had slept in some pretty uncomfortable places during his years in the SAS, so any night when he didn't freeze, get bitten by the local insects or have to sleep on rocks or sand was a good one. But the cabin was cramped and he felt as if he was sleeping in a coffin, while the boat creaked and groaned as it moved on the water. He doubted he slept for more than four or five hours in total, and never for more than an hour at a time. When sleep eluded him, he read the books on seamanship that Willoughby-Brown had given him. He heard the other man get up at just after six, then some pretty unpleasant noises from the toilet, and eventually Willoughby-Brown was banging and crashing in the galley. Shepherd hadn't bothered taking off his clothes so he pulled on his training shoes and joined him.

'Not much choice for breakfast, I'm afraid,' said Willoughby-Brown, plonking two boxes of cereal onto the table. 'Weetabix or Alpen.'

'Alpen always reminds me of hamster food,' said Shepherd. He helped himself to two Weetabix and slopped milk over them, then sat down and tucked in. Willoughby-Brown had made coffee and took it onto the deck to drink it while he smoked. Shepherd joined him once he'd finished his cereal.

'So what's the plan?' asked Shepherd, sitting down on the opposite side of the wheel. There were sailors on several of the boats to either side of *Second Wind*, mainly middle-aged men in windbreakers and thick pullovers, busying themselves with jobs that needed doing on boats.

'We'll go out for a few hours and I'll put you through your paces. Then you're off to Florida.'

'Meyer's in Florida?'

'You're not ready to meet him yet,' said Willoughby-Brown. 'We need to get you familiar with big boats and that's out of my league. I've arranged for a guy in Jacksonville to show you the ropes. His name's Barry Minister – most people call him BM.'

'Seems a long way to go for a sailing lesson,' said Shepherd.

Willoughby-Brown blew a tight plume of bluish smoke up at the mainsail. 'One, he's the best in the business, Nothing he doesn't know about sailing. Two, we can trust him. I've used him before and he's one hundred per cent reliable. Three, you're unlikely to bump into any of Meyer's contacts in Jacksonville. Four . . .' He looked across at Shepherd. 'Do I need a four?'

'I wasn't trying to second-guess you, Jeremy,' said Shepherd, 'just pointing out it's a long way to go, that's all.'

'You were a lot more flexible when you weren't having sex on a regular basis,' said Willoughby-Brown.

'Well, to be fair, I haven't been home for nearly three months – at least, not for more than a day or two.'

'And the au pair's missing you?'

Willoughby-Brown grinned and Shepherd knew he was trying to rile him. He refused to give the man the satisfaction and smiled easily. 'Katra will be fine. Just I could do with a few days R and R.'

'You don't find sailing relaxing?'

'No, Jeremy, I don't.'

'I find it the most relaxing thing in the world, Daniel. The sky above, the water below, the sails full of wind, completely responsible for my own destiny.'

'Master of your own domain?'

'You clearly don't get it.'

Shepherd shrugged. 'It's transport. A way of getting from one place to another, and generally not an efficient way of doing it.'

Willoughby-Brown sighed. 'Clearly you don't see the romance of it.'

'Clearly not.'

Willoughby-Brown flicked what was left of his cigar over the side into the water. He didn't look happy. 'Okay, let's get started. I'll untie us. You take the wheel.'

'Aye, aye, Captain.'

Debbie in the colonel's office had given Standing a list of three therapists in London. One was a woman – Dr Sharon Doyle – with a string of letters after her name and an office in Harley Street. He figured that if he was going to spend hours in therapy he'd rather it was a woman – at least he'd have something pleasant to look at. When he phoned for an appointment, the receptionist already knew who he was and said there was a slot free at three o'clock. Standing hadn't expected her to be available so soon but he had nothing else to do so he caught the Tube to Regent's Park and was in Dr Doyle's office at three o'clock prompt.

Dr Doyle was indeed pleasant to look at, a pretty brunette in her early thirties with her hair in a bob, and full lips that always seemed to be on the verge of smiling. Standing had expected a sofa but there were two winged armchairs either side of a low coffee-table on which there were two bottles of Evian water and crystal tumblers. She was holding a notepad and a Mont Blanc pen, and shook hands with him before waving him to the chair that faced the door. 'So, I'm assuming you know how this works,' she said. 'We're going to chat over the next few weeks and together see what we can do to improve your anger-management skills. I've signed the Official Secrets Act so anything you tell me is confidential and will stay that way, though obviously there are things you shouldn't and mustn't tell me.'

'You see a lot of guys from the Regiment?'

She nodded. 'Some serving and others who have left. The job you do is stressful, to say the least, but returning to civilian life can be even more so.'

'A lot of guys can't cope,' he said. 'I'll be honest. I'm not sure that I could. I really don't want to leave the Regiment, Dr Doyle. It's my life. My whole life. I don't have anything else.'

'Well, I'm sure that's an exaggeration,' she said. 'Why don't we start with a little background? Tell me about your family situation.'

'I don't really have a family.'

'Mother? Father?'

'Sure. Everyone has a mother and father, don't they?'

Dr Doyle smiled. 'I meant are you close? Did you have a happy childhood?'

'No. And no.'

She looked at him expectantly and eventually he saw there was no point in not talking. 'My dad was a bastard,' he said quietly. 'He still is, probably. He beat me up when I was a kid and knocked my mother around. He ended up killing her.'

Dr Doyle's eyes widened. 'Oh, my God,' she said. 'I'm so sorry.'

'He was in the kitchen, shouting at her the way he always did when he was angry with her. He punched her, like he always did. I guess he forgot that he was holding a knife. Killed her instantly. It went straight into her heart. He phoned the police and sat down next her.'

'Where were you?'

'In the next room, watching TV with the sound turned up, like we always had it when they were fighting.'

'We?'

'Me and my sister. She was three.'

'And how old were you?'

'Eleven.'

'That must have been awful.'

'It was a long time ago. Things don't seem so bad with hindsight. We were still watching TV when the police came. I remember them taking him away in handcuffs. I remember the blood on his shirt and his hands. But I don't think we knew what had happened. There was this really nice police-woman who sat with us. Wendy, her name was.' He smiled. 'Funny that. I don't remember much about that day, but I remember Wendy. Then in the evening a woman from the council came and took us away. We never went home.'

'That must have been terrible.'

'Like I said, time numbs you. I remember Lexi crying herself to sleep. We were put with a foster family for a few weeks, then something happened and we were moved to another. That was shit. They were just in it for the money and the food was crap. The guy was just plain creepy. He kept trying to get into the bathroom, and once when I was watching TV, he put his hand on my knee. I punched him in the face and the next day I was moved to another family.'

Dr Doyle frowned. 'They split you up?'

'They didn't care. I was put with another couple who were using fostering as a business. They had six boys in three bedrooms, sleeping in bunk beds. Cornflakes for breakfast, egg and chips for dinner. Sometimes just the chips. I had to move school, and then I was moved again a few months later. It became a pattern.'

'And how often did you get to see your sister?'

'Once a month, maybe. But then she was adopted and I saw less of her.'

'And your father? What happened to him?'

'Life imprisonment,' said Standing. 'But, these days, life doesn't mean life. He might be out again in another ten years.'

'You've never been to see him?'

'Why would I? He knocked me around and he killed my mum.'

'For closure. To have him apologise for what he did, maybe.'

'Apologising won't bring my mum back.'

'You sound angry.'

Standing's eyes narrowed. 'Of course I'm fucking angry. He killed my mum and I lost my sister. I've a lot to be angry about.' He realised he was clenching his fists. He took a deep breath and forced himself to relax. 'I'm sorry.'

'For what?'

'For getting angry.'

'Anger is a perfectly reasonable emotion,' said Dr Doyle. 'Everyone gets angry. It's how we control the anger that matters. And you controlled it, just then. You took a deep breath and you weren't angry any more.'

'I guess so.'

'Do you get angry a lot?'

Standing laughed harshly. 'Isn't that why I'm here?'

'You're here not because you get angry but because you have problems controlling your anger.'

Standing reached for a bottle of water and drank from it. He wiped his mouth with the back of his hand. 'I'm a soldier,' he said. 'If I didn't get angry, I'd be a pretty crap one. If you're in a firefight, you don't have time to stop, think and control your emotions. You react. You move. You fight back.'

'Absolutely,' said Dr Doyle. 'From what I hear you're a brilliant soldier. You react instinctively. You know where to move, what to do and how to react. I'm told that time and time again you've saved the lives of your colleagues.'

Standing nodded. 'I'm good under fire,'

'Oh, no, Matt. You're not good. I'm told you're a natural. You're able to assess risks and calculate angles. You know where's safe and where to fire from, where the enemies are and where you need to be. They teach tactics and strategies but with you the rulebook goes out of the window, doesn't it? You do it without thinking.'

Standing grinned. 'It's a gift.'

'Yes, it is. For a soldier. But I think you've found it can be a hindrance in the real world.'

'You're saying that soldiering isn't the real world? Because I can tell you, it's as real as it gets.'

'I apologise,' she said. 'Bad choice of words. But you know what I mean. Behaviour that can save your life in a war zone can get you into trouble in civilian circles.'

'No argument there,' he said. He stared glumly at the floor.

'Cheer up,' she said. 'It's fixable.'

He looked up. 'It is?'

'Of course. Otherwise I'd be taking money under false pretences. There are exercises you can do, techniques I can teach you that will help. To be honest, you have an advantage that most people don't – you have an outlet where you can unleash your anger. You can fire a gun at an enemy. You can fight and you can kill. Most people are stuck in lives where they have no choice but to quell their anger. You at least have a release. But what we need to do is to teach you to confine that release to combat.'

'Okay,' said Standing. 'I'll give it a go.'

'But first I need to try to understand what it is that sparks your anger. You got upset when I talked about your mother. You clenched your hands, and I could see the anger in your eyes. It was quite scary, actually.'

'I've never hit a woman. Never have and never will.'

'Are you sure about that?'

Standing's eyes hardened. 'You think I'm lying?'

'I'm sure you'd never intend to hit a woman. But the way your temper is, you've never lashed out at a woman? Never?'

Standing shook his head emphatically. 'Never.'

'That's interesting,' said the therapist.

'Why?'

'Because it suggests you do have control. That you would lash out at a man but not at a woman. The anger is the same, but in one case you hit out, in another you don't. What's the difference?'

'Men don't hit women.'

'But they do. Your father is an example of that. Not only do they hit women but sometimes they kill them.'

'I'm not like my father.'

'No, you're not. But you can see the similarities, can't you, between the two of you?'

Standing folded his arms. 'No.'

'I don't mean you're like your father, Matt. I mean you both have anger-management issues. But the fact that you have never hit a woman suggests you have more control than he does. Which is a good thing.'

Standing nodded. 'I guess so.'

Dr Doyle scribbled on her notepad. 'I'd like to know a little bit more about your sister. How old is she now?'

'Sixteen,' he said.

'Do you see much of her?'

'Not really, no.'

'I suppose your job makes it difficult?'

'It's more complicated than that.'

'How so?'

'It's a long story.'

'We've got all the time in the world.' She looked at the clock on the wall and smiled. 'Well, actually we've got forty-five minutes. But I'm listening.'

'I'm not allowed to go to her house,' said Standing, flatly.

Dr Doyle waited for him to continue, and when he didn't, she smiled encouragingly. 'Because?'

'Because I had an altercation with her parents. It was a long time ago but it turned nasty and they got a restraining order, saying I couldn't go near the house or approach them. I'm pretty sure it still applies.'

'So what happened?'

Standing sighed. 'You have to understand I was a bit wild back then. I'd been in care almost half my life and in a succession of foster homes, some okay but most of them pretty bad. I was always big for my age and a bit gawky and no one wanted to adopt me. Not like Lexi – she was adopted within months. Cute as a button, blonde hair, blue eyes, they were queuing up to take her. So she had a home and family and I had . . . I had fuck-all.'

'And that made you bitter?'

Standing shook his head vehemently. 'Hell, no. I was happy for her. I was glad that she had a good life. They were good people. They *are* good people, I mean. He's a manager in some office or other, she's a housewife. They have a son a bit older than me. Andrew. And they couldn't have more kids so they adopted. They gave her everything. And I wasn't jealous. I just wanted to be with her. She was my sister and I wasn't allowed to see her.'

'That doesn't sound right,' said Dr Doyle.

'If I wanted to see her I had to talk to my social worker

and she had to talk to the parents and it seemed to take for ever to get anything arranged. I was never allowed to see her on her birthday because she always had a party, and I was so much older that they said I'd be a disruption. They didn't want me at Christmas because I wasn't family. I wasn't *their* family, was what they meant.' He sighed as the memories flooded back. 'One year I'd bought her this teddy bear as a present. She had a teddy bear when she was small but once we were taken into care she never saw it again. I had a paper round so I saved my money and bought her this really expensive bear. A German one.'

'A Steiff?'

Standing nodded. 'She'd seen one in a toy shop once and wanted it but our father wouldn't buy it for her. I saved and saved and bought it the week before Christmas. Wrapped it and put a bow on it. But that Christmas, like pretty much every Christmas, the social worker said I couldn't see her. It was about three days later. Her new parents picked me up in their car and took us to a park. It was freezing cold and it had been raining so we couldn't play. All we could do was sit on a bench. They'd bought her a video game thing for Christmas. Sony made them – they cost a small fortune back then. PSP, I think it was called.'

'I remember. My son nagged and nagged until I got him one. He played with it for a few weeks and then it got shoved in a drawer.'

'Lexi couldn't take her eyes off it. Hardly looked at the bear. Her mother ended up holding it while she played the game.'

'She was a small child, you can't blame her.'

Standing's jaw tightened. 'I don't. It's not about blaming her. I'm just telling you the way it was. She was my sister and they did everything they could to keep us apart. Then, when I was sixteen, I'd had enough. I went around to the house without talking to the social worker first. I just went. They wouldn't let me in. They said I had to go away or they'd call the police. All I wanted to do was to talk to my sister and they treated me like a criminal. The guy grabbed me by the arm and twisted it and I hit him. Hard. Right on the chin. He went down and banged his head against a hall table. Cut it open. I didn't mean to, I just . . .' He left the sentence hanging.

'You just reacted?'

'It was instinct. He'd grabbed me hard and I pushed him. It wasn't a conscious decision. There was no thought – there was no time to think. Grab. Push. Crash. I ran but where could I run to? The cops had me within hours and I was charged with GBH.'

'That seems extreme?'

'The father made it sound worse than it was, as if I'd attacked him out of the blue. I was up before the magistrates and they were going to send me to the Crown Court, but then my brief gave them this whole spiel about me wanting to join the army and serve my country and that a criminal record would blight my career.'

'Was that true?'

'I'd been thinking of signing up, sure. I was still in care. How could the army be any worse than that? Anyway, one of the magistrates was a former officer with the Paras and he convinced the others that if I signed up immediately they should let the case drop. You have to remember that at the time Afghanistan and Iraq was in full flow and they probably figured that dodging bullets in the desert would be a better punishment than sitting in a cell with a PlayStation.'

'You can join the army at sixteen?'

'Yes. But you have to be eighteen to go to a war zone.'

'So you signed up?'

He grinned. 'I was in Iraq two days after my eighteenth birthday. And I finally got the family I'd been missing. The army does everything for you. It feeds you, it clothes you, it gives you things to do, it trains you, it teaches you. It doesn't care who you are or where you came from, all it cares about is that you're a good soldier. And I was. I was bloody good. By the time I was three years in, my sergeant said I should try for the SAS and I did. Sailed through Selection. Loved it. Just loved it. It was what I was born to do.' He sat back in his chair and folded his arms. 'Now they want to kick me out.'

Dr Doyle shook her head. 'That's not what this is about,' she said. 'They're not looking for ways to kick you out, they're looking for ways to keep you in. You're not a lost cause, far from it. You've got anger-management issues, and we can deal with them.'

'You think?'

'I'm sure of it, Matt. It's what I do. What you did earlier, when you got angry. You took a breath. That was you instinctively trying to control your anger. We can work on that. Let's try something they call square breathing. You inhale for four seconds, hold that breath for four seconds, then exhale for four seconds, then hold again for four seconds. Try it. You can count the seconds in your head. Something like "Inhale, two, three, four, hold, two, three, four. Got it?'

'Sure.'

He followed her instructions and after a few repetitions he realised it was working. The combination of taking more air into his lungs and concentrating on the count was relaxing.

'See?' said Dr Doyle. 'It's a very simple exercise. It's a great way of falling asleep, as well.'

'I'll try.'

'Whenever you feel yourself in a stressful situation, start the square breathing.'

'Snipers do something similar when they're shooting,' said Standing.

'Yes, I know. Obviously they have to be totally relaxed when they pull the trigger, and tension can throw off the shot. Now, you've heard the old saw about counting to ten before doing anything drastic. If you do find yourself in a confrontational situation – say, for instance, you are confronted by a superior officer and he pushes you. Before you push him back, count to ten.'

Standing chuckled. 'Ten? How do I do that if I react instinctively?'

'You train yourself so that the instinctive reaction is to start counting,' said the therapist. 'You learn to stop and think before you act. You aim for ten, but the mere fact that you start counting should be enough to take the red mist out of the equation.'

'Okay.'

'Good. Use the square-breathing technique regularly throughout the day, and the counting to ten when you're in a confrontational situation. And come back and see me in a few days and we'll discuss how you're getting on.' She looked at the clock. 'I bill by the hour but I think we've covered enough ground today,' she said. 'I find that therapy works in small doses.'

'Perfect,' said Standing. He stood up and shook her hand. 'Thank you,' he said. 'I'm glad I chose you.'

'And why did you choose me?' she asked.

'You seemed the best qualified,' he said, and he could see from the way she smiled at him that she knew he was lying.

Willoughby-Brown kept Shepherd out at sea for the best part of eight hours, and it was four o'clock in the afternoon before he was in his BMW X5, heading back to London. He was physically exhausted and mentally drained. Willoughby-Brown had worked him hard, sailing the yacht single-handed in a series of often quite complicated manoeuvres. He was constantly testing Shepherd on nautical terms and definitions, which were easy because Shepherd's memory was pretty much infallible, but the sequences involved in tacking, jibing and heaving to were complicated and more a matter of muscle memory, a totally different skill that required repetition. Handling the steering and the lines was physically demanding and every muscle in his body was aching.

He called Katra on hands-free as he drove past Gatwick airport. 'Katra, baby, are you okay?'

'I'm fine, Dan. What about you?'

'Busy, busy, busy. Sorry.'

'You're on the way home?'

He could hear the hope in her voice and grimaced. 'I'm sorry, baby, no. I have to go to Florida tomorrow.'

'Florida?'

'Short notice. I'm sorry.'

'Okay,' she said, and he heard her disappointment in the single word.

'I'll make it up to you when I get back,' he said. 'I promise.'

'Be careful,' she said. 'Don't make promises you might not be able to keep.'

Now she sounded resentful but Shepherd could empathise. He'd barely seen her over the last three months and he'd had to let her down several times at short notice. It went with the job, and she said she understood, but understanding didn't necessarily mean she was happy about his long absences. When she had been the family's au pair it hadn't mattered, it was solely a question of logistics, but they'd been sleeping together for a year now and she expected – deserved – more. 'I'm really sorry, baby. I'm not happy about this either but they haven't given me any choice. Hey, what perfume do you want? I'll pick some up at Duty Free on the way back.'

'Dan, it'll take more than a bottle of perfume to buy your way back into my good books,' she said. She sniffed, and he knew she was fighting back tears.

'I wasn't trying to bribe you, baby,' he said, even though he actually was. 'We'll have a holiday when I'm done. Just the two of us. Somewhere hot and sunny.'

'Florida?'

'Sure. If that's what you want. I'll take you to Disneyland.'

She laughed. 'I'm not a kid,' she said. 'And Disneyland is in LA. Disneyworld is Florida.'

'I'll take you to see the mouse wherever you want,' he said. 'Or how about the Florida Keys? Five-star hotel, the beach, the works.'

'Okay, Dan,' she said. 'You've bribed me.'

'I really am sorry about this,' he said, and he meant it.

'I know you are. I know how hard they work you. I just wish that sometimes they would realise you have a family.'

'They do,' said Shepherd. 'They just don't take it into consideration. But as soon as this case is over we're off to the Keys. I promise.'

'Okay,' she said, but she sniffed again. 'Do you think you'll be back next weekend?' she asked. 'Liam said he'd be here.'

'Really? He didn't tell me.'

'He's got leave. He's definitely coming.'

'I'll do my best to be there,' he said. 'Love you, baby.'

'Love you, too,' said Katra.

Shepherd ended the call with a heavy heart. He hadn't

actually lied to her but he couldn't see himself tying up the Meyer case in time to go home the following weekend. He called Jimmy Sharpe and tried to sound more cheerful than he felt. 'Razor, you old reprobate, how's life?'

'What do you want, Spider? I'm busy,' growled Sharpe, in his granite-hard Glaswegian accent.

'Fancy a drink?'

'So you do want something. Why am I not surprised?'

'Now why do you say that, Razor? Can't an old mate take you out for a pint?'

'The reason I say that is because I only ever hear from you when you want something. But what the hell? Yeah, I need a drink. What time?'

The National Crime Agency was based in a modern brick and glass building south of the Thames, midway between Lambeth Bridge and Vauxhall Bridge and a stone's throw from the MI6 building. Unlike MI6, the NCA didn't have a river view but it was generally agreed that it had better canteen facilities. Jimmy Sharpe tended to avoid HQ as much as possible, in the same way that Shepherd was reluctant to set foot inside Thames House. The whole point of working under cover was that as few people as possible knew your face. Shepherd arranged to meet Sharpe in a pub close to Waterloo station and got there first. He was halfway through his Jameson's and soda when Sharpe arrived, wrapped up in a heavy overcoat. He was in his late fifties, greying, and he'd put on a few pounds since they'd last met but he still had the bearing of a man you wouldn't want to get into an argument with.

'Spider, good to see you,' said Sharpe. He gave Shepherd a powerful bear-hug. He was an inch or two shorter than Shepherd but unless they were standing toe to toe Shepherd always felt that Sharpe was the taller man. 'Kronenbourg,' he said, 'before you ask.'

'Do you want food?'

Sharpe looked at his watch. 'Better not,' he said. 'The wife was watching *Masterchef* last night and I think she's got something special planned tonight.'

'Grab us a table,' said Shepherd.

'Real men stand when they drink,' said Sharpe. He laughed when he saw the look on Shepherd's face and punched him lightly on the arm. 'Just busting your balls, Spider. And get me some pork scratchings.'

'You'll ruin your appetite.'

'It's a snack,' said Sharpe.

Sharpe went to get a table while Shepherd was at the bar. 'So, how's work?' asked Shepherd, when he eventually sat down.

'Work is shit,' said Sharpe. He raised his pint in salute. 'Cheers.' He drank deeply, then smacked his lips. 'First of the day.'

'Shit how?'

'They've put me on a major paedophile case. I've been on it for almost a year, on and off, and it's doing my head in. It's bloody awful. Even the wife has noticed how moody I'm getting.'

'Do you have to look at the stuff?'

'Thankfully not. We've got specialised teams who do that. I've no idea how they cope. We're told the nature of what's been found, and we see a breakdown of what's there, but someone has to watch it all, and note down what's being done.' He shuddered. 'It blows your mind. Not so much that people would want to watch it, but that someone actually sets out to abuse kids just to make a video. And when I say kids I don't mean small kids or toddlers, I mean babies. The youngest is six months. A grown man having sex with a baby, how sick is that?'

'How much longer will you be on it?'

'It's open-ended. It's huge, Spider. We started in 2014 with six hundred arrests. Most came through credit-card use, idiots who were stupid enough to use their own cards to buy child porn. We pulled them in and seized their computers. Then we started on the file-sharing, netting the guys who weren't paying for it but were making their own and swapping it. But for every computer seized, someone has to watch every video, look at every picture. It takes for ever. Once we have a breakdown of what they've been looking at, the case gets handed to the investigators.'

'But why you? You're an undercover specialist.'

'That's why I was seconded, initially. I was posing as a paedo, and that was a whole lot of fun, as you can imagine. Robbers, hitmen, drug dealers, they're criminals but often enough they're okay as people. You've met plenty of guys who are perfectly reasonable except that they break the law.'

Shepherd nodded. 'A few.'

'They're criminals, but they're ordinary decent criminals, as they call themselves. Nice to their mothers, good with kids, stand their round in the pub.'

'Salt of the earth,' laughed Shepherd.

'You know what I mean. But these scumbags, they're not human. They're like snakes. Reptiles. A different species. Luckily they don't usually get together, only contact each other online, but even then I had to go home and shower after I'd been online with them – I felt that dirty. Once we started bringing them in, they were using me for the questioning. The superintendent in charge thought they'd see me as a friendly face.'

'Oh, shit, really?'

Sharpe grimaced. 'Yeah. Basically saying that I looked like a paedo. Nice, huh?' He drained his glass and grinned mischievously. 'Your round.'

'I bought the last one, Razor.'

'Yeah, but you obviously brought me here to pick my brains so you're gonna have to pay for your pound of flesh.' He made a shooing motion with his hand. 'Maybe bring me a malt chaser. I'm developing a thirst.'

Shepherd went back to the bar and returned with fresh drinks.

'So enough about me, how's life with the spooks?' asked Sharpe.

'Same old. I'm on surveillance a lot of the time. Not much call for undercover work when all the bad guys are brown-eyed and bearded.'

Sharpe wagged a finger at him. 'Now don't tell me you're racially profiling because you know that's not allowed.'

Shepherd laughed and sipped his whiskey and soda.

'That shoot-out was you, yeah? Trafalgar Square, Hyde Park and the South Bank?'

'Yeah, I was there.'

'It was a close one?'

'We only had one casualty on our side but, yeah, we cut it way too close.'

'Willoughby-Brown?'

Shepherd nodded.

'He's a glory-hunter, that one. He'd be looking for the big score.'

'Well, he got that, all right. But we lost an officer – Lofty Loftus. You ever come across him?'

Sharpe shook his head.

'He was a good guy, old-school. They stuck him like a pig. No reason for it, they could have just knocked him out or tied him up but they killed him.' He screwed up his face. 'Bastards.'

'Yeah,' agreed Sharpe. 'Bastards.'

'And it's never-ending. They just keep coming. It's like what the IRA said about Thatcher. She has to be lucky all the time. They only had to be lucky once. We're putting cell after cell out of commission, but they're still going to get through eventually. It's a matter of the odds. We might stop ten or fifty or a hundred attempts, it doesn't matter. There'll always be another group that wants to try their luck.'

'So what's the answer?'

'I really don't know. It's as depressing as hell. Some of the jihadists we took down were ISIS fighters trained out in the Middle East, but a lot were British. Born here, went to school here, played football in the park, went to the local library.'

'Yeah, well, just because a dog is born in a stable, that doesn't mean it grows up to be a horse.'

'Razor . . .'

'I know, I know, we're not supposed to say that. But I believe it's in their genes. Maybe three or four generations down the line they'll start to think like Brits but until then they're always going to be different.'

'If we start treating them as different, of course they'll behave differently.'

'Spider, these kids have been given every advantage they could want, and they still hate us. They hate us, mate. They think we're lower than animals. It's in the Koran.'

'Have you actually read the Koran, Razor?'

'As a matter of fact I have. "We shall cast terror into the hearts of the unbelievers" is one of the lines I remember. And "Fight them; Allah will punish them by your hands" is another. So, not really the religion of peace.'

'Yeah, that's from what they call the Sword Verse. What

about "But those mine enemies, which would not that I should reign over them, bring hither, and slay them before me", that's pretty aggressive. And "Think not that I am come to send peace on earth: I came not to send peace, but a sword." It's all violent stuff, isn't it?'

Sharpe nodded. 'Damn right.'

'Yeah, but those second two quotes are from the Bible, Razor. Luke chapter nineteen verse twenty-seven, and Matthew chapter ten verse thirty-four.' He raised his glass and grinned.

'You're a tricky bugger,' said Sharpe.

'I'm just showing that selective quotes don't prove anything. There are plenty of peaceful imams around, just as there were priests happy to help the IRA when they needed it, civilian deaths or not.'

'But it's the religion that's the problem, no question,' said Sharpe. 'Even if the schools do their job and the parents have the best of intentions, the mosques are the breeding ground for the jihadists.'

'It's the bad imams that are the problem, not the religion,' said Shepherd. 'There's plenty of good Muslims around. The vast majority. We've got a fair number working at Five now. The ones I've met there are as British as you and me. More English than you, that's for sure.'

Sharpe laughed and raised his glass.

'Several of them drink, and think nothing of it. Some don't, but then drink isn't always a religious thing. Plenty of teeto-tallers in Five and Six. Vegans, too. A couple of girls wear headscarves but most don't. Western clothing, designer-label handbags, high heels, make-up.'

'My mum never went out without a headscarf when I was a kid,' said Sharpe. 'And, to be fair, a lot of the lassies in Glasgow would benefit from the full burka.'

'The point I'm trying to make, despite your piss-taking, is that there are plenty of Muslims here who are no different from us. They're as patriotic and law-abiding as we are, and they're as dismayed as we are at what's happening in the name of their religion. Though to hear Willoughby-Brown talk about it, you'd think we were being infiltrated by the Taliban on a daily basis.'

Sharpe raised his eyebrows. 'Tell me more.'

'Just something he said. He's got a source he's keeping close to his chest and he said it's because he's worried about confidentiality. He said there's been a lowering of standards when it comes to recruiting from the Muslim community and the jihadists are taking advantage of it.'

'Like they've done at the airports.'

'He mentioned the airports, yeah.'

'Don't sound so surprised. You've been through Terminal Three. You've seen what it's like there. And look at the immigration service. Then we wonder why there are so many hooky passports floating around.'

'He said the cops were being infiltrated, too.'

'I reckon he's right. And he's definitely right about standards being lowered. Back in my day, you had to be built like a brick shithouse to be a copper. These days, if you're the right ethnic mix, you don't even have to be able to walk up a flight of stairs.'

'To be fair, the job's changed,' said Shepherd. 'The days of chasing after the bad guys blowing a whistle have long gone. Nowadays they call for mobile back-up.'

'Yeah, but still, when the shit hits the fan, do you want a midget watching your back?'

Shepherd laughed. 'I think you're overstating the case.' He picked up his glass and sipped. 'Anyway, a midget might come in useful if you wanted to infiltrate a circus.'

'Aye, and there's a few bearded ladies in the Met, these days.' He leaned over and clinked his glass against Shepherd's. 'We should hang out more often.'

'Yeah, I miss the old days, working with Sam. They were good.'

Sharpe smiled. 'And finally we get to the point.'

Shepherd tilted his head on one side. 'What do you mean?'

'I did all the interrogation courses, plus I've got nigh on thirty years' experience interviewing,' he said.

'No one's questioning your ability, Razor.'

Sharpe's smile widened. 'Sam's fine, if that's what you're asking.'

'You think I asked you for a drink just so that I can talk to you about Sam Hargrove?'

'Do you want to deny it?' He shrugged. 'No problem, I apologise. Let's change the subject and talk about football.'

Shepherd looked at him for several seconds, then grinned. 'Fine, yes, okay, you've got me. I need to pick your brains.'

'Pick away. Just don't try to kid a kidder.' He settled back in his chair and folded his arms.

'So how is Sam, these days?'

'Same old, same old.'

'Getting near retirement, right?'

'Him and me both.'

'You'll never retire, Razor. You'll die in harness.'

'Maybe. But Sam has visions of days watching cricket at Lord's and evenings walking his dogs with his wife.'

'Do you think he's taken his eye off the ball?'

Sharpe looked quizzically at him. 'Why would you say that?'

'It's been a while since I've seen him. I just wondered . . .'

'If he's gone senile?'

'Don't be like that.'

'How do you expect me to be? He's my boss, and you want me to badmouth him? What's your interest, Spider? Does he have something to worry about?'

'Can we talk off the record?'

'Fuck off, Spider.' Sharpe was smiling but his eyes had hardened.

'I'm in a difficult position. Try to appreciate that.'

'Yeah? Well, you need to appreciate the difficult position you're putting me in.'

'Not if it's off the record.'

'We both know that means nothing. A conversation is a conversation.'

Shepherd leaned towards him. 'I'm putting my job on the line here, Razor. I need some guarantees. If Willoughby-Brown finds out that I've talked about this, I'm toast.'

Sharpe's eyes narrowed. 'So Willoughby-Brown is trying to do to Sam what he did to the fragrant Miss Button?'

'Different scenario,' said Shepherd.

'What the fuck's going on, Spider?'

Shepherd took a gulp of whiskey and soda. 'Have you come across Lisa Wilson?'

'Sure. She's a good operator. Worked on a couple of cases with her when she joined the NCA's undercover unit a couple of years ago.' He frowned. 'Is this about Lisa? Or Sam?'

Shepherd sighed. 'Both.'

'Fuck me,' said Sharpe.

'This has to stay between you and me, Razor.'

'Understood. But what's Willoughby-Brown up to?'

'He thinks Lisa's gone over to the dark side and that Sam has dropped the ball. Do you know what she's working on now?'

Sharpe shook his head. 'The unit doesn't function like that. Sam assigns case officers and they pull undercover operatives from the pool. It's not like we all get together for morning prayers and share information. And we're rarely in NCA headquarters.'

'She's been told to get close to a drug dealer. Good-looking, charismatic, ticks all the boxes. Could she have fallen for him?'

'How would I know?'

'Does she have a husband? Boyfriend?'

'Not that I know of.'

'But committed? To the job?'

Sharpe chuckled. 'You know as well as I do that you can't do this job if you're not a hundred per cent committed. It takes over your life. No one who wants a nine-to-five works under cover.'

'What's her background?'

'Didn't they show you her file?'

'They did, but the file never tells the whole story.'

'From what I remember she was a beat cop in south London. Then she got an attachment to the Drugs Squad and that's where she came across some of the NCA guys. One of them recommended her to Sam.'

'What sort of family?'

'Regular middle class, I think. Difficult to tell. She's a bit of a chameleon.'

'That's what Willoughby-Brown said. But he was referring to the way she could change her appearance.'

'That too,' said Sharpe. 'But I meant she's an emotional chameleon.'

'How so?'

Sharpe took a drink as he gathered his thoughts. 'Okay. So, the first time I met her was on a drugs case. I was posing as a buyer from Glasgow. She was my girlfriend.' He grinned at the look of surprise on Shepherd's face. 'I know, who'd have thought it, right? We got some looks when we walked into places, I can tell you, because she went the tarty route. Short skirts, low-cut tops. She was a distraction, and it worked. Great cover – I don't think anyone would ever have placed her as a cop. Anyway, we spent a week schmoozing the bad guys, throwing around money like there was no tomorrow, Cristal, the Mayfair Bar, the full monty. The NCA is a lot more generous with its budgets than SOCA ever was. Anyway, the whole time I was with her, I thought she was Scottish. She had the accent, she spoke the slang. It didn't even occur to me that she wasn't. But when the operation was over and we were briefing the CPS solicitor, he was a Brummie and, bugger me, she had a Birmingham accent. Not too strong, not like she was taking the piss, she just had the accent. And she was always doing that mirroring thing. Not just with me, with everyone. You know what I mean? You smile, she smiles. You fold your arms, she folds her arms.'

'It makes people feel comfortable,' said Shepherd. 'It builds trust.'

'Yeah, I've read all the body-language books, too. And it works. But she does it naturally. I'm sure it isn't deliberate. And she seems to adapt her personality to whoever she's with. With me in private she was always respectful. Deferential, you know what I mean. Like everything I said was gospel. She'd ask me something and then listen like every word I gave her was gold. She'd ask me if I wanted a coffee and just put her hand on my arm. Not sexual, not at all, like I was her dad.' He chuckled. 'Or her grandfather.' He took another drink. 'When we were out with the targets, she was all sex. I mean, she just walked differently, talked differently, the way she held herself. Not overtly – she wasn't flashing her tits or anything. It was more eyes and the way she moved. You could see the guys with their tongues hanging out. They spent so much time ogling her they didn't see the trap closing.'

'Sounds like she's good at her job.'

'She's a natural. I was minding her on a job she did in Exeter last year. The local cops had a guy they were sure had killed his wife but they just couldn't get the evidence. He was on that Tinder dating site so they put her on and he matched her within hours. The plan was to get him to confess to her. So it was going to take time. She was fixed up in a flat in the city centre, wired for sound and vision, and I had the flat upstairs. That was so I could watch what was going on and kick down the door if things went wrong.'

'So she was on her own a lot with the guy?'

'A hell of a lot,' said Sharpe. 'It took weeks. I spent hours watching them, and it was like she was a totally different person. Her voice was different, her mannerisms, the way she moved. She'd dyed her hair, too, because the target was into blondes. She had it cut short because that was how he liked it. But she changed her personality, too, to become the sort of girl he wanted. And she didn't seem to be doing it consciously.'

'And the target, what was he like?'

'Good-looking guy but not too bright. Married his wife for her money. She was few years older, owned the house, and there was a trust fund her parents had set up for her. She had a good team of lawyers, who made him sign a pre-nup. If they ever divorced, he'd get nothing. He'd been fooling around and she'd set a private detective on him. He found out and a few weeks later she disappeared. Her car was found in a car park at Heathrow and he told his friends she'd said she wanted to spend some time on her own. Her family didn't believe him and went to the cops. There was no record of her taking any flights and they couldn't find her on CCTV. Her father used to be a local councillor and was friends with the deputy chief constable so the local cops asked the NCA for help.'

'So, no body?'

'No body, no evidence of violence, no threats, nothing. If the father hadn't been connected it would probably have been written off as a missing person at most.'

'And the guy still had access to her money?'

Sharpe nodded. 'Joint bank accounts, and they owned a chain of hairdressing salons. So money was still coming in and he had the house. All he had to do was carry on as normal and after seven years have her declared officially dead.'

'And how did it go?'

'Like a dream,' said Sharpe. 'He liked Lisa's Tinder profile, they chatted online for a few days, she gave him her number and they talked on the phone for almost a week before he said he wanted to meet. They met for a coffee. Then dinner. Went to a movie. We had to take it slowly. But after a couple of weeks he was coming around to her flat and drinking wine, watching Netflix, getting all cosy.'

'She wasn't sleeping with him?'

'Of course not! That would have blown any case out of the water.' He frowned at Shepherd. 'Is that what Willoughby-Brown thinks? That she's sleeping with her target?'

'He didn't say so in as many words but, yeah, I think that's on his mind.'

'She definitely didn't cross the line with this guy. Not that I saw. She kissed him, held his hand, hugs, that sort of thing. But she managed to keep sex at bay.'

'How?'

Sharpe grinned. 'She said she had a medical problem. One of those women's things, a twisted cervix or something, and that she wasn't supposed to have sex until the doctors had given her the all-clear.' He waved away the look of disbelief on Shepherd's face. 'When I say it, it sounds ridiculous. But when she sold it, he bought it. He said he'd wait a few weeks. Anyway, she kept reeling him in, then started talking about her father. The story she told him was that her father was a bastard who was threatening to cut her out of his will if she didn't go home and take care of him.'

'And the target told her how to solve her problem?'

'Even gave her the number of the guy who'd taken care of his wife. She ended up getting two birds with one stone – the target and the killer. They both ended up pleading guilty.'

'Nice job.'

Sharpe nodded. 'She was brilliant. No question. I'd have no problems working with her again. So, what evidence is there that she's gone bad?'

'The intel she's been sending back has dried up recently.'

'Maybe the guy suspects something. If that's the case, she should be pulled out.'

'He wants me to check her out.'

'Without telling Sam?' He raised his eyebrows and exhaled through pursed lips. 'That's not good, Spider.'

'That's why I'm here.'

'Sam's not going to be happy when he finds out.'

'Hopefully he won't,' said Shepherd. 'If she's on the straight and narrow I'll tell Willoughby-Brown so and all's well that ends well. Sam will never know.'

'Yeah? And if she isn't? How's that going to impact on Sam?'

'You said she's not the type to switch sides. I respect your judgement.'

'Don't blow smoke up my arse, Spider. This is wrong and you know it is.'

'I'm not arguing,' said Shepherd. 'But what can I do? I

can't say no. I don't get to pick and choose my assignments. And you can't say anything to Lisa. Or Sam.'

'I won't, obviously. But for fuck's sake, Spider. What a mess.'

'I know, I know.' He sipped his whiskey.

'Who's out there with her now?' asked Sharpe.

'What do you mean?'

'Does she have an uncle? Someone watching over her?'

'The target moves around too much. Spain, the West Indies, South America. There'd be no way anyone could keep up with her.'

'That's not good,' said Sharpe. 'Who's going to help her if she gets into trouble?'

'It's not my operation, Razor. I'm late to the party. If it had been my show I'd have worked something out.'

Sharpe drained his glass, then burped. 'You know, there is a way out of this.'

'What's that?'

Sharpe put the empty glass down in front of him. 'Quit. Tell Willoughby-Brown to shove his job and work for the NCA. Sam would bite your hand off.' He grinned. 'You can think about it while you're getting me another drink.'

Standing woke up instantly, as he usually did. One minute he was fast asleep, the next his eyes were open and his mind was clear. It was just after six o'clock and again he'd slept on the sofa without bothering to fold it out into a bed. There was never any mid-ground with Standing. He was either awake or he was asleep. He'd served with a lot of soldiers who always seemed to want an extra few minutes in the sack, but ever since he'd been a small child Standing had never seen the point of staying in bed once he'd woken up. Unless there was a girl with him, but that was a whole different ball game. As there wasn't, he rolled off the sofa and padded naked to the kitchen area to switch on the kettle. As he waited for it to boil he checked his phone. There was no message from Lexi and no one had called. He checked her Facebook page but she hadn't updated her status.

He pulled on a pair of shorts and a sweatshirt, then made himself a cup of coffee and drank it as he watched the BBC News Channel. Coffee finished, he went downstairs and jogged south along Queensway, crossed Bayswater Road and entered Hyde Park.

The park was 350 acres and criss-crossed with paths but Standing ran around the edge, which he knew was close to three miles. He finished the circuit in exactly twenty minutes, and while he was breathing heavily he wasn't out of breath: SAS troopers had to be able to run four miles in less than thirty minutes. He dropped down onto the grass and did thirty press-ups followed by fifty sit-ups, then got into the plank position and held it for a full three minutes.

His workout finished, he jogged back to his apartment and checked the phone. Still nothing. By the time he had shaved and showered, pulled on a clean shirt and jeans it was seven o'clock.

He was starting to worry about Lexi. He checked her Facebook page again. Up until the final posting, she had been putting up pictures, comments and links more than a dozen times a day. He rang her number, which went through to voicemail.

Maida Vale was just twenty minutes by Tube with one change at Paddington station. He figured she'd probably leave for school about eight, so he had plenty of time.

Standing was outside the house where Lexi lived at just before seven thirty. Mr and Mrs Chapman had done well for themselves, buying the four-bedroomed semi long before prices had skyrocketed well beyond the reach of nice, middle-class families. It was a mock-Tudor with black beams, white panels and leaded windows. The garden had been paved as parking was at a premium in the area and there were two cars – a Volvo and a Mini.

Standing knew he'd be asking for trouble hanging about on the pavement so he moved further down the road to a corner but even that was too exposed. If he was in a war zone he'd simply break into an unoccupied house and use it as an observation post but that approach wasn't going to work in leafy Maida Vale. There was a bus stop further along the road and he walked to it. He could just make out the front of the house so he waited there, his hands in his jacket pockets, his shoulders hunched against the morning chill.

After fifteen minutes a bus turned up but Standing stepped back to let it go. He was joined by a middle-aged woman with a briefcase, who studiously ignored him until the next bus arrived. She got on and the bus drove off. Then the Volvo pulled out into the road and headed in his direction. He turned his back on the car and managed to sneak a look as it went by. Mr Chapman was driving and he was alone. He glanced at his watch. Eight o'clock. He stamped his feet to keep the circulation going. Buses came and went. Most of the time he was alone at the bus stop. The time ticked slowly by. Eight thirty. Nine. By the time his watch showed nine thirty, Standing figured that Lexi wasn't going to school. He frowned as he considered his options. It had been more than ten years since he had been to the house, but he was pretty sure that the court order was still in effect. But what if something had happened to Lexi? He couldn't keep ringing an unanswered phone and sending text messages that were never replied to. And there was a limit to how long he could stand outside in the street.

He had never had a problem with Mrs Chapman; it was her husband who was set against him. If he was polite and smiled a lot, maybe she wouldn't slam the door in his face and call the police. Worst possible scenario, if she did call the cops, it had been ten years since they had dealt with him, which meant they had no current address so it wouldn't be easy for them to track him down. He took a deep breath, then spent two minutes practising square breathing. It was worth a go, he decided.

He walked back to the house and up to the front door, rehearsing what he would say. He took a deep breath and pressed the bell. Maybe Lexi herself would answer the door. That would be the best possible result. He heard a soft footfall and then the door opened. It wasn't Lexi, it was Mrs Chapman. It had been many years, of course, but she looked much older than he remembered, and smaller. He knew she was in her early forties but if he had passed her in the street he'd have pegged her as much more. Mid-fifties. Sixty, maybe. Her eyes were watery, her hair was lacklustre, her skin dry and wrinkled. She wasn't wearing make-up and she was dressed for comfort rather than style in a knee-length baggy dress and a cardigan.

'Mrs Chapman, I'm really sorry to bother you, and I know I shouldn't be here, but I've been having no luck trying to get hold of Lexi on the phone and I really want to talk to her.' He was speaking far too quickly so he paused and took a breath. 'Sorry,' he added.

She gazed up at him, then her eyes widened in recognition. 'Matt?' she said. 'What are you doing here?'

It was as if she hadn't heard a word he'd said. 'I just want to have a word with Lexi. Then I'll be on my way.'

'Lexi? Alexia?' Her mouth opened. 'Did nobody tell you?'

Her words hit Standing like a pile-driver to the stomach. 'Tell me what?' he said, though cold fingers of dread were already tightening around his heart. Time seemed to have stopped.

'Oh, Matt, oh, Matt,' she whispered. She opened the door. 'You'd better come in.' He stepped into the hallway and she closed the door.

'What's happened, Mrs Chapman?' he asked, but she was already walking down the hallway to the kitchen.

'I'll make you tea,' she muttered, almost to herself. 'You need tea.'

He hurried after her. She went straight to the kettle and switched it on, then seemed to sag against the counter. He put out his hand to touch her but pulled it back. He wasn't supposed to be in her house and he definitely wasn't supposed to have physical contact with her. 'What's happened, Mrs Chapman?'

A long, slow moan escaped her, the sound of a deflating balloon, and the claws of dread were so tight on his heart that Standing could barely breathe. He sat down at the kitchen table, waiting for her to speak but already knowing what she was going to say. She slowly turned to face him. 'Alexia's dead, Matt. She died two weeks ago. The funeral was on Tuesday.'

Standing shook his head. 'No,' he said.

'I'm sorry,' she whispered. 'She was cremated.'

'Why did nobody tell me?' he asked, but even as the words left his mouth he knew what the answer was. He wasn't family. In the Chapmans' eyes, he didn't exist. He put his head into his hands. He'd seen death before, at a distance and at closer quarters. He'd had friends die, and twice he'd been there when it had happened. But Lexi was his sister.

His little sister. He felt a touch on his shoulder and realised that Mrs Chapman had come over to him. 'Somebody should have told me,' he whispered.

'It all happened so quickly,' she said, sitting down opposite him. 'One moment she was here, the next she'd gone.'

'Was she sick?' asked Standing. 'She never said anything.'

'It was drugs,' said Mrs Chapman.

Standing looked up, shocked. 'What?'

'Drugs,' said Mrs Chapman.

'Lexi never took drugs. She was sixteen.'

'We were as surprised as you. And we said the same thing. But the police were sure. She'd overdosed on heroin.'

'Heroin? Lexi took heroin?'

Mrs Chapman nodded.

'Where? Not here, surely?'

She shook her head. 'It was in a house in Kilburn.'

'A friend's?'

'No, just a house that drug addicts used. They called an ambulance but she was dead by the time it got there.'

'So it was an accident? Is that what they said?'

'That was the coroner's verdict. Death by misadventure. Misadventure? What sort of word is that? It implies she was on an adventure, doesn't it? An adventure that went wrong.'

'Did you know she was taking drugs?'

'Of course not!' She stared at him in disbelief. 'How could you say that? What sort of parents do you think we are?'

'I didn't mean anything, Mrs Chapman. I'm sorry. I just meant – I wondered if you knew where she was, that's all.'

'She said she was going to a friend's house to study. That was about five o'clock. It wasn't a school night so we said okay. The next thing we knew it was nine o'clock and there were two police officers on the doorstep. Greg answered the door. I was watching the TV. I knew from the look on his face that something was wrong. Then I saw the police officers and I just collapsed. You know when you're going to be told really bad news, you just know.' Tears ran down her face and she ripped off a piece of kitchen towel and dried her eyes. 'We went to identify the body. Greg said I shouldn't go, that he'd do it, but I wanted to see her.' She sighed. 'It was as if she'd gone to sleep. She looked as if she'd wake up at any moment. I wanted to touch her and hold her but they said I shouldn't. They made us stay behind a window and they pulled a cloth off her face. It was defi-nitely her and they covered her up again.'

'Did the police catch anyone?' asked Standing.

'Catch anyone?' repeated Mrs Chapman.

'Somebody must have given her the drugs.'

'I don't know.'

'You don't know?' spat Standing. 'How can you not know?'

Mrs Standing flinched as if she'd been slapped, and Standing immediately felt guilty. It wasn't her fault. And while Standing had lost a sister she had lost a daughter, albeit an adopted one. 'I'm sorry,' he said, putting up his hands. 'I didn't mean to snap. I just . . .' He couldn't find the words.

'I understand,' she said, dabbing at her eyes.

'Did the police try to find out what happened?'

'They know what happened. Alexia took an overdose. The policewoman we saw said that sometimes people got careless or took a drug that was stronger they were used to.'

'Policewoman? Who was she?'

Mrs Chapman stood up. 'I've got her card somewhere. She was a very nice lady. Very sympathetic.' She went over to the fridge and pulled a business card from under a fridge magnet in the shape of an apple. 'This is her.' She gave him the card. It belonged to a family liaison officer.

Standing looked at both sides. 'Can I keep this?' he said.

'I suppose so,' she said. 'We haven't heard from her since the funeral.'

'You said the funeral was on Tuesday?'

Mrs Chapman nodded. 'There were so many people there. Everyone loved her.' She bit down on her lower lip. 'I'm sorry you weren't told. You should have been there.'

'I was . . .' He was going to say he was in Syria but that would raise a whole load of questions that he didn't want to answer. '. . . overseas. I've only just got back.'

She forced a smile. 'Anywhere nice?'

'Not really. No.' Her face fell and he realised he'd snapped at her again so he forced a smile.

'Are you still in the army?' she asked.

Standing nodded, still smiling. His face was aching with the effort of showing his teeth.

'Alexia was always so proud of you. I'm sorry you couldn't see her.'

'I saw her sometimes,' said Standing. 'Not here, obviously. But sometimes I'd come to see her at weekends.'

'She never told us.' She took a deep breath. 'Of course she wouldn't tell us. Greg wouldn't have allowed it. He wouldn't have been happy.'

'Sure, and it's all about how your husband feels, isn't it?'

Mrs Chapman looked startled and Standing made himself smile again. 'I'm sorry,' he said.

'Do you want tea?'

'Yes, please.' He didn't, but he wanted her to keep occupied because if she thought about it she might prefer that he got the hell out of her house.

She stood up and went back to the kettle.

'Do you know why she was taking drugs?' he asked.

She shook her head. 'We had no idea. She had gone a little quiet and spent a lot of time in her room, but that's teenagers for you, isn't it? Andrew was the same before he went to university.'

'Andrew took heroin?

'No, of course not. We never had any problems like that with Andrew. But he went quiet. Solitary. It's what teenagers do, isn't it?'

'I suppose so. Was she doing okay at school?'

'We'd ask her but she usually just said, "Fine" or "Good" and leave it at that.' She gave him a cup of tea. It was delicate china with peach-coloured flowers on it. The handle was so slender that Standing feared it would snap between his fingers. 'Milk and sugar?'

'Please,' he said. 'Two sugars.'

'We have lumps,' she said, pushing a bowl towards him.

He picked up two lumps with his fingers and regretted it immediately when he saw disgust flash across her face. He stirred it in with a tiny spoon that looked as if it might be silver.

'I'm sorry that no one told you,' she said.

'Like I said, I was overseas. I doubt I could have come back for the funeral, even if I'd known about it.'

'I suppose that's something,' she said quietly.

'Mrs Chapman, can I see her room?'

She frowned, not understanding.

'I'd just like to see her room. Would that be okay?'

She looked uncomfortable, but then she said, 'I don't see why not.'

She took him out of the kitchen and he followed her upstairs. She took every step slowly, as if climbing was an effort. When she reached the top she kept a grip on the banister for several seconds, then walked along the landing and opened a door. She flashed him a smile. 'I go in every day, just to sit,' she said. 'Usually around the time she used to get back from school. I keep hoping I'll hear the back door open and she'll shout that she's home.' She sighed. 'But she never does.'

Standing walked into the room. The bed was made and there was a stuffed bear sitting on the pillow. He smiled when he recognised it. It was the Steiff bear he'd bought for her all those years ago, dark brown and wearing a bright red waistcoat.

He sat down, picked it up and held it to his chest. 'I can't believe she still has it.'

'That was her favourite bear,' said Mrs Chapman. 'She loved it.'

'I got it for her, ages ago.'

'I know. She used to sleep with it.' Tears were brimming in her eyes and she dabbed them with a handkerchief.

A phone rang downstairs. 'I'll have to get that,' said Mrs Chapman, and left him alone. Standing looked around the room as he heard her walk slowly down the stairs. There were dozens of posters of bands he'd never heard of, composed mainly of young men in denim with tattoos and piercings. There were a dozen photographs around the dressing-table mirror and he recognised one. He'd given it to her once when he'd met her outside her school. He'd tried writing letters to her but her father – her adopted father – had always intercepted them and presumably thrown them away. The photograph was of himself in the middle of a group of guys in the desert. No weapons, because he figured that would upset Mr Chapman, just a group of guys in desert gear and sunglasses, squinting under the unrelenting sun next to a bored-looking camel. He was pleased that she'd kept it.

There were feminine touches in the room, too, signs that Lexi was no longer a little girl. There was a collection of lipsticks and bottles of perfume, and a pile of fashion magazines by the bed. Standing hugged the bear and felt something hard against his arm. He looked at the bear, wondering what it was. He felt with his thumbs and realised there was something in the pocket of the bear's waistcoat. It was a locket, small and heart-shaped, either gold or gold plate, on a thin chain. He opened it, which wasn't easy as the catch was tiny. There was a picture inside. Lexi and an Asian man. Standing frowned. It was a man, not a boy. Late twenties. Maybe older. He was leering at the camera but Lexi was smiling, as if she was happy. And proud. Standing's frown deepened. What the hell was going on?

There was a knock on the door and Mrs Chapman opened it. 'I'm so sorry but I have to go out.'

Standing slipped the locket into his pocket as he stood up. 'No problem,' he said. 'How's Mr Chapman taking it?' He put the bear back on the pillow.

'He's being very calm. Too calm. It's hit him hard but he won't talk about it.'

'Guys tend not show their feelings, I guess.'

'He's very angry, still,' she said. 'He's looking for someone to blame.'

Standing nodded. 'So am I,' he said. 'Can I ask you for a favour, Mrs Chapman?'

'What?' She sounded apprehensive as if he was going to ask for something she didn't want to give.

He pointed at the dressing-table mirror. 'Can I take a photograph? A photograph of Lexi?'

For a moment she looked as if she was going to say no, but then her hand fluttered, like an injured bird, and she nodded. 'Of course.'

Standing took a picture of Lexi standing in front of a Ferrari, her arms outstretched as if she was claiming owner-ship. He showed it to Mrs Chapman and she nodded again.

He put it into his pocket and went downstairs. She followed him, then moved past him to open the front door. He saw tears welling in her eyes once more.

'I'm so sorry,' he said.

'I know,' she said, dabbing at her eyes with a handkerchief. 'But, please, don't come here again. My husband wouldn't like it. He's never forgiven you . . . for . . .' She left the sentence unfinished and dabbed at her eyes again.

Standing stepped out of the house and she closed the door softly behind her. Even through the door he could hear her crying. Then there was a soft thud and he knew she had sat down on the floor. He walked down the driveway, gritting his teeth, willing away the tears that were building in his own eyes.

Shepherd flew to Orlando on a Virgin Atlantic plane packed with holidaymakers heading for Florida's theme parks. The travel department had bought him an Upper Class seat, including a limo to the airport and a spell in the Virgin clubhouse, where he was able to shower, shave and eat an excellent breakfast, washed down with several cups of coffee. He even had a complimentary haircut. His seat folded completely flat so he was able to sleep pretty much the whole flight and he arrived at Orlando feeling fresh and rested. Immigration was smooth and quick. The Hispanic woman who stamped his passport gave him a beaming smile and welcomed him to the US. It was the first time he had flown to Orlando and it was by far the best experience he'd had. Most of his previous US flights had been to JFK or LA and the queues at both were always horrendous, the staff surly at best.

Barry Minister was waiting for him in the arrivals area, wearing a yellow shirt, covered with red and blue parrots, and denim shorts, cut off just above the knee. The guy was professional enough not to be holding a card with Shepherd's name on it. Instead he was leaning against a pillar, chewing a toothpick. As Shepherd walked up to him he noticed a circular piece of carved stone hanging around his neck and several lengths of string tied around his left wrist. Shepherd smiled. 'Hi, Barry. I'm the one you're waiting for.'

'The eagle flies south in the winter,' said Minister, straightening up. He sounded American but there was more than a touch of Australian in his accent.

'What?'

He took the toothpick from between his lips. 'The eagle flies south in the winter.'

Shepherd frowned in confusion.

Minister shook his head. 'Mate, if you don't know what you're supposed to say, I've got the wrong man.' He turned to walk away, then came back and grinned. 'Only messing with you, mate. The look on your face. Priceless.' He put the toothpick back into his mouth and stuck out his hand. 'They call me BM.'

Shepherd shook it. 'Dan.' He finally got the joke. 'Oh, right.'

'Good to meet you, Dan. You'll get used to my sense of humour.' He nodded at the small holdall Shepherd was carrying. 'That's all your luggage?'

'I'm only going to be here for a day or two.'

Minister took Shepherd out of the terminal into the bright Florida sunshine, and to a car park where he had a white Ford Escape. Ten minutes later they were driving down a six-lane highway, heading north to Jacksonville.

'So you're Australian?' asked Shepherd.

'I'm a Kiwi, mate,' said Minister. 'But I left New Zealand in my teens so my accent is all over the place.'

'And how did you end up in Florida?'

Minister laughed. 'Do you want the long or the short version? I was backpacking, started in the Far East, did Thailand and Vietnam, Laos and Cambodia, then started crewing yachts out there. Did a few runs to the Med for rich guys who wanted their boats moving but didn't have the time to do it themselves, then got offered a job as first mate on a yacht belonging to a Russian oligarch. I say yacht, it was a bloody ocean-going ship with a helicopter pad and a garage for his collection of sports cars.'

'Paid well?'

'Actually, it tends to be shit money with the oligarchs. The lifestyle's great – that's what you do it for. All the best ports, the chefs take really good care of the crew, and there's always plenty of booze around. But in terms of cash in the bank, you'd make more money delivering pizzas.' He shrugged. 'Good experience, though. But it's driving rather than sailing. I prefer to feel the boat as it goes through the water, to hear the wind over the sails and the waves splashing against the prow.'

'Quick question,' said Shepherd, raising his hand. 'Bow and prow. What's the difference?'

Minister grinned. 'Bloody hell, you really do need the basics, don't you?'

'Yeah, but I've got a good memory. You only have to tell me once.'

'Okay, the bow is the forward part of the boat. When we say fore or forward we mean towards the bow. The back part of the boat is the stern.'

'That I know,' said Shepherd. 'It's bow and prow I'm not sure of.'

'The prow is the forward-most part of the bow, and it's above the waterline, strictly speaking. But the words are pretty much interchangeable.'

'Thanks,' said Shepherd. 'Sorry, didn't mean to interrupt. So, did you quit the oligarch's boat to get back to sailing?'

'Yeah. I got my captain's licence and I could have stayed working on the super-yachts but they're misnamed. There are no sails involved and I wanted to get back to wind power. I worked for a company that organised sailing holidays but it was a pain dealing with rich kids who'd rather have been somewhere else and parents who did nothing but bellyache, so I went back to moving boats around. Sailed across the Atlantic a few times, then found my way down to the West Indies. Barbados, St Lucia, Martinique, Dominica. Loved it. Loved the weather, the people, the sailing, so I hung around for a couple of years, getting what jobs I could, captain if I could find a vacancy, first mate or even crewman if there were no captain's jobs going. That's when I came across the DEA.'

'Professionally?'

Minister laughed. 'I wasn't smuggling, if that's what you mean. But I was on a boat where the captain was. He was picking up parcels and dropping them off in Florida. He didn't tell anyone else what he was up to, so in a way I was lucky the DEA approached me. They could have just pulled the boat in and sent us all down. The captain was a bit of a bastard, and I don't think he would have taken the rap on his own. And who would have believed that the crew weren't involved? Anyway, a DEA agent sidled up to me in a bar and we had a few drinks and he sounded me out. When he realised I was kosher he told me who he was and asked for my cooperation.'

'And you were okay with that?'

'Hell, yeah. The captain could have had us all doing ten years in an American prison – he didn't give a toss. It would have been different if he'd offered the crew the choice, but bringing drugs onto a boat on the sly is the worst thing you can do. If the crew had been at sea and had found out, they'd probably have thrown him overboard.' He saw the smile on Shepherd's face. 'I'm serious,' he said. 'Someone tries to fuck you over like that, they deserve what they get. There are no cops at sea and he wouldn't have been the first captain to be cold-cocked and thrown overboard.'

'I'm guessing that after the DEA had used you once, they wanted more?'

'Sure. And I was happy enough to help. They paid well and helped me get a Green Card. It was pretty exciting too. You know what I mean?'

'It can be dangerous, though, no?'

'They look after me.'

'And how did you come across Jeremy Willoughby-Brown?'

'He was over here a few years ago, not long after I'd moved to Jacksonville. He was on a case involving the IRA.'

'The IRA?'

'One of the new offshoots. Real IRA or something. He was vague about exactly who they were. A couple of Irish guys had chartered a yacht with their families and he wanted it bugged. It was a big one with a full crew and he managed to get me on board. I planted the bugs and stayed on for a week, then faked an illness and bailed out. He seemed happy with what I did.'

'And what did he tell you about me?'

'That you were a sailing virgin and I had to break you in.'

'Nice image,' said Shepherd.

Minister grinned at him. 'Don't worry, I'll be gentle.'

Standing went into what was now becoming his regular Italian restaurant for lunch. The waitress gave him a beaming smile and told him he could sit anywhere. He took a table by the window, ordered lasagne and a bottle of Peroni, and took out his iPhone. He opened Facebook. He had started an account as a way of keeping in touch with Lexi and she was his only friend. He went to her page and flicked back through her postings. The last she had made was two days before she'd died. It was a selfie, her and another girl, both gurning at the camera. Lexi didn't look like a heroin addict. She looked like a happy, boisterous teenager.

He scrolled down. There were several other pictures of the same girl, and other female friends. He continued to scroll through her timeline. She seemed to have a lot of friends but was clearly closer to the blonde girl than anyone else. He had to go back six months before there were any photographs of her with boys, and the pictures that she had posted were of groups, usually half a dozen or more, flashing what they clearly thought were gang signs at the camera. He didn't see any pictures of anyone who looked like the man in the locket. So he was a secret, something that had to be kept hidden.

The blonde girl's name was Zoë Middlehurst. Standing went to her page and checked through her postings. She had two brothers, both younger than her, and lived in St John's Wood. There were several photographs of her and her friends on the zebra crossing near Abbey Road Studios, recreating the iconic album cover by the Beatles. The previous Christmas she had posted pictures of her family in front of a tree surrounded by wrapped presents. The proud Mr and Mrs Middlehurst were there. He was in his thirties with receding hair and a moustache to compensate, while she was a few years younger and looked tired, as if he left most of the hard work to her. Mr Middlehurst didn't have a Facebook page but his wife did. Most of her postings were of food she'd cooked or meals she'd eaten. There were a few holiday snaps, herself, her husband and three children by a swimming pool, standing around a camel, lying on a beach, and in all of the pictures Mrs Middlehurst seemed close to tears.

Mr Middlehurst had a LinkedIn profile. He'd been to Reading University, had graduated with a second-class degree in accountancy and worked for a large firm in the City. He'd had just three jobs since leaving university.

He went back to Zoë's Facebook page and tried to get an address, but there wasn't one, and any photographs of the house had been taken inside. She did say which school she went to, which was enough.

He took out the card Mrs Chapman had given him. The family liaison officer was Constable Sarah Ellis, based at Paddington. He tapped out the number. A man answered and Standing asked for Constable Ellis. Two minutes later she was on the line. Standing said he was Alexia Chapman's brother but she cut him short. 'Andrew is Mr and Mrs Chapman's only son,' she said. 'She only has one brother.'

'No, I'm the real brother,' he said. 'Same mother, same father. Andrew is her step-brother.'

'That's the first I've heard of this,' she said. 'Are you telling me that Alexia was adopted?'

'About twelve years ago,' said Standing. 'We were both in care. The Chapmans adopted her and I stayed where I was. I was overseas when she died.'

'I'm sorry about your loss,' she said. 'What was your name again?'

'Standing,' he said. 'Matt Standing. Matthew.'

'How can I help you, Mr Standing?'

'I've just got back to the UK and I spoke with Mrs Chapman today. She explained what had happened, but I wanted to see if there had been any progress on the case.'

'Case? What case?'

'My sister's case. She died of a drug overdose, right? What's happening about that?'

'Mr Standing, I'm a family liaison officer. My job is to help families through stressful situations. I'm not an investigating officer.'

'Okay, no problem. Who should I talk to?'

'I'm sorry, what is it you want to talk about?'

Standing wondered if the woman was being deliberately obtuse or if she really didn't understand the question. 'My sister was sixteen years old, and someone supplied her with drugs that killed her. Surely the police would be looking to find out who that was and to charge them with murder. Or, if not murder, at least manslaughter.'

'I don't think anyone forced your sister to take drugs, Mr Standing.'

'She was sixteen years old.'

'Yes, I know. It's very sad, and it's an awful thing to have happened, but no one put a gun to her head.'

'Maybe not, but if a shop sold her alcohol, they would be prosecuted. How can you not prosecute the person who sold her drugs?'

'That's really not an issue for me,' said the policewoman. 'As I said. I'm family liaison.'

'Is there an investigating officer I can speak to?'

'Mr Standing, I understand how upset you are, but I really don't think it would be productive for you to pursue this.'

'Why do you say that?'

'Because in my experience there are rarely prosecutions after a drug user overdoses. That's just a fact.'

'So are you saying that my sister's death isn't being investigated?'

'It has been investigated. There was an inquest.'

'Mrs Chapman said. Death by misadventure.'

'Exactly.'

'With no mention of how she got the drugs, or who gave them to her.'

'The purpose of an inquest is to determine the cause of death,' she said. 'And that was done.'

'Who gave evidence at the inquest? For the police?'

'Bear with me, Mr Standing. Let me check my notes.' He heard the phone being put down on a desk, then nothing for several minutes. He was starting to wonder if the line had gone dead when she came back. 'It was a Detective Constable Adam Kaiser. He's based at Kilburn. Hopefully he will be able to answer your questions.'

It was clear from her tone that she wanted rid of him, so he thanked her and ended the call. He thought about phoning DC Kaiser, but bearing in mind how it had gone with her, he figured that a face-to-face meeting might be more productive.

The waitress returned with his lasagne and beer, and he tucked in. He had almost finished when his phone rang. It was the therapist, Dr Doyle. Or, at least, it was her receptionist, calling to make an appointment for another session. 'I'm actually feeling okay,' said Standing.

'Dr Doyle says you should be aiming for at least three sessions a week at this stage,' said the receptionist. 'How are you fixed for tomorrow?'

'Tomorrow's not good,' said Standing. 'I've got things to do.'

'The day after, then?' said the receptionist. 'First thing in the morning.'

When Standing hesitated, the receptionist cut in: 'Mr Standing, I have to be honest with you. Dr Doyle has already been in touch with your commanding officer regarding the first session and she tells me they're very keen that you keep the momentum going. If you appear reluctant to continue with the therapy, they might take it as a sign that you're not committed to making the changes they require.'

Standing laughed harshly. 'That sounded like a threat,' he said.

'Just a statement of fact,' said the receptionist, archly. 'But you can take it how you will.'

'The day after tomorrow, then,' said Standing. 'First thing.'

'Excellent,' said the receptionist. 'Have a wonderful day.'

Standing finished his meal, paid his bill and walked down Queensway to a Snappy Snaps photo shop. He took the photograph out of the locket and asked the guy behind the counter if he could blow it up. The man explained that the picture was so small they'd have to scan it and even then the quality wouldn't be great. Standing asked him to do the best he could, and in less than fifteen minutes he had a ten-by-eight photograph in his hands. As the guy had warned, the features were far from sharp but the faces were clear enough.

He picked up a couple of bottles of lager and took them back to his apartment. He propped the picture against the television, then lay on the sofa and watched the news as he drank one of the lagers. After a few minutes he sat up and folded the picture in half. He wanted to look at his sister, not the man she was with. He wanted to find out who he was, and what he meant to Lexi, but he didn't want to look at his grinning face.

The marina to which Minister took Shepherd was much bigger than the one where Willoughby-Brown kept his yacht. It was the size of a small town, with hundreds of boats of all sizes, from small single-masted yachts to craft that looked as if they could carry a few dozen passengers in comfort. Minister saw him peering at one of the larger vessels. 'You wouldn't get much change from fifty million dollars for that one,' he said.

'Who owns a boat like that?' asked Shepherd.

'The mega-rich,' said Minister. 'But there's a lot of them in Florida. A lot of drugs money ends up in boats. You'll see a fair number registered in Panama and Colombia. But the oligarchs come here for the sunshine, and a lot of internet money ends up afloat. But, trust me, these are small compared with the ones owned by the oligarchs and the Arabs. It's been a while since I checked but the biggest super-yacht is owned by some sheikh. It's called *Azzam* and it cost six hundred and sixty million dollars. Top speed of thirty-two knots and has fifty suites.'

'Some people have money to burn.'

'Literally,' said Minister. 'A decent-sized super-yacht burns through five hundred gallons of diesel an hour. They reckon the average super-yacht owner spends four hundred thousand a year on fuel, three hundred and fifty thousand on docking and a million or so on maintenance.'

They reached a barred gate and Minister used a keycard to open it. They walked along a wooden jetty, their footsteps echoing. Overhead, black-and-white seagulls banked in the wind. Minister's boat was midway along the jetty. It was called *Dreamcatcher* and was registered in Jacksonville. It was about twenty feet wide with two hulls and a cockpit between them. There were two wheels in the cockpit, two sets of throttles and, between them, a console packed with screens and dials. A white leather high-backed chair stood behind each wheel, and behind them an entertainment area with white leather sofas and a white table large enough to seat eight people.

'Is this yours?' asked Shepherd.

'Sort of,' said Minister. 'The DEA seized it a few years ago. The owner is doing several life sentences and most of his assets were taken, though I hear the money is all squir-relled away. Oft-times the DEA auctions the ill-gotten gains, but they've given this to me, providing I do the odd job for them. They say if I'm a good boy they'll sign it over to me in three years, so I'm keeping my fingers crossed.'

'What sort of jobs?'

'Moving people around, mostly. Dropping people off in South America or the West Indies. Picking them up. People who need to stay off the radar. Some surveillance work. If there's someone in a small port they want watching, I can moor next to them, no questions asked.' He grinned. 'No one suspects a Kiwi. Anyway, they don't ask much and the rest of the time I just goof around on my own, take the odd charter out to the islands, bit of whale-watching.'

'Sounds like the life,' said Shepherd.

Minister nodded. 'For me, it is. Soon as they sign it over I'll start sailing it around the world. But there are worse places to be than Florida.' He waved Shepherd over to a bench seat on the port side. 'Grab a pew.' He opened a small fridge and pulled out a bottle of beer. 'Are you okay with Coors? Or I've got Miller Lite if you're watching your weight.'

'Coors is fine,' said Shepherd.

Minister tossed the bottle to him and Shepherd caught it. Minister grabbed a second bottle and flopped down on the seat opposite. He used his disposable cigarette lighter to prise off the cap, then leaned over and gave it to Shepherd. Shepherd knew he was being tested but it was a trick he'd mastered years earlier so he deftly popped off the cap and gave the lighter back. Minister raised his bottle in salute. 'Welcome aboard, Dan!' he said.

'Thanks for having me,' said Shepherd. He drank. The American beer was close to tasteless but it had been a long drive and he was thirsty so he took another pull.

'So, how much do you know about cats?' asked Minister.

'Other than that they've got two hulls, not much.'

Minister smiled. 'Well, to be fair, that's it in a nutshell. A traditional sailboat has only one hull centred around a heavy keel. Basically the weight of the keel keeps the boat upright. A catamaran is balanced on two hulls, so you don't need the keel. They are way more stable and they have a lot more room to play with. You can use the space between the hulls as a cabin, a cockpit, a place for sunbathing. Or, as the bad guys were quick to realise, to hide a shed-load of drugs. The cat is the boat of choice for most smugglers, these days, just because there's so much more space on them. You can tuck away four times as much in the way of drugs on a cat as you can on a monohull of the same length.'

'Got it,' said Shepherd.

'Now, in terms of cruising, holidaymakers much prefer cats. There's more privacy because you've got cabins in both hulls, more space generally, and they don't pitch around as much. You anchor at night and a monohull, even a big one, is going to be pitching and rolling. A cat is much more stable. You get a better night's sleep. Do you get seasick?'

'I don't seem to, no. But I've not been in a really rough sea.'

'You're lucky,' said Minister. 'Okay, so sailing a cat and sailing a monohull are two different ball games. Cats are much faster, mainly because they don't have the keel to slow them down. The two hulls also means the boat doesn't tip over like a monohull does, so you're not fighting gravity all the time. It's a lot less tiring. The lack of a keel also means you can sail in much shallower waters.'

'So, all good. Makes you wonder why anyone would sail anything else.'

Minister laughed. 'The purists won't touch them,' he said.

'It's the difference between driving an automatic or using a gearstick. Automatics are easier, but car enthusiasts want to be choosing their own gear. Monohulls are more responsive, generally, especially in light winds or when you're trying to sail upwind. Often you'll see the wind drop and the cats will stop but the monohulls will still be making headway. When you're sailing a monohull you can feel the wind on the sails, but a cat doesn't give you that input, which means you can find yourself overpowered without realising it. You know about overpowering, right?'

Shepherd nodded.

'And reefing?'

'Willoughby-Brown showed me the basics.'

'The principle is the same. But with a monohull, you can tell when you need to reef because you'll see the hull heel over. A cat can't heel so it's harder to tell when you're over-powered. And in heavy weather, they can be bitches to handle. But a good sailor always avoids bad weather, so hopefully that won't be an issue.'

'Good to know.'

'Luckily for you, the weather forecast says we're due some high winds and rain tomorrow, so I'll be able to give you a taste of what it's like.'

'Lovely,' said Shepherd.

Minister clinked his bottle against Shepherd's. 'You'll be fine. What we'll do today is go over the boat from bow to stern. I'll show you all the lines, fill you in on all the jargon. We'll head out to sea first thing tomorrow.'

'Sounds like a plan,' said Shepherd.

Kilburn police station was a short walk from the Tube, a brick building with a wheelchair ramp along one side and a short flight of steps on the other. Standing chose the stairs and pushed open the door. It was just after nine a.m. Inside there was a large reception room, a security door to the left, with a keypad and card reader, and a dozen plastic seats in three rows to the right. The chairs were facing a counter behind which sat a single uniformed constable. She was in her thirties with thinning hair and a look on her face that suggested she'd rather be anywhere else than dealing with members of the public. She was talking to a young woman with two crying toddlers in a double pushchair, but the woman kept interrupting her. 'The bitch keeps slagging me off on Facebook and it's doing my head in,' she said.

'I understand that, miss, but, really, that's not an offence. Just block her.'

'I did block her but she came back.'

'Well, block her again.'

'I want her arrested.'

'We can't arrest someone just because they're being rude on Facebook,' said the constable.

'I'm being bullied,' said the woman. She was big, and Standing reckoned she weighed at least a hundred kilos. He doubted she would be intimidated by anyone. He sat down and folded his arms. There were only two other people waiting, a young man in a baseball cap and another woman, who was breastfeeding a baby while glancing around aggressively as if she was daring anyone to pick fault with her. She saw that Standing was watching her and, even though he smiled, she glared at him as if she wanted him dead. Standing concentrated on reading the anti-drug, anti-gun and anti-crime posters that covered the walls. The woman and the constable went back and forth for another five minutes before the woman stormed off, swearing loudly and saying it was a bloody disgrace, her being a taxpayer and all. The constable sighed and took a drink from a water bottle. Standing looked around but neither the man nor the mother seemed in any hurry to approach the counter.

He stood up and tried to look as non-threatening as possible, just a regular citizen visiting his local police station. 'I'd like to see Detective Constable Kaiser,' he said to the policeman. 'DC Adam Kaiser.'

'Is he expecting you?'

'No.'

'Can you tell me what it's in connection with?'

'A case he was on. Alexia Chapman.'

'And what's your connection?'

'I'm her brother.'

The woman picked up a phone, spoke for less than a minute, then replaced the receiver. 'He's going to be tied up all day. He suggests you drop him an email and he'll respond to that.'

'I'd rather talk to him face to face.'

The woman's eyes hardened. 'As I've already explained to you, DC Kaiser is busy.' She took a business card from a rack and handed it to him. 'This is the email address.'

Standing took the card. 'It's generic,' he said.

'Yes. You mark it for the attention of DC Kaiser. It'll be forwarded to him.'

'I'd rather wait.'

'As I said, he'll be busy all day.' Her tone was harder now. It was clear she just wanted him to go.

'I've got nothing better to do,' said Standing. 'You never know, he might get a free slot sometime. Can you just let him know I'll be waiting here?'

The woman was now staring at him with open hostility but he simply smiled and sat down on one of the plastic chairs. Waiting wasn't a problem for him. Compared with sitting in a bomb-damaged building with no water and electricity, unbearably hot during the day, freezing cold at night, a nice comfortable plastic chair in an air-conditioned reception area was a piece of cake. Admittedly, he didn't have a plastic bag to shit in, but there was a pub next door if necessary. He sat with his hands in his lap and practised square breathing. The female officer didn't appear to call the detective to tell him that Standing was waiting, so when she left her post at midday and was replaced by a middle-aged officer with steel grey hair and an equally unfriendly disposition, Standing went up again and asked for DC Kaiser. He was told once more that the detective was unavailable. By then there were half a dozen people waiting with him. Most were kept for half an hour or more before whoever they were waiting for came to the counter. Standing wasn't sure if it was a definite policy to keep people waiting but it seemed consistent.

At six o'clock the grey-haired male officer was replaced by another woman, this one a cheery West Indian with bright red lipstick. She gave him a big smile when he went up to the desk, and happily called DC Kaiser. But she relayed the same message. DC Kaiser was busy and suggested he sent an email.

Standing thanked her, sat down again and went back to square breathing. The clock on the wall said seven when an Asian man in a dark grey suit appeared behind the counter. He had jet-black hair that he flicked away from his eyes as he spoke to the officer. He was about ten years older than Standing, taller and thinner, and was wearing wire-framed glasses that gave him the look of a librarian. The officer pointed her pen in Standing's direction, and Standing looked away. He had the feeling they were about to throw him out and he wasn't sure how he should react.

He looked back just in time to see the Asian man pat the

officer on the shoulder, then walk away. A few seconds later the man emerged from the door to Standing's left and came over to him. 'Mr Standing?' he asked. He was wearing a raincoat over his suit.

Standing stood up. 'Yes?' He squared his shoulders for the confrontation that he was sure was coming.

'You've been waiting for me, I understand?'

Standing frowned in confusion. 'I'm sorry?'

'DC Adam Kaiser. You were asking to see me.'

It was the last thing Standing had expected to hear. No one had said that DC Kaiser was Asian, but why would they?

'Are you all right, Mr Standing?'

'Yes, no, I'm sorry. I'm just tired, that's all.'

'How long have you been waiting?'

Standing shrugged. 'Ten hours or so. I got here just after nine.'

The detective raised his eyebrows. 'And you've sat here all day?'

'I needed to talk to you. They said you were busy so I said I'd wait. You are DC Kaiser, right? Handling the Alexia Chapman case?'

'Yes, I am. I said I was busy because, to be honest, I really didn't want to talk to you.'

'Yeah. I figured that.'

'And you had nothing better to do all day than sit here?'

'I need to talk to you.'

'You're a patient man, Mr Standing.'

'Actually, I'm not. Far from it. But you didn't give me a choice.'

'Do you live locally?'

'Not really. But I'm staying in Bayswater.'

The detective consulted his watch. 'I've got to get home. I'm on homework duty tonight with my eight-year-old and

my wife will give me hell if I'm late. Do you want to walk
to the Tube station with me?'

'Sure.'

The detective headed out and Standing followed him. 'Do
you smoke?' asked the detective.

'Smoke? No.'

'Well, I do.' The detective lit a cigarette as they walked.
'So you're Alexia's brother?'

Standing nodded. 'That's right.'

Kaiser looked across at him. 'See, I was told the brother
was called Andrew. Andrew Chapman. And you're Matt
Standing. Run that anomaly by me, will you?'

'Alexia was adopted when she was three. By the Chapmans.
She changed her name. I'm still Standing.' He smiled. 'No
pun intended.'

'Your parents are dead?'

'My mother is, yes. After she died we were taken into care.
Alexia was adopted. And now she's dead and I don't understand what happened.'

'She overdosed. Heroin.'

'How does a sixteen-year-old girl start taking heroin?'

Kaiser blew smoke up at the sky. 'Are you serious? I've
come across twelve-year-olds on crack. Sixteen isn't young
any more. Sixteen-year-olds are taking drugs and having kids
and doing what the hell they want.'

'But she had a good family. Her mum and dad are nice
middle-class people.'

'I know. I've met them. And they were as surprised as you.
But middle-class kids take drugs. They get bored, they're
usually under a lot of pressure at school and at home, and
they've got money.' The detective sighed. 'I'm sorry for your
loss, but it happens.'

'Who gave her the drugs?'

'That I don't know.'

'Someone gives heroin to a sixteen-year-old girl and you don't try to find out who it was?'

'Mr Standing, there are probably a dozen drug dealers within a five-minute walk of here who will sell you any drug you want. A lot of them will deliver. You send a text message and ten minutes later a guy on a pushbike will come and take your money. Thirty seconds after that another guy on a bike will spit out a package and the deal is done.'

'And you don't try to stop it?'

Kaiser chuckled and flicked ash onto the pavement. 'Welcome to the world of modern policing,' he said. 'It's all about resources and the Met doesn't have the resources to bring in every drug dealer in London. And where would we put them? Our prisons are full as it is.' He took a long drag on his cigarette and held it up. 'Meanwhile these are ten quid a pack. The world's a mess.'

'Where did it happen?'

'Your sister? A house not far from here. It was used as a shooting gallery but it was shut down after your sister died.'

'Shooting gallery? She was injecting?'

'You thought she was chasing the dragon? No, she was injecting. Had been for months, according to the coroner. She was clever – she was hiding the track marks in her feet, so she was no novice.'

Standing could barely believe what he was hearing. 'I don't know what to say,' he said.

'There's nothing *to* say,' said the detective. 'It happens. Nice kids from nice families take drugs. In fact, it's usually easier for kids from nice families to get drugs because they usually get lots of pocket money and have parents with busy social lives.'

'But heroin . . . In my day the naughty kids smoked cigarettes. I didn't know anyone who did drugs.'

'I did,' said Kaiser. 'I knew kids at my primary school who smoked weed. And glue-sniffing was big when I was a boy. Now, with the price of drugs down and them being so readily available, the kids that used to sniff glue go straight to E or smack or coke. It's endemic.'

'But why?'

'Why are drugs endemic? Because people like to take them, end of.' He held up his cigarette. 'My drug of choice. Nicotine. They're not illegal – not yet, anyway – but if they were made illegal, would I stop? Probably not.' He waved his hand at the people around them. 'One in three people have tried drugs and there's maybe three million in the country who regularly take them. There's a need, so dealers move in to fulfil it. You can't blame them for looking to widen the market, and they do that by getting kids hooked. They're already breaking the law selling to adults so selling to kids is no big thing.'

'And you're not trying to stop them?'

'The Drugs Squad is, but they're going after the big fish. No one gets pulled for personal use, these days. But, sure, if we found a guy selling drugs to kids we'd throw the book at him.'

'And after Lexi died, you didn't go looking for her supplier?'

'I'm sorry, no. I know you want some sort of retribution, but your sister injected the heroin into her vein herself. Her fingerprints were on the syringe.'

'But you could have gone after her dealer.'

'After she died, everyone ran from the house, like rats leaving a sinking ship. Her friend was the only one who stayed.'

'But you should have been able to get her dealer's number from her phone. She must have called him, or messaged him, right?'

'We never found it,' said the detective. 'It wasn't on her and we didn't find it in the house. We figured someone must have stolen it.' They had arrived at the Tube station and the detective nodded at the entrance. 'This is where I leave you,' he said. 'Really, I'm sorry for your loss.'

'You said the house where she died is near here. Can you show me?'

The detective glanced at his watch. 'I've really got to go,' he said. 'My wife's gonna have my guts for garters.'

'I'd just like to see where it happened.'

'It'd be a pointless exercise. The owners cleared everything out and boarded it up.' He could see from the look on Standing's face how much it meant to him so he sighed. 'Okay. Come on.'

He walked away quickly and Standing hurried after him. They crossed Kilburn High Road, went down a side street and took another turn. It was the fifth house along, a terraced house over three floors. Corrugated-iron sheets had been fixed over the windows and there was a large metal plate covering the front door. Bright yellow stickers announced that the building was under the care of a local security company.

'There were squatters in it – security was nowhere near like it is now,' said the detective. 'It was a one-stop shop for pretty much any sort of drug you wanted. Weed, heroin, crack. They didn't keep the drugs on the premises. The users would turn up and pay and the drugs would be delivered. Everyone on the premises only had enough for personal use, so it was difficult to bust them. Until your sister OD'd, when all hell broke loose, obviously.'

'Who was running the place?'

'It was a local gang. They split after it happened.'

'Asians?'

Kaiser nodded.

'They weren't arrested?'

'Mr Standing, arrested for what? Organising a drugs den? With only a relatively small amount of drugs on the premises?'

'My sister died.'

'Yes, she did. But she injected herself. I'm sorry, but that's the way it is.'

Standing nodded slowly as he looked up at the house. 'What floor was she on when she died?'

The detective looked pained. 'Why do you ask?'

'I just want to know.'

The detective swallowed. 'She was there. On the pavement.' He pointed near the front door.

'The pavement?'

'Her friend tried to get her outside. She thought she could walk it off. But she collapsed and that was when they called an ambulance. She was dead when it got here.'

'Was the friend Zoë Middlehurst by any chance?'

Kaiser looked at Standing sharply. 'How do you know that?'

'I think Mrs Chapman mentioned it,' Standing lied.

Kaiser nodded. 'Yeah, that was her.' He looked at his watch again. 'Look, I'm sorry, but I've really got to go.' He patted Standing's shoulder and hurried off.

Standing stood staring at the pavement. Tears pricked his eyes and he blinked them away. He took deep, slow breaths, four seconds in, hold, four seconds out. He did that for a full minute, then swore out loud and stepped forward, slamming his fist into the metal plate that was covering the door.

★   ★   ★

The cabin that Minister allocated to Shepherd was bigger than the whole of Willoughby-Brown's yacht. There was a double bed, a built-in wardrobe with mirrored doors that made the cabin look even bigger, an armchair, a large TV and an ensuite shower room. Unlike Willoughby-Brown's yacht, the catamaran barely moved during the night and he slept so deeply that he didn't wake up until Minister banged on the cabin door. 'Wakey, wakey, rise and shine!' shouted Minister. 'Breakfast's ready and I want mine.'

Shepherd pulled on his clothes and went through to the galley where Minister had put plates of scrambled eggs, bacon and toast on the table, along with mugs of coffee. 'So what's the plan?' asked Shepherd, as he sat down and picked up his knife and fork.

'We'll take her out and put her through the paces,' said Minister. 'She's easy enough to sail single-handed but you need to be fairly nimble. Usually you'd have a captain, a first mate and a deckhand if you were carrying guests, plus a chef and maybe a waitress-chambermaid. But I've sailed her to the West Indies and back with no bother, and I could probably sail her around the world if I wanted to.'

The two men finished their breakfast, then Minister washed up while Shepherd shaved, showered and changed into clean clothes. By the time he was back in the cockpit, Minister had the engine running and was consulting a screen that gave the local weather conditions.

'Have you got a local chart?' asked Shepherd, as he took the chair next to Minister.

Minister tapped on another screen, which filled with a chart showing the water depth and the location of the buoys at the entrance to the marina. Shepherd memorised it without any effort. 'We tend to rely on the GPS here,' said Minister, 'but the chart's useful just in case the system ever goes down. Right, you untie us and then I'll let you take us out to sea.'

Shepherd stepped onto the jetty, untied the cat and climbed back on. Minister ran through the controls with him, then talked him through guiding the vessel away from the jetty and out to the sea. Despite its size, the boat was responsive, and Shepherd had no trouble negotiating his way through the marina. Once out in the open sea, Minister showed Shepherd how to unfurl the sails and the cat was soon slicing through the waves. There was none of the pitch and roll Shepherd had experienced on Willoughby-Brown's yacht – the cat was much more stable and the visibility way better.

'I don't see the telltales,' said Shepherd, looking up at the sails.

'Telltales are for wimps,' laughed Minister. 'Plus they'd be difficult to see from the cockpit. We don't need them. You can tell from the way the sail is behaving whether you're doing it right or not.' He clapped Shepherd on the shoulder. 'Don't worry, mate, I'll see you right. I bet Willoughby-Brown uses telltales.'

'He does, yes.'

'Fucking fair-weather sailor.'

'What do you think of him?' asked Shepherd.

Minister looked across at him. 'As a sailor?'

'As a . . . whatever he is.'

'You want me to tell tales out of school?' He grinned. 'I told you, I'm not a fan of telltales.'

'I admire your loyalty,' said Shepherd.

'You sound like you've got reservations about the guy.'

Shepherd shrugged. 'I've known him a long time, but I hardly know him, if you get my drift. He keeps his cards close to his chest.'

'Meaning you don't trust him?'

'Trust has to be earned, right?'

Minister nodded. 'Always a good technique, answering a question with a question.'

Shepherd laughed. 'Sorry. Force of habit.'

'I'll be honest, I don't know him that well. He was fine to work with back in the day. He knows his tradecraft. He's a pro.'

'That's true enough,' said Shepherd.

'But he's not one of those driven guys, you know, the type who are on a crusade. The DEA is full of them. Guys who truly believe that drugs are the work of the devil and would turn in their nearest and dearest if they found them with a joint.'

'And you don't?'

'Don't what?'

'Think that drugs are the work of the devil?'

Minister smiled slyly. 'I can see I'm going to have to choose my words carefully,' he said.

Shepherd laughed. 'You're among friends.'

'Okay, I'll trust you. Drugs cause a lot of misery, but so do cigarettes and booze, and everyone knows that far more people die from alcohol than drugs. No question of that. Drug-taking is rife among the sailing community, especially out in the islands. And why not? Why can't a guy sit on his own boat and smoke a joint as he watches the sun go down? Who's he harming? And suppose you've got a lot of water to cover, you're on a deadline. What's wrong with a guy doing a line of coke just to keep his spirits up?'

'I guess if you're in international waters, nothing.'

'Exactly. There isn't anything morally wrong with drugs that I can see. It's just that at the moment we have laws against them, same as the Yanks used to have laws against alcohol. Most of the DEA know that all they're doing is enforcing the law, and I get that. It's the ones who regard it as a crusade that I have a problem with. Most of the agents I deal with are just regular guys earning a pay cheque. I've smoked dope with several, when we're well away from land. They're not against drugs *per se*, and they all realise the futility of what they're doing, but it's how they pay their mortgage. I always wondered how the people who worked for Five felt about being told they were joining the war on drugs.'

'That was before my time,' said Shepherd. 'It was after the Soviet Union fell apart and all the spies had nothing to do. The Security Service was looking for something else to occupy its time and the powers-that-be settled on the IRA, drugs and organised crime. But, yeah, it was a big change.'

'How do you feel about drugs cases?'

Shepherd frowned. 'In what way?'

'Well, I'm guessing the case you're on involves drugs. That's why you need this crash course in sailing. I'm guessing you're trying to bring down a big-time smuggler.' He held up his hands. 'Stop me if I'm being too nosy,' he said. 'Willoughby-Brown told me nothing and I'm just curious.'

'I can't tell you about the case, but happy enough to talk generally,' said Shepherd. 'I know what you mean. I was a cop before I joined Five and I worked a lot of drug cases. When you go after a murderer or a rapist, you know they need to be put away. If you don't catch them they're going to hurt or kill someone else. Armed robbers hurt and terrorise civilians so they need to be behind bars, and obviously terrorists are the scum of the earth. When it comes to people killing and maiming civilians just to prove a political or religious point, then I guess you can count me as a crusader. But drug dealers, the big guys who arrange the major shipments, in a way they're just businessmen who are breaking arbitrary laws. Some of them, anyway. Some are vicious scum and need locking up. The Colombians and the like, who use terror and violence to grow their business. But the big-time marijuana importers, I'm not sure they deserve twenty-year sentences. Not if they haven't hurt anybody. But then I don't get to make the laws, and I don't get to choose my cases.'

'Did you read that Howard Marks book? *Mr Nice*?'

'Yeah. He was a character.'

'The DEA went after him, and he got twenty-five years. He never did more than a few in the UK. I heard he worked for MI6 for a while.'

'So they say.'

'It's a messy business, isn't it?' said Minister.

'We operate in a grey area, that's for sure,' agreed Shepherd.

'I can tell you one thing about Willoughby-Brown. He was always driven – not like a crusader, but driven to get to the top. He was a big networker while he was out here. DEA, CIA, FBI, Homeland Security, he was always making contacts. It's obviously paid off. He seems to have managed to climb the greasy pole, all right, hasn't he?'

'Yeah. He knows how to play politics. And he's not averse to climbing over others to get to where he wants.'

'He's a fan of yours.'

'What?'

'Yeah, he said he was sending over one of his top men and that I was to take good care of you.'

Shepherd laughed and shook his head.

'What's funny?' asked Minister.

'If I know Jeremy, he was well aware when he said it that you'd tell me.'

'He's that devious?'

'Oh, yes.'

'Bastard,' said Minister. 'Okay, interrogation over. Now we'll run through some reefing. Look over at the leeward hull.

See how it's being pushed down into the water? And look at the scoop. There's water up to the steps. Now, you can't tell from the position of the boat that we're overpowered, but those are two signs that we need to reef. Basically we let the apparent wind speed make our reefing decisions. If we don't, we're always going to be late to the party. There's an old sailor's saying – if you think you should reef, you should have done it already. Words to that effect, anyway. So, on a cat like this, you put in your first reef anywhere between eighteen and twenty knots. When we get to twenty-five you want reef number two, and put in the third when we get close to thirty knots. Now, in the unlikely event we find ourselves in a wind of more than thirty knots, we put away the jib and sail with a fully-reefed main. Any worse than that and we'd be looking at spilling wind by luffing. Did Willoughby-Brown cover that?'

Shepherd shook his head.

'It's simple enough. You steer towards the wind to disrupt the airflow over the sail. That will make the sail flap, or we call it luffing. Luffing also happens when the boat is tacked.'

'Ah, I get it,' said Shepherd. 'I saw that when I was out with Willoughby-Brown. Just didn't know it was called a luff.'

'There's a lot of jargon, and unfortunately you'll have to remember it all,' said Minister. 'It's a sure way of spotting a beginner or a wannabe. Anyway, luffing lets you sail in very strong winds without damaging the sails or the lines. Okay, let's get to it.'

Minister spent the next hour showing Shepherd how to reef the cat, and the effect it had on the boat's handling. Shepherd eventually got the hang of it, and Minister nodded his approval. 'Right. I'll show you now how to park the cat. It's the equivalent of heaving to in a monohull. It's a phrase you want to drop in, if you can.'

Shepherd nodded. 'Park the cat,' he repeated.

'Basically you deep-reef your main, drop the traveller all the way to leeward, then pull the mainsheet hard in. Once you've done that, you point the bow into the wind and you can sit there quite nicely, no matter what's going on around you. Say you're sailing at night and you're taking a pounding, you can park and get some rest. We do it if we need to make repairs at sea.'

Shepherd grinned and Minister looked at him quizzically. 'Something funny?'

'Yeah. You just gave me a whole raft of jargon and I understood every word. I think we're making progress.'

Standing arrived at Dr Doyle's office at eight thirty but, although the receptionist had said first thing, it wasn't until nine o'clock that he was shown into her inner sanctum. 'Sorry to have kept you waiting,' she said. She was already sitting in her armchair with her notepad on her lap.

Standing sat down opposite and crossed his legs. 'No problem,' he said. He wondered if keeping him waiting was a test to see if he'd get angry. He smiled at how wrong she was. Waiting wasn't a problem for him. If it was, he wouldn't have been able to spend days on end in unpleasant ops, rationing food and water, and shitting into plastic bags. A half-hour wait in a room with comfortable chairs and a pile of magazines was no hardship.

'How's it going?'

'All good,' Standing replied.

'You're sticking with the exercises? The square breathing?'

'Yes, no problem.'

She smiled. 'Good,' she said. 'Now, I've been giving some thought to your father.'

'That's more than I have,' said Standing. 'But you knock yourself out.'

'I was thinking you should go and see him. Talk to him. Is that possible?'

'Sure. Even murderers are allowed visitors. But why would I want to see him?'

'We talked last time about the similarities between the two of you.'

Standing frowned. 'The way I remember it, we talked about the differences.'

She scribbled in her pad. 'Well, yes. But I thought that sitting down with your father and talking things through with him might help you understand your own issues more clearly.'

'I'm not him.'

'I'm not saying you are. But your anger-management issues didn't arise spontaneously. They sprang from somewhere. And maybe your father is a cause. A partial cause, perhaps, but a cause nonetheless.'

'And how does me talking to him help me?'

'Perhaps he could explain why he behaved the way he did. And you might see parallels with your own behaviour.'

'I don't beat people up for fun,' said Standing.

'You think your father did?'

'He used to give me a beating every now and again and it seemed to be for the hell of it.'

'Did he ever explain why he felt it necessary to hit you?'

'What? Are you serious? He felt it necessary to beat the crap out of a nine-year-old boy? That's what I should ask him? And maybe I should ask him why he felt it necessary to stick a knife in my mother. I can't believe . . .' He realised she was watching him carefully, assessing his reaction. He was being tested. Standing took a deep breath and sighed. 'You're winding me up,' he said.

'Well, to be honest, I'm exploring the triggers that cause

your anger,' she said. 'And your father is certainly one. Look at how you've tensed. Your voice changed and so has your body language. I can see and hear how angry you are.'

'But I'm not lashing out.'

'No. But you have a code, don't you, about not hitting women? And again that code might have come from your father. You saw how he treated your mother and you've promised never to behave like that.'

Standing frowned. 'So you're saying that sometimes I copy my father, and sometimes I do the opposite of what he did? How does that work? How do I decide which is which?'

'The human psyche is a very complicated thing,' said Dr Doyle.

He forced a smile. 'Which is why you charge so much, I suppose.'

'You don't have to worry about the bill,' she said. 'The Ministry of Defence is taking care of it.'

'I was being flippant.'

'Yes, I know. And humour is a terrific way of dealing with conflict. If you could learn to tell a joke to defuse a situation, you might be less likely to lash out physically.'

Standing flashed her a tight smile. 'I'll try that next time I come up against the Taliban.'

'You know what I mean, Matt. We're not talking about combat. We're talking about day-to-day confrontations. Now do you understand the difference between anger and anger impulse?'

'I'm guessing the impulse comes before the outburst.'

She smiled. 'Exactly. And when we were talking about your father, I could see examples of anger impulses. Your face reddened, your neck was tense, your voice got louder and you kept sighing.'

'You were making me angry. What did you expect?'

'But you weren't angry, were you? You were getting angry, and that's the difference. If we can make you more aware of the impulses, we can teach you to deal with them, to turn a negative into a positive.'

'I'm not sure I follow you.'

She leaned back in her chair. 'As we've talked about before, anger can be productive. In combat, it's a survival skill. Elsewhere it's a perfectly normal human emotion. Anger isn't a mental illness and we're not treating it as such. In fact, dealing with anger appropriately can make it a healthy emotion. That's why we refer to it as anger management. It's not about suppressing or internalising the anger, it's about expressing your feelings – and your frustrations – in a calm and collected manner. We need you to learn coping mechanisms and start following positive pathways to release your anger. The key to that is recognising your anger impulses.'

'Okay,' said Standing, but he wasn't sure that he agreed with her. He was never aware that he was getting angry, not on those occasions when he'd lashed out physically. One moment he was fine, the next he was in fighting mode, and it always felt to him as if the transition was immediate, as if a switch had been thrown. But he was happy enough to give the therapist the benefit of the doubt – his SAS career depended on it.

'But, first, I want to spend some time teaching you a relaxation technique that you may find useful.' She pointed at the side of his chair. 'There's a yoga mat. Spread it out on the floor, will you?'

Standing did so. Then she asked him to slip off his shoes and lie down on the mat.

'Normally you'd do this in a darkened room,' said Dr Doyle. She was still sitting on her chair but leaning forward to get a better look. 'It's a relaxation technique but it involves tensing your muscles, so if at any point you cramp or feel pain, stop straight away. It's not about pushing yourself.'

'Got it,' said Standing, staring up at the ceiling.

'So, first, try to relax. Let your mind go blank. I know that's difficult when there's someone in the room, but do the best you can.'

Standing closed his eyes. 'Okay.'

'Breathe deeply. You can square breathe if you want, whatever feels the most comfortable. Let your arms relax, unclench your teeth, let your feet fall outwards.'

She let Standing lie still for a couple of minutes. He didn't feel at all relaxed: he felt vulnerable and defenceless lying on a yoga mat in the middle of an office.

'Okay,' she said eventually. 'Now that you're relaxed we'll start the exercise. You're going to start working on each main muscle, but keep breathing deeply and evenly while you do it. You're tensing the individual muscles while remaining totally relaxed. You hold the tension for a few seconds, then relax the muscle. Do that for three or four repetitions. Then move onto the next muscle.'

'Okay.'

'So, start with your left foot. Curl your toes and clench your foot. Hold it for three seconds, then relax. Have you got it?'

'Got it,' said Standing. He worked his left foot in the way she'd described and soon felt it grow warm.

Over the next thirty minutes she talked him through all his major muscles, ending with his face and neck, making him force yawns and frowns to work all the parts of his face. By the time he had finished he felt as tired as if he'd done an hour in the gym. She told him to relax for five minutes, then sat back in her chair. 'You should try to do that once a day if you can,' she said. 'Maybe when you go to bed. You'll find you get a really good night's sleep afterwards.'

'No problem,' he said. He reached for one of the bottles of water on the coffee-table and drank from it.

'And I want you to start keeping an anger journal.'

Standing stopped drinking. 'A what?'

'An anger journal,' she said. 'I want you to start writing down the feelings you have when you get angry, and what led up to it. Then we can go through it together and come up with strategies that will dissipate the anger before it becomes a problem. Are you okay with that?'

'Of course,' he said. He grinned. 'Whatever it takes, Doc.'

Shepherd woke to the smell of breakfast cooking. He pulled on a T-shirt and a pair of jeans and padded through to the main cabin. Minister was in the galley, bare-chested, which Shepherd thought quite brave, considering bacon was sizzling in the frying pan. 'Thought I'd let you sleep in,' he said, as Shepherd went over to the coffee-maker.

'What time is it?'

'Eight,' said Minister. He stirred a frying pan filled with scrambled eggs. 'Do you want toast?'

'Sounds good.'

Minister waved with his spatula. 'Toaster's over there.'

Shepherd slotted in two slices of bread, then went back to making his coffee.

By the time Shepherd had made the toast and buttered it, Minister was putting out the eggs and bacon. The two men sat down. Minister smothered his food with tomato ketchup. 'So, how about a quick Q and A, see how much you remember?'

'Go for it,' said Shepherd. He cut his piece of toast in half and put one piece next to his eggs.

'Definition of topping lift?'

'The line that runs from the end of the boom to the mast.' Shepherd took a mouthful of scrambled eggs.

'It's used for?'

'Holding the boom up when the sail isn't set.'

Minister nodded. 'Breast line?'

'A dock line that runs at a right angle to the centre of the boat.'

'Cunningham?'

'The line that puts tension in the luff of a sail.' He grinned. 'I love that word. Luff.'

'And a Cunningham is a type of what?'

'Downhaul.' Shepherd took a sip of coffee.

'What's a fairlead?'

'A hook or a ring used to guide a line, so as to reduce friction.'

'Good,' said Minister. 'Halyard?'

'A line that raises a sail.'

'Jibsheet?'

'A line that controls the jib.'

'Padeye?'

'An eye that a line runs through.'

Minister sat back and flashed him a thumbs-up. 'You, sir, are good to go. I've never met anyone who's picked up sailing so quickly. You're a natural.'

'I've had a good instructor.'

'Well, I'm more than happy to sign you off,' he said. 'I don't think there's anything more I can teach you.'

'I don't know about that,' said Shepherd. He waved his fork over the plate. 'How do you do your eggs? These are amazing.'

Minister laughed. 'Three eggs per serving, but only use the whites from two. Add a knob of butter, a dash of cream and keep stirring them in a frying pan. My mum's recipe.'

'My boy likes scrambled eggs with cheese.'

'Sounds like a rebel.'

Shepherd chuckled. 'He is, in his own way.'

Wandsworth Prison was a harsh building with grey stone turrets and arched windows, surrounded by high walls topped with razor wire. Every square foot seemed to be covered by CCTV cameras, and as Standing stood in the visitors' line he counted three pointing in his direction. The prison looked like one of the old warehouses that used to line the River Thames before they had either been knocked down or converted into luxury flats. Wandsworth Prison had stayed as a warehouse, a place where criminals could be stored until they either died or were released. According to the prison's website, it was built in 1851 based on what was known as the Humana Separate System, with corridors radiating from a central control point and each prisoner having his own toilet. It was soon full to capacity and the toilets were removed to pack in more men, who had to slop out each morning until the mid-1990s when the in-cell toilets were reinstated. It was still the largest prison in the United Kingdom with almost nineteen hundred prisoners in residence.

Most of the visitors queuing up to have their paperwork inspected were clearly regulars. They were mainly women, and probably half of them had children with them, from babes in arms to teenagers. They spent the time gossiping together or on their phones and seemed used to the wait.

There were five visiting slots: eight a.m., ten a.m., eleven fifteen a.m., one forty-five p.m. and three fifteen p.m. Standing had been allocated the first slot and he'd taken the Tube to Tooting Bec, then the 219 bus. He had joined the queue at seven thirty. During the next half-hour another thirty or so visitors arrived, and more than a few cut into the queue ahead of him. That annoyed Standing, but he practised square breathing and after a while it stopped bothering him.

At exactly eight o'clock he heard an expectant buzz, and they filed in to be processed. Half a dozen prison officers, three male and three female, handled the process efficiently and with good humour, clearly recognising many of the visitors and greeting them by name. Their paperwork was checked, everyone provided ID – Standing had brought his passport with him – then handed over anything sharp, along with their mobile phones, and walked through the sort of metal detector found at airports. Standing had heard all the stories about rubber gloves and internal checks but there was none of that, though female officers did peek inside the nappies of the babies, and the children were inspected as closely as the adults.

They were held in a corridor until everyone had been checked, then taken as a group down a windowless corridor to a large room where several dozen small tables had been set out in neat rows with plastic chairs at either side. The prisoners were already sitting down, identified by the bright orange vests they were wearing over their prison-issue sweatshirts. Children squealed and shouted and ran across to greet their fathers, and prisoners waved sheepishly at their loved ones, happy to see them but embarrassed, too.

Standing's father was at a table at the far end of the room, a burly prison officer close by, leaning against the wall, his arms folded. He was greyer than Standing remembered, and heavier, but the face was the same. Cold, almost reptilian eyes, thin lips that parted to reveal crooked tobacco-stained teeth, and ears that stuck out slightly. Standing had the same ears. He hoped that was all he'd inherited from the man sitting at the table. It was the smell that Standing remembered most about his father. Stale sweat, tobacco and booze, with a splash of Old Spice across his cheeks and neck when he shaved. The smell that hit him when he reached the table was different. There was still the stale sweat and tobacco, but now there was no booze or aftershave. His father looked up at him with clear hostility. He folded his arms as he stared up at Standing. 'You're the first visitor I've ever had,' he said eventually.

'Yeah, well, you were never one for socialising, were you?' said Standing. He pulled out a chair and sat opposite his father.

'I nearly turned you down.'

'Why didn't you?'

His father shrugged but didn't reply.

'How are things?' asked Standing, eventually, more to end the silence than anything else.

The man shrugged again but didn't say anything.

'Fuck me, I'm not a cop,' said Standing. 'You don't have to take the fifth.'

'What do you want?'

'I'm not allowed to visit my own father?'

'You haven't visited in . . . what? Twelve years? I'm assuming you're here for a reason. So spit it out and fuck off.' He leaned back in his chair as he stared defiantly at Standing.

'I can see being inside hasn't mellowed you,' said Standing, but his father continued to stare at him, stony-faced. Standing placed his hands on the table, palms down. 'Fine,' he said. 'Play the hard man all you want. Lexi's dead.' He wasn't proud of the satisfaction he took from the way his father's jaw tightened and eyes narrowed. Not that he thought of Des Standing as his father – he hadn't done that for many, many years. Des Standing had provided half the genetic material that formed his DNA, but that didn't make him a father and never had done.

'What happened?'

'She overdosed. On heroin.'

'She leave a note?'

'Why would you care if she did?' Standing leaned forward, his hands still pressed against the table top. 'Are you worried she might have blamed you? That she killed herself because of you?'

'I just want to know what was going through her mind.'

'Why?'

He tilted his head to the side. 'You don't think a father would care about his daughter?'

Standing sneered at him. 'Father? How the fuck were you a father to Lexi? Just because you fucked her mother without a condom doesn't make you a father. The word should make you fucking choke. You were never father to her. Or to me.' He shouted the last three words and the entire room fell silent. Heads turned towards their table. Two heavyset prison officers started moving towards them and the one standing close by pushed himself away from the wall and stared at them, as if expecting trouble. Standing raised his hands and smiled. 'Sorry, guys, my fault. I'll use my indoor voice from now on.'

The two officers looked at each other, then back at Standing. The one by the wall pointed a warning finger at him. 'Yellow card,' he said.

'No problem,' said Standing. He put down his hands and glowered at his father. 'You were never a father to her or to me,' he said softly.

'It wasn't easy for any of us.'

Standing shook his head scornfully. 'Don't play the fucking victim, Des. I was there, remember. Right up until the moment you killed Mum.'

'I put my hands up for that and I'm doing my time. I'm taking my punishment.'

'Yeah, well, I hope they never let you out,' said Standing. 'And pretending to care about what happened to Lexi, you can just fuck off.' He sat back and folded his arms, then realised he was mimicking the way his father was sitting. He straightened up and put his hands back on the table.

The two men sat in angry silence for a couple of minutes. 'When is the funeral?' his father asked eventually.

'You thinking of getting out for the day, maybe doing a runner?'

'Fuck you.'

'Yeah? Fuck you too.' This time Standing kept his voice down. His father looked away, gritting his teeth. 'They already buried her,' said Standing eventually. 'Cremated her, actually. Maybe I could get them to send you the ashes. Easier to take care of them than a living, breathing girl.'

'Who are you really angry at, Matt?'

Standing's eyes narrowed. 'What do you mean?'

'You know what I mean. You've not seen me for going on twelve years. Now suddenly you're shouting and swearing and giving me the evil eye. That's a hell of a long time to bear a grudge, innit?'

'Until the day I die, mate.'

He forced a smile. 'Yeah, you say that, but you've got any revenge you wanted. I'm in a concrete box twenty-three hours a day, and if they ever do let me out I'll be too old to enjoy it.'

'You're alive and Mum isn't. I know who got the better deal.'

The two men sat in silence again. A young woman was crying at a table close by, her head buried in her hands. The man she was visiting reached over and touched her shoulder but she pushed him away.

'The thing that gets me is that you never said sorry,' said Standing. 'You never apologised.'

'I pleaded guilty. I put my hand up.'

'That's not the same as apologising.'

'To who? To Sally? What good would that have done?'

'To me,' hissed Standing. 'And to Lexi. You killed our mother. You took her away from us and had us thrown into care. You ruined our lives. '

'Ruined, is it? Your life?'

Standing glared at his father but didn't reply.

'If you want to hit me, hit me. The screws won't stop you – they'll probably give you a medal.'

'Fuck off,' said Standing.

'You want to. You know you want to.'

Standing had bunched his hands into fists. He forced himself to relax. 'No, you're the one that wants it.'

'I want to be punished, that's what you think? Didn't know they taught you amateur psychology in the army.' He cleared his throat noisily. 'You know, in a way you should be grateful to me.'

'Grateful?' Standing looked at him in disbelief.

'You are what you are because of me. There's no getting away from that. If things hadn't worked out like they did, maybe you'd be stuck in some dead-end job now, serving coffee or working in a garden centre. Instead you're a soldier, travelling the world.' He grinned. 'And killing people with no comeback.' He leaned forward. 'Is that why you signed up? To take out your anger on someone else? You can't shoot me so you go out and shoot ragheads instead?'

'I've barely given you a day's thought since they took you down,' said Standing.

His father grinned and sat back in his chair. 'And yet here you are.'

The woman had stopped crying and was blowing her nose. The man she was visiting was crying now, tears running down his cheeks.

'I came because I wanted to know if you'd seen Lexi. If she'd visited you.'

'She hated me more than you do.'

'So that's a no?'

'That's a no.'

Standing pushed back his chair and got to his feet. Heads swivelled in his direction and he raised his hands to show that he wasn't a threat.

'That's it?'

'You thought I was going to give you a cake with a file in it? You can rot in here for all I care.'

'There's a lot of anger in you, boy. I can feel it.'

Standing's hands bunched into fists again and he clenched his teeth. He could feel the adrenalin coursing through his system and he had to fight the urge to throw himself across the table, grab his father by the throat and squeeze the life out of him.

'Let it out,' said his father, his eyes sparkling. 'Come on, you know you want to.'

Standing took a deep breath, held it, then exhaled. 'Fuck you,' he said eventually.

'I knew you wouldn't have the balls to throw a punch,' laughed his father.

Standing's eyes blazed and he took a step towards him, but then he turned on his heels and walked quickly towards the exit, counting to ten as he went.

Shepherd slid his passport into the automatic reader and waited patiently while the camera focused on his face and compared it with the photograph stored in the passport's chip. It was pretty impressive technology and he was grateful he didn't have to have a face-to-face with a Border Force employee. He was old enough to remember when immigration officers wore suits and welcomed you back to the United Kingdom. Most now seemed to be dressed as paramilitaries and it was rare they managed a smile. The automatic passport readers had become the friendlier option.

The doors hissed open. He took the escalator down to the baggage-reclaim area and walked through the blue Customs zone. Willoughby-Brown was waiting for him in the arrivals area, wearing a camel-hair overcoat. 'Good flight?' he asked.

'Virgin Upper Class. So yes.'

'You're a valued employee. Nothing is too much trouble,' said Willoughby-Brown. 'How did it go with BM?'

'Nice guy,' said Shepherd.

'Isn't he? That *Dreamcatcher* is one heck of a boat, isn't it?'

'Yeah, but I'm not a big fan of boats, I have to say. But if I had to choose, sure, I'd go with a cat.'

'And you're up to speed with the whole life-on-the-ocean-waves thing?'

'Sure. Why are you here, Jeremy?'

Willoughby-Brown patted his shoulder. 'You're so suspicious, Daniel. Come on, let me buy you a coffee.'

Shepherd followed him with a heavy heart. There was only one reason why Willoughby-Brown would come to the airport and that was to turn him around and send him on a flight out. If that was the case, Katra wasn't going to be happy.

Willoughby-Brown got the coffees and two chocolate muffins. He broke off a piece of his and popped it into his mouth. 'Meyer is in Marbella. Lisa is with him. He got in last night and we're not sure how long he'll be there. We think he's got a meet with a supplier so he could be gone in a day or two. We need to strike while the iron's hot.'

'Okay,' said Shepherd, hesitantly.

'We put together a legend for you – well, two, actually. You'll be a bank robber by the name of Rich Campbell, sent down for ten years in 2001, released in 2007. All the files are good for that, PNC, prison records, the whole shebang. But you took on a new identity in 2008, and became Jeff Taylor. The story you can tell if it comes up is that the guys in your crew blamed you for getting caught and you feared for your life. You left London, changed your name and headed for the Med. You became a sailor, crewman, then a mate, and eventually got your skipper's licence. That's the legend. Jeff Taylor. Professional captain. You've got all the necessary paperwork and a valid skipper's licence. There's a CV showing the vessels you've sailed on, and if anyone checks, you'll come up as good as gold. You have a place in Portsmouth, a small flat, which has been kitted out by our dressers just in case anyone breaks in for a look-see.'

'So everything will be in the Jeff Taylor name?'

Willoughby-Brown nodded. 'But the Rich Campbell fingerprints are on file along with your picture, and you'll show up on the Police National Computer. So if someone starts digging it won't take much to realise that the Jeff Taylor is a cover and you're really Campbell. The thing is, of course, that Meyer is going to be very interested in Campbell. You'd be a very useful addition to his team, a sailor who isn't afraid of violence and is good with guns. Plus, the fact he knows your "true" identity means he thinks he has one over on you.'

'You think Lisa will check up on me?'

'Either she'll pass on your details to Sam Hargrove, in

which case the NCA will do the checks, or she'll do it herself.
If the latter, that's a serious red flag, obviously.'

'I see a problem right there. Sam Hargrove is going to
recognise me and he's going to want to know what the hell
I'm up to.'

Willoughby-Brown grinned. 'We've thought of that. The
Rich Campbell picture has been doctored, just enough to
make it look a lot less like you. Campbell's got different
colour eyes. Plus He's got a shaved head. I've seen the
pictures, they're different enough.'

'Nice.'

'The story is that you had plastic surgery to throw the
gang off the track. Hargrove won't realise it's you, trust me.'

'That's all well and good, but what if she sends him an
up-to-date picture?'

'Just make sure she doesn't get one. Don't let her take a
selfie with you and you'll be fine. She'll have your name
and a description and that's enough to get your basic details.
She can have your Jeff Taylor phone number, and she can
see your passport. Just make sure she doesn't get a picture
of it. If she wants to dig deeper she'll need to get your prints.
DNA will draw a blank. I agree the photograph is an issue.
Watch her when she's got her phone in her hands. A floppy
hat and dark glasses always conceal a multitude of sins.'
Willoughby-Brown took a brown manila envelope from his
coat pocket and slid it across the table to Shepherd. 'There's
a Jeff Taylor passport inside, with the skipper's licence and
a CV. The dates in the CV match the stamps in the passport.
There's an AmEx card and two Visa cards – the spending
records fit with the passport stamps – a UK driving licence,
and a few other bits and bobs, including a Vodafone SIM
card, with a contract in Taylor's name. And some cash . . .
quite a lot of cash. Accounts tell me they'd like to see at

least some receipts. Your ticket's an e-ticket so just go to check-in.'

'When's my flight?'

Willoughby-Brown looked at his watch, a cheap plastic Casio that seemed at odds with the expensive overcoat. 'Two hours. You'll need to get a move on because security is a pain. Apparently there's a terrorism threat.' He chuckled.

'What about back-up in Spain?'

'One of Six's people will be there to meet you. We've got a plan to get you close to Meyer but he can explain it to you.' He took out his phone and showed Shepherd a photograph of a man in his thirties, grey-haired with a movie-star smile, as if he was posing for the shot. 'His name's Tony Docherty.'

'And he'll be my back-up while I'm there?'

'Tony can stay on if you feel you need him. The problem is that Meyer tends to move around a lot. He'll be hard to keep up with.'

Shepherd nodded. 'Okay. I'll see how I get on.'

'So, all good?'

Shepherd smiled coldly. Actually, it wasn't good. It was all moving too quickly. He'd barely had time to draw breath since leaving for Miami. Now he was being rushed into an undercover operation when really he'd have preferred some time to get into his role. But he knew Willoughby-Brown would take that as a sign of weakness so he said, 'Yes, Jeremy. All good.'

Zoë Middlehurst's school was on her Facebook page. It was about a mile from where Alexia had lived. Standing caught the Tube to St John's Wood station at about three o'clock and walked to the school. Most of the children were picked up by their parents and by three fifteen there was a queue of vehicles – mainly SUVs – outside the school. Standing knew he had to be careful – he was too young to be a parent – so he walked slowly down the road, faking a phone call. Some of the older pupils walked home or headed for the Tube and he was fairly sure that Zoë would walk. She left the school at three thirty on the dot, with two friends. She wore her skirt short and her tie loose around her neck, the top buttons of her shirt open. She looked younger than she did in the pictures on her Facebook page, probably because she wasn't wearing make-up. Standing figured the school didn't allow it.

He followed the three girls at safe distance, mumbling into his phone. After a couple of hundred yards her friends left her and went down a side-road. Standing put his phone away and jogged up to her. 'Zoë?'

She turned to him. 'What?'

He drew level with her but kept his distance, not wanting to crowd her. The last thing he wanted to do was to spook her. 'My name is Matt and I'm Lexi's brother, I know—' He was going to explain that he was her real brother, not her adopted brother, but before he could get the words out she stepped forward and hugged him, pressing her cheek against his chest. 'Matt!' she said. 'I'm so, so sorry.'

'You know who I am?' he said, confused by the sudden show of affection.

She let go of him. 'Of course! Lexi talked about you all the time. She was so proud of you.' She bit down on her lower lip and looked close to tears. 'I'm so sorry about what happened.'

He forced a smile. 'Me too,' he said. 'Can I talk to you about it?'

She nodded slowly. 'I guess so.' She started walking again and he fell into step next to her.

'The police said she injected heroin and overdosed. They said you were trying to help her out of the house.'

'I wanted to get her to hospital but it was too late. It was . . . horrible.'

'What about you? Had you taken heroin as well?'

Zoë shook her head. 'No. Never. Just ecstasy.'

'Were you going to?'

'I don't want to talk about it,' she said.

'Okay,' said Standing. 'Sorry.'

'Lexi said you were in Afghanistan.'

'I've been around.'

'What's it like there?'

'Hot.'

She laughed. 'She said you were in the SAS. Is that right?'

Standing smiled. He had told his sister he was in the Regiment, which he wasn't supposed to, but he'd wanted her to be proud of him, so he'd told her war stories. Not the gruesome kind, not the killing kind, just stories about defending the free world against terrorists. He'd made her promise not to tell anyone else, but teenage girls did like to talk. 'We're not supposed to tell anyone,' he said.

'But you wear ski masks and stuff?'

'Not in the desert,' he said. 'Zoë, do you have Lexi's phone?'

'Why do you ask?' she said quickly. Too quickly, Standing thought. Her rush to answer had confirmed what he suspected.

'Because you were with her when she died, and because the police didn't find her phone. I didn't see it in Lexi's room, either.'

'You went to Lexi's room?'

He nodded. 'First time ever. And the last.'

'She said her parents wouldn't let you in the house. She said you hit her father.'

'I didn't, but that was what he said and the police believed him. Where is her phone, Zoë?'

'In my room.'

'Will you give it to me?'

'Why?'

'I want to see what's on it. Who she called before she died.'

'It's password protected.'

That's okay. Can I have it?'

She nodded. 'Do you want to come home with me?'

He smiled. 'I'm not sure your parents would be thrilled about you getting home with a strange man.'

She laughed. 'You're not strange. And they won't be home. They're never in at this time.'

'You're sure?'

'Yeah. I only took Lexi's phone because I didn't want the cops getting nosy. I'd die if anyone ever went through mine.' She fell silent as she realised what she'd said. She walked with her head down for a while and Standing saw she was crying. He wanted to comfort her but she was just a kid so he kept his distance. She wiped her eyes with the sleeve of her blazer. 'Sorry,' she said.

'No problem,' he said. 'I miss her too.'

'They didn't let me go to her funeral,' she said. 'Because of the drugs, you know.'

'Did the police ask you a lot of questions?'

'Not really.'

'They didn't want to know where Lexi got the drugs from?'

'No.'

'You bought them?'

Her smile stiffened. 'I don't want to talk about the drugs,' she said.

'Okay,' he said. He knew there was no point in pressing her because he'd only scare her off. They walked in silence for a few minutes. Eventually Zoë pointed at a house, a stucco-fronted semi-detached with two empty parking spaces. 'That's where I live. Told you no one would be home.'

'I'll wait here,' he said.

'You can come in. It's okay.'

'It's not a good idea,' he said.

'Because you're a stranger?'

'I know it sounds silly, me being Lexi's brother and all, but yeah, you shouldn't be allowing strangers in your house.'

'But you're not a stranger.'

'To you I am. I'll stay here. Really.'

She looked at him quizzically. 'You're funny.'

'There are some scary people in the world, Zoë. You need to be careful.'

She laughed but there was a harshness to the sound. 'Tell me about it,' she said.

He was going to ask her what she meant but she turned and ran to the house, her heels clicking on the pavement, like snapping twigs. She pulled out a keychain with a fluffy pink ball on the end and let herself in.

Standing paced up and down. How old was Zoë? Sixteen? The same as Lexi. What the hell was a sixteen-year-old girl doing taking drugs? And why weren't her parents taking better care of her? How could they go to a house in Kilburn and take drugs without their parents knowing? These weren't parents on a sink estate surrounded by neglect and decay – the house was worth millions and the kids at Zoë and Lexi's school all seemed to be from good families. It didn't make any sense to Standing. No sense at all. His heart was pounding so he took several slow, deep breaths to calm himself, then switched to square breathing. After a few minutes Zoë reappeared and gave him an iPhone.

Standing put it into his pocket and took out the photograph. He handed it to her. 'Zoë, who's this?'

Her mouth fell open in surprise. 'What the fuck?' she said.
'Where did you get it?'

'Lexi had it in a locket.'

'Yeah, I know.' She thrust it back at him. 'You shouldn't
have that. It's personal.'

'I know,' he said. 'But who is the guy?'

'That's Frankie.'

'Frankie? Frankie who?'

She shrugged. 'Just Frankie.'

'Her boyfriend?'

'You shouldn't have that,' she said. 'You mustn't tell
anyone.'

'Tell them what?'

She was agitated now, switching her weight from leg to
leg, bobbing from side to side. 'This is fucked up,' she said.
'You have to throw that away. Just forget about it, right?'

'I just want—'

'I've got to go,' she said, hurrying away. She practically
ran to the house and disappeared inside.

Standing looked at the photograph in his hand. 'So who
the fuck are you, Frankie? And what the fuck were you doing
with my sister?'

There were two of them, big men, Algerians, and they both
had knives. Flick-knives. One was pearl-handled, the other
wood, but the blades were the same length, just over eight
inches. They weren't big knives, but the men who were
holding them were clearly expert in their use, and in the
right hands a small knife was just as lethal as a large one.
They held them low and ready to stab. A flick-knife wasn't
designed to slash: it was a straight in-and-out weapon. The

blades were narrow, too, so a guaranteed kill would require multiple stabs, three at least, all in the same area. Three to the heart, a kidney or the chest, and the victim would bleed out so quickly that they would be unconscious within seconds and dead within a minute.

One was to Shepherd's left, the other to his right. Despite their size they were on the balls of their feet, as nimble as ballet dancers. Shepherd had his hands up, fingertips curled, ready to strike or grab. They had to make the first move: he was unarmed and they had the knives. One against two was always difficult, and one unarmed man against two with knives was almost impossible. He was watching their eyes as best he could because it was the eyes that would give away their intentions.

The man to his left made a small stabbing motion but it wasn't an attack, more an attempt to capture his attention, so Shepherd looked at the other man's face just in time to see his eyes tighten and the nostrils contract as he inhaled. The attack came almost immediately and Shepherd was already moving, sweeping up with his left arm to parry the knife away, then striking the man in the chest, between the throat and the sternum. The assailant fell back and hit the wall hard, knocking the breath out of him.

The other man lunged towards Shepherd, knife arm outstretched. Shepherd grabbed his wrist and twisted, then kicked him behind the left knee, forcing him to the ground. As he grunted in pain, Shepherd pulled the knife from his grasp and took a step back. The man stayed down, looking up at Shepherd, grinning. 'Nice move,' he said. He got slowly to his feet, breathing heavily, then wiped his mouth with the back of his hand.

Shepherd turned to the man sitting on the bed. 'What do you think, Tony?'

Tony Docherty, MI6's man in Marbella, was sitting with his back against the wall, legs outstretched, drinking a vodka and tonic he'd made for himself from the minibar. It was his third since they'd started rehearsing. He raised his glass. 'It looked good to me.'

'Yeah, but did it look real?' asked Shepherd.

'I nearly pissed myself watching,' said Docherty. 'I didn't get the feeling they were really trying to kill you, though. There was a slight lack of commitment.'

One of the Algerians nodded. Docherty had only introduced him as Farouk. The other was Salim. 'We could shout,' said Farouk. 'Curse, maybe.'

'That might work,' agreed Docherty. 'The silent-assassin thing makes you think something's going on. More noise generally and you'll look like pissed-off muggers.' He raised his glass at Farouk. 'You okay for him to hit you like that?'

'Yes, but no harder, please.' He grinned at Shepherd. 'You hit hard, in the face or the throat, and I would not be getting up.'

'That's the last thing we want,' said Shepherd. 'I have to fight you off, but we don't want you hurt so bad that you can't get away.' He looked at Docherty. 'What do they do afterwards? Have they got somewhere to lie low? They can't come back here, obviously.'

'There's a safe house not far away where they can hide out for a day or two. And we have two vehicles close by. They'll have keys for both if they can't get to the safe house for any reason. But Meyer isn't the sort to call the cops. They'll be fine.'

'Okay, guys, we're good to go. Just one thing. Depending how it goes, I might let you cut me,' Shepherd told them. 'So don't worry if you see blood.'

Farouk frowned at Docherty and said something in French.

Docherty replied, apparently fluent. 'If that's what you want,' Farouk said.

'It'll make it more real,' said Shepherd. 'But don't you go stabbing me. I'll take the lead. Maybe a cut to the forearm – I'll put my arm against the blade and put the pressure on.'

Farouk spoke to Docherty, again in French. 'He's worried about cutting you,' said Docherty.

'It's on me,' said Shepherd. He went over to Farouk and got him to hold the knife out. Shepherd placed his arm against the blade, just hard enough to make an impression on his shirt sleeve. 'All I have to do is push and I'll get a cut. Nothing too deep, but there'll be blood, and blood always has an effect on people.' He patted Farouk's shoulder. 'Don't worry, I've been cut before.'

Farouk exhaled but clearly wasn't happy.

'Now, when do we do it?' Shepherd asked Docherty.

'Last night he took a walk through the marina and ended up at a fancy sushi restaurant. He had dinner and drinks and walked back to the boat.'

'Was he alone?'

Docherty shook his head. 'A girl, and another guy. The captain of the boat.'

'Not a bodyguard?'

'He's with the boat. Doesn't look like a bodyguard but, then, no offence, neither do you. You can obviously handle yourself, though.'

'So the thinking is they'll do the same tonight? Take an evening walk, eat and return to the marina at about what time?'

'It was eleven last night.'

Shepherd wrinkled his nose. 'They could go clubbing. They could get a car back. There's a lot could go wrong. How long is the boat booked in for?'

'They didn't arrive on the boat,' said Docherty. 'They flew in. The boat is here year-round. The captain seems to be a friend.'

'And the girl?' Willoughby-Brown had said Docherty hadn't been told about Lisa Wilson and what she was doing. The fewer people who knew she was an undercover cop, the better.

'Girlfriend, I guess,' said Docherty. 'They walked hand in hand. Pretty, long black hair. Fit. Good legs.'

Shepherd looked at the Algerians. 'Be especially careful not to hurt the girl,' he said.

The two men nodded.

'So what do we do?' Shepherd asked Docherty. 'Keep them under surveillance and then you tip us off when they're on the way to the boat?'

'I've got two good men on it,' said Docherty, 'both on scooters. I'll be out in the marina. I've got a boat fixed up not far from the one Meyer's staying on so they can lie low there until they're needed. If anyone spots them leaving the boat it won't be an issue – the booking is untraceable. Once they are back in the marina I'll give Farouk and Salim the go-ahead. They move in, you pull your Good Samaritan act, they run for the hills. Hopefully you'll be in like Flint.'

'I think you'll find it's in like Flynn,' said Shepherd.

'Nah, it's that movie in the sixties,' said Docherty. '*In Like Flint.*'

'Yeah, there was a movie with James Coburn called *In Like Flint*. But the saying is "in like Flynn", because Errol Flynn – the movie star – got laid a lot. Apparently.'

Docherty raised his eyebrows. 'Well, you learn something every day.' He raised his glass. 'Thanks for that.'

'Pleasure,' said Shepherd. He glanced around his room. Docherty had booked him a single room in the name of

Jeff Taylor at the Benabola Hotel and Suites, but they spent most of their time in a three-bedroom penthouse because it had views over the Puerto Banús marina where Meyer was staying and a large sitting room where Shepherd could rehearse with the Algerians. The hotel was just four miles from the centre of Marbella and a forty-minute drive from Málaga airport. The two Algerians and Docherty had taken a room each. The sitting room was large and comfortable with sofas and a big-screen TV on one wall. There were three bathrooms and an open-plan kitchen. Not that any of them was cooking: several room-service trays were scattered around, along with beer cans that had been emptied by the Algerians. Shepherd had no problem with them drinking: the smell of alcohol would make the forthcoming attempted mugging seem more realistic. He was less happy about Docherty dipping into the minibar but he seemed more than able to handle his drink so it wasn't an issue. There was a pair of powerful binoculars on the desk and Shepherd picked them up. He went over to the window and focused them on the marina below. 'Which one is Meyer's?' he asked.

'It's not actually his, so far as we know,' said Docherty. 'It's registered to a company in Panama but that could be a shell, of course.' He walked over to stand by Shepherd and pointed down at the marina. 'Third jetty along. See where the big boat is with the circular white radar thing on the top? With the two satellite dishes?'

'Got it,' said Shepherd.

'Go along the jetty towards the sea. Fifth boat. Two motor boats, a two-masted yacht, a catamaran, and his is the catamaran next to that one. You can't see much of it – that big bugger's in the way – just the front.'

'The bow,' said Shepherd.

'I thought the bow was at the back,' said Docherty, waving his glass.

'That's the stern. The bow is at the front. The prow is the top bit of the bow.'

'You sail?'

Shepherd chuckled. 'I know the basics.' He put down the binoculars. 'Okay, so now we wait.'

Standing sat at corner table in Starbucks with a coffee and an egg-salad sandwich in front of him. He was holding Lexi's iPhone. It was a 7, the latest model. Zoë had been right: it was password protected and that was a problem. If he got the password wrong six times he would be locked out for a minute. Seven failed attempts meant a five-minute lockout, eight was ten minutes and nine was an hour. After ten failed attempts he would be locked out and all the data on the phone would be deleted. The earlier iPhone models had four-digit passwords but Lexi's required six. He figured he might as well try the obvious one first. 123456. Fail. He wrinkled his nose. He tried her birth date – month, day and last two digits of the year. Fail. He reversed the first two numbers – day, month and year. Fail. He cursed under his breath and realised he was tensing up. He sipped his coffee and practised square breathing for a few minutes. There was no point in getting angry. This was a problem that needed solving and getting angry wouldn't help him solve it any quicker. He had seven attempts left. Lexi was a young girl: she wouldn't be bothered with remembering a random number. She'd choose something easy, something she could tap in without thinking. The problem was that there were a lot of easy combinations and she could have chosen any.

The keypad also had letters on it so he tried ALEXIA. Fail.

He sipped his coffee. 123789. Fail.

That was five fails. Next time he would be on a lockout. He put the phone down and sipped his coffee again as he stared at it. He ate his egg sandwich, then took out his own phone. He googled 'unlock iPhone 7 London'. He was rewarded with more than six hundred thousand possibilities. Many were shops and websites offering to repair or unlock mobile phones. He scrolled down the list and saw that several were in Edgware Road, just three stops away from Maida Vale on the Bakerloo line.

He walked to the Tube station, and fifteen minutes later he was in a phone shop where a middle-aged Pakistani man said that for twenty pounds he'd unlock it on the spot. The man didn't ask if the phone belonged to Standing, just put the twenty pounds in the till and gave the phone to a young assistant, who took it to a back room. He returned five minutes later with the unlocked phone. Standing left without a receipt.

He walked past a Middle Eastern bank, a Lebanese restaurant, outside which a dozen middle-aged Arab men were smoking hookah pipes, a shop selling saris and a pharmacy, its window covered with Arabic signs. Most of the people he walked by were Arabs or Asian, and it was easy to forget that he was actually in England. He crossed the road, heading for Edgware Road Tube station. There was a Costa Coffee shop and he went in and ordered coffee and another egg sandwich, then took them to a corner table. The shop seemed to be full of middle-aged Arab men sitting in groups, either reading Arabic newspapers or talking in their own languages. Several stared at him as he sat down, their eyes hard, as if they objected to him being in their territory. Standing wondered how they'd feel if they knew what he'd been up to in Afghanistan and Syria, how many of their countrymen he'd killed. He took a bite of his sandwich and realised immediately that it was better than the one he'd had in Starbucks. The coffee was, too.

He took Lexi's phone out of his pocket and stared at the screen, his heart heavy. He had a bad feeling about what he was about to find, but he knew he had no choice. Her screen-saver was a close-up of a guy with a nose piercing and a tattooed neck. He frowned, wondering who it was, then realised it was probably one of the singers in the posters on her bedroom wall. He went to her menu and clicked on 'Photos'. There were hundreds. Most were selfies: Lexi prac-tising various pouty looks. But there were others too. Of the man in the picture in her locket. Some of him on his own, then the two of them together. In some of the pictures she was holding bottles of Bacardi Breezer. In others she was smoking a hookah pipe. There were other pictures of Lexi with girls, but there was only the one man. And he was a man, Standing was sure of that. Early twenties, at least. Maybe twenty-six or twenty-seven. Not much older than Standing. Eight years older than Lexi.

He went to 'Messages'. There were a lot. The most recent were from himself. The ones before that were from her mother and father, asking what time she was coming home.

The message before was from Frankie. The man in the picture. *See you there at six, babe.*

She had replied almost immediately: *I'm not sure I want to go.*

His reply: *Do as you're told.*

She'd replied, *OK*. And added a heart.

He looked at the date. It was the day she'd died. He took a deep breath and let it out slowly.

He went through to the list of calls Lexi had made and received. The last calls she had received but not answered were on the day she'd died. From her parents. The last call she had made was on the same day, but earlier. To Zoë.

He heard growling laughter at the table to his right, and when he looked over he saw three bearded men staring at him. They'd been talking about him, he realised. He stared back and felt the familiar rush of blood that let him know his body was preparing to fight. There were three of them but they were overweight and out of condition and he was as fit as a man could be. He wanted to push away the table, throw himself at them and beat them all to a bloody pulp. It would be so easy. A punch to the face, breaking a nose and loosening teeth, maybe a slash to the throat to break a trachea, a thumb in the eye to blind, a kick to the groin, a stamp on the head. He was breathing heavily and his knuckles whitened as his grip tightened on the phone. For a second the men returned his stare, then one by one they turned away, hunched over their coffees.

Standing stood up, put Lexi's phone into his pocket and walked over to the table. 'You bastards don't know how fucking lucky you are,' he said. 'Normally I'd kick the living shit out of you for giving me the stink-eye like that, but you know what? It's your lucky day. I'm having anger-management therapy and this is brilliant practice.' He smiled but his eyes stayed as cold as ice. 'So you gentlemen have a nice day.' He made a gun with his right hand, pointed at the man furthest away from him and winked. 'Bang, bang,' he said, then walked out of the coffee shop, breathing slowly and evenly as he counted up to ten.

The marina was known to pretty much everybody as Puerto Banús but its full name was Puerto José Banús, named after the Spanish property developer who had built it in the early seventies. It had grown over the years to become the largest marina and shopping complex on the Costa del Sol, with more than five million visitors a year. Expensive cars prowled the narrow roads, model-pretty girls exposed their expensive boob jobs on the beaches, and big men with teak suntans and gold bracelets, sovereign rings and chunky gold watches downed Cristal champagne as if it was Pepsi. During the days when Spain didn't have an extradition treaty with the UK, Puerto Banús had become the epicentre of the Costa del Crime, and as Shepherd walked through the marina he was constantly scanning faces.

He was more likely to be recognised on the Costa del Sol than almost anywhere else in the world. As he walked he heard plenty of British accents, usually south London, but there were Irish and Scottish, too, and a lot of Russian. In 2010 the British police had raided the Costa del Sol as part of Operation Shovel, and Shepherd had spent three months under cover in Marbella, paving the way for the day when 120 suspected British gangsters had had their doors kicked in. After the raids a lot of the British criminals had moved out, but the attractions of the area soon had them drifting back. Morocco was just forty miles away, across the Mediterranean, source of many of the drugs that ended up in Europe. It had become such a successful drug-smuggling route that several Colombian cartels now shipped their cocaine from South America to Morocco and from there into the lucrative European markets. The Russian Mafia had also discovered the advantages of Marbella and had arrived in droves. Shepherd had worked against a number of Russian gangs, another reason for him to be taking extra care in Puerto Banús.

He was wearing a pair of black jeans, a green Lacoste polo shirt and a Breitling watch. He had a gold chain around his right wrist and another around his neck. He was carrying two phones, a throwaway with a Spanish pay-as-you-go SIM that Docherty would use to contact him to tell him the mugging was going down, and an iPhone with the Jeff Taylor card in it.

Docherty's surveillance team had followed Meyer and Lisa to a seafood restaurant, and Farouk and Salim were on standby in the marina. The throwaway phone buzzed in his back pocket, letting him know he'd received a message. He checked it. *On way.* Shepherd put it away. It had taken Meyer and Lisa just under fifteen minutes to get to the restaurant. He checked his watch and headed away from Meyer's boat along a walkway. He had plenty of time. There were parties on some of the boats, music playing and champagne corks popping, girls in designer labels and men twice their age standing in groups, laughing loudly and slapping each other on the back. Shepherd played the part of a tourist looking at boats he could never afford, occasionally stopping to check out some of the bigger ones. His phone buzzed again: *5 mins.*

Shepherd started to walk back along the jetty. In the distance he could see Meyer and Lisa, walking arm in arm into the marina. His heart began to pound as the adrenalin kicked in, and he took slow, even breaths. He was just a tourist, taking an evening stroll. He pulled the throwaway phone out of his pocket and tossed it into the water. Ahead of him, Farouk and Salim emerged from a side jetty. They were wearing T-shirts, showing off their bulging forearms, loose cargo pants and trainers. They were talking to each other but walking purposefully towards Meyer and Lisa, who were laughing and paying no attention to the Algerians. Meyer was wearing blue trousers and a long-sleeved Tommy Hilfiger shirt. Lisa had on a skin-tight canary yellow dress and high heels that were totally unsuitable for the jetty. She was putting her feet down carefully so that she wouldn't get caught in the gaps between the wooden planks. Her hair was jet black and much longer than in the photographs Willoughby-Brown had shown him. Shepherd hadn't realised how short she was. Even in high heels she barely reached Meyer's shoulder.

There were some overhead lights but they were few and far between. Farouk and Salim waited until Meyer and Lisa were in a pool of darkness before they made their move, sprinting forward and pulling out their knives.

Salim pushed Lisa hard in the stomach with the flat of his left hand and she toppled back onto the jetty, yelping as she fell. Meyer put up his hands and cursed but Farouk was too quick, backhanding him across the face.

'Give me your fucking wallet!' shouted Farouk, waving his knife in Meyer's face. 'Or I'll cut you to the bone!'

Salim knelt down next to Lisa and put his knife against her throat. 'Take off your watch and your rings!' he shouted.

'Leave her the fuck alone!' shouted Meyer. He went to grab Salim but Farouk kicked his knee and shouted at him to stay where he was. Meyer clenched his fists, ready to fight. Even from twenty feet away Shepherd could see there was no fear in his eyes, even though he was facing a big man with a wicked knife. Farouk slashed at Meyer, who rocked back but stayed where he was, his hands up, refusing to give ground.

Salim saw that Meyer was preparing to fight. They were under instructions not to hurt him but that didn't mean they wouldn't defend themselves. Salim got to his feet and pointed his blade at Meyer's face. 'Just give us your fucking wallet!' he said. 'And your fucking watch.'

'Oy!' Shepherd shouted, at the top of his voice, breaking into a run.

Farouk and Salim turned to look at him and Meyer took the opportunity to kick, catching Salim close to his groin.

Salim grunted and lashed out with the knife without thinking. The blade missed Meyer's arm by inches.

Farouk kicked out and caught Meyer in the stomach, knocking him back, arms flailing.

'Leave them alone!' shouted Shepherd.

Salim threw himself on top of Meyer, using his legs to hold the man's arms down. He grabbed him by the throat with his left hand and put the point of the blade against his temple. Lisa screamed in terror.

Shepherd reached Farouk and bobbed to the side as Farouk jabbed at his face. He parried the knife to the left, chopping at Farouk's wrist with his hand. Then he let his left hand move over Farouk's arm and down. Shepherd locked eyes with Farouk. His left arm was against the blade of Farouk's knife. Shepherd gritted his teeth, pushed his flesh against the blade and felt a slicing pain followed by a trickle of blood. Farouk did as he'd been told and kept the knife still so that Shepherd did all the damage. Shepherd cursed and pulled his arm away cleanly, then hit Farouk in the chest, hard enough to push him backwards but not to do any serious damage. Farouk regained his balance and came at Shepherd with the knife. Shepherd side-stepped, grabbed his wrist, twisted and flipped Farouk onto his back with a crash that shook the jetty. The knife clattered along the wooden planks and plopped into the water.

Salim stopped choking Meyer and stood up. Farouk got to his feet, looked as if he was about to continue the fight, then Salim shouted at him and the two men ran towards the lights of the main street, their trainers slapping on the jetty.

Shepherd stood where he was, breathing heavily, his hands still bunched into fists as he stared after them.

Meyer rolled over and pushed himself up, then hurried to

help Lisa to her feet. 'Did they take anything?' asked
Shepherd.

Meyer held up his wallet. 'No,' he said. He turned to Lisa.
'What about you, darling?'

She held up her left hand, tears in her eyes. 'He tried to
take my watch,' she said. 'He was going to cut me. That
bastard was going to cut me.'

Meyer put his arms around her and she collapsed against
his chest, sobbing. Meyer looked at Shepherd. 'I owe you
big-time,' he said. 'Thanks.'

'No problem,' said Shepherd. 'I fucking hate muggers.'

'Yeah, you and me both.' He held out his right hand as
he clasped Lisa with the left. 'Marcus.'

Shepherd shook hands. 'Jeff.'

'This is Lucy.'

'Hi, Lucy,' said Shepherd. 'Pleased to meet you.'

She twisted around to look at him and her tear-stained
face broke into a smile. 'Thank you,' she said.

'If I ever see them again I'll rip their fucking balls off,'
said Meyer, looking towards the main road.

'We should call the cops,' said Lisa.

'No,' said Shepherd, quickly. 'No cops. Really, it's fine.'

Lisa noticed the blood on his arm and gasped. 'You're
bleeding,' she said.

'It's nothing,' said Shepherd.

'They cut you,' said Meyer. 'You should go to hospital.'

Shepherd examined his arm. It was a long cut, but not
deep. 'It's okay.' He grinned. 'I'll live.'

Meyer shook his head. 'You need stitches.'

Shepherd lowered his voice. 'If I go to a hospital they'll
tell the cops. And I really don't want the hassle.'

'Not for a knife-wound,' said Meyer. 'For a gunshot,
maybe.'

'I'd just rather not take the risk,' said Shepherd. 'Have you got a first-aid kit?'

Meyer chuckled. 'Not on me,' he said.

'There's one on the boat,' said Lisa.

'Yeah, you're right,' said Meyer. 'Okay, come to our boat and we'll get you fixed up. We can give you a drink too, the least we can do.' He grinned. 'For our Good Samaritan.' He waved down the jetty. 'This way.'

They walked together towards the boat, Meyer with his arm around Lisa. She had taken off her high heels and was carrying them in her left hand. 'So who do you think they were?' asked Shepherd. 'They didn't look like Spaniards.'

'Moroccans, probably,' said Meyer. 'Or Algerians. There's a lot of them over here illegally. A guy was killed for his watch last month.'

'I hope it was a Patek Philippe,' said Shepherd.

'Sadly, it was only a Cartier,' said Meyer. 'I mean, for fuck's sake, dying for a Cartier. How sad is that?'

Shepherd laughed. 'Fucking sad.'

'It's not the place it used to be,' said Meyer. 'Used to be as safe as houses. Now you've muggers coming over from Africa and the Russians shooting things up with AK-47s.'

'Still, the weather's nice,' said Shepherd.

Meyer slapped him on the back. 'Good to hear you've still got your sense of humour,' he said. He pointed towards his boat. 'That's us.'

Close up, Shepherd could see that it was a similar design to BM's catamaran in Jacksonville, but about fifty per cent bigger. It was registered in the Bahamas and called *Windchaser*. At the stern of the starboard hull there was a Yamaha jetski on a metal cradle, and at the back of the port hull there was a row of compressed-air cylinders and scuba equipment.

'Nice boat,' said Shepherd. 'What is she? Eighty foot?'

'Ninety,' said Meyer.

'She's a Catana, right?'

'Right. You're a sailor?'

'I'm a captain, when I can get the gig,' said Shepherd. 'First mate if not.'

'Excellent, you can talk boats with Jeeves.'

'Jeeves?'

'There he is,' said Meyer, pointing at a guy in a white shirt and white shorts emerging from the cabin. He waved at him. 'Hey, Jeeves, get over here.'

The man walked down the steps at the stern of the port hull and on to the jetty. He was in his thirties, tall with a shock of ginger hair and freckles across his cheeks and nose. 'This is Jeff,' said Meyer. 'He's had a bit of an accident. Help him on board, will you?'

'Sure,' said the man. He took Shepherd's right arm and ushered him onto the boat.

'Your name's not really Jeeves, is it?' asked Shepherd.

The captain smiled. 'Phil Jeeves,' he said. 'But everyone just calls me Jeeves.'

Shepherd offered his right hand. 'Jeff.' The two men shook.

'Jeff here saved us from a couple of nasty-looking muggers, and paid the price,' said Meyer. He gestured at Shepherd's injured arm. 'Have you got a first-aid kit?'

'Sure,' said Jeeves, and hurried down to the cabin. He returned carrying a large white box with a green cross on the top. He opened it and peered inside.

'Have you got any antiseptic?' asked Shepherd. 'I've no idea how dirty that knife was.'

Jeeves took out a tube of ointment and a couple of cotton-wool balls. Shepherd wiped away the blood, then smeared the antiseptic cream over the cut. Jeeves grimaced. 'That could do with stitches,' he said.

'It'll be okay,' said Shepherd. 'Have you got any superglue?'

'Superglue?' replied Meyer, frowning. 'What for?'

'I'll show you.' He looked at Jeeves. 'You must have some, right?'

'Sure,' said Jeeves. He went over to one of drawers in the galley and opened it. He looked inside, moved a few things around, then pulled out a tube of Loctite. 'I used it a couple of months ago – it should still be okay.' He gave it to Shepherd.

There was a small needle in the nozzle and Shepherd pulled it out. A blob of glue immediately formed on the tube's tip, glistening under the lights. 'Perfect,' he said. He gave the tube to Lisa. 'Can you be the nurse?'

'What?' she said, clearly bewildered.

'Are you serious?' asked Meyer.

'Medics used superglue during the Vietnam War to close wounds,' said Shepherd. 'It's fine so long as the wound isn't bleeding too badly and isn't over a joint. Ideally you'd want medical-quality glue but Loctite will do the trick.'

'You've done it before?' asked Meyer.

'Well, no, but I've seen it done and it works a treat.' He held the cut edges of skin together and nodded at Lisa. 'Go on, just run the glue along the edges of the cut.' She did as she was told and he was surprised at how steady her hand was. When she'd finished he pressed the edges together and they immediately sealed. He held the skin for a few seconds, then released it. The cut had closed. He held up the arm and grinned. 'There you go. As good as new.'

'You're a bloody marvel,' said Meyer. 'So, what can I get you to drink?'

'Bubbly would be good,' said Shepherd.

'Cristal?'

'You read my mind.' Cristal was the champagne of choice

for most of the gangsters Shepherd had come across. It was first made in 1876 for Alexander II of Russia, who asked producer Louis Roederer to create a clear glass bottle with a flat bottom, ostensibly so that no one could plant explosives under it. Whether or not the assassination fear was true, it was still one of the most expensive champagnes around. Shepherd didn't particularly enjoy champagne but it was as much a part of his Jeff Taylor persona as the gold watch and the chains around his wrist and neck.

Meyer waved at the captain. 'Jeeves?'

'I'm on it,' said Jeeves.

Meyer turned back to Shepherd. 'I do love saying that,' he said. 'It's very P. G. Wodehouse, isn't it?'

Jeeves returned with the champagne and four glasses threaded between his fingers. He gave the glasses to Lisa and popped the cork with barely a whisper. When they each had a glass, Meyer raised his in salute to Shepherd. 'To Jeff, the white knight who galloped to our rescue.'

Shepherd grinned. 'To be fair, you looked like you were giving as good as you got before I arrived.'

'If they hadn't had knives I'd have beaten the shit out of them.'

'But they did have knives,' said Lisa. 'They could have killed us, Marcus. You could see it in their eyes. It was scary.'

'But they didn't, did they? They ran off like the cowards they were.' He gestured at Shepherd with his chin. 'So where did you learn to fight, Jeff?'

'Did a bit of boxing as a kid,' said Shepherd. 'But you know what life's like when you're sailing from port to port. It's not all champagne and caviar. Sometimes it's drunks and knives.'

'We try to steer clear of the downmarket places,' laughed Meyer. 'But I know what you mean.'

'So, this is an awesome boat,' said Shepherd. 'Crew of three?'

'Five when we're chartering,' said Jeeves. 'We have a hostess and a chef. Guests need to be pampered.'

'What are the engines?'

'Two Perkins 210 horse power.'

'I bet she can move.'

'We tend to keep her at about ten knots under sail, but we've had a few days when we've covered three hundred miles.'

'Nice,' said Shepherd. 'Have you sailed her single-handed?'

Jeeves nodded. 'Yeah, but it's challenging. You'd want two to be comfortable. So you sail?'

'I'm a big fan of cats,' he said. 'Haven't captained anything bigger than sixty feet, though.'

'Do you want to take her out tomorrow?' asked Meyer.

'Hell, yeah,' said Shepherd.

'Why don't we do that?' Meyer said to Jeeves. 'Put her through her paces. Maybe do a spot of diving.'

'Sounds like a plan,' said the captain.

'But not too early,' said Meyer, raising his champagne glass. 'We've got some serious drinking to do tonight.'

Standing woke at six. He went for an hour's run in Hyde Park, shaved, showered, grabbed a coffee and a sandwich in Queensway, then headed for the Tube. He was outside the Chapmans' house at eight and hid from view when Greg Chapman got into his car and drove off. He waited a few minutes, then walked up to the front door and rang the bell. Mrs Chapman answered and frowned when she saw who it was. 'Matt? What are you doing here?'

He took the photograph of Lexi and Frankie from his pocket and gave it to her. 'Mrs Chapman, did you ever see

Lexi with this man?' She continued to stare at him in surprise and he pushed the picture at her. 'Look at it, Mrs Chapman.'

'I'm calling the police,' she said, backing away. 'My husband said I should call the police if you came back.'

'I just want to talk to you,' said Standing. 'This man, did you see him? Did he come to the house?'

'No, of course not,' she said, but she wouldn't look at the picture. He pushed it to her chest and she put her hands on it.

'Just look at it,' pleaded Standing.

She shook her head and let the picture fall to the floor, then stepped away from the door. She didn't make any attempt to close it. Standing pushed the door further open and saw that she was holding her mobile to her ear. 'Please don't call the police, Mrs Chapman. I'm just talking with you here. We're having a conversation.'

'He's back,' she said, into the phone. There was a pause. 'He's at the door now.'

She walked back down the hall to the front door and thrust the phone at him. Standing realised she wanted him to talk to whoever was on the line. 'Hello?' he said hesitantly.

'What the fuck are you doing at my house?' shouted Greg Chapman. 'The court told you stay away.'

'I just wanted to talk to your wife about a photograph I found.'

'What are you talking about?'

'I have a picture of Lexi with a man and I wondered if you knew about him.'

'Alexia's dead!' shouted Chapman. 'And I don't want you upsetting my wife! I want you to leave now!'

'Mr Chapman, I'm not upsetting your wife. I just showed her a photograph, that's all.'

'I'm calling the police!' snapped Chapman, and the line went dead.

Standing gave the phone back to Mrs Chapman. 'I'm sorry to have bothered you,' he said. 'I really didn't mean to cause you any grief. I'm sorry.'

She took the phone from him and he realised her hands were trembling. The photograph had fallen on the floor and she picked it up. She brushed a lock of stray hair away from her face as she looked at it. 'Who is he?' she asked.

'I think he's a boyfriend.'

She shook her head vigorously. 'Oh, no, Alexia didn't have a boyfriend.' Her lip curled in disgust. 'And she certainly wouldn't . . .' She left the sentence unfinished.

'You can see how happy she is in the picture,' said Standing. 'And he was messaging her all the time.'

She looked at it again. 'Maybe it's someone from school.'

'No, he's an adult. He's at least twenty-five. Maybe older.' She thrust the picture back at him. He took it but held it up. 'That's a boyfriend-girlfriend picture, Mrs Chapman. Surely you can see that.'

'Alexia didn't have time for boyfriends,' she said firmly. 'She only went out to study with her girlfriends. She was a good girl.'

'I've seen the messages she sent to him. She said she loved him. She called him her boyfriend.'

'That's not possible.'

'She died of a heroin overdose, Mrs Chapman. Maybe this man gave her the drugs. Did you think about that?'

Mrs Chapman began to cry, and Standing put the photograph back into his pocket. 'I think his name is Frankie,' he said. 'Did she ever mention a Frankie?'

She took out a handkerchief and dabbed at her eyes. 'No.' She sniffed. 'But she never really told us about her friends.

Just Zoë. She used to go to Zoë's house to study. She said
she found it easier to work with her. I said they could come
here but she said Zoë preferred to stay at home so she went
there. She didn't have time to go gallivanting with boys.'

'Mrs Chapman, the night Lexi died, where did she say
she was going?'

'Why do you keep calling her that? Her name was Alexia.
No one calls her Lexi.'

'Okay, I'm sorry. Where did Alexia say she was going, the
night she died?'

Mrs Chapman sniffed and dabbed at her eyes again. 'Why
are you being so horrible to me?'

'She said she was going to study with Zoë, didn't she?'

Mrs Chapman continued to sniff and wipe her eyes.

'She lied to you, and you know it. She said she was going
to study and she went to that house in Kilburn, injected
herself with heroin and died. How could you not know what
was going on?'

'She was a good girl,' Mrs Chapman repeated.

'You keep saying that, but she wasn't, was she? She lied
to you and she took drugs. You were supposed to be taking
care of her but you let her kill herself. You should have
checked. You should have spoken to Zoë's parents, and you
should have been watching her. But you didn't and now she's
dead.'

Mrs Chapman was sobbing now and she leaned against
the wall.

Standing heard the squeal of brakes and turned to see a
police van pull up at the kerb. Uniformed cops in stab vests
piled out and hurried across the pavement towards him.
Standing raised his hands. 'There's no problem, guys!' he
called. 'I'm going!'

'Stay where you are!' shouted a cop in his early twenties,

his forehead flecked with acne scars. He held a black metal baton above his head.

'I don't want any trouble,' said Standing. 'I'm done here. Nothing happened – it's all good!'

'Get down on the ground, now!' shouted the cop.

'I'm not getting down on the fucking ground,' said Standing. 'I haven't done anything wrong.' There were six cops now, fanned out in a semicircle. One was a sergeant, the oldest of the group.

A second cop drew his baton and swung it out, then began to swish it back and forth, his eyes ice cold and his jaw set tight. He was in his thirties, with the build of a rugby player, his head shaved.

Standing looked at the sergeant. 'I came to speak to Mrs Chapman. Things got a bit heated but there was no physical contact. Now I'm leaving. It's all good.'

'According to Mr Chapman, you assaulted him,' said the sergeant. He was on Standing's left and Standing turned to face him, his hands still in the air.

'That was eight years ago, and all I did was push him.'

'He said you assaulted him today. That's what he told the nine-nine-nine operator.'

Standing shook his head. 'He's not even here.' He waved his arms around. 'Can you see him? No. Because he's not bloody well here. I spoke to him on the phone. That's all.'

'That's not what we were told.'

'Then you were told wrong.'

'Well, we'll have a chat with Mr Chapman, shall we? And then we'll know for sure.' The sergeant looked at Mrs Chapman. 'Where is your husband?'

'I'm not sure. He said he was on his way back.'

'See?' said Standing. 'He's not bloody well here. I told you that.' He saw movement in the periphery of his vision and turned to see the young cop swinging his baton down towards Standing's left elbow. Standing moved without thinking, stepping to his right and putting out his left arm. His hand connected with the cop's wrist and grabbed it, then pulled him in the direction he was already going. The cop's momentum carried him forward and Standing struck with his right elbow, catching him under the chin. The cop's eyes rolled back in his head and he staggered to the side. Standing let his left hand slide over the cop's fist, grabbed the baton and twisted it out of his grasp. The cop fell into the road and lay face down. Something smashed into Standing's right leg, a few inches above the knee and he grunted. It was the other cop. Standing looked over his shoulder and saw him raise his baton for a second strike. He dropped down and spun around, using his left leg to sweep the cop's feet from underneath him. The cop yelped and dropped his baton as he fell. He hit the ground hard and lay there, stunned.

As Standing straightened, he found himself face to face with another officer, this one female, who was holding a bright yellow Taser and pointing it at Standing's chest. Standing locked eyes with the woman and could see the indecision there. He swung the baton in his left hand and threw it at her as he ducked to the left. She fired a fraction of a second before the baton hit her stab-vest and the two metallic prongs whizzed by Standing's face, missing him by inches, trailing two microwires behind them. Standing pointed a finger at her. 'Back off, darling,' he said. 'I don't fight women.'

He saw her eyes flick to the side and he turned, just as another cop fired his Taser and the two prongs hit Standing in the middle of his back. Immediately fifty thousand volts coursed through his body. Part of his brain was able to monitor the pain and it actually wasn't that bad – it was certainly bearable – but the current locked all his muscles so that he couldn't even breathe, never mind move. His whole body went into spasm, then his legs gave way and he fell to the pavement, twitching and flopping around like a fish out of water.

Shepherd woke with an aching head, the result of drinking three bottles of Cristal with Meyer, Lisa and Jeeves on the boat. Meyer had offered to let him sleep in one of the cabins but Shepherd had said he might as well go back to his hotel as it was only a short distance away. They had swapped phone numbers and promised to meet on board the boat at lunchtime.

Shepherd padded over to his minibar, took out a bottle of Evian water and drank it all, then headed to the bathroom to brush his teeth and get rid of the taste of stale champagne. Then he sat on the bed and called Willoughby-Brown on his personal mobile. 'I'm in,' he said, when Willoughby-Brown answered.

'Yes, I know,' said Willoughby-Brown. 'Docherty filled me in last night. Said you were knocking back champers like there was no tomorrow.'

'Had to be done, Jeremy,' he said. 'Though I'm paying the price now.'

'Well, Meyer's definitely interested,' said Willoughby-Brown. 'Your phone records were checked this morning.'

'That's fast,' said Shepherd.

'You clearly made an impression. So now he's sure you're Jeff Taylor, captain for hire.'

'Yeah, but I made a big thing about not calling the cops so he must realise I'm jittery about something. Let's see what happens next.'

'How does Lisa seem?'

'In what way?'

'Professional?'

'She seems the part. They're very comfortable together.'

'Is she sleeping with him?'

'For God's sake, Jeremy, what do you want me to do? Start peeping through portholes? They're hardly likely to have sex in front of me, are they?'

'You're as astute at observing body language as I am,' said Willoughby-Brown. 'Are they physical together?'

'They were holding hands when they came back from the restaurant. But they're not lovey-dovey.'

'Other than the captain, anyone else on the boat?'

'No.'

'And do they share a cabin?'

'I don't know, but I'll try to check when I'm on the boat. But even if she is sleeping with him, that's not a sign that she's gone over to his side. You know as well as I do there have been plenty of cases of undercover agents having relationships with targets. It's hard not to in some cases.'

'The voice of experience, is it?'

'I'm not going there, Jeremy. I'm just making the point that even if they are sharing a cabin that doesn't mean she's stopped working.'

'Maybe not, but it would explain the drop in the quality of the intel the NCA is getting.'

'How does she report back?'

'At the moment, email. Initially she had a handler but now that she's travelling with Meyer, she files her reports electronically. But that's become sporadic.'

'Understandable if they're at sea.'

'Even when she's ashore, she isn't filing much.'

'And what about last night?'

'Nothing yet. Okay, so what's the plan? How do we move this forward?'

'Brunch on the boat. Then we're doing a spot of sailing.'

'You're okay with that?'

'I'm good. Jeeves showed me around last night. The layout is very similar to BM's boat.'

'Jeeves? They've got a butler?'

'Phil Jeeves, the captain. He handles charters on the boat but it's clear from the way he gets on with Meyer that there's more going on. I'll keep you posted.'

'Do you want Docherty to hang around now that you're in?'

'Might be useful,' said Shepherd. 'There's not much he can do while we're at sea, but he can keep an eye on the boat and he's useful for any intel I need.'

'Is his drinking under control?'

It was a strange question, and Shepherd wondered why Willoughby-Brown had asked it. Did he seriously expect Shepherd to tell tales out of school? And if he had any doubts about Docherty's ability to do the job, why send him in the first place? 'I hadn't noticed him drinking,' lied Shepherd. 'If anyone's doing any drinking at the moment, it's me.'

'Worse tipples than Cristal,' said Willoughby-Brown.

'It's just fizzy white wine to me,' said Shepherd. 'Give me a Jameson's and soda any day of the week.'

'You're such a Philistine.'

'I don't even know what that means,' said Shepherd. 'Okay, so I presume you'll let me know if they start doing any other checks on me?'

'I'm watching like a hawk,' said Willoughby-Brown.

Shepherd ended the call and thought about Willoughby-Brown's analogy – hawks usually watched things before ripping them to pieces.

★   ★   ★

The Taser didn't knock Standing out: he was incapacitated but conscious. It was only when he was in the back of the van, his hands plasticuffed behind him, that he regained the feeling in his arms and legs. The cops had put him face down on the floor and one of them placed a boot firmly in the middle of his back. He kept quiet all the way to the police station, knowing there was nothing he could say that would change the outcome of what was happening.

The van pulled into a car park, the doors opened and he was dragged out, then frogmarched inside the police station. They took his wallet and phone. Then he was fingerprinted, a DNA swab was taken from inside his mouth and a gruff custody sergeant asked for his name, address and date of birth. When Standing gave the name of the serviced apartment in Bayswater, the sergeant asked for his home address. 'That's where I'm living,' said Standing.

'Driving licence?'

'I don't have one.'

'You don't drive?'

'I can drive but I never passed a test.'

'Passport?'

'Who carries their passport with them?'

'Don't get lippy with me, I'm just asking you for identification,' said the sergeant.

'I don't have my passport with me. The only ID I have are my credit cards.' He nodded at the wallet. 'See for yourself.'

The sergeant picked up Standing's wallet. There were two credit cards – a Visa and an AmEx. He checked the names on both and nodded. 'I suppose that'll have to do. But the fingerprints and DNA do the same job as Santa Claus – they'll soon tell us if you're naughty or nice.' He nodded at a shirtsleeved PC. 'Put Mr Standing in number four,' he said.

'Four still smells of sick,' said the PC. 'We're waiting on some bleach.'

'Four's the only cell we've got,' said the sergeant. He flashed Standing a tight smile. 'We've a bit of a rush on,' he said. 'You'll get used to the smell.'

'Am I being charged?'

'Don't rush me, Mr Standing. We have our own way of doing things here.'

The PC took Standing down a brick-lined corridor with six metal doors. One was open, and even before he got to the door the acrid stench hit his nostrils. 'Oh, come on, you can't lock me in there,' he said.

'Beggars can't be choosers,' said the PC.

'Isn't it against my human rights?'

The PC laughed. 'Talk to your lawyer.'

Standing stepped into the cell. It was three paces long and two wide, with a concrete sleeping plinth on which there was a blue plastic mattress and a green blanket. There was also a stainless-steel toilet, and that was it. The only light came from two fluorescent tubes overhead, protected by safety glass. The PC pulled the door closed but opened a small hatch. Standing sighed. After a few deep breaths the stench wasn't quite so bad. He sat down on the bed, put his hands in his lap and practised square breathing.

Shepherd arrived at *Windchaser* at eleven o'clock. Meyer already had a bottle of Cristal open, twinning it with fresh orange juice. He raised his glass when he saw Shepherd walking down the jetty. 'Good morning, Jeff,' he called.

Shepherd waved. 'Hair of the dog? Excellent!' He climbed on board and Meyer gave him a glass of Buck's Fizz. Meyer sat down on one of the bench seats and stretched out his legs. 'How's the arm?'

Shepherd rolled up his sleeve and showed him the cut. The superglue had done the job and it was healing nicely. 'All good.'

'You were lucky it didn't cut a vein or something.'

'All's well that ends well,' said Shepherd. 'As my old mother used to say.'

'So where are you from?'

'Originally? Manchester. But I've moved around a lot over the years.'

Meyer nodded. 'Yeah, your accent is difficult to place.'

Shepherd grinned. 'It tends to move around, same as I do. If I'm in Scotland I get a Scottish accent, in Newcastle I sound like a Geordie. It's not that I'm taking the piss, I just seem to acquire accents really quickly.'

'Lucy's the same,' said Meyer. 'Does my fucking head in. We met a couple of Scousers a while back and straight away she was talking pure Liverpudlian. Put her with Jocks and she talks like a Scot.'

'Where is she?' asked Shepherd, looking around.

'She's gone shopping with Jeeves. I do like my croissants fresh.'

'Hell, yeah.'

'Do you scuba?'

'Yeah. Not a lot but I've got my PADI certification.'

'You don't need that,' said Meyer. 'We've got all our own equipment, and Jeeves is a registered instructor.'

'I'm up for it.'

'Excellent. We'll take her out for a sail and you can see what you think of her. Then we'll come back and dive La Torre.'

'The Bull?'

Meyer laughed. '*Torre*, not *toro*. *Torre* is Spanish for "tower". It's a few hundred yards offshore. They used it to load cargo onto ships during the fifties and sixties but it's abandoned now. It's become an artificial reef and there's all sorts to see. There's three wrecks, too, and Jeeves knows where they are.'

Shepherd held up his glass. 'Maybe go easy on the bubbly, then?'

'Just a glass or two,' said Meyer. He looked over at the jetty. 'Here they are.'

Shepherd turned to see Jeeves and Lisa heading their way, laden with filled carrier bags. Lisa was wearing one of Meyer's shirts over a black bikini. She was barefoot and looked tiny next to the lanky Jeeves. He was saying something to her and she was laughing as if she didn't have a care in the world. If she was acting, she was doing one hell of a job.

A face appeared in the inspection hatch in the door and a pair of amused eyes looked at Standing. He was lying on the plastic mattress using the blanket as a pillow but he had been wide awake since six o'clock. He sat up and looked at his watch. It was almost midday. 'Any chance of a coffee?' he asked. 'And there's no toilet paper.'

Whoever was scrutinising him chuckled but didn't say anything. The visitor straightened and there was the sound of a key in the lock. The door opened. DC Kaiser was standing outside, a smile on his face. He was wearing a dark suit, with a gleaming white shirt and a tie that would have done credit to a Conservative councillor door-stepping for votes. 'What's that smell?' asked the detective. 'Did you throw up?' He pushed his spectacles further up his nose and grimaced.

'It was like that when they put me in here,' said Standing.

'Well, it serves you right.'

'Why do you say that?'

'What were you playing at?'

'I just wanted to know if the Chapmans were aware of what Lexi had been up to,' said Standing.

'Not the Chapmans,' said the detective. 'What the fuck were you doing attacking the police? How was that going to end well?'

'What? Is that what they're saying?'

'You cold-cocked one cop and almost dislocated the shoulder of another. And if you hadn't been Tasered I guess it would have been a lot worse. What was it? Karate?'

'It was just rough and tumble,' said Standing. 'If I'd really been trying to hurt them, I would have done. Mate, they attacked me.'

'They're police officers,' said the detective. 'As a general rule they don't go around attacking people.'

'That's not what happened to me,' said Standing. 'I was talking to the sergeant, as nice as pie, when one of his team tried to break my arm with his baton. I did what I had to do to stop him and while I was doing that his pal tried to break my knee.' He pointed at his right thigh. 'If you want I can take off my trousers and show you what he did to my leg.'

'I'll pass on that, but thanks for the offer.'

'He smacked my leg and I kicked him to the ground. It was over in seconds It wasn't a brawl, it was me defending myself. I was unarmed. Then, to add insult to injury, I was bloody Tasered.'

'I think after they saw what you'd done to the two guys, Tasering was the only option. And the sergeant said you were attacking him.'

'Listen, the last time I checked, you lot class a Taser as a firearm. And when someone points a firearm at you and his finger is on the trigger, all you can do is attack.'

'You could have killed somebody.'

'I could have, but I didn't. I was in control. And I never touched the female officer, the one who tried to Taser me. I just threw a baton at her. The men, yes, I defended myself vigorously but if I'd wanted to kill anybody I'd have smashed their throats or broken their necks. And let's not forget the bastard who shot me in the back.'

'Tasered you in the back. But, to be honest, you were lucky. If it had been a firearms team, they'd have shot you with real bullets, the way you were carrying on.'

'Yeah, in my experience the Met SFOs are a decent enough bunch,' said Standing. 'They certainly don't go around shooting people in the back, like the morons I met yesterday.'

'You were a threat. You'd already taken out three officers. He was perfectly justified in Tasering you.'

'I wasn't armed and I was defending myself,' said Standing.

'Yeah, so you keep saying, and I keep telling you it doesn't make a blind bit of difference.' He leaned against the wall, then saw how dirty it was, straightened up and brushed the shoulder of his suit. 'How come you know SFOs?'

'What?'

'You just said the SFOs you knew were decent guys. Not many people know what an SFO is.'

'Senior firearms officer. Yeah, I've run across a few in my time.'

Kaiser looked at him over the top of his glasses. 'Professionally?'

In fact, Standing had met close to fifty SFOs over the years, post the Seven Seven London Tube attacks, when the Met's SCO19 had increased its training of armed officers. A lot of the cops were trained at the SAS's killing house at

Hereford, a state-of-the-art facility where troops – and cops – could practise live-firing at electronic targets. 'Well, they weren't shooting at me, if that's what you're implying.'

'I'm just wondering what branch of the army you're in, that's all.'

Standing shrugged but didn't say anything.

Kaiser stared at him for several seconds, then must have realised he wasn't about to get an answer to his question. 'Anyway, as my dear old mum keeps telling me, every cloud has a silver lining. It seems that Mr Chapman did embellish what happened when he spoke to the nine-nine-nine operator. Now he says that you didn't actually hit him.'

'He wasn't there.'

'Yes. That has since become clear.'

'I didn't even step inside the house.'

Kaiser nodded. 'Mrs Chapman confirms that, too. And while there was an injunction to stop you going within five hundred yards of the Chapmans or their house, it appears to have lapsed. So you were within your rights to ring their bell and initiate a conversation with her.'

'And the cops?'

'Again, you were lucky. The officer who used his baton the first time has had a few issues recently. Bit of a short fuse, you might say, a bit too keen to get physical.'

'So I'm not the first person he's tried to hit?'

Kaiser grinned. 'I couldn't possibly confirm that. But I've spoken to the sergeant and he agrees that when he used his baton you weren't posing a threat and were quite calm and reasonable.'

'That's decent of him.'

'Actually, he's a good guy. Most of the Territorial Support Group guys are, especially when you consider the shit they have to put up with, day in and day out. He's old-school

TSG and while he's happy to bang heads together, he bends over backwards to help the true civilians.'

'I'm sure he happily takes little old ladies across the road,' said Standing. 'But he let his men try to beat me up, then shoot me with a Taser.'

'How was that, by the way?'

'The Taser? I've had worse.'

'Worked, didn't it? Nice bit of kit, that. I think they should issue them to all us detectives.'

Standing couldn't help but smile. 'Yeah. It does what it says on the can. So, to cut a long story short, you're letting me go, right?'

'Probably best,' said the detective. 'Under the circumstances.' He looked around as if to check that there was no one within earshot. 'Look, there's a pub called the Old Bell, not far from here. I get off at six and might well stop off on my way home.' He looked at his watch. 'Right now, though, I've got mountains to climb and dragons to slay. The custody sergeant is going to process your paperwork and then you're out of here.' He gestured with his chin. 'Maybe catch you later.' He winked and headed out of the cell. He left the door open, but a few seconds later, a PC came and closed it. It wasn't the same constable who had locked him up the previous night. He was older and apparently friendlier, asking Standing if he wanted a roll and coffee or tea. Standing asked for a coffee, then sat down on the bed and practised square breathing as he wondered what the detective wanted to tell him.

Shepherd left *Windchaser* at about six o'clock in the evening. It had been an enjoyable day and several times he had almost forgotten he was working, that he was under cover and that Marcus Meyer was a target. Jeeves had disappeared into the galley from which he had produced fluffy smoked-salmon omelettes to go with the fresh-baked croissants and baguettes. There was fruit, and a selection of cheeses, washed down with an endless supply of champagne. Breakfast over, they had taken *Windchaser* out to sea and spent several hours sailing up and down the coast. Everything was friendly and light-hearted but it soon became clear to Shepherd that he was being tested. Jeeves let him take the helm, and gave him instructions on where to go, watching carefully to see how he handled the boat.

He had him tacking and jibing and, when the wind picked up, told him to reef the sails, then nodded approvingly when Shepherd did it perfectly.

Jeeves had him sail to La Torre and, once they reached it, casually asked Shepherd to park the cat. Shepherd had no problems, but he was grateful for Barry Minister's tuition.

Jeeves had stayed on board while Shepherd, Meyer and Lisa had donned scuba gear and spent half an hour exploring the tower and interacting with the wildlife. The water was just eleven metres deep so it was easy diving and the visibility was good.

They got back on board and Jeeves took them to a sunken wreck, a cargo ship almost sixty metres long, which countless bright-coloured fish, octopuses and conger and moray eels had made their home.

They arrived back at the marina at four o'clock and Jeeves had Shepherd do the whole approach, then switch to the engine to guide the cat back into its berth. The rest of the afternoon had been spent drinking champagne, talking and playing backgammon. They took it in turns. Meyer was good – he knew all the moves. Lisa played for fun and often made mistakes, but equally often was lucky, which counted for a lot in the game. Jeeves was slow and methodical: he insisted on staring at the board after he'd thrown the dice. Shepherd could have beaten them all soundly but he paced himself and lost as many games as he won. He'd come across a lot of gangsters who played backgammon during his years as an undercover cop and had read several books on the game. His photographic memory meant that he knew pretty much the right move to make in every circumstance, which meant he could play virtually on autopilot.

Meyer and Jeeves were the easiest to play against because generally they did the logical thing, but Lisa was harder as, time and time again, she would make a move that didn't appear to be logical. But when she left a counter out on its own and vulnerable, more often than not he wouldn't hit the number to take it out. She had the most fun, there was no question of that, laughing and joking and punching the air whenever she threw a double.

Meyer's phone rang throughout the afternoon and he was constantly disappearing below deck to take the calls. Sometimes he reappeared seemingly pleased with himself, at others he came back with a face like thunder. On one occasion he was below decks shouting in Spanish.

As the sky started to darken, Meyer asked Lisa where she wanted to eat and she suggested Japanese. He said he'd prefer Lebanese and she said that was fine with her. Meyer didn't invite Shepherd so eventually he said he'd head back to his hotel. Meyer raised his glass. 'It's been a fun day,' he said. 'We should do it again.'

'Definitely,' said Shepherd. He waited to see if Meyer had something specific in mind but Meyer's phone rang and he hurried down below to take the call. 'Thanks for letting me sail her,' Shepherd said to Jeeves. 'Hell of a boat.'

'If ever I need a first mate, I'll call you,' said Jeeves, raising his glass.

'Anytime,' said Shepherd. He turned to Lisa. 'Have fun tonight,' he said.

'You too,' she said. She waggled her fingers to say goodbye. She was fairly drunk, hardly surprising considering the amount of champagne they'd put away.

Shepherd climbed off the boat and onto the jetty. Meyer was still below decks on the phone as he headed back to his hotel.

Standing took the Tube back to Bayswater. He showered, shaved, walked to Queensway and ate a late breakfast in the Bayswater Arms. In the afternoon he changed into a sweat-shirt and shorts and spent an hour exercising in Hyde Park. At just before six he was in the Old Bell, nursing a pint of Guinness.

The detective was late: it was closer to seven when he walked into the pub. He went over to Standing and nodded. 'Sorry. Briefing on a new case, I couldn't get away.' He took off his raincoat and slung it over his shoulder.

'No problem,' said Standing. 'Do you want a drink?'

'Fuck, yeah. It's been one of those days. Get me a pint of lager. Kronenbourg.' He slid onto the stool next to Standing.

'Lager?'

The detective looked at him sideways. 'Is that a problem? I'm over eighteen.'

'I'm sorry, I'm confused,' said Standing.

'I can see that,' said the detective. 'About as confused as when you first met me, right? You weren't expecting an Asian. The look on your face was a picture.'

'Well, to be fair, Adam Kaiser is hardly an Asian name, is it?'

'Actually, Adam is a common Muslim name. He's the father of the human race, according to Islam. And I get that

Kaiser sounds German, but it's a Muslim name, too. It means "emperor". It gets used as a first name, too.'

'So you are a Muslim?'

Kaiser grinned. 'Guilty as charged.'

'So why am I buying you a lager?'

'Because I'm a Muslim who takes a drink. I don't have to follow all the rules, do I? There's a Jewish sergeant at the station who loves bacon sarnies. No, I don't eat pork but, yes, I'm okay with alcohol. Now are you buying, or not?'

Standing ordered the lager. 'So you were born here?' he asked, as the barman went to the pumps.

The detective looked around. 'In this pub? Nah.'

Standing grinned. He liked the cop's sense of humour. 'England, I mean.'

'Sure. My mum and dad lived in Uganda and were kicked out by Idi Amin back in 1972. They started a new life here, from scratch.' He leaned closer to Standing, who got a whiff of sweet-smelling aftershave. 'Just so we're clear, this is all off the record.'

'Sure.'

'I mean it. We never met. We never spoke. I was never here.'

'I'm just sitting drinking with myself,' said Standing. He grinned and raised his glass. 'Okay?'

'Okay,' said Kaiser, sitting up again.

'That's why you chose this place,' said Standing. 'Minimal CCTV. And that's why you came in the back way.'

'There are cameras everywhere,' said Kaiser. 'The film footage and mobile phones are how we solve ninety per cent of our cases, these days.'

The barman returned with the detective's lager. Kaiser picked up the glass. 'First today.' They clinked, and Kaiser drank deeply. 'You're not from around here, are you?' he asked, as he put his glass down on the bar.

'I was born in London,' said Standing. 'Streatham. But I signed up when I was sixteen.'

'It's changed.'

'London?'

'Everywhere. The whole fucking country. But, yeah, London. And this bit of London more than most.' He shrugged. 'And it's made doing my job a nightmare, like I'm doing it with one hand tied behind my back.'

'How so?'

Kaiser sipped his pint. 'You know about profiling, right? Racial profiling. Giving someone a pull because their face fits.'

'Sure.'

'Ask any copper about profiling, they'll tell you it works. You want to find a serial killer who's knocking off women, look for a middle-aged white man. Fred West, the Yorkshire Ripper, Harold Shipman. White and middle-aged. You want to find a crack dealer, go looking for young black men. If you were looking for terrorists thirty years ago, you'd be looking for white men with Irish accents. These days, you're looking at Asians with beards.' He glanced around, as if he feared he was being overheard, and lowered his voice. 'But the way we are now, we're not allowed to do that. The TSG, they know that if they stop and search a black teenager he's more likely to be holding drugs or carrying a weapon than a middle-aged white woman. Stands to reason. But if they focus their stop-and-search operations on the basis of colour they get called racists. You've heard how the Muslims cry foul when they're searched at airports. But you tell me, how many non-Asians have tried bringing down planes or have driven trucks into crowds of Christians recently?' He pointed at himself. 'And look at me. I'm as Asian as they come, right? If I can see that, why can't the powers-that-be?'

'I hear you,' said Standing. 'But what's your point?'

'My point is that we can't do our jobs because the powers-that-be are scared shitless of being accused of racism. Everyone's walking on eggshells.' He leaned closer to Standing. 'Mrs Chapman said you showed her a picture.'

'Yeah. A guy Lexi was hanging around with.'

'Show me.'

Standing pulled the photograph from his jacket pocket. The detective took it. 'Do you know him?' asked Standing.

'I know the type. Where did you get this from?'

'She had it in a locket, the two of them together. Like boyfriend-girlfriend.'

'Must have been a bloody big locket.'

'I had it blown up.'

'And you asked Mrs Chapman if she knew her daughter had been sleeping with the guy?'

'Words to that effect, yeah.'

'And that he'd been supplying her with drugs.'

Standing nodded.

'You seem very well informed.' He gave him back the photograph.

'I suppose I am. His name's Frankie.'

'Well, I can tell you that's not a Muslim name,' said the detective.

'That's what I thought.'

'The picture was in a locket?'

'Yes.'

'But how did you know that she was sleeping with him and that he was supplying her with drugs?'

'I saw the text messages they sent.'

The detective frowned. 'So you have her phone?'

'Yeah.'

'How did you get it?'

'I'd rather not say. But here's the thing. Even without the phone, the cops could get a record of her calls and messages.'

'True.'

'So did you?'

'No.'

'Why not?'

The detective sighed. 'I was told not to,' he said quietly.

'Now, why would anyone tell you not to investigate the death of a young girl?' asked Standing.

'There was nothing to investigate about the death. Your sister was in a drugs den and she injected herself.' He saw that Standing was about to interrupt so he held up his hand. 'Yes, I know, we should have investigated the dealer, and I wanted to, but I was told to stop.'

'By whom?'

'An inspector. But he was acting on orders from above. It wasn't his decision. That's what he told me. Officially, he said, we didn't have the resources to mount a major investigation into small-time dealers.'

'And unofficially?'

'Unofficially? Orders from on high not to go queering our pitch with the Muslim community.'

Standing's jaw dropped. 'What? Are you fucking serious?' Heads turned in his direction and he realised he had raised his voice.

'Don't shoot the messenger, Matt,' said the detective. 'And keep your voice down.'

'Sorry,' said Standing.

'But you see the irony, right?' said Kaiser. 'A Muslim cop is told not to do anything to offend the Muslim community. Bloody ridiculous.'

'I see it.'

'And I can see how that upsets you. It upsets me, too. That's why I'm here. I want to steer you straight, that's all, before you get into any more trouble.'

'Okay.'

'So, you've heard about these child-exploitation gangs, right? Muslim guys, mainly of Pakistani origin, grooming underage girls for sex.'

'I've read about it,' said Standing.

'They call non-Muslims *kafir*s and in their eyes that makes them less than animals. And that's how they treat white girls, like animals. Less than animals. They groom them, get them addicted to drugs and pass them around. Sometimes they use them to shoplift. Sometimes they sell them for sex. And because they don't think of these girls as human, they don't care how young they are. I've heard of girls as young as nine being sucked in.'

'For fuck's sake,' said Standing. 'Why don't you put a stop to it?'

'If it was up to me, the whole lot of them would be behind bars. But the same thing is happening here as has been happening in Rotherham, across the north of England and the Midlands. In Rotherham alone they reckon as many as fifteen hundred young girls were abused. It's huge. The council and the cops are reluctant to expose just how big the problem is in case they get accused of Islamophobia.'

Standing pushed the picture towards the detective. 'And you don't know who he is?'

Kaiser shook his head. 'They use the younger, good-looking guys to pull the girls in. They meet them outside school, coffee bars, McDonald's, anywhere young girls hang out. They pay attention to them, flatter them, buy them meals, take them to the pictures, act like they're loving, caring boyfriends. Once they've pulled them in they get them on drugs and hand them over to the older men.'

'So why don't the girls go to the police?'

'Most are too ashamed. Usually at some point photographs will be taken and the girls can be blackmailed. If a girl does tell her parents or her social worker, the cops might get called and they might step in, but never in an organised way. A guy might get warned to leave a girl alone, but there won't be any charges.'

'Even if there are drugs involved?'

The detective drained his pint. He pointed at his empty glass and Standing finished his own, waving for the barman to bring fresh drinks.

The detective leaned closer to Standing and murmured, 'Okay, here's the thing. Your sister isn't the only kid to have overdosed. We had three in the past year, before she died. Young girls, no real suspicious circumstances to speak of, just injecting too much heroin. It happens, right?'

Standing didn't reply.

'But the three weren't random. They were all involved with the same group of Asian guys. They were based around a discount shop in Kilburn. One of those places where everything costs a quid. These guys are scumbags.'

The barman returned with their drinks. The two men fell silent until he had walked away.

'So, we knew that the scumbags in the shop were seducing young girls. Young white girls. Grooming them. Then screwing them. We knew about the shop, and we knew that several of the men who visited it worked as minicab drivers based out of an office in Kilburn. We did a quick recce and found they had a back room with sofas and a big-screen TV, video games, all the stuff that kids like. They'd let girls hang out there, and we were pretty sure that's where they were plying them with drink and drugs. So me and my DS put together a proposal to have the place under more intensive surveillance, maybe try to get a camera inside. But at the very least we could have eyes on the place and see who was coming and going. Once we'd identified the main players, we could move in. Hopefully pull in the dealers, too. I even offered to go under cover, take a job with the minicab firm, get to them from the inside. Me and my DS put forward a hell of a good case, but the inspector vetoed it.'

'What did he say?'

'Said there weren't the resources available, and that there was a risk of allegations of racism. Cultural complications, he said. More trouble than it was worth.'

'That's what he said? More trouble than it was worth?'

'Words to that effect,' said Kaiser.

'He was cutting them slack because they're Asian?'

'Happens all the time,' said the detective. 'Back when I was walking a beat a memo went around telling us not to discipline Asians or blacks for spitting in the street. We were told that it was a cultural thing. So we were to let them hawk and spit. I told my sergeant that was bollocks. I'm Asian and I don't spit in the street. My mum would've given me a clip around the ear if she'd caught me spitting. Anyway, I was told to just follow the orders.' He shrugged. 'That was ten years ago, but it's way worse now. Remember that nutter who stabbed the cop to death at the Houses of Parliament?'

Standing nodded. 'Sure. Rammed pedestrians with his car, then stormed the building with a knife.'

'He killed one of ours, Matt. He knifed a brother officer to death. And what did the Met say a few hours later? They said they realised that the Muslim communities would be anxious about what had happened because of the past behaviour of right-wing extremists. They said they would work with them to put their fears at rest.' He gritted his teeth. 'The cop's blood was still on the pavement and our bosses were worried about the feelings of the Muslim community. I'm a Muslim, right, but it's not skinheads I'm worried about. It's the thought of bearded nutters with knives killing cops on the street that keeps me awake at night. But our bosses just don't get that. Politically correct gone mad, like they say.'

Standing could see that the detective was breathing heavily and trying to calm himself. He recognised the signs and knew exactly how Kaiser felt. Anger had to be controlled because lashing out didn't solve anything.

Eventually the detective forced a smile. 'So, anyway, my inspector said if girls were choosing to hang out at the store, and no one was forcing them, it was down to them. They might be making bad choices, but that's what people do, isn't it?' He sipped his drink. 'Long story short, the inspector killed the investigation. Killed it stone dead.' He wrinkled his nose. 'But here's the funny thing. About a week later that back room was turned into a storage space. Filled with stock. They got rid of the sofas and the TV, and the girls stopped going around. Same guys running the shop, but they just stopped having girls there.'

Standing frowned. 'Do you know why?'

'No idea, but you wonder if someone warned them off, right?'

'The inspector?'

'Who the fuck knows?'

'So they've stopped the grooming?'

The detective shook his head. 'They just moved to the minicab office. They use a room there, second floor.'

'Is that where they took Lexi?'

'That I don't know. But the place in the pound shop was closed six months ago.'

'You were told to drop it. Why didn't you?'

Kaiser laughed. 'Do you always do as you're told?'

'Good point,' said Standing.

'My daughter's eight, and it scares me shitless that these scumbags might still be around when she's a teenager. What these bastards are doing, it's evil. They choose their victims carefully. Usually girls from broken homes, abusive parents. Poverty. They pay attention to them. Give then presents, make them feel special. It's grooming. It's what paedophiles do. They choose the right victim, then persuade them, slowly and carefully, until they get them to do what they want them to do.' He shuddered. 'It's fucking evil.' He sighed. 'But, like I said, no one's going to do anything.'

'We'll see about that,' said Standing. 'This inspector, the one who killed the investigation. What's his name?'

'I doubt he'll talk to you.'

Standing grinned. 'I can be persuasive.'

Shepherd woke to the sound of his mobile. Before he even opened his eyes he knew it was Willoughby-Brown. He groped for it and sat up.

'You'll like this,' said Willoughby-Brown. 'Your fingerprints have just been run through IDENT1.' It was the UK's national fingerprint database. Until 2005, fingerprints were taken with ink and paper, then converted into digital images stored on the National Automated Fingerprint Identification Service. That system was replaced by IDENT1, with fingerprints taken electronically by the Livescan system used in all police stations and the Lantern portable scanners that officers carried. The database contained more than seven million sets of fingerprints and IDENT1 was responsible for identifying more than a million and a half suspects every year.

'Any idea who checked?'

'It was done through Liverpool. St Anne Street police station. We have the name of the officer who ran it and he's now under surveillance.'

'So it's Meyer getting it done, not Lisa?'

'Looks that way. Any idea how they got the prints?'

'I was on the boat all yesterday so I touched lots of things. Including several glasses. Plenty of opportunity to lift my prints. What about the NCA? Has Lisa filed anything?'

'Funny you should ask. Yes. She's said you've met with Meyer and given a description. She's identified you as Jeff Taylor and says that Meyer is thinking about using you for one of his deliveries.'

'That's interesting.'

'Isn't it? What will be even more interesting is what happens once they get the Rich Campbell legend. I'll keep you updated.'

Willoughby-Brown ended the call and Shepherd lay on his back, staring up at the ceiling. The fact that Lisa had filed a report on Jeff Taylor suggested she was still in operational mode. But she was very close to Meyer, far closer than undercover agents generally got to their targets. It was interesting, true, but it was also confusing. If Lisa had switched allegiances, why would she file information that could lead to Meyer's arrest?

There was a sign in the window of the Everything For A Pound shop that said the weekday opening hours were from nine in the morning until eight at night. By ten to eight there was only one customer, a woman in a burka who was spending an eternity choosing plates. Standing was across the road, watching her in the reflection of a betting-shop window. Eventually she carried half a dozen plates to the counter, where a middle-aged Pakistani wrapped each one in newspaper and placed them in a plastic bag. A younger man was tidying shelves. Standing had hoped that at least one of them would leave before closing time, but it seemed they were both going to be there until eight.

Eventually the woman left with her purchases. Standing checked his watch. Five to eight. Time to move. He was wearing gloves, and a parka with a fur-lined hood. He hadn't seen much in the way of CCTV in the street, and when he'd been in the shop earlier in the day there had been no cameras inside. He figured that in a shop where everything cost a pound, shoplifting probably wasn't a problem.

He kept his head down as he jogged across the road and pushed the door open. A bell dinged. The man behind the counter didn't look up. The younger guy was a few feet away from him, arranging a display of glasses.

Standing turned and flicked the 'OPEN' sign to 'CLOSED'. There were two large bolts, top and bottom, and he slammed them home, then turned and walked purposefully towards the counter. The older man was staring at him, wide-eyed, but had frozen. That was what most people did when faced with a threatening situation. Soldiers could be trained to react but civilians were not: usually they stood rooted to the spot. Mouths would drop open, foreheads would frown, eyes would widen, but otherwise, bodies would go into self-preservation mode and that meant not moving.

The younger man hadn't noticed what Standing had done and was concentrating on the glassware. Standing walked quickly but he didn't run. The man behind the counter opened his mouth to speak. Standing reached the counter, grabbed the man's hair and slammed his head down, hard. Then he pushed him back so that he fell against the wall behind him.

At the crash the younger man turned. Standing hit him

in the solar plexus. The blow sent the man's diaphragm into involuntary spasm, which meant he couldn't breathe. Standing hit him a second time, and as his victim slumped to the floor, he grabbed the man behind the counter and dragged him along the floor to the storeroom. He pushed open the door, threw him inside, then went back for the other, who was now curled into a ball, gasping for air. Standing dragged him through the door and dropped him next to the older man.

He took a roll of duct tape from his pocket and bound the wrists of both men behind their backs, then slapped tape over their mouths. He stood up. His breathing was slow and even, and he doubted that his pulse had broken eighty. Less than a minute had passed since he had walked in from the street.

He went back into the shop and flicked three light switches on the wall by the cash register, plunging the place into darkness. There was a display of plastic-handled knives by the glassware. He selected a carving knife and took it back into the storeroom. The younger man was still having trouble breathing but the older man lay on his side glaring at Standing, blood trickling from his nose.

Standing hadn't been able to see inside the storeroom when he'd visited the shop, but it was fit for purpose. A door led out to the back, probably for deliveries, and it was locked. There were no windows, just racks of goods that were yet to be put on display. To the left was a small fridge with a kettle, mugs, coffee and tea.

Standing flicked down the hood of his parka. It didn't matter whether they saw his face. This would go one of two ways and neither involved the police. He stood over the older man. 'I'm assuming you're the boss, so I'm going to take that tape off your mouth and talk to you. If you're not the boss and he is, then the first and only words out of your mouth are to tell me that. Do you understand?'

The man nodded fearfully.

'Excellent,' said Standing. He bent down and ripped the duct tape off the man's lips and threw it onto the floor. 'Now, are you the boss?'

'Yes. Look, take the money from the till – there isn't much but just take it and—'

Standing kicked him in the side, hard, bent down and patted the man's trousers until he found his wallet. He took it out, removed the driving licence and studied the name. 'Jafari. Your name's Jafari?'

'Yes.'

Standing tossed the wallet onto the floor and slid the driving licence into the pocket of his parka. He continued to pat the man down and found his mobile in his back pocket. He pulled it out. 'Right, here's the thing. I've got what they call anger-management issues. That means I tend to fly off the handle. I act first and think second. Sometimes, when I'm really angry, I kill people. I'm not making that up. I have killed people. Do you believe me?'

The man swallowed. 'Yes.'

Standing kicked him in the ribs. 'Are you sure?'

The man closed his eyes and groaned. 'Yes. I believe you.'

'Right. Because this isn't going to end well if you lie to me. I already know the answer to most of the questions I'm going to ask you, and if you do lie to me I'm going to hurt you.'

'Okay, okay.'

Standing showed him the knife. 'And by "hurt you" I mean cut off a finger. Or a toe. An ear, maybe. Or your dick.'

'Okay, okay,' said the man, louder this time.

Standing took out the picture of the Asian man who'd

been with Lexi and held it in front of his face. 'Who is this?'

'I don't know him,' gasped the man.

'See, I know that you do know him,' said Standing, stamping on the man's knee. 'And I'm going to stay here until you give me his name.'

'I don't – I swear.'

Standing kicked the man in the ribs and he yelped. 'That's just a tap. Next time it'll be your kidney and you'll be pissing blood for a week.' He drew back his foot and the man curled up into a foetal ball. 'Faisal,' the man whimpered . 'His name's Faisal.'

Standing kicked him again. 'Now I know you're lying. That's not his name.'

'It is. I swear.'

Standing stuck the boot in again. 'Don't fuck with me,' he said. 'His name's Frankie.'

'They call him Frankie but his name's Faisal. Faisal Khan.'

'You know him?'

'Yes. I know him.'

'From where?'

'I know his father. They go to my mosque.'

'What's the father's name?'

'Salman.'

'Salman Khan?'

'Yes.'

'And where do they live?'

'I don't know.'

Standing kicked him in the back, and the man screamed. 'I don't know! Local, he's local. I think in that tower block on the way back to Maida Vale. The council one. But I'm not sure.'

Standing took the man's phone out and looked at the

screen. It was password protected. 'What's the password for your phone?'

The man gave him a four-digit number and Standing tapped it in. He flicked through the address book. He found a number for Faisal but no text messages. The log had been cleared so there was no way of seeing when the two men had last spoken.

'How else do you know Faisal?' asked Standing.

The man coughed. 'What do you mean? I don't understand the question.'

'You meet him when you're being a good Muslim, down at the mosque. What about when you're being a bad Muslim and fucking underage girls?'

'I don't do that! Why do you say that? I have three daughters.'

'You let him bring girls here, to this room. Didn't you?'

'Yes, but just to hang out. They played video games. It was like a club.'

'A club? A fucking club? Do you think I'm stupid?' He kicked him in the side.

'They were just hanging out!'

'They were bringing them here to fuck them!'

'I didn't know. I swear!'

Standing kicked him, twice, then stopped. It was possible that he didn't know what had been happening in the room. The man began to cry softly.

'Why did you stop?' asked Standing.

The man sniffed. 'Stop what?'

'Why did you stop letting Faisal and his friends bring girls back here?'

'They decided to stop coming, that's all I know.'

'Did somebody call you?'

'What? No!'

'You're sure? The cops didn't call you and warn you off?'

'No. They just stopped coming. And they stopped paying. So I turned it back into a storeroom.'

Standing stood over the man as he went through his phone. He checked the photographs but there were just family shots. The man. A wife in a headscarf. Six children. Three boys. Three girls.

'You know what Faisal was doing in here?'

'Just playing around. Kids' stuff. They had video games and comics.'

'What about drugs?'

'No! No drugs. Of course no drugs. Why would I allow drugs in my shop?'

'Booze, then.'

'Booze?'

'Alcohol. Faisal was giving them alcohol.'

'No. Not here. I am a good Muslim. I would never allow alcohol here.'

'You thought they were just playing games?'

'Faisal, he said he wanted somewhere to hang out. Said he'd pay me a hundred a week just to use the room. He brought in a couple of sofas and a TV. He said it was like a youth club.'

'And who did he bring with him?'

'His friends.'

'Boys? Girls?'

'Both.'

'Asian girls?'

The man shook his head.

'Just white girls? And Asian men. You didn't think there was something strange about that?'

The man closed his eyes, tensing for another kick.

'Did the father ever come here?' asked Standing.

'Sometimes.'

'To this room, I mean. To play with the girls.'

'No. He just came to the shop.'

'And did he pay you for the room? Or did Faisal?'

'Faisal. Faisal always gave me the money.'

'Does he have a job?'

'I don't know.'

Standing kicked him in the ribs. 'Does he have a job?'

'He works as a taxi driver sometimes. But he's like freelance. Sometimes he works, sometimes he doesn't.'

'Which taxi firm?'

'In the high street.'

'And his father. Does he work?'

'He's on benefits. He's got a bad leg. Gets all sorts of allowances and his wife is down as his carer.'

Standing put the phone into the pocket of his parka. 'I'm going to keep your phone, along with the pictures of your family. And I'm keeping your driving licence, so I know where you live. If I hear you've spoken to the police, I'll kill you. I'll kill you and your family. And, trust me, I have cop friends so if you do talk to the police I will know.'

'I won't,' said the man.

'You won't what?'

'I won't talk to the police.'

'And you won't talk to anyone else. Not a whisper, to anyone. If I hear that you've told anyone about what happened here, I'll kill you.' He gestured with the knife at the younger man. 'And you need to make sure that he keeps his mouth shut. I don't give a fuck who he is, because if he talks to anyone it'll be you I kill. Do you understand?'

The man nodded. 'Yes.'

'Yes what?'

'Yes, I understand.'

'If either of you tells Faisal or Faisal's father that I was asking about them – well, you know what will happen.'

'Yes. I know.'

'Tell me. Tell me what will happen.'

The man swallowed. 'You will kill me and you will kill my family.'

'Do you believe that?'

'Yes.'

'Are you sure? I don't hear any conviction in your voice.' He bent down and pressed the blade of the knife against the man's little finger on his left hand. 'Maybe I should cut a finger off, give you something as a reminder. Just in case you think I'm not serious.' He slid the knife along the flesh and blood flowed.

'No!' screamed the man. 'I believe you! I believe you!'

'Best you do,' Standing said. He stood up and kicked him hard in the ribs. 'I'm going to leave the knife by the door. You can cut yourself free when I've gone. But for now you stay on the floor while you count to a hundred. You can count, can you?'

'Yes,' sobbed the man.

'Then start now,' said Standing. He left the storeroom and walked to the shop door, dropping the knife on the counter as he went by. He slid back the bolt and let himself out. He practised square breathing as he walked to the Tube station. Four seconds in. Hold for four seconds. Four seconds out. Hold for four seconds. Repeat.

The middle stages of an undercover penetration were always the hardest. The initial phase was, more often than not, a matter of waiting for the right moment to make an approach. Shepherd had already done that, courtesy of the two Algerians. By the time the end phase came around, trust had usually been won and it was just a matter of assembling the evidence to bring the target down. But the middle phase was where it could all go badly wrong. If Shepherd came over as too keen, Meyer would become suspicious. But if he maintained too low a profile, Meyer might lose interest. The fact that Meyer now believed Shepherd was Rich Campbell, former bank robber on the run from vindictive colleagues, might mean that he'd want to know more. Or he might decide Campbell was more trouble than he was worth and distance himself accordingly. All Shepherd could do was wait and see.

Shepherd went for an early-morning run before he had breakfast in the dining room. Later he went for a walk along the beach and took the opportunity to phone Katra. 'Where are you?' was the first thing she asked.

'Spain,' he said.

'Lucky you.'

He heard the resentment in her voice. 'I'm working.'

'I can hear seagulls.'

'I'm on the beach.'

'You're working on the beach?'

He laughed. 'Believe it or not, I am,' he said.

'When are you coming back?'

'I'm not sure.'

'I miss you,' she said.

'I miss you too.'

'Hurry home.'

'I'll try,' he said, even though he knew there was nothing he could do to speed things up. He ended the call and looked at his watch. It was eleven o'clock.

He walked back to the hotel and spent an hour in the gym, forty-five minutes on a treadmill and the rest of the time with free weights. Then he showered, changed into clean clothes and went upstairs to Docherty's suite.

Docherty was sitting on the terrace with his binoculars and a glass of gin and tonic on a table next to him, with a copy of the *Daily Telegraph* and a half-eaten club sandwich. 'Help yourself to the minibar,' said Docherty. There was a Nikon camera with a two-foot lens on a tripod next to him.

'I'm good,' said Shepherd, dropping into the seat on the other side of the table. He jerked his thumb towards the marina. 'Anything happening?'

'The girl went shopping at just after nine. There was a wine delivery at ten. She returned about half an hour ago. Jeeves has been doing some boat stuff.'

'Meyer hasn't left?'

Docherty shook his head. 'He was up and about when the girl got back but they're both below decks. He's probably giving her one.' He grinned at the disgust that flashed across Shepherd's face. 'Come on, don't tell me you wouldn't give her one, if you had the chance.' So far as Docherty was concerned, Lucy Kemp was just a pretty girl hanging out with a known drug dealer. He didn't know her real name or that she was an undercover cop.

'She's not really my type,' said Shepherd.

'Good to know,' said Docherty. 'Because she's just the type I go for. I like them small with long black hair.'

'You should go to Thailand,' said Shepherd.

'Nah, I'm not into Asians,' said Docherty. 'Not that I get the chance to fool around anyway.' He raised his glass. 'I'm married with three kids and the wife keeps me on a very short leash.'

'How are Farouk and Salim?' asked Shepherd.

'Back in Algeria until Meyer moves on,' he said. 'Farouk was worried about the cut.'

'Tell him I'm fine,' said Shepherd.

'He said there was a lot of blood.'

'There was, but I heal quickly.'

Docherty sipped his drink. 'What's the plan?' he asked.

Shepherd shrugged. 'The ball's in Meyer's court. All I can do is wait.' He put his Jeff Taylor phone on the table. 'I suppose a beer wouldn't hurt.'

'Help yourself,' said Docherty. 'It's all on the taxpayer.'

Standing got to Zoë Middlehurst's house at just before four o'clock. The two car parking spaces were empty so he figured her parents weren't home and rang the bell. Zoë had changed out of her school uniform and was wearing a black T-shirt and leggings. 'Oh, Matt,' she said, when she saw who it was. 'What's up?'

'I need to talk to you, Zoë.'

'What about?'

'Lexi.'

'I don't think there's any point,' she said.

'Just a few minutes,' he said. 'I've seen her phone, Zoë. I know she called you on the day she died.'

'That's not a secret,' she said. 'She wanted me to come and take her home.'

'So you didn't go to the house in Kilburn with her.'

Zoë shook her head.

'She went with Frankie?'

'I guess.'

'Can I come inside, Zoë? I don't want your neighbours wondering why a strange man is standing on your doorstep.'

'You're not strange,' she said.

He smiled. 'You know what I mean.'

She thought about it for a few seconds, then pulled the door open. Standing stepped into the hall. There were stairs to their right and two doors to the left. She took him down the hall to the kitchen where several textbooks were scattered across a stripped-pine table beside a glass of Coke. 'I was doing my homework,' she said.

'I won't be long,' he promised. 'What time do your parents get back?'

'Mum's home by six, unless she's out drinking. Dad gets back when Wall Street opens. So, late.' She flopped down on a chair and took a sip of the Coke. The schoolbooks reminded him how young she was. And that he was alone in the house with a schoolgirl. He suddenly felt guilty about what he was doing, but knew that he had no choice. Only she could answer his questions about what had happened to Lexi on the day she'd died.

He smiled, trying to put her at ease. 'So, I saw that Lexi called you that night.'

Zoë nodded. 'As I said, she wanted me to come and get her. Frankie had left her at the house and she said the other men there wouldn't let her go.'

'What?'

'They weren't kidnapping her or anything like that. They just kept giving her drinks and saying she should stay. She called me and asked me to come and get her. And that's what I did.'

'Why didn't you go to the house with her?'

'Why would I do that?'

'For the drugs?'

'I never touch drugs. Well, not heroin. Ecstasy, sure, but everyone takes ecstasy.'

'So she went on her own?'

'No, like I said, she went with Frankie. I told her she was stupid, but she still went. She always went.'

'Why? Because he gave her drugs?'

'She said he was her boyfriend, but he was using her.'

'Using her how?'

Zoë picked up a pen and began doodling on a pad.

'Using her how, Zoë?' Standing repeated.

She screwed up her face. 'You won't like it, Matt,' she whispered.

'You have to tell me. I need to know.'

She sighed. 'When they first started going out, he was nice. He bought her flowers and perfume, he took her to Pizza Express, he paid for an upgrade for her phone. Then he started giving her drugs. Ecstasy. Weed. She used to smoke it in a place he used in Kilburn.'

'The pound shop?'

She looked up. 'How do you know about that?'

'I just do. Did you go?'

'Sometimes. Frankie had a PlayStation 4 and he always had Bacardi Breezers. He'd order pizza and that. He and Lexi were always fooling around and he was trying to get me to go with one of his mates, but I wouldn't.'

'Why not?'

Zoë wrinkled her nose. 'I always thought Frankie was sleazy but Lexi loved him.'

The word 'loved' hit Standing like a punch to the stomach, but he tried not to show how much it upset him. 'And he gave her drugs at the pound shop?'

Zoe nodded. 'Yeah, first it was just cannabis and ecstasy, but then he got her to try heroin. Chasing the dragon, he called it. You heat it on silver foil and smoke it through a straw. I tried it once but just the once. Lexi loved it.'

'And he started her injecting?'

'I don't know. I didn't know she was injecting, honest to God, not until I went around to the house to get her. I thought she just smoked.' She shook her head fiercely. 'I told her he was only using her. I told her.'

'What do you mean, using her?'

Zoë stared out of the window. Her left leg was jigging up and down, a sign of nerves. Standing let the unanswered question hang in the air for almost a minute before repeating it. 'What do you mean, using her?'

She winced. Then she turned to him with tears in her eyes. 'You don't want to know,' she whispered.

'I do,' he said. 'Tell me.'

She sighed again. 'He gave her drugs when he was first going out with her. Whenever she wanted cannabis or ecstasy or heroin, Frankie gave it to her. Then about three months ago he changed. He said he had to pay for the drugs, which meant she had to pay him. Of course she didn't have any money, just what her parents gave her. So Frankie said she'd have to do things for him.' Her cheeks reddened and she looked away.

'What sort of things, Zoë?'

'You know,' she whispered, averting her eyes.

'Sex?'

She nodded.

'He made her have sex with him?'

'Not with him. She wanted to have sex with him. She was a virgin before she met Frankie and he was her first. But Frankie said she had to have sex with his friends. For the drugs.'

Standing's throat had gone dry and he could barely swallow. 'And did she?'

'She said no – at least, that was what she told me. She said she just gave them blow jobs.'

Standing's heart was racing and he forced himself to stay calm. He didn't want Zoë to know how upset he was because then she'd clam up. 'Where was this? The pound shop?'

'They stopped using the pound shop. The guy who owned it started using the back room for something else. So Frankie took her to a minicab firm in Kilburn. They had a room upstairs. That's where she used to do it.'

'You're sure about this?'

She was still avoiding his gaze. 'She hated it. She said she didn't want to but Frankie said she had no choice and she always did what he wanted. Sometimes he drove her to houses where she had to . . . you know . . .' She left the sentence unfinished.

'And you don't think she was screwing them? These guys?'

'She always said it was just blow jobs, but about two weeks before she died she got really upset. She wouldn't tell me what was wrong. Frankie had taken her somewhere and . . .' She trailed off.

'You think he made her have sex with them?' he asked.

'Yes,' she whispered. 'I told her she should chuck Frankie. Have nothing to do with him any more. Tell him to fuck off. I said she should tell her parents, or the police. Or even one of the teachers. What he was doing was wrong, wasn't it?'

Standing nodded. 'Of course it was. Very wrong.'

'That's what I said. I said she should tell Frankie that if he kept passing her around she'd tell the cops. I said that if he thought she was going to go to the cops he'd have to stop.'

'When was that?'

'About two weeks before she . . .'

'Died?'

She sniffed. 'Yes.'

'Do you think she told Frankie she would tell the police?'

She sniffed again. 'She wouldn't, though, because she didn't want to get him into trouble. She just wanted him to tell the other men so that they would stop . . .' Another unfinished sentence.

Tears were running down her face and Standing wanted to comfort her, but he didn't want any physical contact to be misconstrued so he stood up and went over to a kitchen roll. He pulled off a few sheets and gave them to her to wipe her tears, then left the house, pulling the front door closed behind him. As he walked down the road he started square breathing. Inhale, two, three, four. Hold, two, three, four. Exhale, two, three, four. Hold, two, three, four. By the time he'd reached Maida Vale Tube station he had almost calmed down. Almost.

'*Windchaser*'s got visitors,' said Docherty. Shepherd got up off the sofa. He'd been half watching a football match between two Spanish teams and snacking on peanuts from the minibar. 'Two IC2 males from the look of it.'

He went out onto the terrace where Docherty was snapping away with his long-lensed camera. Shepherd picked up the binoculars, but by the time he had focused them on the jetty, the two men had boarded the boat.

Docherty took the camera off the tripod and handed it to him. Shepherd flicked through the photographs. Docherty had snapped the two men walking along the jetty and getting onto the boat. In several images he had caught their faces. Shepherd zoomed in on one of the photographs. Both men were dark-haired. One had a five o'clock shadow, the other was clean-shaven. They wore light suits and open-necked shirts. The clean-shaven guy was in his late twenties or early thirties, the other maybe a decade older and wearing a light-coloured hat and sunglasses. Shepherd flicked to the next picture. The faces were more visible and Shepherd recognised the younger man. 'That's Randy Garcia,' he said, showing the close-up to Docherty.

'Randy?'

'His real name is Juan Garcia but he's a bit of a one for the ladies so the DEA call him Randy. For the sex and after the actor. He works for the Hernandez cartel – his great-uncle is Jesus Hernandez. Big-time cocaine exporters. Vicious bastards, they've killed at least four DEA agents over the years and ten times as many Colombian government officials.' He checked more of the pictures, trying to get a clearer view of the older man, but the hat and glasses made identification difficult. 'The other guy might be Oscar Lopez, one of the cartel's enforcers, but I couldn't swear to it.'

'So they're putting together a drug deal?' said Docherty. 'It's a pity we can't get a bug on the boat.'

'That's why Meyer has his meetings afloat,' said Shepherd. 'Very hard to eavesdrop.'

'Do you think you can get a bug on board?'

Shepherd grimaced. 'I could try, but if it was discovered it would be pretty obvious where it had come from. Too risky, I reckon.'

'So what do you think's going on?'

'I guess he's arranging a delivery,' said Shepherd. 'The Colombians move a lot of product through Spain, these days. The open-border thing means that once it's there they can get it to anywhere else in mainland EU without any Customs checks, and there's so much stuff crossing the English Channel that checks there are cursory at best.'

He went back into the room and started watching the football again. After twenty minutes Docherty called through from the terrace. 'The eye candy is leaving.'

'Alone?'

'Yeah. Probably shopping. She lives the life of Riley, that one, doesn't she?'

Shepherd popped some peanuts into his mouth and chewed thoughtfully. The waiting was frustrating but there was nothing he could do to speed things up. Either Meyer would approach him or he wouldn't. If Shepherd was too pushy, Meyer would be suspicious. The worry was that he would leave Marbella without making contact. If that happened, Shepherd's options would be limited. He could hardly turn up at Meyer's next port of call.

He stared at the Jeff Taylor phone on the coffee-table in front of him. 'Ring, you bastard,' he said. 'Ring.'

'*Windchaser*'s setting sail,' called Docherty.

Shepherd went out onto the terrace. The catamaran was edging away from its berth. Jeeves was standing behind the wheel on the port side. Meyer and the two visitors were sitting in the cockpit, holding glasses of champagne. Docherty was clicking away on the camera. Shepherd picked up the binoculars again. The Colombians were smoking cigars. The younger one was definitely Juan Garcia. The older one still had his hat and glasses on but Shepherd was fairly sure it was indeed Oscar Lopez. He had seen Lopez's DEA file five years ago and he was one mean son of a bitch. Lopez took care of discipline within the Hernandez cartel and dealt with any outside threats. According to the file, he was a fan of the Colombian necktie, where a victim's throat was slashed from side to side and the tongue pulled through the open wound. Shepherd knew that the Colombian necktie was actually a myth – it was a physical impossibility – but the fact that the DEA believed it was a sign of just how much Lopez was feared. The agency was sure that he had killed at least four of their agents, but as all the murders had occurred in Colombia there was no evidence and no witnesses.

Windchaser headed for open water. Shepherd looked at his watch. 'I'm guessing they'll be at sea for a while,' he said. 'I'll hit the gym.'

'Do me favour and get me a couple of vodka miniatures, will you?' asked Docherty. 'And another tonic water.'

★ ★ ★

The inspector who'd vetoed the operation against the groomers was called Graham Reynolds, and Adam Kaiser had said he lived in Stanmore, in north-west London, about an hour from Bayswater on the Jubilee line. Standing checked the electoral roll and found a Graham Reynolds at a Stanmore address. An Angela Reynolds was also shown as living there, presumably his wife.

Standing had decided he'd be better off meeting the inspector away from the police station: it was unlikely he'd say anything on the premises but on his home turf he might open up. He decided to head up to Stanmore in the early evening so he bought a long black coat and a pair of black leather gloves from a menswear store in the Whiteleys shopping centre in Queensway.

He arrived in Stanmore at five thirty. The Reynoldses' house was semi-detached in a narrow road a short walk from the Tube station. Standing walked by slowly. There was a parking space that had once been a garden but it was empty. Standing didn't know if Reynolds drove to work or not but he decided to wait. If he knocked on the door and the inspector wasn't in but his wife was, all it would take was one phone call for a van of police to arrive and he was in no mood for another Tasering. There were no obvious places where he could stand and watch the house without appearing suspicious, so he walked slowly down the road, then retraced his steps. Every now and again he would take out his phone and fake a call, looking as if he was waiting for someone.

Six o'clock passed. Then six thirty. At just before seven a white Toyota turned into the road. Standing was about a hundred yards away and walking towards the house when the car turned and parked. He quickened his pace and got to the house just as Reynolds was climbing out. He was short and slight, less than five eight, and probably weighed seventy kilos. He was wearing a light blue fleece over his uniform and carrying a North Face backpack.

'Graham Reynolds?' said Standing, quietly.

Reynolds spun around, his right arm moving instinctively to protect himself. Standing stood with his hands out of his pockets, his fingers spread wide to show that he wasn't carrying anything.

'Who are you?' asked Reynolds.

'I just wanted a quiet chat, away from the station,' said Standing. 'I didn't mean to startle you. I'm sorry.'

'Who are you?'

Standing smiled. 'Here's the thing, Inspector Reynolds. I'll happily tell you who I am, and I can show you ID, but if I do that, it puts you in an awkward position.'

Reynolds frowned. 'How so?'

'At the moment I'm just a stranger, someone you've never met and hopefully will never meet again. I just want a chat. Nothing more. If you're ever asked about this meeting you can easily deny it ever happened. But it's a lot harder to deny that once I've identified myself.'

'And if I just tell you to go away and leave me alone?'

Standing shrugged. 'Then I'll do that. Look, I didn't go to the police station because I knew you probably wouldn't see me, and I'd no doubt you wouldn't tell me what I want to know. Because if I go to the station then it's official and it's on the record. This is neither. I know you're a good cop. I know you wanted to investigate the grooming that's been going on in Kilburn. And I know you were stopped. As a good cop, that's got to weigh on you. You were prevented from doing your job, a job that needs to be done. I just want to know why.'

Reynolds continued to stare at him. Standing could practically hear the man running through his options. He himself clearly wasn't a threat: any threats would have been made already. The fact that Standing had turned up outside his home meant that he wasn't just a random member of the public. But if he was in law enforcement he would have identified himself. So would a journalist. So why would a member of the public want a private chat about an operation that had been pulled?

'You're not a member of a right-wing group out to attack Muslims?' Reynolds asked eventually.

Standing shook his head. 'It's nothing like that,' he said. 'I just want the right thing to be done, and at the moment that's not happening. Just a chat, Inspector Reynolds. No notes, no recordings, no comeback. I just want to know what happened.'

Reynolds glanced at the house. 'My wife's going to be wondering what I'm up to.'

'Tell her I'm a journalist looking for a quote on a story,' said Standing.

'You're not, I hope.'

'You have my word that I'm not a journalist, and never have been.' He smiled. 'I'm not much of a writer.'

Reynolds gestured down the road. 'Let's walk.'

Standing pointed in the opposite direction. 'Can we walk that way? That's where the Tube is.'

'You don't drive?'

'Never took my test.'

Reynolds began to walk and Standing matched his pace. 'The way I understand it, you were keen to investigate an Asian grooming gang that was operating in Kilburn. They were taking young girls into a pound shop and plying them with drink and drugs.'

'How do you know that?'

'I just do,' said Standing. 'But you stopped the investigation, ostensibly for cost reasons, though there was a suggestion it was a cultural thing.'

'That's the official line, yes.'

'But it's not the truth?'

Reynolds didn't say anything.

'That must have pissed you off, right? You were ready to go, you had the bad guys in your sights, then someone higher up tells you to stop. Basically they didn't want you to do your job. In which case, what's the point, right?'

Reynolds sighed. He took a packet of cigarettes from his pocket and offered it to Standing. He shook his head and the inspector lit one for himself. He waited until he'd blown smoke up at the darkening sky before continuing. 'I got called into my boss's office. He's a superintendent. He's behind a desk most of the time but he's a real copper and initially he'd given me the go-ahead to start the investigation. The plan was to put the shop under surveillance, see who was coming and going, ideally get some CCTV in there. We already knew that several young white girls had been taken there by Asian men so we needed to get a view on how big a problem it was and how many of the girls were under age. I get called in and I assume it's to talk about resources and manpower but I'm told that it's all off. My boss is with a deputy assistant commissioner. The DAC doesn't say much. He's just there to prove that what I'm being told is from the top. My boss tells me that the operation I've planned is going to cut across a long-term operation being run by another agency, and that we have to hold off on ours.'

'Other agency?' said Standing, frowning. 'Did they say who?'

'My boss didn't while the DAC was there. Just that my operation was being put on ice, for the time being. The DAC thanked me for all my good work, assured me that this was in the best interests of the fight against serious crime, and said that if anyone asked I was to say the operation had been curtailed for budgetary reasons. I'm sent on my merry way and the DAC gets into his limo and is driven back to Scotland Yard. Once he's gone, my boss has me back in the office and shuts the door. He's as annoyed as I am and brings me up to speed. It's MI5. They're running an anti-terrorism case and our operation risks exposing it.'

'Did he say what the case was?'

'He didn't know. But the obvious conclusion is that it's Islamic fundamentalists and some of them are involved in the child grooming. If we pull them in on grooming charges, the anti-terrorism operation falls apart. According to my boss, the anti-terrorism operation is way bigger and involves more targets. Five don't want their operation compromised so we stand down.'

'Four girls died. Doesn't that count for anything?'

'Four girls died of heroin overdoses. There were no suspicious circumstances.' Standing opened his mouth to speak and the inspector held up a hand to silence him. 'Yes, I know what you're going to say. Of course there's something wrong when young girls die of drug overdoses and, yes, someone must have given or sold them the drugs. But the deaths themselves weren't criminal acts. Two of the girls died in their own bedrooms and were found by their parents. One died outside, in a park, the fourth in a shooting gallery in Kilburn. But they all injected the drugs themselves. They all made bad choices.'

'Or someone deliberately gave them much stronger heroin, knowing it would kill them.'

The inspector stopped walking and turned to him. 'What makes you say that?'

'It's possible, right?'

'Anything's possible. But why would anyone want them dead?'

'It's not rocket science, is it?' said Standing. 'The girls were coerced into having sex. With gifts, with sweet talk, with booze, with drugs. Whatever, they started having sex, then maybe photographs and video were taken, pressure was applied, and then the girls find themselves being passed around. That's what happened up north, right, in Rotherham and all those places? Thousands of young white girls abused by Asian gangs.'

'It's a big jump between grooming and murder.'

'It's a logical one, though. Say the girls aren't happy about what's being done to them. They see what's been happening up in Yorkshire and that these men are finally being sent to prison for what they did. Maybe they start to think about going to the police. The guys find out and decide to take action.'

'You mean you think the girls were murdered?'

'It's possible. The girls were all being used by the Asian gang.'

'The ones who died. That's what we heard. But we hadn't confirmed it. That was going to be part of the investigation.' He narrowed his eyes. 'Who the hell are you?'

'Just a guy who wants to know what happened. Okay, I won't take up any more of your time. And thanks for talking to me.' He offered his hand and the inspector shook it. 'I realise you could have just told me to go fuck myself.'

The inspector smiled. 'I thought about it,' he said. 'But you were right, it did annoy me. It still annoys me. Kids are being abused and I'm being told to do nothing about it.' He shook his head angrily. 'It annoys the hell out of me. But what can I do? I've got twenty-five years in and I'd like at least one more promotion before I retire. And that's not going to happen if I start making waves.' He turned away and began to walk back to his house.

'Oh, Inspector, one last thing,' said Standing.

Reynolds stopped. 'What?'

'The pound shop? Did you close down the back room?'

'I was told to back off, and I did.'

'You didn't make a call, tell him to shut it down? Because he did. The room's used as a storeroom now.'

Reynolds looked at him quizzically. 'You seem to know a lot about this.'

'They've moved to a minicab office in Kilburn.'

'That would make sense.'

'Why?'

'One of the men we were looking at runs a cab company.'

'What's his name?'

'Hussain. Ali Hussain. There's four of them own the business. Fifty or so drivers on the books, though last I heard a lot are moving to Uber.'

'Why were you looking at Hussain?'

'He was a regular visitor to the pound shop.'

'Anything else on him?'

The inspector shook his head. 'Nothing known. I must go. My wife's got the dinner on.'

'Thanks,' said Standing. 'Thanks for everything.'

'I was never here,' said the inspector. 'And neither were you.'

There was a decent gym in the hotel so Shepherd spent the best part of an hour exercising. When the lift doors opened on his floor, he was surprised to see Lisa standing in the lobby. 'I'd just given up knocking,' she said. She was wearing a yellow halter top, a short skirt that showed off her tanned legs, and high heels, but still looked tiny.

'I was in the gym.'

She nodded at his sweat-soaked shirt. 'I can see.'

'I'm just going to shower,' said Shepherd.

'Probably a good idea.'

'I thought you were out on the boat?'

'Then you were obviously mistaken.' She grinned. 'Marcus wanted a boys' trip. So I'm surplus to requirements. Me being a girl and all.'

She made no move to leave so Shepherd unlocked his door and went inside. She followed him, then went to the minibar, squatted down and opened it. 'There's no champagne,' she said.

'I know. How remiss.'

'What sort of hotel doesn't have champagne?' she asked.

'This one,' said Shepherd. 'There's white wine.'

'Nah,' she said. She took out a bottle of beer. 'What do you want?'

'I'll have a beer,' he said. There was an opener on the side of the minibar and she used it to open the two bottles. She gave one to him and clinked hers against it. 'Cheers, Jeff. My White Knight.'

He grinned. 'Cheers, Lucy. My Damsel In Distress.'

They drank. 'I'm going to have to shower,' he said.

'Don't let me stop you.'

Shepherd put down his beer and took his phone into the bathroom. He put it by the basin while he stripped off and stepped into the shower. He hit the cold water and gasped as it flowed over him. He closed his eyes and let the water play over his hair.

'Do you always do that?'

Shepherd jumped and whirled around. Lisa was leaning against the doorway, tapping her bottle against her chin, an amused smile on her face.

'Do what?'

She gestured at the phone with her bottle. 'Take the phone with you into the bathroom.'

'Sure. And do you always follow men into the bathroom?'

She grinned. 'Sure. Want me to join you?'

Shepherd laughed, assuming she was joking. He grabbed the soap and turned the water up to warm. He looked over his shoulder. She hadn't moved.

'Well?' she said.

'Well what?'

'Do you want me to join you?'

'What about Marcus?'

'What do you mean?'

'You're his girlfriend, right?'

She laughed. 'Well, I'm a girl and I'm his friend. But I'm not his girlfriend.'

'Oh, come on, I've seen you together.' He realised she had no intention of leaving so he began to lather himself.

She raised her eyebrows in mock surprise. 'You've seen me fucking him?'

'No, of course not. But . . .'

'But what?'

'You walk hand in hand. You're close.'

'He's a friend.'

'You're not sleeping with him?'

She laughed again. 'You're an idiot.'

'I don't fool around with other guys' girls,' said Shepherd.

'How very Victorian of you,' she said. 'You really don't know, do you?'

'Know what?'

'Marcus is gay.'

Shepherd's jaw dropped. 'Get out of here.'

'He doesn't make it obvious but, yeah, he's gay. I mean,

he likes having pretty women around, and he's charming and funny, but there's never anything physical with us. And he's the same with guys. When he hangs out with gay guys, he fools around, but in all the time I've known him I don't think he's had sex with anyone.'

Shepherd put the soap back on its holder and rinsed himself off. 'I'm gob-smacked,' he said.

'Don't tell him I said anything,' said Lisa. 'He doesn't like being gossiped about.'

'What about Jeeves? Are he and Marcus an item?'

'An item?' She giggled. 'Who says that, these days?'

'You know what I mean. You stay on the boat. Are they . . .?'

'Fucking? No, Jeff, they're not. Look, Marcus is pretty much asexual. And Jeeves isn't gay. He's always trying to get into my pants when Marcus isn't looking.' She shook her head. 'You really have no gaydar. You just can't tell, can you?'

'It's because I don't really care. Gay or straight, people are people, good or bad. Unless a guy goes around in a dress or camps it up, I'm probably not going to notice, that's true.' He shook his head. 'I really thought you and he . . .'

'Because we hold hands? He's very tactile, with women anyway. And don't get me wrong, we hang out a lot and he's great fun. He's charming, he makes me laugh, he's bloody great to go shopping with, but sex? It's just not on the agenda.'

He turned the shower off and grabbed a towel. 'If it was, would you be tempted?'

She tilted her head on one side. 'What do you mean?'

'I dunno. He sounds like the perfect boyfriend, other than the fact that he's gay.'

'Even if he was straight, nothing would happen,' she said.

'Because?'

He tried to get past her but she blocked his way, an amused smile on her face. 'Because he's not my type.'

'So what is your type?' Immediately the words had left his mouth, Shepherd regretted them. She moved closer, her lips parting, and he knew she was going to kiss him. His mind whirled. How the hell was he supposed to react? She was an undercover cop, he was an MI5 officer, both on active operations. He had a girlfriend, and this woman might well be working for a big-time drug importer. She reached up with her right hand, slipping it behind his neck.

Suddenly the phone rang, startling them both. She laughed nervously and Shepherd picked it up. He squinted at the screen. 'It's Marcus.'

She laughed. 'Speak of the devil.'

'Hey, what's up?' said Shepherd into the phone.

'Is Lucy with you?'

'Yeah, she wanted to hit my minibar.'

'Fancy an early dinner? Lobster? My treat?'

'Sounds good.'

'Come down to the boat. We'll crack a bottle of bubbly, then head off.'

He ended the call. 'We've been summoned,' he said.

She stood on tiptoe and kissed his cheek. 'To be continued,' she said, and patted him on the backside.

Camouflage was the key to stalking a target if you had to get up close and personal without arousing suspicion. If you were attacking from a distance, the target wouldn't see you, so you could dress for efficiency. But Standing needed to wait close to the entrance to the building where Faisal Khan lived so he had to blend in. He was wearing his long black coat and he went to a charity shop in Kilburn High Road and bought himself a multi-coloured wool hat with ear flaps that looked as if it might have been a souvenir from a holiday in South America. Then he bought a large bottle of cheap cider from an off-licence and walked back to the high-rise. There was a garden area with a few benches close to the entrance to the block and he chose one that gave him a clear view, sitting down with his legs spread wide, the bottle of cider in his lap. He had looked up his quarry on Facebook. There were hundreds of Faisal Khans but he found the right one eventually. From the postings, Faisal came across as a good Muslim boy, who loved his family and his religion, who played five-a-side football with a local team and enjoyed working out in the gym. There was no mention of a job, and the only girls who featured in the pictures were Asians wearing *hijab*s. He was able to download a much clearer photograph of the man and had that on his phone.

He sat patiently, every now and again pretending to take a drink from the bottle. Most people who walked by avoided eye contact with him, more so when he let out a long, satisfying burp or muttered to himself. People came and went. Early in the afternoon it was mainly young women, usually with toddlers in pushchairs, and old folks carrying shopping. From five o'clock onwards people were returning from work – men and women with tired, unsmiling faces, many walking from the nearby Tube station. The occupants of the tower block reflected the multi-racial mix of the city and probably ten per cent were Asian.

Standing kept the photograph of Faisal in his hand and looked at it frequently to refresh his memory. There were two false alarms, one at ten past five and the other twenty minutes later, when he saw men who were a close match. On the second occasion he had actually stood up and headed for the door of the block until he realised the man was considerably taller than Faisal.

It was just before eight o'clock and night had fallen when

Faisal Khan appeared. He was driving a red Peugeot 106 with wire wheels and a large spoiler at the back. He parked and walked towards the entrance, his mobile phone pressed to his ear. Standing checked the photograph on his smart-phone. It was definitely Faisal. He stood up, shoved the bottle into the pocket of his coat and ambled towards the man, muttering loudly.

Faisal tapped in an entry code and pushed open the door. Standing slipped in behind him, keeping his head down, and followed him through the lobby to three lifts. The middle one was the first to arrive. Faisal was talking into his mobile. 'Yeah, bruv, I'm heading into the lift so I'll lose my signal, yeah.'

He got into the lift and stabbed at the button for the seventh floor. Standing followed him and pressed the one for the top floor. The doors closed. As the lift started to move, Standing reached over and grabbed the phone from Faisal's hand.

'What the fuck, bruv?' shouted Faisal. He tried to get his phone back but Standing put it into his coat pocket, seized him by the throat and rammed him back against the side of the lift. He kept up the pressure, easily avoiding Faisal's attempts to claw at his face, and started to count. His grip was blocking the blood flow in the carotid artery and the jugular vein and, if applied for too long, would result in death. Faisal's eyes bulged and his chest heaved as Standing reached eight. After he got to ten Faisal's eyes closed and his legs lost their strength. Standing kept applying pressure and used his other hand to force the man up against the side of the lift. He counted to fifteen, then took away his hand. Faisal's head slumped forward, unconscious.

Standing bent at the knees and hefted him over his shoul-ders. The lift reached the seventh floor and the doors rattled open. He pressed the button to close the doors and they were soon heading up to the top floor.

Standing carried Faisal out and looked left and right. There was a fire door to the left and he pushed it open. Concrete stairs led down and up. He went up and reached another fire door. This one was locked and the key was in a glass-fronted red metal case. A notice warned of the penalty for unauthorised use. Standing used his elbow to smash the glass and pulled out the key. He unlocked the door and carried Faisal onto the roof. The door clicked shut behind him and he slipped the key into his pocket.

He dropped the unconscious man onto the floor and stood over him. 'Wake up,' he said, and when there was no reaction he kicked him in the side. Faisal grunted but didn't come round. He pulled the bottle of cider from his pocket and poured it over the man's face. Faisal coughed and spluttered as the cider trickled into his open mouth, then rolled over, choking. Standing gave him another kick in the side and this time the man groaned. 'Wakey, wakey,' said Standing.

Faisal rolled onto his back, still coughing. His eyes fluttered open and he frowned in confusion. Standing bent down, grabbed the scruff of his jacket and pulled him into a sitting position, his back against the concrete parapet that ran around the roof. Faisal wiped his mouth with the back of his hand. 'What the fuck, bruv?' he croaked.

'Where do you get off grooming underage girls?'

Faisal glanced around, trying to get his bearings.

'You heard me, Faisal. What do you think you're doing, taking young girls and passing them around your mates like they were nothing?'

'What the fuck are you talking about, bruv? I don't groom no girls.'

'You buy them presents, you give them booze and drugs and then you fuck them. Right?'

'Are you fucking high, bruv? Cos you're making no sense.'

'That pound shop in Kilburn. That's where you used to take them. Now it's the cab office. Don't fuck me around, Faisal. I know what you do and I know where you do it.'

'What the fuck do you want, bruv? You want to mug me? I've got maybe fifty quid on me. You went to all this trouble for fifty quid? You are fucking demented.'

'I don't want your money, Faisal. I want to know who runs your grooming group. Who's the ringleader?'

'You keep saying grooming. Fuck that, no one grooms them.'

'How old are you?'

'Old enough.'

'Twenty-five? Twenty-six?'

'What's it to you?'

'The girls you're grooming, they're – what? Fourteen? Fifteen? Sixteen?'

Faisal shrugged. 'I don't ask. Don't ask, don't care.'

'And you give them drugs?'

'They ask for drugs. Nobody forces anybody to do anything. If a girl wants drugs, she can have drugs. If a girl wants to suck my cock . . .' he grinned '. . . who am I to say no, right? It's a free country, innit?'

'Not when men screw underage girls and think it's okay.'

'Fuck off, man,' said Faisal. 'Are you telling me you'd turn down free sex if it was offered? With a fit young girl who'll do exactly as she's told?'

Standing felt the anger flare inside him and drew back his foot to kick the man.

Faisal glared up at him. 'You think I'm scared of you? I'm not scared of you, man. You don't scare me.' His hand disappeared inside his jacket and reappeared clutching a large knife, its blade protected by a cardboard sheath. He flicked the knife to the side as he got to his feet and the cardboard flew through the air. 'Yeah, now who's scared?'

'Tell me about Lexi,' said Standing.

Faisal frowned. 'Lexi? Lexi Chapman? Is that what this is about? What are you – some relative or something?'

'Or something,' said Standing.

'And you're pissed because she topped herself? Ain't my fault, bruv. Silly bitch overdosed. Shit happens, right?' He jabbed the knife at Standing to punctuate his words.

'She was sixteen when she died. Fifteen when she met you.'

'Never asked her age, bruv. Don't ask, don't tell. She was young, though, I can tell you that.'

'I know exactly how old she was, *bruv*,' said Standing, his voice loaded with sarcasm.

Faisal's eyes narrowed. 'So who the fuck are you? You're not her father.'

'I'm her brother.'

Faisal frowned. 'Didn't know she had a brother.'

'Don't ask, don't tell?'

Faisal shrugged. 'Don't give a fuck.' He jabbed the knife at Standing's face but Standing didn't flinch. 'Now you need to get the fuck away from me before you get cut.'

'You cut many people with that?' asked Standing.

'Some. Why?'

'It doesn't look like it would do a lot of damage, that's all. And the handle. I'm guessing your hand would slip right off it if you stabbed anyone with any real force. You need a quillon for a knife to be effective.'

'Say what?'

'A quillon. A crossguard. A metal bar at right angles to

the blade, between the blade and the hilt. If you're going to slash, a quillon isn't that important, but if you're planning to stab someone and you don't have a quillon, your hand will probably slip onto the blade and you'll end up cutting yourself.'

It was clearly too much information for Faisal. 'What are you? The knife whisperer?'

'I've had some experience with knives, yeah.'

'Like a butcher?'

Standing nodded. 'Yeah. Like a butcher.'

Faisal waved the knife from side to side. 'Yeah, well, I've got the knife and you haven't so maybe you'd best be on your way, bruv.'

'See, I'm really not sure stabbing is the way to go,' said Standing. 'Stabbing is the equivalent of a gunshot. In and out, leaving a single wound. But, like a gunshot, placement is the key. You can get shot several times but if no vital organs or blood vessels are damaged you can keep moving. Sure, a shot to the head will stop you every time but I've seen guys take three or four rounds and still be able to return fire.'

'What the fuck are you talking about, man?'

'I'm just saying that you might want to rethink the stabbing technique, that's all. Stabbing an artery is bloody difficult, but relatively easy to achieve when you slash. Stab an arm, it hurts and you bleed. But slash an arm severing muscle and tendons and the arm becomes useless. You have to put in the effort, though. You have to slash deep or the cuts will just be superficial.'

Faisal had a blank look in his eyes.

'And, like gunshots, you want to go central mass. The chest and stomach. Bigger target, less effort. I always find a combination of stab and slash is best. Stab then slash. Works every time.' He nodded at the knife in Faisal's hand. 'But, seriously, that's not the knife you'd want to be using. I mean, it looks the business, it's big and all, but it's not a great blade. Me, I always prefer a double-edged dagger. Nice and sharp, with a milled fuller. The fuller reduces the weight of the blade, without sacrificing strength, and limits lateral flexion.'

'What?'

'It stops the blade twisting. It also helps you pull it out because it reduces the suction effect. That's why you hear the fuller called the "blood groove", but it was never about the blood. It was about making the knife strong and light.' He nodded at Faisal's knife. 'That's heavy and, frankly, probably not too strong.'

'It'll do the job,' said Faisal.

'I suppose,' said Standing. 'So who gave Lexi the drugs? The heroin?'

'Why do you want to know?'

'I want to know who killed her.'

'She killed herself, bruv. She injected herself. It was her call.'

'So it was you? You gave her the drugs?'

'Fuck off, bruv. If it hadn't been me it would have been someone else. She was well up for it.'

'Well up for what?'

'For everything, man. She loved sex, she loved drugs. I couldn't keep her away from me, bruv. I didn't have to try that hard. She wanted it. She wanted me. She wanted the brown sugar and she wanted my brown cock. She loved it, man, she fucking loved it.'

Standing stepped forward, his hands bunching into fists, his jaw clenched. Faisal took half a step back and raised the knife, then stabbed it at Standing's throat. Standing's left hand shot out instinctively, knocking the knife to the side. His punch was also instinctive and caught Faisal on the chin with such force that his neck cracked. Faisal staggered back and fell over the guardrail, his arms flailing even though the blow had almost certainly knocked him out.

Standing tried to grab his legs as he disappeared over the edge but his fingers only managed to touch the bottom of his trousers and then he had disappeared into the darkness. Standing started counting in his head as he breathed in. When he got to three he heard a dull thud from 180 feet below. He turned away and walked back to the door, still counting. Inhale, two, three, four. Hold, two, three, four. Exhale, two, three, four. Hold, two, three, four.

On the way to the Tube station he shoved the coat and hat into a clothing recycling skip and the empty cider bottle into a glass bin.

The restaurant Meyer had chosen overlooked the sea and they were given a corner table on the terrace. The maître d' knew him by name and shook his hand, then kissed Lisa on both cheeks and patted Jeeves's shoulder. Meyer introduced him as Billy but Shepherd recognised the man from an NCA file he'd seen a few years earlier – his name was Rupert Cunningham and he was a convicted fraudster with several charges still outstanding.

Billy gave them the first bottle of Cristal on the house and during the evening Meyer bought another four. The food was excellent, possibly the best Shepherd had ever eaten in Spain, and the lobsters were huge and succulent.

As always with Meyer, conversation was amusing, never boring. He had a fund of stories, mainly his adventures at various ports around the world. He was clever enough to skirt around what he actually did for a living, but his tales were populated by villains of various nationalities.

Shepherd told his fair share of tall stories, mainly tales

he'd picked up from Barry Minister, but it was Meyer who did most of the talking, holding court like a king surrounded by his courtiers. Shepherd found himself genuinely liking the man, but he was professional: he recognised the signs and forced himself to focus on the fact that Meyer was a criminal, whose product caused untold misery and who was almost certainly responsible for the death of a DEA informer.

They left the restaurant just before midnight. Shepherd assumed they were heading home but Meyer had other ideas. A Mercedes was waiting for them and drove them to a nightclub in the hills overlooking Marbella where another maître d' welcomed them, this one a glamorous blonde in a tight-fitting black dress that showed off a clearly enhanced cleavage. Again it was evident that Meyer was a regular: he and Lisa were kissed and hugged, and Jeeves got a smile. Meyer introduced Shepherd as his good friend Jeff, and Shepherd was rewarded with a kiss on the cheek before she took them to a VIP section, unhooked a red rope and waved them through. They had barely sat down before the first of several bottles of Cristal arrived, each accompanied by a lit sparkler. Meyer and Lisa danced together while Shepherd and Jeeves talked sailing.

It was after two when Meyer eventually called for the bill. Shepherd tried to pay his share but Meyer would have none of it, waving away his money. 'You're my guest, Jeff,' he said. 'End of.'

Shepherd thanked him and put his money away. In the circles Meyer moved in, who paid was a matter of status. The top dog picked up the tab, the beta males expressed the requisite amount of gratitude.

The Mercedes was parked outside, waiting for them. Jeeves sat in the front and Lisa sat between Meyer and Shepherd. As soon as the doors slammed, Lisa put her head against

Meyer's shoulder and fell fast asleep. Meyer grinned over the top of her head at Shepherd and winked. 'She's a lightweight.'

'How many bottles did we drink?' asked Shepherd.

'You can never have enough Cristal,' said Meyer. 'It was a good night.'

'Yeah. I had a blast. Thanks.'

'It's good getting to know you, Jeff,' he said. 'We should have a chat about business opportunities sometime.'

'That'd be great,' said Shepherd. 'I'm not getting any interest here. I was thinking of heading over to Greece, see if I can pick up some charter work there.'

'Don't do anything rash,' said Meyer. 'Give me a chance to put something together.'

Lisa snored softly, then put her arm in Meyer's lap. He laughed. 'Bless her.'

They dropped Shepherd at his hotel before driving over to the marina. He phoned Willoughby-Brown as soon as he got back to his room and brought him up to speed. 'And he didn't mention that he'd pegged you as Rich Campbell?'

'Didn't come up,' said Shepherd.

'I wonder what he's playing at?'

'Maybe he's running more checks. How's the Portsmouth flat?'

'Still secure. And it's not exactly difficult to break into.'

'He did suggest we do business together, so he's definitely interested,' said Shepherd. 'Now, here's a question for you, Jeremy. Has Lisa ever been asked to get a bug on the boat? Get it wired for sound?'

'Not that I know of, but I'm not privy to everything that NCA is doing. Why?'

'It was something Docherty said. Meyer has all his meetings at sea, precisely because he can't be overheard. That means his conversations afloat would be incriminating, for sure. It's why he leaves Lisa ashore when he has business to discuss.'

'So we get a bug on board? That makes sense.'

'The question is, why hasn't it been done already? Was she asked? If she was and she refused, I'd like to know why.'

'There are valid reasons,' said Willoughby-Brown. 'If she got caught, it would be the end of her.'

'Yes, but she comes and goes as she wants, and Meyer clearly trusts her. The NCA has the same sort of technical experts that Five has. I'm sure they could have come up with something that would have done the job. Or rigged her phone. Might be worth asking the question.'

'Could you get a bug on board?'

'That ship has probably sailed,' said Shepherd. He chuckled. 'That was accidental. But the issue is, I'm still the newcomer so there's going to be an element of suspicion. Let's see what happens next. But maybe start thinking about it. Jeeves is always on board so we wouldn't be able to make it anything permanent. It would have to be something portable.'

'I'll put it under consideration,' said Willoughby-Brown. 'What about you wearing a wire?'

'I'm loath to risk that, unless we know for sure he's going to have an incriminating conversation,' said Shepherd. 'It's bloody hot here so we don't wear much in the way of clothing. Plus there's the wind, so anything strapped to your body is going to show at some point.'

'We'll put our thinking caps on,' said Willoughby-Brown. 'What's your plan now?'

'There's nothing much more I can do,' said Shepherd. 'The trap's baited. It's just a question of how tempting the bait is.'

'Nice analogy,' said Willoughby-Brown. 'You be careful.'
'Always,' said Shepherd.

Standing woke at six, spent an hour exercising in Hyde Park, showered and shaved, then had breakfast in Queensway before catching the Tube to Edgware Road. It was the same Pakistani man behind the counter in the phone shop, and the same young assistant who went out back to unlock Faisal's phone, an iPhone 7, but the price had gone up to thirty pounds and again there was no receipt. Standing waited until he got back to his apartment before checking what was on the phone. There were pictures. A lot of pictures. With a lot of different girls. All young. In some the girls, and Faisal, were naked, or semi-naked. Standing's stomach churned as he flicked through them, knowing what he was going to find eventually. When he saw the first naked photograph of Lexi, tears sprang to his eyes and he blinked them away. He threw the phone onto the sofa and stood up, then paced up and down taking deep breaths. After two minutes he sat down and picked up the phone again.

In some of the photographs, Lexi was naked and smiling at the camera, clearly happy at what was going on. There were photographs of her lying on a bed, and in others she was standing next to Faisal in a bathroom. He was holding her with one hand and the camera with the other, taking the picture in a mirror. Lexi was holding him, kissing him, playing with him. In one of the pictures she was on her knees in front of him, clearly giving him oral sex. Standing's hand was shaking and his eyes misted again. He wiped them with the back of his hand.

He took deep breaths to calm himself before he checked the videos on the phone. The most recent was a group of Asian men standing around a bed. They were laughing and jeering. The camera moved through the crowd. There was a figure on the bed. White-skinned. Dark-haired. Standing wanted to look away but he couldn't. The camera moved closer. An Asian man was lying on a girl. A white girl. She was young. Very young. He'd been holding his breath and he let it out when he saw that it wasn't Lexi. The camera went close in on the girl's face. There was a faraway look in her eyes as if she wasn't aware of what was going on, and Standing figured she'd been drugged.

The Asian climbed off the girl to cheers from the crowd. Another man, this one in his sixties, pulled down his trousers and took his place.

Standing stopped the video. There were others, dozens, but he couldn't bring himself to look at them.

His phone rang and he jumped. It was the therapist's office. 'Mr Standing?' said a woman's voice. It wasn't Dr Doyle.

'Yes?'

'This is Dr Doyle's office. I just wanted to check that you were going to be here at eleven.'

Standing cursed under his breath. He'd completely forgotten that he had a therapist's appointment. He looked at his watch. It was ten o'clock. 'Yes, of course I'll be there,' he said. He ended the call, picked up Faisal's phone again and went through the messages. Again, there were hundreds. He scrolled back to the day that Lexi had died. There were several messages to and from a man called Ali. Standing figured that might well be Ali Hussain, one of the owners of the minicab company. When he read the messages he became even more convinced. *Make sure she goes. You have the heroin? Make sure she injects. Is the bitch there yet?* Standing checked the calls log. There had been more than a dozen from Ali during that afternoon, and several from Faisal to Ali. Standing had a sick feeling in his stomach. The two men had clearly been planning something involving Lexi, and he had a horrible feeling that he knew what it was.

He went back to the messages. There were plenty of texts between the two men in recent days, most of them about girls. There was a long conversation with texts back and forth about a girl called Emma. Ali was asking if she was ready and Faisal said she was hooked on heroin and would do as she was told. He had sent pictures of Emma, naked on a bed, either drunk or stoned. In some of the pictures Faisal was sitting next to the girl, pushing an empty Bacardi Breezer bottle between her legs. She looked young. Fourteen or fifteen at the most. Standing gritted his teeth, furious that the cops were allowing this to happen. Part of him wanted to give the phone to Inspector Reynolds but then he would have to explain how he'd got it and that would open up a whole can of worms. He switched it off and put it into the safe, then grabbed his jacket and headed out.

There was a delay on the Tube – someone had thrown themselves under a train at Paddington – so Standing arrived at Dr Doyle's office five minutes late. He apologised profusely to the receptionist, and again to the therapist, but she said, as she sat down in one of the armchairs, 'Getting around London can be problematical at the best of times. Wait until we have another Tube strike. Then you'll see what I mean.'

'Hopefully I won't be here for too long,' he said. 'I want to get back to the Regiment.'

'I understand that,' she said. 'And obviously that's what we're working towards. So, how are you getting on with your anger journal?'

'Yeah. Okay.'

'Did you bring it with you?'

Standing reached into his jacket pocket. He brought out

a small notebook he'd bought from a Ryman's office-supplies store in Queensway and handed it to her. He'd scribbled into it the previous evening, putting a different date at the top of each page and writing down things that he figured she would think he would find upsetting. Things like people pushing in front of him on the Tube, surly shop assistants, waitresses who got his order wrong, music being played too loudly at night when he was trying to sleep. All of it was made up: things like that generally didn't upset him. He wrote how he had reacted to each of the fictional events, and how deep breathing and square breathing had helped him to relax. What he didn't write was that he'd threatened to kill a shopkeeper and sent an Asian child-abuser to his death from the top of a tower block. Some examples of his anger-management issues were best kept to himself.

She nodded as she read through what he'd written. 'This is good, Matt,' she said, approvingly. 'This is very good. And how are you managing with the relaxation exercise I showed you?'

'Yeah, good,' said Standing. In fact, he hadn't bothered even trying it. He felt there was no need. He fell asleep as quickly and as easily as he woke up. When he was tired he went to bed and slept. It was as simple as that. He put his head on the pillow, closed his eyes, and within minutes he was fast asleep. He assumed that she thought someone with anger-management issues would lie awake at night tossing and turning but he had never had any problems on that score. It was partly the nature of being in the SAS. On operations you were never sure when you'd get the chance to eat or to sleep, so you grabbed the opportunity whenever it presented itself. 'I'm surprised at how well it worked.' If he was going to lie to her, he might as well go the whole way.

She nodded happily and jotted in her notepad. 'That's

good to hear,' she said. She finished writing, looked up, and smiled. 'This time I thought I'd show you another exercise. This one is much shorter but it can be just as effective.'

'I'm all ears,' said Standing.

She stood up, put her pen and notepad on her chair and motioned for him to join her. 'So, first you stand up straight and tall. As if you were on parade. But let your arms hang naturally by your side.'

Standing did as he was told.

'Now, breathe in slowly through your nose, but as you do that I want you to tense all the muscles in your body. Every muscle. So clench your fists, pull your stomach in, clench your buttocks, hunch your shoulders and go up onto your tiptoes. Sort of make out you're the Incredible Hulk.'

He tried to do as she described but he felt ridiculous and started laughing.

She laughed with him. 'I know, I know! This is an exercise you're going to want to do in private,' she said. 'But you need to tense everything and hold it for a count of five. Then breathe out and relax back into your original standing position.' She showed him how to do it and he couldn't help but smile.

'I know how stupid it looks,' she said. 'But, trust me, it can help relax you in a very short space of time. Three to five repetitions should do it.'

Shepherd's phone rang. It was Meyer. It was early afternoon and Shepherd was in his room, watching an in-house movie and nursing a hangover.

'What's your pool like, Jeff?' Meyer asked.

'There isn't one,' said Shepherd.

'That's a pity, I fancy a swim. How about the sea? You up for a swim?'

It was a strange request, so Shepherd assumed that Meyer wanted something more than a dip. 'Yeah, sure.'

'Meet you on the beach outside your hotel? Ten minutes?'

'Sounds like a plan,' said Shepherd.

Meyer ended the call and Shepherd phoned Docherty. 'Meyer wants to meet on the beach dressed for swimming, so I figure he wants to make sure I'm not wearing a wire, which means he wants to tell me something.'

'I'll make sure to get some pictures,' said Docherty.

'What about Jeeves and the girl?'

'Jeeves is working on the boat, the girl's sunbathing. Topless, as it happens. I've some very nice pictures I can show you.'

'Please don't,' said Shepherd. He ended the call and went over to the wardrobe. He'd bought a pair of shorts and a couple of shirts soon after he'd arrived in Marbella, along with underwear and socks. One of the pairs of shorts was suitable for swimming so he slipped them on and chose a Lacoste short-sleeved shirt. The beach was right outside so he decided to go barefoot. His watch was waterproof but it was chunky and he figured it might make Meyer nervous so he put it into the safe.

Meyer was waiting for him on the beach wearing tight red trunks that left little to the imagination. It was the first time Shepherd had seen him without a shirt and he noticed a puckered scar near to his left shoulder, like an old bullet wound. Meyer grinned when he saw Shepherd was looking at it. 'A war wound,' he said.

'What was it, nine mil?' asked Shepherd.

Meyer nodded.

'Nasty.'

'You should see the other guy,' said Meyer. He laughed harshly. 'Actually, you can't. He's dead.'

'Was it a gunfight?'

Meyer shook his head. 'Came out of the blue. Did a deal with a couple of scallies who came up short on the cash front. They thought it'd be cheaper to pay someone to kill me than come through with the money they owed. Big mistake.' He gestured at the sea. 'Come on, let's have a swim.'

Shepherd took off his shirt and Meyer's eyes widened when he saw the scar under Shepherd's right shoulder. 'Fuck me, that's a bullet wound, all right. That's huge.'

'Yeah. Tell me about it.'

'Who shot you?'

'Taliban,' said Shepherd, dropping his shirt onto the sand.

'In Iraq?'

'Afghanistan.'

'What sort of gun was it?'

Shepherd shrugged. 'Who the fuck knows?' Actually he knew all too well what had done the damage. He still had the round in a drawer somewhere in his house in Hereford. It was a 5.45mm round from a Kalashnikov AK-74. The AK-74 was a small-calibre version of the AK-47, initially developed for parachute troops but had eventually become the standard Russian infantry rifle.

Meyer frowned. 'There's no exit wound,' he said.

'The doc took it out from the front,' said Shepherd. 'It hit the bone and went downwards. I was lucky – it could have severed an artery and I wouldn't have been here today.'

'If you'd been really lucky, the shot would have missed,' said Meyer. 'So how does a sailor end up in Afghanistan being shot at by the Taliban?'

'It's a long story.'

'You didn't mention it.'

'It was another life, Marcus.'

'Did you get a medal for it?'

Shepherd laughed. 'No, I didn't.'

Meyer slapped him on the back.' Come on, let's see how far out we can go.'

'I'm not the world's best swimmer,' said Shepherd.

He followed Meyer into the water. As soon as it reached their waists, Meyer drove forward and began to swim in an energetic crawl. Shepherd went after him, but using a brisk breaststroke. He wasn't a fan of swimming, as exercise or recreation. He enjoyed running, and ran for fun as much as for fitness, but it always seemed to him that swimming was something you did when you fell off a boat. Meyer was pulling away from him so Shepherd switched to a crawl. Meyer was swimming directly away from the beach and didn't seem to be slowing. Shepherd breathed evenly, putting his face into the water every second stroke, and concentrated on maintaining a steady pace. He had no idea how long he could swim because it wasn't something he did regularly. He knew exactly how long he could run, and at what speed, and in his SAS days he'd known how long he could march, depending on the speed of the march and the weight on his back. But swimming was alien to him and his arms were already tiring.

Meyer continued at his pace, cutting cleanly through the water, still heading away from the beach. Shepherd switched to breaststroke. His legs were stronger and more efficient than his arms so it made sense to let them do most of the work.

When they were well out to sea, Meyer trod water and waited for Shepherd to catch up with him. 'You okay, Jeff?' he asked.

'All good,' said Shepherd.

'Tired?'

'Getting there. I guess you're not worried about sharks.'

'Sharks? There's no sharks here.'

'There are almost fifty species of shark in the Mediterranean,' said Shepherd. 'Including the Great White.'

'Are you sure?'

'Sure I'm sure.' He grinned. 'But they don't usually attack. We'll be fine.'

Meyer began swimming again, this time parallel to the shore, away from the marina. He was still doing the crawl, but slower than before, and Shepherd's breaststroke was enough to keep up with him. Off to their left a speedboat roared by. Shepherd hadn't been joking about sharks, but attacks in the Mediterranean were rare. There was much more chance of being mown down by a fast-moving boat.

Meyer was slowing, and Shepherd got the impression he'd been showing off before. They were still half a mile from the shore. If Meyer didn't turn back soon he might run into problems. 'Marcus, I'm fucking knackered!' shouted Shepherd. 'Can we head back?'

Meyer trod water. 'You wimp!' he yelled.

'Yeah, I know,' said Shepherd. 'What can you do?'

Meyer laughed and swam back towards the beach. Shepherd followed. His breaststroke was still relaxed and methodical, and he reckoned he could maintain the pace for at least another hour. But Meyer's crawl had become scrappy and undisciplined, and Shepherd could hear his laboured breathing. He kept back. This was about face. Meyer was the alpha male in the relationship and he wouldn't be happy if Shepherd had to rescue him.

The shore was getting closer, which seemed to spur Meyer on. He was gasping for breath now and his hands were slapping into the waves instead of cutting cleanly through them. Shepherd gained on him, ready to intervene if Meyer ran into problems, but after a couple of dozen strokes the water was shallow enough for them to stand. Meyer turned and grinned, though he was breathing heavily. Shepherd pretended to be more tired than he was. 'I'm out of condition,' he panted.

'You did great,' said Meyer. Meyer slapped him on the back and they walked the rest of the way to the beach, then on to where Shepherd had left his shirt.

'You know, you can tell me the truth,' said Meyer, shading his eyes from the fierce sun.

'About what?'

'About everything,' said Meyer. 'We could be a big help to each other. You know, you scratch my back and I'll scratch yours.'

'You've lost me, Marcus.'

Meyer chuckled. 'Do you think I'm stupid?'

'No, of course not. Why do you say that?'

'Okay, let me run this by you. I don't think for one minute that Jeff Taylor was shot in Afghanistan. But I do think Rich Campbell might have stopped a bullet.'

Shepherd stopped, feigning surprise. 'How the fuck . . .?' He left the sentence unfinished.

Meyer stopped too. 'Oh, come on, Rich. I didn't get where I am today without knowing a thing or two. I run checks. I checked you out.'

'Who else knows?'

Meyer patted his face. 'Don't worry, your secret's safe with me.'

'How did you find out?'

'I just did. Let's leave it at that.'

Shepherd shook his head. 'Fuck, if it was that easy for you to find out, anyone can.'

'Give me some respect,' said Meyer. 'Not everyone has the contacts I have.'

'How much do you know?'

'Pretty well everything. I know you changed your name because there's a price on your head. But your Jeff Taylor identity is solid. Unless you check your fingerprints. Once they're on file, they're there for ever.'

'That's what you did? You checked my prints? For fuck's sake.'

'Relax, Rich. Actually, fuck it, I'm calling you Jeff. You're Jeff to me. But it's Rich I'd like to do business with.'

He started walking across the sand again and Shepherd hurried after him. 'What do you mean?'

'You must have guessed by now that I'm not exactly a legitimate businessman. I've got a few irons in the fire, and I could do with a former squaddie turned bank robber turned sailor. I've got a job for you, if you're interested. It'll make full use of your talents.'

'Exactly what talents do you have in mind, Marcus?'

'Sailing. Plus you obviously don't care about breaking the odd law.'

'Drugs?'

'Are you okay with that?'

'What sort of drugs?'

'Drugs are drugs,' laughed Meyer.

'No, they're not,' said Shepherd. 'Not when it comes to sentencing.'

'Fair comment,' said Meyer. 'It's cocaine. Colombian cocaine. The best. But it's hidden so well that your chances of being discovered are practically zero.'

Shepherd pulled a face. He didn't want to appear over-eager. The harder Meyer had to try, the more he'd trust Shepherd. 'Practically zero means there's still a chance of getting caught. And cocaine means serious prison time.'

'Not the way I do it,' said Meyer. 'Let me at least show you what I have in mind.'

'Here?'

'The Caribbean. St Lucia.'

'And how do we get there?'

'I'm going in a few days. I'll meet you there. I'll show you my set-up and you can decide if you want to go for it or not.'

'And how much do I get?'

'How much do you want?'

Shepherd frowned. 'How much of the drug are we talking about?'

'Does that matter? You'll never see the gear – it's built into the boat. Could be a kilo, could be a ton.'

'A ton of cocaine?'

'Maybe. Maybe not. The less you know, the less you have to deny.'

'Marcus, a ton of cocaine has a street value of millions.'

'Sure. But street value and true value are two different things. But, yeah, we're talking big money.'

'So I'd get – what? A million?'

Meyer laughed and patted him on the back. 'Let's talk about it in St Lucia,' he said. 'But, trust me, I'll make it worth your while.'

Shepherd nodded thoughtfully. 'Okay. That sounds fair.'

'Excellent,' said Meyer. 'You make your own way there and I'll book you a room in the Capella Marigot Bay. You'll like it. The service is second to none.'

'What about you? Where will you stay?'

'I'll have a boat.'

'You always stay on boats?'

'More often than not. Boats are way more secure, so long as you have them swept and you know everyone on board. On that subject, there's something I have to tell you.'

Shepherd wondered if Meyer was about to talk about his

sexuality, so he prepared himself to show the requisite amount of surprise.

Meyer leaned closer to him, as if he feared being overheard 'Watch yourself with Lucy.'

Shepherd raised his eyebrows, wondering what Meyer meant. Did he know what had happened in his hotel room? 'In what way?' he said, trying to keep his voice steady and relaxed.

'For a start, her name's not Lucy Kemp. It's Lisa Wilson.'

Shepherd's heart raced but he forced himself to stay calm, even though he knew what was coming next. He stopped walking and put his hands on his hips. 'You're winding me up.'

Meyer stood in front of him. 'She's a fucking cop. I kid you not.'

'No fucking way.'

Meyer nodded. 'NCA. National Crime Agency. I found out about two weeks ago,'

'What the fuck are you playing at?' said Shepherd. 'Does she know who I am?'

Meyer patted his shoulder. 'Don't worry, she thinks you're Jeff Taylor. I've kept the Rich Campbell thing to myself.'

'If she finds out who I am, I'm fucked.'

'She won't find out, stop worrying. I had you checked out by a guy in the Liverpool cops who works for me. She doesn't know.'

'This is ridiculous. She's a cop? An undercover cop? Why the fuck is she still around? You need to get rid of her.'

Meyer grinned. 'Come on, you know what the Mafia say, don't you? Keep your friends close and your enemies closer. She's a conduit to the cops, so I know exactly what she can and can't tell them. I know what information she has access to and what she hasn't. If I get rid of her, they might replace her, and next time I might not spot the grass. So I keep her on a short lead and all's well with the world.'

'Except she's a fucking cop!'

Meyer grinned. 'Well, yes. But better the devil you know, right?'

Shepherd shook his head. 'You're playing with fire. And I'm the one that could get burned.'

'Your secret's safe with me,' said Meyer. 'I know exactly what she sees and hears. I'm careful what I tell her. A couple of times I've used her to funnel stuff back to the NCA that'll cause problems to my competitors. It's all good.'

'How is it all good? She knows I'm with you. What's to say she hasn't told her bosses?'

'Told them what? That a jobbing sailor called Jeff Taylor saved her and me from a couple of muggers and has been hanging out with us?'

'And talking about smuggling drugs?'

'In general terms. And it'll only be her word against ours. You've seen the clothes she wears, there's no room for a recording device. Not in those swimsuits.'

'Conspiracy to import drugs? And what if we do start moving gear? If she finds out and we get caught . . . Fuck me, mate, they'll throw away the key.'

'She doesn't know anything. Trust me.'

'I do trust you. I wouldn't be considering going into business with you if I didn't. But I can't afford to be hanging around with an undercover cop.'

'It won't be for long,' said Meyer.

'What do you mean?'

Meyer pulled a face. 'Look, I'm not that happy about what's happened. When I found out, my first thought was to tie a concrete block around her legs and throw her overboard. It wouldn't be the first time, either. But who's she got watching her, especially in Europe? If I try anything there could be a SWAT team up my arse in next to no time.'

'So just tell her to fuck off.'

'And, like I said, if I do that I'll always be looking over my shoulder. Look, between you and me, I'm going to be taking care of it. Sooner rather than later. But I'll do it so there's no possibility of any comeback. Until then, just be careful what you say when she's around.'

'When you say take care of it, what do you mean?' asked Shepherd.

Meyer tapped the side of his nose conspiratorially. 'Need to know,' he said.

Surveillance was all well and good but there were times when all the watching in the world wouldn't do you any good and the only thing to do was to launch a full frontal assault. Standing knew that Ali Hussain was one of the owners of a minicab firm in Kilburn, and one of the leaders of the child-grooming ring. And, from the text messages between him and Faisal, it was clear he'd supplied the heroin that had killed Lexi. But Standing had no idea what Hussain looked like, other than that he was a middle-aged Asian, a description that probably fitted a quarter of the residents of Kilburn. He'd tried looking for Ali Hussain on Facebook but there were hundreds to choose from. Checking the electoral roll was equally unproductive: there were just two many men with that name.

The cab office was easy enough to find. It was above a hairdresser's, with its own entrance on the street, an open door with a flashing light above it and a sign that said 'MINICABS'. Surveillance was easy enough: there was a bus stop opposite and Standing spent an hour there, watching the comings and goings. He had bought a well-worn dark green parka with a fur-lined hood and had an Iceland carrier bag with a few provisions in it.

At any one time there were up to half a dozen minicabs parked near the office, mainly in a nearby side-street. Asian men were constantly coming and going, and any one of them could have been Hussain. Customers also came and went, walking up the wooden stairs to make a booking, then re-appearing, sometimes accompanied by a driver, others meeting him on the pavement. The firm was clearly busy and employed a lot of drivers, virtually all of them bearded Asians. Standing realised pretty quickly that no matter how long he sat and watched, he'd never be able to spot Ali Hussain.

The foot traffic fell off about midday, presumably as some of the drivers went for lunch, and Standing decided to make his move. He pulled his hood up, crossed the road and headed up the stairs. The last three drivers he'd seen go up had all come down, and he hadn't seen any customers go in. At the top he found another door with a metal-barred window at head height and a sign above that repeated the message downstairs – 'MINICABS'. A CCTV camera pointed at the door and Standing kept his head down.

There was an intercom set into the wall and he pressed the green button at the bottom. Almost immediately the lock buzzed and he pushed the door open. There were two desks to his left, and on the wall behind them a large whiteboard with names and car registration numbers, presumably the drivers who were working. Two Asian men sat behind the desks, one wearing a headset, both looking at computer screens. The guy with the headset was chattering away in Urdu. Standing couldn't speak the language but he recognised it when he heard it.

To the right, a cheap plastic sofa had once been white or

cream but had turned a grubby grey over the years. In front of it was a pine coffee-table with a dozen or so empty fast-food containers on it. An Asian man in his fifties was sitting on the sofa, shovelling curry into his mouth,

The man who wasn't talking looked at Standing. His beard was greying and his skin was wrinkled, like old leather. He was wearing a white topi skullcap. 'You want a cab?' he asked.

'I want to talk to Ali Hussain,' said Standing. There was a door at the far end of the room. It opened, and he saw it led into a toilet. A bearded Asian wearing baggy *salwar kameez* came out and sat on the sofa. The man with the headset was still talking but the other three were all gazing at Standing.

'What about?' said the man with the skullcap.

'I owe him some money,' said Standing.

'How much?'

'Fifty quid.'

'You can leave it here,' said the man. 'I'll make sure he gets it.'

'I want to give it to him personally,' said Standing. 'What time does he come in?'

The man shrugged. 'Difficult to say.'

'But he's an owner, right?'

'The man shrugged again but didn't say anything.

'So what do you think? When will Ali be here?'

The man waved his hands. 'You should just go. You are wasting your time here.'

Standing continued to smile at the man, but turned slightly so he wouldn't see him slip his hand into his pocket. He had pre-set Faisal's phone so that all he had to do was touch the screen to call Ali Hussain's number. 'I guess I'll come back later,' he said.

'Up to you,' said the man. He looked at the two men sitting on the sofa and spoke to them in Urdu. They got up and faced Standing. The younger man was holding a plastic fork and Standing smiled, wondering if he was planning to stab him with it.

'I'll be off,' he said. 'If Ali does come in, tell him Peter was looking for him.'

'Peter,' repeated the man. His phone began to vibrate on his desk and he looked down at it. He frowned when he saw who was calling.

Standing pressed the screen to end the call and almost immediately the phone stopped vibrating. He headed for the door, keeping his head down to avoid the CCTV camera.

Shepherd waited until he was back in his hotel room before phoning Willoughby-Brown. 'We've got a problem, Jeremy.'

'I'm listening,' said Willoughby-Brown.

'Meyer knows who Lisa is. He knows her name and he knows she's an undercover cop.'

'That's impossible,' said Willoughby-Brown.

'No, it makes perfect sense,' said Shepherd. 'Somehow he found out who she is and that's why her intel has dried up.'

'And you know this how?'

'Because he just bloody well told me. Said I shouldn't say too much while she's around because she's an undercover cop working for the NCA.'

'Then why is she still there?'

'Keep your friends close and your enemies closer.'

'Bastard,' said Willoughby-Brown, under his breath.

'He's planning on killing her,' said Shepherd. 'We need to pull her out.'

'We can't do that. She doesn't work for us.'

'Then tell Sam Hargrove. Tell him that Meyer is on to her and that he has to bring her back.'

'What exactly did Meyer say?'

'First he said he wants to see me in St Lucia. Says he wants us to work together.'

'So he's bitten? That's great news. Well done, you.'

'Yes, but in the same breath he said he knew Lisa works for the NCA and that I should be careful what I say around her. Then he said he was going to take care of it.'

'Which could mean anything. It doesn't mean he plans to kill her. Let's be honest, he knows she's a cop and he knows the trouble he'll be in if he kills a police officer.'

'When you first put me on this case you said that Meyer had killed a DEA informant.'

'I said the informant had disappeared and that it was possible Meyer had killed him, yes.'

'So she's in danger. Look, we know now that Lisa hasn't gone over to the dark side. She's not sleeping with Meyer and she's not helping him. She's doing her job to the best of her ability but because Meyer has rumbled her she's not getting any worthwhile intel. It's time to pull her out.'

'No can do, Daniel,' said Willoughby-Brown. 'How's it going to look? Meyer tells you she's a cop and hours later she heads for the hills. He's going to realise PDQ that you tipped her off.'

Shepherd cursed under his breath, knowing that Willoughby-Brown had a point. If they pulled Lisa out he'd have to leave too, which meant the whole operation would amount to nothing.

'I'm assuming from your lack of a snappy comeback that you've realised I'm right,' said Willoughby-Brown.

'We need to watch her.'

'Well, you can't. You're off to St Lucia.'

'I'm well aware of that, Jeremy. But somebody needs to watch her, especially when I'm away. What about Docherty? He's got a room overlooking the marina. He can keep an eye on her.'

'I'm getting the bills, Daniel. He's got a three-bedroom suite.'

'It's perfect for watching Meyer's boat.'

'If Meyer does kill Lisa, he's hardly going to do it on the deck, is he?'

'She needs back-up,' said Shepherd. 'Or she needs to be told what's going on. Her cover has been blown but she doesn't know.'

'I hear what you're saying. But I doubt he's going to do anything over the next couple of days, by which time you'll be in St Lucia and, assuming he has the drugs there, he can be arrested.'

'He never goes near the drugs, you said.'

'If the drugs are in the boat, and he's there, asking you to sail it to Europe, that's all we need. Look, I can see you're worried and I understand your reservations, so I'll talk to Docherty. I'll make sure he has her back while she's in Spain. You're already booked on the flight to St Lucia?'

'It's sorted,' said Shepherd. 'I'll be there tomorrow.'

'What about Meyer? When's he going?'

'He wasn't specific.'

'But he's flying, right? It'll take weeks by boat.'

'No, he's flying. He was just vague about the details.'

'I'll have a watch put on all the scheduled flights but it's going to be harder if he goes private. But I'm on it. What about Wilson? Will she be going with him?'

'That's what I don't know,' said Shepherd. 'My worry is that he does something to her before he flies out to St Lucia.'

There was a knock on his door. 'I've got to go.' He ended the call and crossed the room. He checked the peephole and cursed under his breath when he saw it was Lisa. He took a deep breath, forced himself to smile, then opened the door.

She was holding a bottle of Cristal and wearing a short low-cut dress over a dark bikini so that the outline showed through. Her high heels brought her head up to his chin and she grinned up at him. 'I come bearing gifts.' From the look of it she'd already had a fair bit to drink.

'Are you sure this a good idea?' he said. He peered into the empty corridor behind her. 'Where's Marcus?'

'He had someone to see,' she said. 'Are you going to let me in or not because this bottle is heavy.'

Shepherd held out his hand and she gave him the champagne. 'You took this from *Windchaser*?' he asked.

She nodded. 'Marcus is fast asleep, Jeeves is AWOL and I really don't want to drink alone.'

Shepherd waved her in and closed the door. There were four glasses on top of the minibar, though no champagne flutes. He took the two wine glasses while Lisa deftly popped the cork. She poured champagne and they both drank. 'So you're going to St Lucia?' she asked.

'Did Marcus tell you that?'

'Sure. We'll be out in a few days. Are you going to work for him?'

Shepherd sipped his champagne as his mind raced. Had Meyer really told her about the job offer? Why would he do that if he didn't trust her?

'What's wrong? Did you think it was a secret?'

Shepherd forced a laugh. 'Of course not. It's just we haven't got to that stage yet. We're just talking.'

'He likes you,' said Lisa. 'And he trusts you. And I can tell you he doesn't trust everybody.'

Shepherd sat down on the sofa and put his feet up on the coffee-table. He still wasn't sure why she'd come to his room and he needed to tread carefully. 'I've not had much joy work-wise so, yeah, it could be a Godsend.'

She dropped down onto the sofa next to him and crossed her legs towards him so that one was brushing his. 'Big money, right?'

'I guess so.'

'He didn't tell you?'

'It's early days.'

She put out a hand and ran it along his thigh. Shepherd's mind was racing. What the hell was going on? He doubted that Meyer had sent her, which meant it had been her decision to come on to him. But why would she do that? Was she working him? Was she trying to get information from him to send back to the NCA? 'I sort of hope you won't take the job,' she said.

'Why's that?'

'It's fun having you around. If you do this thing for him, you'll be at sea for weeks, right?'

'I guess so.'

'Did he say where you'd be sailing to?'

Shepherd looked into her eyes. She smiled back at him as if she didn't have a care in the world but he realised she was working him, probing for details of exactly what he was going to be doing for Meyer.

'I'm assuming Europe,' said Shepherd. 'He'll explain everything to me there, he said.'

She sipped her champagne, then slowly scraped her fingernails along his neck. 'I'll miss you,' she said.

'Yeah, I'll miss you too,' he said. 'Are you not going to St Lucia?'

'No, I'm going,' she said. 'Marcus is booking the flights. But he's got some Colombians he needs to talk to.'

'They can be dangerous, Colombians.'

'Is that the voice of experience?'

'No, but I read. They kill people, right? A lot of people?'

'That's what they say.' She laughed. 'But the ones Marcus deals with seem okay.'

'I think they're all okay until the day they decide to put a bullet in you.'

'He's never let them down,' she said. 'And he makes them a shedload of money.'

'He does a lot with them, does he?'

'When Marcus does a shipment, it's tons, Jeff. Tons of cocaine. He doesn't fuck around.'

Shepherd nodded. 'That's what I thought.'

'And he pays his captains good money, too. What has he offered you?'

'Still under negotiation,' he said.

She squeezed his leg. 'Don't sell yourself cheaply,' she said.

'I won't.'

She leaned over and kissed him. He was expecting the move but she still caught him by surprise and, despite himself, he responded. She reached up and slipped her dress down over her shoulders, then unclipped her bikini top to allow her breasts to swing free. Shepherd broke away. 'What are you doing?'

'What does it look like I'm doing?'

She tried to kiss him again but this time he gently pushed her away. 'This isn't a good idea,' he said.

'Are you serious?'

'I know it sounds crazy, but yes. I don't think Marcus would be happy if we did . . . you know . . .'

Her jaw dropped. 'Are you telling me you want to ask Marcus's permission before you fuck me?'

Shepherd laughed. 'When you say it like that, it sounds ridiculous, I know. But he's offered me a job, Lucy. A big job. And it comes down to trust. If he finds that I went behind his back he's not going to trust me.'

'You're not going behind his back. I keep telling you, me and him, there's nothing between us. He's gay, for fuck's sake.' She stood up and held her arms to the side. Her dress slipped even further down. 'Do you have any idea how many men want to get into my pants? And here I am, offering it to you on a plate.'

Shepherd couldn't help but look at her breasts. 'Believe me, no one is more tempted than I am, right now.'

'Men offer me money, Jeff. A lot of money.'

'You know that's not a good thing, right?'

She groaned in frustration and sat down again. 'Do you have any idea how long it's been since I got laid?' she said.

'I'm guessing a while.'

She rolled over so that she was sitting on his lap, her legs either side of his. 'I'm horny, Jeff. And I like you.'

'I like you, too.'

She looked into his eyes with a fierce intensity. 'No, I really like you.'

'I really like you, too.'

She put her hands either side of his face and kissed him. His lips parted and her tongue slid between them, and she pressed her groin down against his. He felt himself grow hard and found himself returning the kiss. She broke away, grinning. 'See? You do want me.'

'Of course I do. That's not the issue. The issue is that I'm working for Marcus and I'm not going to do anything behind his back. Let's wait until we're in St Lucia, at least.'

'For fuck's sake!'

'It'll be more romantic. I won't be worried that Marcus is going to phone at any moment.'

She groaned again and flounced off the sofa. 'You know what I'm going to do, Jeff?' she asked.

'I have absolutely no idea.'

'I'm going back to the boat to take care of myself.'

'Okay.'

'And if Jeeves is around, it might just be his lucky day.'

Shepherd held up his glass. 'You enjoy yourself.'

She growled at him, like an angry tigress. 'You're seriously not going to fuck me?'

'Not today.'

She stamped her foot in frustration, refastened her bikini top and pulled up her dress, then walked to the door, her high heels clicking on the wooden floor. She pulled the door open and turned to glare at him. 'St Lucia?'

'Yes.'

'You'd better not back out,' she said, pointing at him. 'Because I will kill you.'

Shepherd grinned, despite the threat, and she blew him a kiss. 'St Lucia,' she said, and then she was gone. Shepherd sighed and put down his glass. He really didn't like the taste of champagne and if anything it made him feel even thirstier. He went over to the minibar, took out a bottle of Evian water and drank it as he gazed out of the window. He couldn't see the marina from his room, but he wondered if she was really going back to the boat, and what she planned to do. Under other circumstances he'd be flattered, and amused, but this wasn't funny. She didn't know he was there to investigate her, or that Meyer knew her true identity and was planning to kill her. The next few days were going to be fraught with danger and he knew he was walking on a knife-edge. He couldn't tell Willoughby-Brown what had happened because it would pretty much end her career, and if he mentioned it to Meyer, he would probably decide to do something to her sooner rather than later. Shepherd had to keep what had happened under wraps, and just hope that everything was resolved in St Lucia before she made another move.

★   ★   ★

Standing pulled on a sweatshirt, shorts and his trainers, and headed for Hyde Park. It was early – it hadn't yet turned seven – and the park was quiet so he spotted the two men almost immediately. They were in their late twenties and were wearing tracksuits that seemed to be brand new with gleaming white Nikes. They had short haircuts, which suggested they were military, and wraparound sunglasses that were out of place under the clouds that blanketed the city. They were running together, their paces perfectly synchronised.

Standing headed away from them. He always preferred to run alone and to set his own pace. He jogged for a while, then did a series of sprints to get his heart rate up, then dropped and did press-ups and sit-ups for a couple of minutes. When he got back on his feet the two men had changed direction and were now heading his way. It wasn't a coincidence, he was sure, and he also didn't think they wanted to chat about the merits of Nike versus Adidas.

He started jogging. There was no point in running away because if they wanted to talk to him they'd get to him sooner rather than later. At least the park was in daylight and the tight running gear they were wearing suggested they weren't carrying weapons. It would be a different story if it was night and they had on bulky coats. He ran south, towards Knightsbridge.

They came up behind him and matched his pace, one either side. Standing looked at the man on his right. A little over six feet, square chin, pug nose, bulging forearms. He was staring straight ahead. 'How's it going?' asked Standing.

The man continued to stare in front of him. 'So far so good,' he said. Scottish accent. Glasgow, probably.

Standing looked to his left. The other was a little under six foot, an inch taller than himself. The guy nodded. 'Nice day for it,' he said. Midlands. Birmingham or Wolverhampton.

He had a swimmer's build, wide shoulders and narrow waist, and short, curly hair.

Standing accelerated and cut to the left, but the two men matched his pace easily. Neither was breathing heavily and both seemed to have no problem keeping up with him. They ran together for two minutes before they reached one of the tarmac roads that criss-crossed the park. Standing turned and ran along the road. The men ran with him.

'Isn't it about time you went back to Hereford, Former Sergeant Standing?' asked Pug Nose.

'I'm on leave,' said Standing.

'London isn't good for your health,' said Curly Hair. 'Time for you to pack your bags and leave.'

Standing stopped. The two men stopped too, one either side. 'Who the fuck are you?' he asked.

'That's not the issue,' said Curly Hair, jogging on the spot. Pug Nose had started stretching. Just three exercise junkies taking a break.

'You're not cops, obviously. So you're spooks? Five? Six?'

'As my colleague said, that's not relevant,' said Pug Nose. 'You carry on the way you've been carrying on and your career will be over.'

'It's not going that great at the moment anyway, truth be told,' said Standing.

'Yeah, well, imagine how much worse it will get if you have a conviction for assault.'

Standing shrugged. 'If you were cops you'd have arrested me by now,' he said. 'So if you're not cops, my being arrested for assault isn't an issue. Anyway, who do you think I've assaulted?'

'A few cops, for a start. And the guy who runs that shop in Kilburn.' He looked over at Curly Hair. 'And what was the name of the man he threw off that tower block?'

'Faisal,' said Curly Hair. 'Faisal Khan. But that wasn't assault, was it? That was murder.'

'That's right,' said Pug Nose. 'Murder it was. How about that, Former Sergeant Standing? What would a murder conviction do to your career prospects?'

'No idea what you're talking about, mate,' said Standing.

Pug Nose grinned at Curly Hair. 'Hear that? He's no idea what we're talking about.'

Curly Hair nodded. 'Yeah. Did you bring your PowerPoint so we can bring him up to speed?'

Pug Nose patted himself down. 'Completely forgot it,' he said.

'It's not your lucky day, Standing,' said Curly Hair. 'Seems like you're just going to have to take our word for it. We know you threw Faisal off that roof, and if you don't get the fuck out of London, your Regiment is going to know.'

'If you think I killed anyone, just call the cops.'

'We don't want this made public,' said Pug Nose.

'And why's that?' asked Standing.

'Because we fucking don't,' said Curly Hair. 'Just take that as read.'

Standing stood with his hands on his hips. They had a confidence about them that suggested they weren't scared of being physical. They'd been well trained, he was sure of that. But there was training and there was combat, and the two weren't the same. 'So are you the guys who scared off the cops?' he asked.

Pug Nose put up his hands. 'Whoa, now you're throwing out allegations.'

'Yeah, you shouldn't be doing that,' said Curly Hair.

'Or was it one of your bosses? Did a guy in a suit have dinner with the assistant chief constable and have a quiet word over the port and cigars? Tell the troops to keep away from Hussain and his child-grooming ring?'

'Just pack up and go, Standing,' said Pug Nose. 'Stop asking questions, stop making waves, stop poking your nose in where it's not wanted.'

'Or else?'

Pug Nose frowned as if he hadn't understood what Standing had said.

'I'm serious,' said Standing. 'What the fuck are you going to do to persuade me? If there was any sort of case to be made against me, it'd be the cops making it. My career? Fuck, I'm not sure I even have a career, but you having a word with the Regiment isn't going to make a difference either way. So I'll ask you again. Or else?'

'What are you trying to achieve,' asked Curly Hair, 'running around like a loose cannon? Where does it get you?'

'It gets the man who killed my sister. That's what it gets me.'

'Your sister was a junkie who overdosed on heroin,' said Pug Nose.

Standing's eyes hardened as he stared at the man but he didn't say anything.

'She killed herself,' said Pug Nose. 'You know that. The cops told you. And it's the truth.'

'Why do you care?' asked Standing. 'What's it to you? What is so fucking important that you want the cops off and get heavy with me?'

'Let's just say it's a matter of national security and leave it at that,' said Curly Hair. 'But you're to drop it, and drop it now.'

'Or else?' said Standing.

'This isn't the fucking playground,' said Pug Nose. He pushed Standing's shoulder, hard enough to knock him back. 'Just do as you're fucking told.'

'Don't touch me,' said Standing. 'Do not lay your hands on me.'

Pug Nose grinned at Curly Hair. 'They do like to talk big, the SAS, don't they? The problem is they believe their own publicity. I've never met one yet who could do anything without a Heckler in their hands.'

Curly Hair laughed. 'They can do that swinging-through-windows thing, though. They're good at that. Like fucking monkeys.'

Both men laughed. Standing turned away. Pug Nose grabbed his left arm and Standing reacted immediately, chopping him across the throat with his right hand and then, when the man stepped back, following up with two quick punches to the solar plexus.

Curly Hair tried to grab Standing around the neck but Standing dropped and threw him over his shoulder, slamming him onto the ground. He stamped on the man's elbow with his heel, cracking it like a dry twig. Pug Nose straightened, cursing, and threw a punch at Standing. He ducked under it, hit him twice again in the stomach, then stepped forward and kneed him in the balls. Pug Nose dropped like a stone and fell next to Curly Hair. Standing was still moving and he stamped on the man's left knee, splintering the cartilage. Only then did he stop. He looked down at them, breathing slowly and evenly. The whole incident had taken just a few seconds. The park was still relatively empty and no one had seen what had happened. Standing jogged away, heading for Queensway. They hadn't mentioned his visit to the cab office, and he wondered why not. Maybe they didn't know he'd been there. Or maybe they did but didn't want him to know that they knew. You could never tell with spooks.

★　　★　　★

Shepherd walked into the arrivals area and frowned when he saw Willoughby-Brown waiting for him. 'Are you going to make a habit of meeting me at airports?' he asked.

'Something's just come up,' said Willoughby-Brown. He was wearing the same coat he'd had on the last time Shepherd had seen him. 'I need you in London for a day or two. And Hereford.'

'Are you serious? Meyer wants me in St Lucia. I'm in and out of London, I'm not supposed to be hanging around.'

'He's still in Marbella. You've got time.'

'I need to be close to Lisa. She's in danger, Jeremy, and she doesn't know it. Has she filed anything recently?'

'Not that I'm aware of. Why?'

'She was grilling me for intel before I left. Felt like she was working me. I need to know what she's passed back to the NCA.'

'There might be a time lag. But I'll check.'

'And this other thing can't wait?'

'It won't take long. Then you can get off to St Lucia and play the White Knight.'

'What's so bloody important?'

'I'll explain in the car.'

'Car? Where am I going?'

'Battersea. The heliport. I've arranged a flight to Hereford. Look on the bright side, Daniel. You'll be able to spend time with the au pair.'

Willoughby-Brown took Shepherd out of the terminal and along to the short-term car park, where a van was waiting with the engine running. The side door slid back to reveal four large leather armchairs at either side of a table. There was an overhead TV screen and racks containing newspapers, magazines and bottles of water. Willoughby-Brown took one of the forward-facing seats and waved for Shepherd to sit on

the other side of the table. The doors whispered shut. There
was a privacy panel separating them from the driver so
Willoughby-Brown had to press an intercom button to talk to
the driver. 'Mickey, we're good to go,' he said. 'The heliport.'

The van started to move and Willoughby-Brown took out
a packet of the small cigars he liked to smoke.

'I thought this was classed as a place of work so smoking
wasn't allowed,' said Shepherd.

Willoughby-Brown pointed at the privacy pane. 'This
means Billy has one place of work and I have another,' he
said.

'What about me?'

'You don't smoke?'

'You know I don't, Jeremy.'

'But you do sometimes. When you're under cover?'

Shepherd sat back in his chair. 'Go ahead and smoke.'

'Thank you,' said Willoughby-Brown, taking out a box of
matches. 'By all means open a window if it annoys you.'

Shepherd smiled sarcastically. 'How could you possibly
annoy me?'

Willoughby-Brown returned the smile but there was no
warmth in his eyes. He lit a cigar, then passed an A4 envelope across the table. 'Did you ever cross paths with a guy
called Matt Standing? SAS. He's been a sergeant a couple
of times but has just been busted back to trooper.'

Shepherd slid two photographs out of the envelope, both
in colour. One was a head-and-shoulders shot of a man in
his mid-twenties, square-jawed and with pale blue eyes He
had dark brown hair, like Shepherd's, but cut shorter. The
second picture looked as if it had been taken in the desert:
his hair was longer and he had a beard. His skin had browned
under the sun and he was carrying a carbine. Shepherd shook
his head.

'Not surprising,' said Willoughby-Brown. 'He's almost fifteen years younger than you and he joined after you left. He made a bit of a name for himself in Afghanistan, Syria and a few other trouble spots.'

'And?' He put the photographs back into the envelope.

'What do you mean?' asked Willoughby-Brown.

'I'm waiting for the point, Jeremy. I went to a lot of time and trouble to get close to Meyer.' He pulled up his shirt sleeve to show him the scar on his left arm. 'Spilled blood for it. So you can see I'm not thrilled to be taken off the case.'

Willoughby-Brown waved his hand dismissively. 'No one's taking you off the case. I just need your help for a day or two. It appears that Matt Standing has gone rogue.'

'Rogue? In what way?'

'He's been beating up police officers. Put two MI5 officers in hospital. And killed at least one Muslim. We want him stopped before he goes any further.'

'Why hasn't he been arrested?'

'Five doesn't want any publicity over our officers. If this goes to court at any level the *Guardian* and the *Independent* will have a field day. I know nobody gives a toss about what appears in the left-wing press, these days but, the internet being what it is, the story will go viral and we don't want that, obviously.'

'Obviously,' repeated Shepherd. 'But if he killed someone . . .'

'No witnesses. The man he killed took a flyer off a very tall building. Just because I know Standing did it doesn't mean the police have a case. I just need you to find him, and get him to stop.'

'Why me?'

'Because he's a younger version of you, Daniel. He'll think like you and vice versa. You can get inside his head, work out where he is and what he's doing.'

'Five can't find him?'

'Until yesterday he was staying at a serviced apartment in Bayswater. After he attacked our people he went to ground.'

'So I'm supposed to find him in a city with more than eight million people?'

'I didn't say it would be easy.' Willoughby-Brown grinned. 'That's why I'm putting my best man on it.'

Shepherd scowled. 'You're putting me on it because you want information from the Regiment.'

'Guilty as charged,' said Willoughby-Brown. 'And on the QT, too. It has to be off the record. Totally unofficial.'

Shepherd gazed out of the window as he considered what Willoughby-Brown was asking him to do. It was a simple task. London was a big city but most hotels required identification, and with half a million CCTV cameras, it was almost impossible to walk around undetected. But Shepherd was never happy investigating his own. It was bad enough mounting an operation against an undercover cop, but he really wasn't happy about going after someone whom Willoughby-Brown so blithely described as being a younger version of himself.

'You say this Standing has gone rogue,' said Shepherd. 'Why exactly?'

'His sister was a drug addict and she overdosed. Standing seems to blame Muslims for her death and is on something of a rampage.'

'And why are you involved?'

'It's complicated, obviously. When it became clear the police couldn't handle it, Five stepped in. As I said, he put two of our officers in hospital so we need to find him and stop him.'

'If Standing is such a danger, why not just release his picture? Or get the Met to use its CCTV facilities.'

'Because if this gets out, nobody looks good,' said Willoughby-Brown. 'The SAS is shown to have a maverick soldier, the police can't catch a lone fugitive and MI5 can't take care of its own, plus there's the whole racial thing. This has to be kept low profile.'

'Swept under the carpet, you mean.'

'Play with semantics all you want, Daniel. Just get the job done.'

'Get what done? What exactly do you want me to do?'

'Find him, and tell me where he is.'

'What then? What will you do to him?'

'Me? Nothing.'

'Now who's playing with semantics? What will happen to him?'

'Hand on heart, I don't know. I really don't know. But he has to be stopped, one way or another.'

'Which is why you can't tell the Regiment? Because if Standing is discovered in a zipped-up kitbag in his bathroom, you'll have the SAS on your back?'

'I don't think it'll come to that.'

'Hand on heart?' Shepherd's upper lip curled back into a snarl. 'Sometimes I hate this job.'

'You're over-thinking, as always,' said Willoughby-Brown, dismissively. 'Just find him and let me worry about the consequences.' He smiled. 'That's why I get paid the big bucks.'

When the van arrived at the heliport, the driver pressed a button to open the side door electronically. 'I'll say goodbye to you here,' said Willoughby-Brown. 'I've got back-to-back meetings all afternoon.'

Shepherd climbed out and hefted his bag over his shoulder. In the distance he could hear the roar of helicopter turbines. He wasn't happy at what he was being asked to do, but at least he could pay Katra a flying visit.

Willoughby-Brown was already looking at his phone as the van door closed.

Shepherd walked into the terminal. An earnest young man in a grey suit was waiting for him. 'Mr Shepherd? We've been expecting you.'

'Give me a minute to make a couple of calls,' he said.

'Of course,' said the man. 'Just let us know when you're ready.'

Shepherd thanked him, then called Major Allan Gannon, his former commanding officer in the SAS and a friend of many years. He explained what he wanted and arranged a meeting in Hereford later that evening.

His second call was to Katra, who was overjoyed to hear his voice, and even happier when he explained that he would be in Hereford in less than an hour. He asked her to meet him in a field where Liam used to play football. 'You're not going to parachute, are you?' she asked, and he wasn't sure if she was joking.

'I think my parachuting days are behind me,' he said. 'See you soon.' It was only when he was slipping his phone back into his pocket that he realised yet again he'd put work before his personal life. He'd called the Major before he'd called Katra. He headed over to the man in the grey suit, who was now holding a clipboard. 'Ready when you are,' said Shepherd.

'Have you flown in a helicopter before, Mr Shepherd?' asked the man, brightly.

Shepherd nodded. 'Only a few hundred times.'

The man was unfazed by Shepherd's sarcasm. 'Excellent. You'll know the drill, then,' he said.

Standing didn't waste time showering or shaving. He changed quickly, into a pullover and jeans, packed his bag and headed downstairs. He didn't bother telling the Indian girl on

Reception that he wouldn't be back, just said a bright 'Good morning' and hurried out. He walked to Queensway and headed into the Tube. The fact that they knew he exercised in Hyde Park almost certainly meant they knew where he was staying so he needed to get away, and quickly.

The problem was where to go. He went down to the platform. Queensway was on the Central line, which gave him two choices – east or west. He decided east and followed the signs to the westward platform. He kept a watch for anyone who appeared to be following him but didn't see anyone. The train arrived and he got on. Then, just as the doors started to close, he jumped off. No one followed him and the only people on the platform were passengers who had got off. He sat down and waited for the next train.

How had they found him? Maybe MI5 were also looking at the pound shop. Had they also been watching Faisal Khan? If they had, why hadn't they grabbed Standing when he'd left the tower block? Maybe Kaiser or Reynolds had spoken to them. But, no matter how they had found him, it meant that his life was going to be much more complicated from now on.

The next train arrived and Standing boarded it. He stood staring at the Tube map above the doors, wondering where he should go. He needed somewhere he could stay where he could pay cash and where he wouldn't have to provide ID, somewhere there were lots of tourists, lots of strangers, but not too far from Kilburn. He settled on the King's Cross area. The Eurostar train from Paris terminated at St Pancras station and there were hundreds of small hotels in the area. He changed at Holborn and caught an eastbound Piccadilly line train.

Twenty minutes later he was walking down a road lined

with houses most of which had been converted into hotels. Almost all had 'VACANCY' signs in the window.

Standing figured the smaller the premises, the more likely they would be to take cash. And the shabbier the building, the less likely they would be to insist on a credit card.

He chose a hotel with stained brickwork, windows that hadn't been washed for a long time and plastic plants in an unruly line on a windowsill. An African man in a cheap suit, reading a book on computer programming, was sitting behind a hole in the wall with a sign saying 'RECEPTION' above it. Next to it was a sign in smaller type saying that the front door was locked at 11 p.m. but that the night porter could be summoned by pressing the doorbell. Standing asked for a room and took out his wallet.

'Do you have a passport?' He had a French accent.

'I don't,' said Standing.

'Driving licence?'

Standing shrugged. 'I don't drive.'

'Credit card?'

'Can I pay cash?'

'I'm supposed to ask for a credit card.'

'I know, but I can pay cash in advance and I should have a credit card in a day or two.' He held out a handful of notes. 'How much is the room rate?'

'How many days?'

'Three.'

Standing tried not to smile as he saw the man trying to work out how much to charge, the official rate plus the notes that would go straight into his pocket. 'Two hundred and forty pounds?' he said, and Standing heard the hope in his voice.

'No problem.' He handed over the money.

The man gave him a key and a big smile. There was no

registration, nothing to sign, and Standing doubted there would be.

The room was on the third floor, overlooking the rear of the property. The window opened and Standing looked out. There was an outbuilding below and, if push came to shove, he could probably jump down without hurting himself too much. From there he'd be able to jump down to the alley behind the property.

There was a single bed that was sagging in the middle and a small wooden chest of drawers next to it that was covered with cigarette burns and white rings from wet glasses. The television was an old box-type model with a circular metal aerial attached to the back. The bathroom was tiny, with a half-size bath and a dripping shower above it. There was no plug in the washbasin and the mirror above it was cracked. It was far from salubrious but Standing had stayed in worse places.

He dropped his bag onto the floor by the bed, lay down and stared up at the ceiling. He was pretty sure that the men in the park had been spooks. They certainly hadn't been cops. And he couldn't see that they had been friends of Faisal or Ali. MI5 had warned the cops off their investigation into the Asian grooming gang, so it was likely that they had also decided to get heavy with Standing. A matter of national security, they had said. Which presumably meant terrorism. Islamic terrorism. So was Ali Hussain a terrorist? Was Faisal?

If it was MI5, the powers-that-be would now know that Standing couldn't be warned off. So what would they do next? He'd felt that their threat to talk to his bosses was an empty one. If they wanted to do that they would already have done it. That meant they didn't want the SAS top brass to know what was going on. Secret Squirrel. Spies did love to play spy games. Standing was sure of one thing – they

would be back. And next time there would be more than
two of them. And they wouldn't want just to talk.

Katra was waiting for Shepherd at the entrance to the field,
standing next to her Saab. She jumped up and down and
waved as the helicopter came into land, circling the field
once before landing into the wind. Shepherd climbed out
and jogged towards her, crouching forward even though the
rotor blades were well above head-height.

She ran towards him and practically threw herself against
him. She was still hugging him as the Agusta 109 took off
again, retracted its wheels and flew east, back to London.
'How long are you staying?' she asked, when he finally untangled himself.

'It's literally a flying visit,' he said. 'I'll be back to London
tomorrow.'

Her face fell.

'But I can take you out to dinner tonight,' he said. 'I'll see
if I can get a table at Castle House.'

'I was going to cook,' she said.

'Even better,' said Shepherd, putting his arm around her
as they walked to her car. 'I've got to see someone at about
six, so I'll be back around seven thirty. And I'll bring some
decent wine with me.'

'Champagne?'

He grinned and nodded, even though he wasn't keen on
it and, in any case, was fed up with it. 'Champagne it is,' he
said.

Standing didn't like being confined, but he wasn't sure how
actively MI5 would be looking for him so he decided to stay
put for a while. He sat down on the bed and logged on to
Facebook on his phone. He searched for Ali Hussain and

went through all the entries, looking for a match to the face he'd seen in the cab office. There were hundreds of people – men and women – with the name and it wasn't until early evening that he was sure his quarry didn't have an account. The electoral roll was equally unhelpful: there were almost two hundred Ali Hussains in London. Not exactly a needle in a haystack, but there was no way he could put two hundred properties under surveillance.

He left the hotel once, to pick up new clothing from various charity shops, toiletries, and a selection of sandwiches, a box of Kentucky Fried Chicken and half a dozen bottles of beer.

Back in the flat he spent the afternoon working out in his boxer shorts, switching between press-ups, sit-ups, planks and various stretching exercises. He followed that with half an hour doing the exercises that Dr Doyle had recommended. Later he showered, then watched the news while eating some of the chicken and a sandwich. All the time his mind was working through all his options. The minicab office seemed to be his only way forward, though if MI5 were still on the case it would put him in the firing line. Standing knew he didn't have any choice. He wasn't going to back down now. Or ever.

Shepherd got to The Barrels early and took his Jameson's and soda outside to the cobbled courtyard. It was a cloudless evening with a slight breeze that ruffled his hair as he sipped his drink. The Barrels was a traditional pub, just down the road from Hereford Cathedral, with five bars and a manager who allowed the televisions to be switched on only for major sporting events. Major Allan Gannon arrived exactly at seven o'clock. He was several inches taller than Shepherd, with wide shoulders, a strong chin, with a dimple in the middle, and a nose that had been broken several times. He was in his early fifties but as fit as any SAS trooper half his age. His grey hair was close-cropped and his eyes were watchful as he walked across the courtyard. He smiled as he reached Shepherd, shook his hand and clapped him on the back. 'I don't see enough of you, these days,' he said. 'You still live in Hereford, right?'

'Sure, I've still got the house. But I've been in London most of the last six months.'

'No rest for the wicked,' said the Major.

'Drink?'

'Thought you'd never ask.' The Major slid onto the bench opposite Shepherd. 'Get me a Guinness – it's been a long day.'

Shepherd went to the bar and returned with the Major's pint, another Jameson's and soda and a couple of packets of peanuts.

'So, how's Liam, these days?' asked Gannon, after they had clinked glasses and sipped their drinks.

'All good,' said Shepherd. 'He's doing Elementary Flying Training at RAF Cranwell and, assuming he passes, he'll move to 670 Squadron for operational training.'

'I suppose he wants to fly Apaches?'

'They all want to be Top Gun, I guess. But he'll be happy just flying. And they took him on as an officer even without a degree, so it's all good.'

'And the lovely Katra?'

Shepherd looked at him warily. 'All good, too.'

'How does Liam feel about you being romantically involved with the maid?'

Shepherd laughed. 'Romantically involved? It isn't a bloody Jane Austen novel. And, yes, he's fine with it. And she was never the maid. Au pair was the official title.'

'I was only messing with you, Spider. She's a lovely girl.

You're punching well above your weight there, you being twice her age.'

'I'm ten years older, that's all.' He realised from the look on the Major's face that he was joking. 'Fine. Joke all you want. I'm very happy.'

'And lucky.'

Shepherd grinned. 'That, too.'

The Major took a long pull on his pint. 'So I'm guessing the fact that you didn't want to meet at Credenhill means this is off the record?'

Shepherd nodded. 'I'm sorry. Yes. It's a funny one, boss. I've got to tread carefully.'

'You're among friends, Spider. So I'm guessing the desire to keep this on the QT is to do with Jeremy Willoughby-Brown.'

Shepherd shrugged but didn't reply.

'I'll take that as a yes,' said the Major. 'You watch your back with that one, Spider. You need to count your fingers after you've shaken hands with him.'

'I try to keep physical contact to a minimum,' said Shepherd.

'Probably best,' said the Major. 'So, you wanted to know about Sergeant Standing. Or Former Sergeant Standing. He's just lost his stripes. He's on leave at the moment.'

'Do you know him?'

'I've met him a few times.'

'What's he like?'

The Major chuckled. 'He didn't hit you, did he? He makes a habit of lashing out, but it's usually officers he thumps.'

'It's not that,' said Shepherd. 'I wish it was.'

'You know they call him Lastman?'

'Lastman Standing? I've heard worse nicknames than that.'

'Lastman because he's the last man you want to have an

argument with. He doesn't really have a filter. If he disagrees with you, he'll tell you, right up front. If you push him, he'll push right back. Try to hit him and you'd better connect because his retaliation will be full on.'

Shepherd nodded. 'He acts on his instincts?'

'Without thinking,' said the Major. 'He doesn't consider the consequences of his actions. Do you know what happened, out in Syria?'

'I'm told he hit an officer. Who hasn't wanted to do that at some point?'

'No offence taken,' said the Major.

Shepherd smiled. 'You know what I mean, boss. A wrong decision can cost lives in combat. And we've all known officers who've made bad calls.'

'But you know how it works in the SAS. Officers consult their men, the old Chinese parliament. Everyone who has a view expresses it. That tends to iron out any wrinkles.'

'So why did Standing feel he had to get physical with an officer?'

'The way he tells it, the officer started it. The officer hit him. Or at least pushed him. Standing went into retaliation mode and didn't stop until he'd put the officer in hospital.'

'And the officer pushed him because?'

The Major nodded. 'Ah, yes, and thereby hangs a tale. Standing was leading a four-man team, who were providing the laser targeting for a drone strike on one if ISIS's top people. This is a guy the Yanks have been hunting for months. They finally get an opening and they send Standing and his team in to light the way. All good. The team hunkers down and six days into it said target appears. Problem is, a truck-load of kids also appears, right outside the target house. The drone's on its way, the clock's a-ticking, and Standing doesn't want the collateral damage.'

'Understandable,' said Shepherd.

'I knew you'd see it that way.'

Shepherd frowned. 'See it what way? We're not in the business of killing kids. If we start killing children then we're no better than the people we're fighting.'

'You and him are alike, you know. You both have this moral compass that constantly points you in the direction of the right thing to do.'

'You make it sound like a bad thing.'

The Major sipped his pint. 'Doing the right thing is just that, doing the right thing. But sometimes you have to look at the big picture.'

'Please don't tell me that the end justifies the means.' Shepherd drained his glass. 'So far, from what you've told me, I'd have done the same. I've been on those drone operations and my view is always that if there's any possibility of civilian collateral damage you hold off. We shouldn't be killing innocents to get at the bad guys.'

'In a perfect world, I'd agree with you,' said the Major. 'But the world isn't perfect and it's not black and white. It's all a murky grey and that means sometimes you have to take difficult decisions. And sometimes those difficult decisions lead us to follow orders that we're not happy with. But that's why we call them orders, not requests.' He took another pull on his pint. 'The target out in Syria was Abdul-Karim Ahmadi. AKA, literally. Cut his teeth making IEDs and graduated to big-time bombmaking. But he's a strategist, too, one of those arguing that they have to take the fight to Europe. It's generally believed that he came up with the idea of hijacking trucks and driving them into crowds, as happened in Berlin and Nice. Cheap, effective and deadly. Taking him out will save lives. There's no question of that.'

'Well, you say that, but once he's taken out, he'll be replaced.'

'That's no reason not to do anything, though.'

'No, but your argument that the end justifies the means is all hypothetical. Could've, would've, should've. Anyway, what happened about the kids?'

'Standing was given a direct order to paint the target's house. He queried the order and Captain Waters read him the Riot Act. So Standing painted a building a couple of hundred feet away. The Yanks weren't happy, naturally. Waste of a perfectly good missile. But it's the fact that all the intel went to waste that's really pissing them off.'

'Then they should have got Delta Force to do their painting instead of subcontracting it out to the Brits.'

'They're keen to share the workload,' said the Major.

'The responsibility, you mean. So that they can say these are joint operations when really it's the Yanks that are calling the shots. So why didn't the captain just put Standing on a charge for disobeying the order?'

'The captain is fairly inexperienced. A more experienced officer might have let it go, or given him a verbal dressing-down. But for some reason known only to the captain, he decided to get physical. It was all over in seconds, but the captain ended up with a broken nose and a cracked jaw.' He took another drink, then shrugged. 'Anyway, the long and the short of it is that Standing has been given a month to get his anger-management issues under control.'

'How's that going to work?'

'He's been given a number of therapists to choose from.'

'Was Carolyn Stockmann on the list?'

'I wouldn't know. Shouldn't have thought so. I don't think anger management is her area of expertise. Does she still do your psychological evaluations?'

'Jeremy put a stop to that. Now I go to a hi-tech firm in the City and they run me through some sophisticated computer programs. It's all bollocks.'

The Major laughed. 'You're telling me.'

'So the therapist, where are they?'

'London. He was issued with a rail warrant for the Big Smoke and given details of therapists there. The idea is for him to get his anger-management issues sorted and then the SAS doctors will assess him to see if he's fit for duty or not.'

'And if not, he's RTU'd?'

'I'm afraid so.'

Shepherd grimaced. Being Returned To Unit was pretty much the death knell for a military career – most troopers who were RTU'd usually left the army soon afterwards. The SAS was the best of the best, and its members regarded all other units as second best. 'I don't suppose you've got an address for him?'

'He gave the Credenhill camp as his home address. But I've got a mobile number.' He took a piece of paper from his pocket and gave it to Shepherd. Shepherd put it into his wallet but he had already memorised the number it bore.

'Next of kin?'

'A sister. Alexia. Lives in London. She's just a kid. Sixteen, seventeen.'

Shepherd frowned. 'Which is it? Sixteen or seventeen?'

'Sixteen, I think. Why?'

Willoughby-Brown had said that Standing's sister had died of a drug overdose and sixteen seemed hellish young for a drug addict. 'No reason,' said Shepherd. 'Just trying to work out what's what. Do you know if he's seen any of the therapists yet?'

The Major shook his head. 'I can probably find out.'

'Could you? It'd have to be on the QT.'

'I'm sure I can manage that. Now, can you tell me what he's done that's so bad they've put you on the case?'

'It's better if I don't. Let's just say Five wants a word with him and they can't find him. Hand on heart, I don't really know much more than that.'

'But Willoughby-Brown can't ask the Regiment officially?'

'That's right.'

'But he knows that if he asks you, you'll ask me. Unofficially.'

'Yup.'

'He's a devious bastard, isn't he? He doesn't care who he uses.'

'He gets things done, though.'

The Major chuckled.

'What?' asked Shepherd.

'You hate the argument that the end justifies the means. And now look at you.'

Shepherd nodded. 'You're right. But there's a world of a difference between using people and killing people.'

The Major raised his glass. 'No question,' he said. 'But going back to Lastman Standing. At least answer me one thing. Has he gone over to the dark side?'

'To be honest, it's the opposite.'

The Major's eyes narrowed. 'He's gone vigilante?' Shepherd didn't say anything, just raised his eyebrows. 'I'll tell you one thing,' said the Major. 'He's the last man I'd want coming after me, that's all I can say.'

Lisa Wilson looked up at a knock on her cabin door. 'Are you decent?' asked Meyer.

She put down the magazine she was reading and sat up. 'What's up?'

Meyer pushed open the door. 'We're going to St Lucia,' he said.

'Lovely,' she said. 'Now?'

'Tomorrow,' said Meyer.

'Sailing?'

Meyer laughed. 'Don't be daft,' he said. 'It's six thousand kilometres – it'd take months. We're flying.'

'How long will we be there?'

'Why? Have you got somewhere else to be?'

She laughed. 'I just want to know what to pack.'

'Travel light,' he said. 'We'll buy whatever we need when we're there.'

'You know I love to shop,' she said.

'Are you hungry?'

'I can eat.'

'Tapas?'

'Perfect.'

Meyer grinned. 'Great. We'll head out in half an hour. Jeeves is coming.'

'To St Lucia?'

'Just for tapas,' said Meyer. He pulled the door shut and went back above deck. Lisa reached for her phone. She sent a text message to Jeff: **Where are you?**

After a couple of minutes her phone vibrated to let her know he'd replied: **Who is this?**

She smiled and sent a second message: **It's Lucy.** She added three kisses for good measure.

She left it a minute or so before sending a follow-up. **Did you forget me already? Bastard!**

There was no reply so she snarled at the phone, 'Come on, you bastard, don't give me the silent treatment,' she muttered. She sent a third text. **Don't forget I want your body.** She added more kisses.

She tossed the phone onto her bed and went to shower and change into a canary yellow dress that she knew showed off her tan. She added mascara to her lashes, then picked up the phone again. Jeff still hadn't replied so she called the number. It rang for several seconds, and then it was answered. 'Jeff, where the hell are you?' she asked. There was no answer. 'Jeff? Stop messing about. Jeff?' She was fairly sure she could hear breathing but there was no reply. Then the line went dead. She frowned, but decided against calling him back.

Shepherd parked the SUV in front of the house and let himself in. 'I'm home!' he shouted. 'And I've got champagne!' There was no reply from Katra so he headed to the kitchen. He was surprised to see her standing by the sink, looking out into the garden. 'Didn't you hear me?' he asked, putting the bottle of Moët into the fridge.

She didn't react and he went over to her. When he put his hand on her shoulder she shrugged him off. 'Katra, what's wrong?'

She turned around and pushed him away, using both hands. The shove caught him by surprise and he staggered back, off balance.

'Baby, what's wrong?' Her eyes were red and her cheeks flushed.

'Why don't you tell me what's wrong?' she said, folding her arms and staring at the floor.

'Baby, I've no idea what you're talking about.'

She sniffed.

'If you don't tell me what's wrong, how can I help?'

She looked up and glared at him. 'Help? How can you help? What do you mean, help? Help me how?'

He took a step towards her. She flinched so he held up his hands. 'I really don't understand what's going on,' he said. 'What's happened?'

She shook her head but didn't answer.

'Katra, if you don't tell me what the problem is, how can I fix it?'

'You can't fix it,' she said. She sniffed and wiped her nose with the back of her hand.

'At least let me try.'

A single tear trickled down her cheek. 'Who is Lucy?'

'Lucy?'

'Don't lie to me, Dan.' She pointed at the phone he'd left on the kitchen table. The Jeff Taylor phone.

He groaned as realisation dawned. 'You checked my messages?'

'It beeped. I just looked to see who it was.'

'That's my work phone, Katra.'

'That makes it all right, does it? She said she misses you and wants to know when you're back.' She sobbed and put a hand up to her mouth. 'How could you lie to me?' Shepherd reached for her but she pushed him away.

'Katra, please . . .'

She sobbed again and rushed out of the kitchen. He heard her run upstairs and slam the bedroom door. He sat down, picked up the phone and checked the messages. He grimaced when he saw the last: *Don't forget I want your body*. And kisses. He cursed under his breath, then checked the other messages Lisa had sent. He groaned and put down the phone. He was angry with himself for not taking it with him, but he hadn't expected anyone to be texting him.

He went upstairs with a heavy heart and knocked on the bedroom door. 'Katra?' There was no answer and he turned the handle, half expecting her to have locked the door. She hadn't. She was curled up on the bed, hugging a pillow, her back to him. 'Katra, can we talk?'

'There's nothing to say,' she said. 'Just leave me alone.'

'It's not what you think.'

'How can it not be what I think?' she said. 'She said she wants your body. And for all I know you want her too. I don't understand. If you want her and not me then just tell me. Why lie to me?'

He went to her side of the bed and sat down. He put a hand on her shoulder. She flinched but didn't shake him away.

'Lucy is part of a case I'm working on. Her name's not even Lucy.'

'You said it was a drugs case. You didn't say it was a girl.'

'It's not. Well, it is in a way. It's complicated, and you know I don't like to talk about my work.'

'She said she wanted you. Why would she say that, Dan? You don't say you want somebody if you don't.'

He lay down next to her and put his arms around her. 'She's in a difficult position, baby. She's alone and very vulnerable at the moment. Because of that she's lonely and she's reaching out to me.'

'Didn't you tell her about me?'

'Baby, I'm under cover. She doesn't know anything about me.'

'You lie to her?'

'I have to. That's what it means when you work under cover. You pretend to be someone else.'

She was silent for a while, but sniffed occasionally. 'Dan?'

'Yes?'

'Do you lie to me?' Her voice was a soft whisper.

He hugged her. 'Sometimes.'

She stiffened. 'Really? When?'

'You know when you cook gnocchi and I tell you they're delicious?'

'Yes?'

'I don't really like them that much.'

She laughed and rolled around so that she was facing him. 'I won't cook you gnocchi ever again,' she said.

'I can live with that.'

'And I don't want you ever to lie to me,' she said, looking into his eyes.

'I'll try not to.'

She frowned. 'What do you mean?'

'Well, you know, you buy a new pair of jeans and you ask me if they make you look fat? Is it okay to lie then?'

'You think I'm fat?'

'Of course not. But maybe in ten years. Who knows?'

'I won't be fat in ten years. I'll never be fat.' Her frown deepened. 'You think I'm getting fat?'

He kissed her, to shut her up more than anything else. She returned the kiss, then pushed him away. 'If ever you think I'm getting fat, you tell me, okay?'

'Okay,' he said.

'Promise?'

'I promise.'

'Good,' she said, and settled down next to him. She was silent for a while, other than her soft breathing, and he began to wonder if she'd fallen asleep. 'Why does she think your name is Jeff?' she said eventually.

Shepherd stiffened. 'Why do you say that?'

'She kept asking for Jeff.'

Shepherd's heart began to pound. 'What do you mean, baby?'

'She called. She kept asking for Jeff.'

'What do you mean she called?'

'About fifteen minutes after she sent the text message. She called and I answered.'

'You answered my phone?' He shook his head. 'Oh, no, baby, please don't tell me you answered my phone.'

'I didn't speak to her. I hung up.'

'Oh, shit.'

''I didn't say anything to her, Dan. She just kept saying Jeff and then I hung up.'

'You shouldn't have done that, baby.'

'I just wanted to hear her voice, that's all. I thought you were having an affair,'

'Well, I'm not. She's a case. A job. And by answering the phone . . .'

She sat up. 'What? What have I done?'

Shepherd forced a smile. 'Nothing. It's okay.'

'I didn't say anything to her, Dan.'

'I know. It's all good.'

She reached over and hugged him, burying her face in his neck. 'I'm so sorry, I should have trusted you.'

Shepherd hugged her back. Yes, she should have trusted him. And she shouldn't have answered his phone. If it was just Lisa calling, then probably no damage had been done. Lisa might wonder who had answered the phone, but so long as Katra hadn't said anything, he could come up with an explanation. What worried him most was if Meyer found out that she had called him. Meyer would be watching her closely and might well be monitoring her phone. If he got suspicious he might track Shepherd's phone. It was a pay-as-you-go throwaway so it wouldn't give him any information but it wouldn't be too hard for him to get information on the phone's location. He might only be able to pin it down to the nearest cellphone tower but even that would be a problem. He was supposed to be en route to St Lucia and Taylor lived in Portsmouth, how would he explain that he was in Hereford? The whole case was in danger of unravelling, and all because he'd left his phone on the kitchen table.

'I love you, Dan,' she whispered.

'I love you too. For ever.'

She kissed his neck, then his lips. He kissed her back, then she pushed him down on the bed and rolled on top of him. 'I'm sorry,' she said.

'You don't have to apologise for anything.'

'I'm an idiot.'

He laughed. 'No, you're not.'

She started kissing him again and he stopped laughing.

Meyer topped up Lucy's glass and poured the last of the Cristal champagne into his own. He had changed into a white linen suit and black silk shirt but was still wearing gleaming white Nikes. He looked at his watch. 'I'm just going to hit the head and then we'll be off,' he said.

He went below deck and along to Lucy's cabin. Her phone was on the bed. He'd known her password for weeks and he tapped it in. He checked her call log and frowned when he saw Jeff Taylor's number. 'Hello, hello, hello,' he muttered to himself. He checked her messages and smiled as he read the texts she'd sent. 'Naughty girl,' he whispered.

Katra kissed Shepherd, then ran her hand down his chest and between his legs. 'Round two?' she asked.

Shepherd chuckled. 'Maybe after dinner and a couple of hours' sleep,' he said.

'You're bored with me already!' she said, and rolled over to gaze up at the ceiling. 'I knew it! It's only been a year but you're already fed up.' She sighed theatrically, then drummed her feet on the bed.

Shepherd laughed and reached over to hug her. 'I'll never be bored with you,' he said. 'But I'm knackered. I've been flying around the world from one hotel to another, plus I've been sailing.'

'Sailing?'

'Catamarans.'

'Why?'

'To get close to this bad guy.'

She ran her fingers down his arm and stopped when she felt the cut there. 'What's that?' she said.

'Nothing.'

She sat up and made him show it to her. 'How did you do it?'

Shepherd didn't want to lie, but if he told her the truth she'd be scared and worried. 'I did it at the marina,' he said. 'A stupid accident.' It was almost the truth, not quite a lie, he told himself. He had made a career out of lying but he hated lying to the people he loved.

'It looks bad,' she said.

'It's a scratch,' he said.

She lay down again and he held her. 'So what are you cooking?' he asked.

'Don't change the subject.'

'I didn't realise there was a subject.'

'You're very good at doing that,' said Katra.

'Doing what?'

'Changing the subject.'

'I'm sorry.'

She stroked his chest. 'I get worried sometimes. When you're away. That's all.'

'I know. I'm sorry. But it's the nature of the job. There aren't many big villains in Hereford. I have to go where they are.'

'Don't you ever get fed up?'

'With the job?' He shook his head. 'I love it, Katra. It's what I am.'

She sighed. 'I know.' She kissed his shoulder. 'And don't

worry, I'll never try to change you. You'll just have to put up with my insecurities.'

'I can do that,' said Shepherd. He rolled on top of her. 'It's not that hard.'

She reached between his legs and giggled. 'Yes, it is,' she said, and kissed him.

If MI5 were on his case, Standing knew he'd be better off not taking public transport. He used his smartphone to log on to Craigslist and found a Yamaha 125cc trail bike for sale in Croydon. It was three years old and, from the photographs, it had been well looked after. It was a private sale so he phoned and arranged to go down to look at it. The seller was a guy in his early twenties who had just bought his first car and was looking for a quick sale. Standing borrowed the man's full-face helmet and drove up and down the road, checking the acceleration and the gears. It seemed fine so he paid the asking price in cash. The seller was so pleased he threw in the helmet and a pair of gloves.

Standing didn't have a licence but he'd ridden plenty of bikes in the SAS. He drove back to King's Cross and into the alley behind the hotel but decided it wasn't a safe place to leave it. He took it to a multi-storey car park close to the station and left it there. On the way back to the hotel he popped into an Oxfam shop and bought a second-hand leather motorcycle jacket, then picked up some more sandwiches, another bucket of KFC and half a dozen bottles of beer, then went back to his hotel. He spent the rest of the night in his room, watching mind-numbing game shows and drinking his way through the beer.

Shepherd's phone rang, jolting him awake. Katra was curled up next to him and murmured in her sleep. He had put his personal phone and his Jeff Taylor phone on the bedside table and it was the Taylor phone that was ringing. It was Marcus Meyer. Shepherd untangled himself from Katra, slid out of the bed and padded onto the landing before answering.

'Jeff?' asked Meyer.

'Yeah, what's up?'

'Are you in St Lucia?'

'Nah, mate. On my way.'

'Yeah? So where are you?'

Shepherd gritted his teeth. He didn't want to tell Meyer where he was, but there was a possibility that he already knew. If he'd found out that Lisa had phoned him it would have been easy for him to get the location of his phone. And if Meyer caught him out in a lie – even an innocuous one – it would destroy what trust had been built up. 'Hereford,' he said.

'Hereford? What the fuck are you doing in Hereford?'

Meyer sounded surprised but Shepherd had the feeling he was faking it. 'My aunt's had a bad fall,' he said. 'I was on my way to Portsmouth when the hospital called. She's broken her hip and the NHS was no bloody help so I've been arranging a private hospital for her. It's all sorted, and I'm on my way to St Lucia now. What about you?'

'We're flying today,' said Meyer. 'You need to get a move on. We don't want the boat hanging around for too long.'

'I'll be flying out tomorrow, hopefully,' said Shepherd. 'The day after at the latest. Sorry about this but she's pretty much my only relative.'

'It's all right, family's family. But soon as you can, yeah?'

'Absolutely,' said Shepherd.

Meyer ended the call. Shepherd frowned as he replayed the conversation in his head. Had Meyer known where he was? Shepherd was fairly sure that he did. So Meyer was checking up on him. That was probably a good thing: it showed that Meyer was ready to move forward. But had Meyer believed his story about a sick aunt?

He realised that Katra was standing at the bedroom door watching him. 'Was that your girlfriend?' she asked.

'It was the target,' he said. 'He wants to know where I am.'

'Is it because I answered your phone?'

'Maybe,' he said.

She hurried over to him and hugged him. 'I'm sorry.'

He stroked her back and kissed the top of her head. 'It's okay.'

'Are you sure?'

'Of course,' he said, though he wished he felt as confident as he sounded. Meyer had been testing him, he was sure of that. The big question was, had he passed? The only way he would know for sure was when he met the man in St Lucia.

'Shall I make you breakfast?'

'Sure,' said Shepherd. He kissed the top of her head again.

Shepherd shaved and showered while Katra went downstairs to the kitchen. By the time he'd dressed she was buttering toast to go with the eggs, bacon, sausages and tomato she'd cooked, and there was a mug of steaming coffee on the kitchen table. He brought the two phones with him and put them on the table while he ate. He was biting into his second piece of toast when his personal phone rang. It was Major Gannon. 'The therapist who's helping Matt Standing, her name is Sharon Doyle and she has an office in Harley Street.'

'Brilliant, thanks,' said Shepherd.

'She's filed two reports already, and both are very supportive.'

'Supportive?'

'According to Dr Doyle, Standing is showing great progress. He's coming to an understanding of the issues he has regarding his anger management, and is responding well to treatment.'

'Treatment? Medication, you mean?'

'Exercises. Basically she's teaching him to count to ten.' He chuckled. 'Which for the SAS is no mean achievement. So where are you?'

'Still at home, but I'm off to St Lucia ASAP,' said Shepherd.

'Nice work, if you can get it,' said the Major. 'Or are you on holiday with the lovely Katra?'

'It's work,' said Shepherd.

'Feel free to take me on as a consultant any time you want,' said the Major.

'I'll add you to the list, boss,' said Shepherd. He ended the call, phoned Willoughby-Brown and passed on the therapist details the Major had given him.

'And this Dr Doyle says Standing has his anger under control?' said Willoughby-Brown.

'That's what I'm told.'

'She clearly doesn't know what he's doing,' said Willoughby-Brown.

'I've got a mobile number for Standing.'

'Excellent. Let me have it.'

Shepherd dictated the number. 'Now what?' he asked. 'Do you need anything else?'

'You can head off to St Lucia for your meet with Meyer,' said Willoughby-Brown.

'He called today, said he's on his way.'

'Do you want me to arrange back-up?'

'I don't think so. We'll be on a boat again so any back-up will be too far away to be any use. What's going to happen about Standing?'

'I can take care of it, Daniel, but thank you for your concern.'

'Don't underestimate him,' said Shepherd.

'Don't worry. I won't.'

He ended the call. Katra was watching him and he could see the concern on her face. 'It's just work,' he said.

'Is everything okay?'

'It's fine.'

'And you have to go to St Lucia?'

'Just for a day or two.'

'And you'll see that girl?'

'It's work, baby.' He reached over and ruffled her hair. 'I'm not interested in anyone else.'

'You swear?'

He looked into her eyes. 'I swear.'

Standing found a place to leave his bike in a side-street where he had a reasonable view of the door that led up to the minicab office. He parked up at just before lunchtime and kept his helmet on. He sat on the bike and switched into surveillance mode, his body inactive most of the time but his eyes and ears constantly on alert. Drivers came and went. Customers made their way up the stairs and would return a few minutes later, either with drivers or to meet a car down the road. So far as he could tell, no one else was watching the office. A BT Openreach van parked up for about half an hour but the West Indian technician went inside one of the shops and returned twenty minutes before driving off. Cars and vans stopped, but none remained for more than half an hour, and there were no pedestrians lurking.

From where he was sitting he couldn't see any observers in the upper-floor windows overlooking the cab office. That didn't mean they weren't there, of course, but he did several walk-bys still wearing his helmet and was fairly sure that there was no surveillance in place.

He popped into a café, bought a ham and cheese sandwich and ate it while sitting on the bike, washing it down with a coffee. There was no sign of Ali Hussain, but the man wasn't a driver so probably didn't leave the office during his shift.

At just after four o'clock two young girls in school uniforms walked along the pavement and headed up the stairs to the minicab office. Standing kept a close watch on the entrance but it was more than an hour before they came out, this time accompanied by two young Asian men. One was a teenager, tall and good-looking, and had his arm around one of the girls. She was blonde and pretty, and though she had on make-up and was wearing high heels, Standing doubted she was more than sixteen. The other girl was shorter and plumper with brown hair. Like the blonde, she had plastered her face with make-up so it was hard to judge her age exactly, but she was young.

The two Asians guided the schoolgirls to a grey Toyota Prius. The young guy got in the back with the blonde and the other sat the brunette in the front passenger seat, then got behind the wheel. Two other Asians, middle-aged, bearded and wearing Puffa jackets, came down the stairs and headed for another Prius.

None of them was the one he was looking for, but Standing had a bad feeling about what was going on. He started the engine, flipped down the helmet's visor and put the bike in gear.

The two cars pulled away from the kerb and Standing followed. They headed north, eventually turning left on the North Circular Road towards Wembley Stadium. They turned right, then left again. Standing held back, not wanting to get too close. The cars headed north. For a while they drove along a road of detached houses, most of which were in a state of disrepair, then they slowed. The Prius with the two girls on board parked outside a house that had been painted dark green with a bright blue door. A thick, badly trimmed hedge bordered the pavement and the front garden had been gravelled over for parking. There were already two vehicles in the driveway – a van with the name of an Asian halal butcher on the side and a battered Volvo estate filled with cardboard boxes. Standing slowed as he drove by. The two Asian men climbed out of the car and waved for the girls to follow them. The blonde got out and stood by the car, swaying unsteadily. The other girl seemed to be refusing to get out. One of the Asians leaned into the car and began to pull her. The other Prius reversed into a parking space on the other side of the street.

A car beeped at Standing and he accelerated away. He drove a hundred yards further on, then turned left and found a parking space. He locked the bike and walked back to the house, keeping his helmet and gloves on.

The two men had taken the girls inside. Night was falling and the streetlights were already on. As Standing flipped up the visor of his helmet and looked up at the house, the front bedroom light went on behind closed blinds. He glanced up and down the road, wondering what to do. What was happening to the two young girls was none of his business. He could call the police but he doubted they would do anything. Part of him, the rational part, knew he should just get back on his bike and go back to King's Cross. But the emotional part, the part that hated injustice and wanted revenge for what had happened to his sister, was itching to storm inside the house and wreak havoc on the men there.

The emotional part won and Standing walked down the driveway at the side of the house. There was an overgrown garden at the rear, with a rusting car up on bricks and bags of rubbish that had been ripped open by cats or foxes.

Standing looked up at the house. Another light showed in one of the rear bedrooms, but the lights were all off downstairs.

Standing went to the kitchen door. It was unlocked so he opened it and slipped inside to be met by a strong smell of curry and stale onions. There was enough moonlight coming in through the window for him to see that the oven didn't appear to have been cleaned in years. There were piles of dirty crockery in the sink and a small kitchen table covered with old takeaway containers.

Standing walked softly across the kitchen. The floor tiles were sticky and pulled at the soles of his shoes as he moved down the hall. He heard noises from the bedrooms. He reached the bottom of the stairs and put a gloved hand on the banister.

He went slowly up the stairs, keeping to the wall to minimise any creaking. As he reached the top he was faced with four doors leading off a long landing. The door to his left was open and he could hear a bed creaking and men talking in hushed voices. The door to his far right was also wide open. It was a bathroom – he glimpsed marble and a shower cubicle. He heard a toilet flush and then an Asian man walked out, buttoning the fly of his jeans. His mouth dropped open when he saw Standing, who moved quickly: he strode along the landing, grabbed the guy by the throat and pushed him back into the bathroom. He back-heeled the door shut and banged the man's head against the marble wall. There was a sickening crunch and the fight went out of the Asian immediately. Standing slammed him against the wall a second time and this time the man went limp. Standing lowered him to the floor.

He went to the door, opened it and peered out. The landing was still empty. The next door was slightly ajar. Standing pushed it open slowly. There were three figures on the bed. The blonde girl, now naked, and two Asians, one of whom had been holding the girl outside the minicab office. He had taken off his trousers but was still wearing his shirt. The other was bearded and in his sixties. He had also dropped his trousers and kept his shirt on. The girl was on her hands and knees between them. The younger man was pounding into her from behind, his hands gripping her slim white hips, while the older man was pushing himself into her mouth. 'Come on, you bitch, open your mouth wider!' he urged, pulling her hair towards him. He sneered down at the girl, showing grey teeth.

A hot rage washed over Standing and he pushed the door wide, crossed to the bed in three quick steps and punched the younger man in the side of the head with all his strength. He staggered off the bed and hit the wall. Standing followed him and punched him twice in the stomach with his gloved fists, left and right, then as the man doubled over, he punched him in the back of the neck. The Asian twitched and went still.

Standing straightened. The older man was staring open-mouthed at him but his hips were still moving back and forth. Standing's rage intensified. He hated the man for the way he was abusing the girl, treating her as if she was a piece of meat. Her back was to Standing so she had no idea what was happening around her.

It took Standing two steps to reach the man and less than a second to punch him in the face so hard that his nose was flattened completely. Blood gushed down his face and he fell back, his head striking the wall. The girl fell forward into his lap.

Standing walked quickly to the door, checked that the landing was still empty, and headed out. The next door was shut and he walked past it. The muttering was louder now, and there was the occasional cheer. He looked around the door into the room. The bedroom was twice the size of the one he'd just been in, with a king-size bed. Six men standing with their backs to him, watching another have sex with the young brunette. She was naked and the man on top of her had only pulled down his pants to his knees. His backside was thrusting up and down and he was trying to kiss her but she was thrashing her head from side to side. She wasn't crying out and her eyes were open and blank. Something had dulled her senses, either drink or drugs, or maybe she was just trying to blot out the horror of what was happening to her.

The blinds had been drawn and the only light came from a small red lamp on a bedside table. There was a single pillow on which the girl was resting her head. The rest of the bedding had been tossed onto the floor.

One man turned and his mouth opened in surprise when he saw Standing, who grabbed him by the throat, punched him in the face, then turned and slammed him against the wall by the door. The rest of the men heard the commotion and spun round. Standing smashed the man in the face, then swivelled. There were now five men facing him, plus the one on the bed.

One was holding up an iPhone, filming what was happening. He was young, early twenties maybe, with a straggly beard and bushy eyebrows. As he turned towards Standing he was still holding the phone up high, still focused on the screen. Standing grabbed it with his left hand and punched the man in the throat. He slumped to his knees, clasping his neck with both hands. Standing punched him in the side of the head and he went down, out like a light.

The helmet was hampering Standing's vision so he pulled

it off, just in time to see a middle-aged Asian lunging towards him with a wicked-looking knife. He slammed the helmet against the man's hand. As the knife fell to the floor, he swung the helmet again, this time catching the man under the chin. His head snapped back and his eyes rolled upwards. Standing hit him a third time, slamming the helmet against the side of his head and he fell like a dead weight.

Two middle-aged Asians, both wearing baggy pants and long shirts, with knitted skullcaps on their heads, rushed towards Standing with their arms outstretched, their yellow fingernails curved like talons. Standing moved towards his nearest attacker, ducked, grabbed his thighs and threw him over his shoulder, slamming him against the wall behind him. The second seized Standing's arm but there was little strength in his grip. Standing broke away and slashed the man across the throat with the side of his hand, splintering the trachea. He dropped to his knees, fighting to breathe. Standing kicked him in the head, knocking him senseless. He was operating on autopilot, reacting instinctively.

Standing heard a scream to his right, and as he turned, a young Asian kicked out at him. The blow landed but there was no strength in it and the foot bounced off his hip. The Asian frowned in disbelief as if he couldn't understand why Standing wasn't in pain. Standing punched him under the chin and he went down without a sound. Less than ten seconds had passed since Standing had entered the room and six men were now lying unconscious on the floor.

The man who had been having sex with the girl rolled off the bed. He was naked and his pendulous belly hung over his private parts, like a late pregnancy. There was saliva on his beard and his chest glistened with sweat. 'Please, sir, I am an old man . . .' he spluttered, waving his hands in front of him. Standing felt the anger flare deep inside him and he struck the man in the face with the helmet. He staggered back, blood splattering, and Standing kicked him between the legs with all the force he could muster. The man's feet left the ground and he crashed against the wall. As he slowly slid to the floor, a streak of blood smeared down the wall-paper.

Standing walked over to the bed. The brunette was naked, her legs apart and her head turned to the side. Standing wasn't sure if she had passed out or if she was just blocking out what was happening. There was a quilt on the floor and he picked it up and draped it over her. She groaned and stared at him with unseeing eyes. Standing picked up the phone that had been used to record her being raped. On the way downstairs he dialled 999. When the operator answered he told her that two girls were being attacked and gave her the address. He said an ambulance was required but when she asked for his name he tossed the phone under the hedge as he walked out of the driveway. He continued along the pavement to his bike. As he drove away he heard police sirens in the distance.

Shepherd took the train from Hereford to London, then a taxi from Paddington station to the rented flat he'd been using while running the north London surveillance operation. The milk in the fridge had gone off so he made himself a cup of black coffee and flopped down in front of the TV. He found it difficult to concentrate, and after he'd finished his coffee, he paced up and down in front of the sofa. Something about the Matt Standing case didn't feel right. Standing was clearly a good soldier, albeit with a tendency to fly off the handle. Shepherd could understand why the SAS wanted him to undergo therapy – that made perfect sense – but it didn't make sense that Standing would then run riot in London. And if he had killed a civilian, why hadn't the police arrested him? It also didn't make sense that Standing would come all the way back to the UK to kill an Asian when he was being paid to do just that in Syria. Shepherd was sure that Willoughby-Brown wasn't telling him the whole story, which was par for the course where his boss was concerned.

There was a bond between the men of the SAS that went far beyond comradeship. They were a family and, like all families, there might be arguments and even fights, but at the end of the day they stuck together, no matter what. Though he'd never met Standing, he was a brother-in-arms and you didn't betray a brother. Shepherd picked up one of his throwaway mobiles, hesitated for a few seconds, then tapped out Standing's number.

'Hello.'

Shepherd hesitated again. Willoughby-Brown had Standing's number and might already be monitoring it. 'Matt?'

'Yes?'

'You don't know me but we need to talk. Urgently. Can you get to Trafalgar Square at nine o'clock?'

'Who is this?'

'Just be there. Near the lions.' Shepherd ended the call. Trafalgar Square was a safe place for a meeting because there were always tourists milling around. But it was also a place where followers could easily blend into the background. If Standing was already under surveillance, they'd have to throw in a few counter-surveillance moves before they could talk.

He grabbed a raincoat, let himself out of the flat and caught a black cab to Charing Cross station, arriving at seven forty-five. He walked along the Strand until he had a clear view of Nelson's Column and the four massive bronze lions around it. He wasn't sure how Standing would be getting there so he continued walking until he was in Northumberland Avenue. That way he could watch the square and see anyone coming from the station.

He realised he had made the right call when he saw Standing walk out of the Tube station. He was wearing a parka with a fur-lined hood and had his head down but Shepherd saw his face when he looked up to cross the road into the square. He waited until Standing had reached Nelson's Column before calling him. 'Matt, okay, I need you to go down into Charing Cross Tube station. Bakerloo line. Northbound platform.'

'Why can't we meet here?' asked Standing, looking around.

'Because I want to check that you're not being followed. If you are, I'll be off.'

'Who do you think is following me?'

'Let's worry about that later. Just walk across the square and I'll introduce myself on the platform. If I'm not there within ten minutes you'll know there's a problem. Find somewhere quiet above ground and call me back.'

'Who the fuck are you?'

'One step at a time, Matt,' said Shepherd, and ended the call.

Shepherd watched as Standing headed for the Tube station. He was looking around as he walked, casually but covering all areas of the square, obviously looking for a tail. Shepherd was further along the Strand, ahead of him. He kept his phone pressed to his ear and pretended to be having a conversation. He reached the Tube station before Standing and went down, then turned towards the southbound platform and waited for Standing to come down the escalator.

As soon as Standing had walked onto the northbound platform, Shepherd followed him. He walked slowly up to

Standing and smiled when Standing looked his way. 'Stay calm, Matt, I'm the guy who called you.'

Standing frowned. 'Do you know me?'

'I know you, but you don't know me,' said Shepherd. 'I used be in the Sass.'

'The Regiment sent you? What the fuck's going on?'

A train arrived. 'Come on,' said Shepherd, taking a quick look around before getting on. Standing followed and the doors rattled shut. There was only one other person in the carriage, an elderly woman deep in an eReader. They sat well away from her.

'What the hell's going on?' asked Standing. 'Who are you and what do you want?'

'I was asked to run a check on you. By MI5.'

'Fucking spooks.'

'They think you've gone rogue. They say you're killing Asians and beating up cops. And that you put two MI5 officers in hospital.'

'They attacked me. And the business with the cops was self-defence. If I'd broken the law, I would have been charged.'

'Yeah, I wondered about that.'

'Who are you?'

'My name's Shepherd.'

Standing's eyes widened. 'Spider Shepherd? Fuck me, you're a legend.'

'Yeah, well, I'd appreciate it if you'd keep that to yourself. I'm not supposed to be talking to you.'

'What did they tell you?'

'Just that you went rogue.'

'And are you supposed to stop me?'

Shepherd shook his head. 'They just wanted intel.'

'And you gave it to them?'

'It's my job.'

Standing gritted his teeth, then visibly relaxed. 'Yeah, I guess so. We all have to do shit work at some point, I suppose. So why are you here?'

'Because you and me, we're maybe not the same but we're similar. We've got a lot in common. And if the shit was about to hit my fan, I'd appreciate a heads up.'

'So that's what this is? A heads up?'

'You put two MI5 guys in hospital. Next time you might not be so lucky.'

'If they don't touch me, I won't touch them.'

'Yeah, well, that's not how it works. Can't you call it a day?'

'Do you know what's happened? What did they tell you?'

'Not much. Just what you'd done and that they wanted it stopped.'

They arrived at the next station. Piccadilly Circus. The doors rattled open and two teenage girls got on, sharing a set of earphones plugged into an iPhone. They sat well away from Shepherd and Standing. The doors closed and the train sped off again.

'They killed my sister, Spider. They got her hooked on heroin and then they gave her an overdose.'

'Who did?'

'A fucking Asian grooming gang. I can show you pictures, video, the fucking works. They groom them and then they fuck them. If they step out of line they fucking kill them.'

'The Asian that died?'

'Was one of them. He was the one that groomed her. Now I'm trying to get the guy who gave her the heroin. I know who he is and I know he did it because I've got the texts he sent to Faisal.'

Shepherd was stunned, wondering why Jeremy Willoughby-Brown had got involved in this can of worms.

'I was at a place tonight where a gang of them were raping

two young girls. They're sick fucks, Spider, and I'm not backing down. You can't stop me doing what needs to be done.'

'I told you already, I won't be the one to stop you.'

Standing shrugged. 'That's good to know.'

Shepherd's eyes hardened. 'If I did try to stop you, what then?'

Standing shrugged again. 'Like I said, you're a legend. But you're fifteen years older than me and I'm just back from Syria. You wouldn't want to take me, Spider.'

Shepherd smiled. 'Yeah, well, hopefully, we'll never know. If you've got evidence, why didn't you go to the police?'

'Tried that. They'd been told to lay off. By MI5.'

Shepherd frowned. 'That doesn't make any sense.'

'No, it makes sense, all right. I think there's a major anti-terrorism operation going on and they don't want me making waves.'

Shepherd rubbed the back of his neck. It was possible, he supposed. It wasn't unusual for two agencies to target the same individual and at some point one would agree to play second fiddle. But Shepherd couldn't see how any operation – even one involving terrorists – would supersede rape and murder.

'So you hear where I'm coming from, right?'

Shepherd nodded. 'Yeah.'

'So what happens next?'

'I get off at the next station and we go our separate ways,' said Shepherd. 'What happens then is up to you. I just wanted to mark your card.'

'And I appreciate that,' said Standing. 'Consider it marked.'

The train slowed as it approached the next station. Shepherd stood up and offered his hand. Standing shook it. 'Thanks,' he said.

'Be lucky,' said Shepherd.

The train stopped at Leicester Square, the doors opened, and Shepherd got off. He didn't look around as the train sped into the tunnel.

As he rode the up escalator at Oxford Circus, Standing opened his smartphone and pulled out the SIM card. He broke it in half and tossed it into the gutter when he reached street level. He knew enough about telephone surveillance to realise that the security services were able to track his phone, no matter what SIM card was in it, so he had to get rid of that, too. He dropped it into a litter bin. He kept looking over his shoulder and didn't think he was being followed, but having met Spider Shepherd he was even more on his guard.

When you were on a mission and you were spotted, more often than not the sensible decision was to pull out. Confrontation often led to casualties. But there were times when pulling out was not an option and this was one of them. There was no backing down from what he intended to do. He was going to have his revenge for the death of his sister, one way or another.

Shepherd arrived at Gatwick airport early in the morning and had breakfast in the Virgin Clubhouse lounge. His phone rang just as he was drinking a second cup of coffee. It was Willoughby-Brown. 'Where are you?' he asked.

'Airport,' said Shepherd. 'Boarding soon.'

'Just so you know, Standing went on the rampage again. He killed two Asians in Wembley and put another half-dozen in hospital.'

'Are you serious?'

'You think I'd joke about something like that?'

'He killed two people?'

'Beat them to death.'

'When did this happen?'

'Early yesterday evening.'

'Why?'

'I'm not sure that when and why are the right questions to be asking.'

'I mean, he's not the type to go around killing at random, is he?'

'He's got anger-management issues, Daniel. The Regiment acknowledges that.'

'There's a big difference between anger-management issues and killing people. What about the cops?'

'What about them?'

'Has he been arrested?'

'No.'

'Why not?'

'There's no evidence. The men he injured aren't talking.'

'So it might not have been him?'

'One guy takes out more than half a dozen men at the same time. That takes a particular skill set, as you know.'

'Do you want me to stay in London?' asked Shepherd.

'No need,' said Willoughby-Brown. 'But I'd like you to tie up the Meyer case as quickly as possible.'

'No problem,' said Shepherd. 'I'm assuming that if I pass muster he'll show me the boat, which will be loaded with the drugs. Lisa can give evidence against him so it should be cut and dried. But who's going to handle the arrest?'

'We can do it through the NCA and let them take the credit.'

'And what about Lisa? What intel has she been sending back?'

'She's informed the NCA that she and Meyer are heading to St Lucia, and she reported the meeting he had with the Colombians.'

'And what about me?'

'Just that Meyer had told her he would be meeting Jeff Taylor out there. So we're good to go. I'll talk to you again when you're over there.'

'Be careful with Standing,' said Shepherd.

There was a slight pause before Willoughby-Brown answered. 'What makes you say that?'

'SAS, Jeremy. "Who Dares Wins." Whatever mission it is that he's on, he'll see it through to the end, come what may.'

'I'll bear that in mind, Daniel,' said Willoughby-Brown, frostily. 'You have a safe flight.'

Standing woke instantly, as always, and lay staring at the ceiling as he ran through his options. He still had only one way of finding Ali Hussain and that was through the minicab office in Kilburn. Which meant all he could do was to sit outside and wait. But after what had happened in Wembley the previous night, would Hussain be on the defensive? Would he link what had happened in Wembley to Standing's visit to the minicab office? If he did, and if he went to ground, Standing might never find him.

He rolled out of bed and spent an hour exercising in his room – a mixture of press-ups, sit-ups and planks – then showered and shaved. He knew he needed to replace his phone and SIM card but he was uncomfortable going outside after what had happened in Wembley. He doubted that any of the men in the house would give his description to the police, but the girls had seen him and he wasn't sure how cooperative they would be. He pulled on his parka and put up the hood as soon as he left the hotel, keeping his head down and avoiding CCTV cameras wherever possible. He found a phone shop and bought a cheap Samsung smartphone and half a dozen pay-as-you-go SIM cards with cash. He was fairly sure that the shop assistant thought he was a drug dealer but she took the cash anyway. He found an office-supplies store and bought a clipboard, a pack of manila envelopes and a messenger bag, figuring that if he was going to keep carrying out surveillance on a motorbike he might as well try to look like a courier. He popped into a café and picked up a selection of sandwiches and a cup of coffee, bought half a dozen newspapers, then took his purchases back to the hotel.

He drank his coffee and ate two of the sandwiches while he read through the papers and charged the phone. There was no mention of what had happened at Wembley, which he took as a good sign. Later he put in one of the SIM cards and phoned Credenhill to give them the new number in case they needed to contact him. He would have preferred to go off the grid completely but regulations insisted that he be contactable by the Regiment 24/7. Then he phoned Dr Doyle's office where the receptionist thanked him for calling and said she had been trying to contact him about his next appointment. Dr Doyle had a free slot at two p.m. and they wanted Standing to attend if he could.

Standing wasn't happy about having another therapy session but he knew that his SAS career depended on it so he promised to be there.

The stewardess asked Shepherd if he wanted a drink. Most of the passengers in Upper Class were taking advantage of the free champagne on offer but he wanted to keep a clear head so he asked for soda water with ice and lemon. It was a long flight – just over eight hours – and he planned to sleep most of the way. He sipped his water as he ran through what Willoughby-Brown had told him. His boss had been vague about why Standing was behaving as he was. There was no way Shepherd could tell Willoughby-Brown that he had spoken to him, and that he knew exactly why the former SAS sergeant was wreaking havoc across London. Shepherd understood why Standing was doing it, and he empathised. The men he was targeting had killed his sister, and nothing was more important than family. Shepherd had no doubt that if something similar ever happened to Liam or Katra he would react in exactly the same way.

If Willoughby-Brown was right and Standing had attacked a group of Asians, killing two of them early yesterday evening, it must have been before Shepherd had met him at Charing Cross Tube station. Standing must have ice for blood because he had given no indication at their meeting that he had been in a fight just a few hours earlier.

What was worrying was that Willoughby-Brown hadn't filled him in regarding Standing's motives. He must have known that the attacks weren't random and that everything Standing was doing was to take revenge on the men who were responsible for his sister's death. Standing had been quick to explain himself to Shepherd, and there was no way Willoughby-Brown wouldn't have known about his sister. That meant Willoughby-Brown had deliberately withheld the information from Shepherd, which was a worry. A big worry. Trust was important in the undercover business, and it was a two-way street. The handler had to trust that the operative was doing the job to the best of their ability. And the operative had to trust that his handler was watching his back and protecting him when necessary. Without trust, there was nothing. There was no good reason for Willoughby-Brown to be keeping Shepherd in the dark, at least none that Shepherd could think of. That suggested Willoughby-Brown was working to his own agenda at a time when Shepherd was about to put his life on the line, which meant that Shepherd could no longer trust him.

Standing picked up his motorbike from the car park and drove to Harley Street, the messenger bag over his shoulder. He passed Dr Doyle's building and didn't see anyone who was obviously watching so he parked up in a side-street, waited ten minutes and drove by again. Still nothing. But MI5's surveillance teams were among the best in the world, so Standing still wasn't convinced it was safe. There was a multi-storey car park in Queen Anne Mews, around the corner from Harley Street, so he left the bike there and walked back to Dr Doyle's surgery, still wearing his crash helmet. As he approached the building, he took the clipboard out of the bag and pretended to study the envelope clipped to it. He rang the bell, and when the door opened he went inside. Only then did he remove his full-face helmet.

He left the helmet, bag and motorcycle jacket in Reception while he went through to Dr Doyle's office. He had his anger diary with him. He had added a few more entries detailing incidents that had never happened and how he had dealt with them. Dr Doyle went through them with him and nodded her approval at the actions he'd taken. Standing took no pleasure in lying to the therapist, but he could hardly tell her what he had really been doing since they had last met.

She had him perform his deep-breathing and relaxation techniques for her, and then they chatted about the incidents in his career that had led to his demotions and how he could better have dealt with them. As the session drew to a close, she said she was very pleased with his progress and sent him on his way.

Standing put his full-face helmet back on and slung the messenger bag over his shoulder before he let himself out of the front door. He knew that if Dr Doyle's surgery was under surveillance, the fact that he'd been inside for an hour wouldn't fit with his courier disguise, so he didn't go back to his bike. Instead he went the other way, walking against the traffic. That meant any vehicle tailing him would either be on the other side of the road or be forced to perform a U-turn. His visor down, he kept a careful watch on the traffic coming towards him and the pedestrians around him. There was a woman pushing a toddler in a stroller, then an old couple walking slowly, him with a walking stick, her with a woollen hat pulled down over her ears. A young man in a tight suit was striding briskly along, barking into his mobile phone in French. In the distance, two teenagers with backpacks. Students, maybe. Too slight to be muscle. He glanced over his shoulder. A businessman. Two housewives. A teenager with his baseball cap the wrong way around. Two Asian schoolgirls wearing dark blue *hijab*s. So far so good. There was a side-road ahead and he crossed, then turned left and walked slowly to see if anyone else did the same. No one did.

He began to relax, but he was still alert. If he was being followed, and they were good, it would take more than one simple change of direction for them to show out. He kept a special look-out for any vehicles that turned into the side-road but the ones that did seemed innocuous and accelerated away without giving him a second look. He crossed the road again and continued north, then took the next left, watching again to make sure that no one followed him.

There were two men on the other side of the road. Big men wearing black nylon bomber jackets, jeans and heavy boots, deep in conversation as they walked in his direction. They were the type, but they didn't even glance at him as they went by. A black cab drove past and the driver looked in his direction. His lips were moving so he was probably talking on hands-free. Standing turned to watch him drive away. A cyclist was heading towards him. A girl. Mid-twenties. Cyclists were a good way of maintaining surveillance in a crowded city like London as they could weave in and out of traffic and pull U-turns quickly if they had to. She maintained her speed as she went by and he couldn't see anything in the way of a radio or phone on her.

The hairs stood up on the back of his neck and he shivered. He took a quick look over his shoulder. The two men in bomber jackets had crossed the road and were now following him. His heart began to beat faster. He was being hunted, no question.

He started to walk faster and took out his clipboard. He made a play of looking at it as he walked. He knew that the charade wouldn't fool anyone but the clipboard was hard plastic and could be used as a weapon. He was sure that this time they would be prepared for him to fight back. He didn't know how long they'd been following him. If they had spotted him on the bike, they'd know he'd left it in the multi-storey. If they were going to take him, the car park would be the best option – things could always go wrong out on a public street. But if they knew where the bike was, why follow him along the street? They could have waited near the bike. Maybe they hadn't seen him until he'd walked into the building. Then when he hadn't come straight out they'd red-flagged him. If that was the case, they would assume he had a bike but wouldn't know where he'd left it. That gave them two choices – to follow him to the bike or to take him in the street.

He turned left and glanced over his shoulder. The two men had given up any pretence of hiding their intentions: they were staring at him with ice-cold eyes and they were heading straight for him. The street, then. It wasn't how he would have done it, but they were the ones making the play.

Standing increased his pace and heard the men do the same. Ahead of him he could see a black van. The driver was also wearing a bomber jacket but he had shielded his eyes with dark glasses. He had both hands on the steering wheel and the engine was running. As Standing drew nearer, the side door of the van rattled open. Two more men appeared. One with a shaved head, one with a beard, both wearing dark glasses. They were wearing the ubiquitous bomber jackets, and gloves. One jumped out and held his arms to the side, blocking Standing's way. The man who remained in the van was holding a black semi-automatic. The sight of the weapon kicked Standing into overdrive.

He charged at the man on the pavement and kicked him in the stomach, putting all his weight into the blow. The man fell back, his arms windmilling, and hit the pavement hard. Before he was on the ground, Standing was already turning towards the van. It felt as if he was in slow motion as his instincts kicked in.

To his right, the two men who had been following him had broken into a run. He hadn't seen a weapon, which meant the man in the back of the van was the immediate threat. He stepped towards the vehicle and kicked out with his left leg, catching the man's wrist and sending the arm whipping to its owner's right.

The moment Standing's left foot touched the ground again he jumped forward, grabbed the man by the collar and pulled him out of the van. He yelped and his hands clawed at the floor but Standing dropped him onto the pavement. He tried to roll over and Standing stamped on his shoulder. He felt the arm pop out of the socket and the man screamed, then went still.

The man Standing had kicked was back on his feet and punched him but Standing was moving and it was a glancing blow to his shoulder. The helmet hampered his vision but it meant his attackers couldn't whack him over the head, which was a big plus. Standing ducked as he turned, tucked his chin into his chest and powered three quick punches to the man's stomach, left, right, left, and the man fell back against the van. Standing used his right foot to sweep the man's legs from under him and he crashed to the pavement.

One of the men running towards him had drawn a gun. That made him the new threat and Standing's instincts took over. He took a quick step, then executed a perfect side kick that struck the man in the stomach and knocked the wind out of him. As Standing straightened, the man bent double, the gun pointing at the ground. Standing grabbed the gun with his left hand and punched the man with his right. His gloved fist caught the man's chin and snapped his head to the side with such force that his spine made a cracking sound. The other man grabbed the collar of Standing's motorbike jacket and pulled him back, throwing him off balance. Standing kept a tight grip on the gun and pulled it away from the man holding it. He spun around and slammed the weapon against the temple of the man holding his jacket. His assailant gasped in pain but kept a tight hold on the jacket as he punched Standing in the side. It was a powerful blow and Standing grunted, but he was firing on all cylinders and barely registered the pain. He struck out with the gun again, this time slamming the butt into the man's balls. The man roared and let go of the jacket. Standing stepped to the side, drew back his right hand and hit the man in the sternum with the full weight of his body behind the punch. The man staggered back, winded, then slumped to the pavement.

The driver's door opened. Standing whirled around, pointing the gun at him with his left hand. It had been years since he had taught himself to fire weapons with either hand and the Glock was almost as comfortable in his left as it was in his right. The driver's face hardened. He wasn't holding a weapon but that didn't mean he wasn't carrying one. 'Back in the van, hands on the wheel!' shouted Standing.

The driver did as he was told.

Standing transferred the gun to his right hand and slid the weapon inside his jacket. He glanced up and down the street. The van had blocked any view of the cars that had gone by and there were no pedestrians. The whole incident had taken less than ten seconds. Standing walked quickly away, breathing slowly and evenly.

The Virgin Atlantic flight landed at Hewanorra International Airport on the southern tip of St Lucia at just before two o'clock in the afternoon. The passengers had to sit on the plane while a set of stairs was pushed over the tarmac, but Shepherd was one of the first off. Within five minutes he'd had his passport stamped and was waved through Customs.

Automatic doors rattled open and he walked out into the arrivals area where there were half a dozen brightly coloured lecterns with the names of hotels on them and half a dozen drivers. A tall man with dreadlocks and a baggy blue suit was holding a piece of card with 'JEFF TAYLOR' written on it in capital letters.

Shepherd said hello to the man, who nodded and grinned, showing a gold tooth at the front of his mouth. 'Welcome to St Lucia,' he said, and stuck out his hand for Shepherd's bag.

Shepherd shook his head. 'I'm good,' he said.

The driver led him to the car park where he opened the

rear door of a ten-year-old Mercedes. Shepherd got into the back.

The drive to the hotel took just over an hour, along a narrow road that wound up and down a hill with dozens of blind corners. The driver was cautious, which Shepherd appreciated as there were dizzyingly precarious drops at regular intervals and the occasional glimpse of clear blue sea far below.

The car rattled along a potholed track with wooden shacks that doubled as bars, then turned into a narrow road that led to the outdoor reception area of the Capella Marigot Bay Resort where a pretty young girl confirmed that his room had been pre-paid, then walked him through the tropical gardens to his suite. Shepherd was no stranger to good hotels but the suite Meyer had arranged for him was something special. Outside, a long terrace overlooked the hotel's swimming pool and the bay beyond, a pale blue sea dotted with pristine yachts and a green hill facing them. On a deck to his left a personal hot tub was already bubbling away.

The girl opened the door and showed him in. It was larger than the flat he'd been staying at in London and much better equipped. There was a sitting area with a sofa, two armchairs and a large-screen TV, and beyond it a full kitchen. Two wooden-bladed ceiling fans whirred overhead and the aircon had been set at an icy blast. She demonstrated the appliances one by one, then opened a door to show him his own personal laundry room. He grinned. 'I'm not planning on doing any laundry,' he said.

Another door led to a large room with a four-poster bed festooned with mosquito nets and coloured pillows, another big-screen television, huge wardrobes and a door that led to a bathroom with a massive walk-in shower and two washbasins.

'I hope you'll be comfortable here,' she said, handing him the door card.

Shepherd gave her a ten-dollar bill, and as she was leaving, his mobile beeped. It was a text: Doolittle's 4 p.m.

'What's Doolittle's?' he asked the girl.

'It's a restaurant and bar on the other side of the bay.'

'How do I get there?' he asked.

'There's a free ferry from the marina,' she said. 'It goes back and forth all day and night.'

Shepherd thanked her with another ten-dollar bill and she left. He opened the fridge and took out a bottle of water, then went out onto the terrace. He was sure it was no coincidence that the text message had arrived just as he had checked in. He sipped his water and looked out over the sea. There were a dozen yachts and catamarans in front of him, most moored in the middle of the bay. A few had dropped anchor close to the mangroves at the base of the hill. There were people on several of the boats but no one appeared to be looking his way.

A dozen people were sitting and lying around the pool, six couples, the youngest of whom were in their forties. Most had tans that suggested they were no strangers to sunbathing, and almost all had cocktails close by. Young waiters flitted to and fro, attending to the needs of their guests. Shepherd wondered what their daily wage was, and how close that would be to the cost of a single cocktail.

The hairs were standing up on the back of his neck, letting him know that his subconscious was pretty sure he was being watched. He smiled to himself and took another sip of water. He was going to have to be careful what he did and what he said. If he was being watched, there was a good chance that he was being listened to as well. He decided against phoning Willoughby-Brown from the suite, just to be on the safe side, and walked down to the marina before calling.

Willoughby-Brown answered almost immediately. 'I'm here,' said Shepherd. 'I'm due to meet Meyer at four o'clock local time.'

'Keep me posted,' said Willoughby-Brown.

'How's the Standing thing going?'

'Funny you should ask,' said Willoughby-Brown. 'He put two of my men in hospital yesterday.'

'How did that happen?'

'They were trying to bring him in but underestimated his abilities, obviously.'

'Obviously,' said Shepherd.

'I can hear the satisfaction in your voice, Daniel,' said Willoughby-Brown.

'Sorry, but the SAS and Five are chalk and cheese when it comes to rough and tumble. How many men did you send?'

'Four. And a driver.'

'Armed?'

'Handguns.'

'I would have sent cops in, with Tasers. You know our people are always reluctant to fire their guns – it's not what they're trained for.'

'Hindsight is always fifty-fifty, of course,' said Willoughby-Brown.

'Twenty-twenty,' said Shepherd.

'What?'

'Hindsight is twenty-twenty. Perfect vision.'

Willoughby-Brown sighed. 'I'll talk to you after your meeting with Meyer,' he said, and ended the call, clearly miffed at being corrected.

Shepherd walked slowly back to his suite, deep in thought.

It didn't make sense that Willoughby-Brown had sent MI5 officers to apprehend Standing. They had no powers of arrest, and clearly what Standing was doing was against the law. That being the case, Willoughby-Brown could have used armed cops or anti-terrorist officers, who would have used overwhelming force to ensure that Standing was taken quietly. For some reason Willoughby-Brown wanted to keep Standing in-house, and he was clearly unwilling to explain to Shepherd why that was.

Standing parked his bike in the multi-storey at King's Cross and went back to his hotel, picking up a pack of beer on the way. He still had untouched sandwiches in his room so he ate them and drank one of the beers while he watched the news. There was still nothing about the attack in Wembley, and no mention of the attempted kidnapping near Harley Street. MI5 was clearly keeping the news under wraps, which would work to his advantage. If they went public and his photograph was plastered across newspapers and television, it wouldn't be long before someone recognised him and turned him in.

He picked up the gun and stripped it, then reassembled it and checked the action. It was in perfect condition, as if it had never been fired. It was a Glock 21, a full-sized .45 pistol with thirteen rounds in the magazine. It had a 4.6-inch barrel, weighed 26 ounces, and it took 5.5 pounds of pressure to pull the trigger. There hadn't been a round chambered in the gun when he'd taken it off the man in the van, which suggested he hadn't intended to use it. The Glock's trigger-safety mechanism meant that it was perfectly safe to carry it with a round in the chamber. And at the time, the man's finger had always been outside the trigger guard. Standing had known immediately that they had no intention of shooting him – the guns were to intimidate him, nothing more. He smiled to himself as he slotted in the magazine. It would take more than a gun to intimidate him. Guns on their own weren't in the least bit threatening, it was the people holding them who wielded the power. A gun was a tool, nothing more.

He slid it under the pillow, lay down on the bed and stared up at the ceiling, wondering what to do next. He'd beaten the spooks twice, but he doubted he'd manage it a third time. They weren't going to give up. But neither was Standing. He was determined to follow this through to the bitter end.

Shepherd walked down to the marina, There were dozens of multi-million-pound yachts and power boats moored up and many more at anchor in the bay At the far end of the marina there was a jetty with large signs advertising the various restaurants that were dotted around. Shepherd headed towards it. He passed a motor launch where a group of bare-chested young men were drinking beer, and nodded to a man in his sixties who was cleaning the rails of his twin-masted yacht. Everyone he met was smiling, a by-product of the Caribbean sunshine and the idyllic setting.

A small ferry, with bench seats enough to sit a dozen people at most, was tethered to the jetty. An awning round the top advertised Doolittle's. The driver was standing in front of the wheel and he grinned at Shepherd. 'Doolittle's?'

'Terrific,' said Shepherd, climbing aboard. An elderly couple were already sitting down, holding hands like teenage lovers. They smiled at Shepherd. He smiled back and sat on the opposite side of the ferry. A few seconds later they were pulling away from the jetty and heading across the bay.

After just five minutes the ferry executed a perfect turn and came to a halt inches from the wooden jetty next to an open-sided bar with a sign confirming that he had indeed arrived at Doolittle's. He stepped off the boat and walked towards the bar. A beautiful young woman with dreadlocks, wearing a tight-fitting dress, flashed him a beaming smile and asked if he was there to eat or drink, but before he could reply there was a shout from across the bar. Meyer and Lisa were playing pool at one of two red-felted tables. Lisa jumped up and down and waved. Shepherd grinned at the woman with dreadlocks. 'I'm with them,' he said.

'Clearly,' she said, with a smile. 'And I'm guessing you'll be wanting another bottle of Cristal.'

'The drink has been flowing, has it?' asked Shepherd.

'Let's just say they came for breakfast and haven't stopped,' she said, with a wink.

Shepherd went over to the pool tables. Lisa rushed over and hugged him, and he shook hands with Meyer, who was wearing white jeans and a blue-patterned long-sleeved Ted Baker shirt.

'How's the room?' asked Meyer.

'The suite? Awesome.'

'It's a great place.'

'Are you staying there?'

Meyer shook his head. 'You know me and hotels.' He pointed at a large catamaran in the bay 'I'm staying on her. I'll show you around tomorrow. The owner's a pal of Putin's and you won't believe the sort of stuff he's got below decks. Gold taps, I kid you not. And he's got bar stools upholstered with whale foreskin.' He pointed a finger at Shepherd, who shook his head in disbelief. 'I'm not making that up!'

'That's not the one I'll be sailing, is it?'

Meyer gestured to the other side of the bay, where a smaller catamaran was moored to a buoy. 'That's yours, assuming you're up for it.'

Shepherd grinned. 'I wouldn't have flown all the way here if I wasn't,' he said.

Lisa poured champagne into a glass and gave it to him. She raised hers. 'To Paradise!' she said.

The two men clinked their glasses against hers. 'You like it here?' asked Shepherd. 'St Lucia?'

Lisa waved a hand around. 'What's not to like?' she said, slurring her words slightly.

'So, how about a bite to eat?' asked Meyer. 'Then I'll show you your boat.'

'Sounds like a plan,' said Shepherd.

A table had already been set for them overlooking the bay. They all had steaks with thick-cut chips and onion rings, and another bottle of Cristal. As always, Meyer was the perfect host, telling stories and making them laugh, but never saying anything that could be used against him in a court of law. He was religious about only discussing business at sea, and while he told plenty of stories about the criminals he'd met over the years and the crimes they'd committed, he kept quiet about his own transgressions. He seemed happy to hold court, which suited Shepherd. He was more than capable of telling war stories, and his near-perfect memory meant he had hundreds of tales and anecdotes that he could roll out if necessary, but as a general rule when working under cover the less you said the better.

They finished the meal with coffee, and Meyer and Lisa shared an ice cream. It was close to five o'clock when Meyer waved for the bill and they walked to where the small ferry-boat was waiting for them. Meyer helped Lisa on and they sat together on the starboard side. Shepherd sat facing them. Lisa seemed a little worse for wear. Meyer had been drinking but not as heavily as usual, and as always Shepherd had been careful with his alcohol intake. 'This is the life,' said Meyer.

He waved up at the villas looking down on the bay 'Good food, good friends, and the prospect of us making a lot of money. Perfect day or what?'

Shepherd faked a grin. 'Perfect.'

Meyer patted Lisa's leg. 'What about you? Good day, right?'

Lisa nodded. 'The best,' she said. She rested her head against his shoulder and closed her eyes.

Some of the villas on the hillside were magnificent. Traditional wooden buildings with sloping roofs and wrap-around terraces were interspersed with modern glass and metal constructions that gleamed in the sun. 'You never thought of getting a place here?' asked Shepherd, indicating the hill.

Meyer shook his head. 'I don't own property. If you own it, they can take it off you.'

'They?'

'The cops, the government. If they ever did make a case against me, the first thing they'd do is seize my assets. All my cash is in offshore accounts and trusts, well hidden.'

'Smart,' said Shepherd.

'Plus, if they know where you live, they can plant bugs and cameras and God knows what. And if you have a place you need staff and they can always be got at.'

'You're starting to sound a bit paranoid,' said Shepherd.

Meyer grinned. 'Just because I'm paranoid doesn't mean they're not out to get me,' he said. 'But if you do plan to get up to mischief, a boat is the place to be.'

The ferry approached a large catamaran from the rear. There were two men already on board but they had their backs to the ferry. 'This is your boat,' said Meyer.

'What is it?' asked Shepherd. 'Fifty feet?'

'Give or take.'

It was called *Plain Sailing* and was registered in the Cayman Islands. The ferry drew up next to the port hull and Meyer climbed over first. He held out his hand for Lisa and helped her on board, then did the same for Shepherd. The ferry moved away, heading back to Doolittle's.

Meyer walked across the cockpit. The two men still had their backs to them, facing towards the bow. They turned as Meyer came up to them. 'So, these guys brought the boat over from Colombia,' said Meyer, and Shepherd knew immediately that he was up to something because one of the men was Oscar Lopez. Lopez was wearing the same hat and sunglasses he'd had on at the marina in Marbella. And, as far as Shepherd knew, Lopez wasn't a sailor. He was wearing a baggy shirt with a palm tree design. It was so loose that Shepherd couldn't tell if he was carrying a gun, and he didn't seem the type who would welcome a hug. He nodded at Shepherd and grunted.

Meyer pointed at the other man. 'This is Jose. Jose Alvarez. He's the captain.'

Alvarez grinned at Shepherd and threw him a mock salute 'Good to meet you,' he said, with a heavy Colombian accent.

'Cheers,' said Shepherd.

Meyer nodded at Lopez. 'And this is Diego. He doesn't speak much English.' Another lie. Shepherd had a bad feeling about the way things were going. Lopez was an enforcer. A killer. And he was a long way from home. There had to be a reason why he was on the boat, and Shepherd was sure it wasn't for the sea air.

He looked around nonchalantly. 'Nice boat,' he said. He sounded calm but his mind was racing, considering his options.

'It's very similar to *Windchaser*, but about ten feet shorter,' said Meyer. 'You can sail it single-handed, but I figure you'd be better picking up a deckhand here. There are always sailors passing through, looking for a charter.'

Lisa had found the fridge and opened it. 'There's no champagne,' she said, and pouted.

'It's not a party boat, honey,' said Meyer. 'Grab me a beer.'

She took out a bottle, popped the cap off with an opener and gave it to him. 'Jeff?'

'Sure,' said Shepherd, and she gave him a beer, then took one for herself.

'How about you take her out, Jeff?' said Meyer. 'See how she handles.'

'No problem,' said Shepherd. He nodded at Alvarez. 'Can I have a look at the chart?'

'I use the GPS display,' said Alvarez.

He pointed at the screen by the wheel and Shepherd looked at it for several seconds. 'Okay,' he said. 'Let's do it.' He jerked a thumb at Alvarez. 'Can you do the anchor for me, Captain?'

Alvarez looked across at Meyer, who nodded, and went to sort out the anchor while Shepherd started the engine. He waited until Alvarez had raised the anchor before pushing the throttle forward and edging the cat out of the bay.

Alvarez stood behind Shepherd, watching over his shoulder. Meyer and Lisa sat on the bench seat on the starboard side while Lopez stood at the rear of the port hull, leaning against the rail. Shepherd had a very bad feeling about Lopez being onboard. A very, very bad feeling.

Standing pulled up on his motorbike in the side-street overlooking the minicab office in Kilburn. He'd thrown away his helmet and motorcycle jacket and bought a new helmet from a shop close to King's Cross station. He'd also bought a Belstaff waxed motorbike jacket and a new pair of gloves, blue instead of black. The MI5 goons hadn't seen his bike so that wasn't a problem, but he still paid careful attention to the vehicles and pedestrians in the vicinity. He'd ditched the courier disguise: his plan was to park up for half an hour, then drive somewhere else. There were several side-roads from which he could watch the entrance to the minicab office. It was the worst possible sort of surveillance – he had to watch out for his target while at the same time look out for anyone who was watching him. As he sat and waited, he practised Dr Doyle's breathing techniques, but he remained totally alert as his heart rate slowed.

Shepherd sailed the catamaran out to sea. It was similar to the boat he'd practised on in Florida and he had no problems putting it through its paces. Alvarez and Lopez were at the stern and Lisa had gone below deck. 'So what do you think? Could you sail her to Spain?' asked Meyer, who was sitting behind the starboard wheel while Shepherd used the port wheel to steer the boat.

'Sure,' said Shepherd. 'But why Spain? I could take this all the way to the UK.'

'Spain's the safer bet,' said Meyer. 'There's more traffic in the Med and it's easier to blend in. Of course you could take her into any of the south-coast ports but all you need is one nosy local to pick up the phone and you'd be busted. Plus we've got a tame boatyard in Marbella where they can strip the drugs out and make the boat good again.'

'Is the stuff on board?' asked Shepherd.

'Built into the hulls,' said Meyer. 'They do it in Colombia. It's damn near perfect – you won't be able to see the joins. They pretty much rebuild the hull with the drugs inside.'

'And how much gear is there?'

Meyer laughed. 'Why does that matter?'

'I guess the more there is, the bigger the risk.'

'Nah, that's bollocks,' said Meyer. 'Once you get over a ton it makes no odds.'

'And Customs won't find it if they come on board?'

'Dogs can't smell it. You'd have to drill to find it and Customs aren't going to do that on spec.'

'What about a scan?'

'They're not geared up for bringing scanners out to boats – they'd have to haul her out of the water to do that and it'd cost an arm and a leg. These days, the only way they catch anyone is from intel and that's my strong point. Money for old rope. Trust me.'

'Sounds good,' said Shepherd. 'But what about . . .?' He nodded at the hatch leading below deck.

'She hasn't spoken to anyone since we left Spain,' said Meyer. 'Seems like her phone developed a fault. I've said I'll buy her a new one but until then she's got no way of contacting anyone.'

Lisa came up from below. 'Speak of the devil,' he said.

Lisa looked a little queasy. 'Are you okay?' asked Meyer.

'I think I drank too much champagne,' she said, sitting next to him.

'Do you think?' laughed Meyer, patting her leg. 'How about we park here, Jeff?' The coastline was half a mile away and there were no other boats nearby.

'Is there a problem?' asked Shepherd.

Meyer waved his beer bottle in the air. 'I just want to kick back for a while.'

Shepherd went about bringing the boat to a stop. Under Alvarez's watchful eye, he deep-reefed the main sail, dropped the traveller to leeward, then pulled the mainsheet hard in. All done, he turned the wheel and pointed the bow into the wind. Alvarez nodded, and Shepherd knew he'd carried out the manoeuvre almost perfectly.

Lopez was leaning against the railing on the starboard side, his hands in his pockets. Neither he nor Alvarez had been drinking. Lopez never took off his sunglasses and his face was always impassive. It was impossible to guess what he was thinking but Shepherd knew he had to be on the boat for a reason and that reason would almost certainly involve violence.

Meyer stood and looked up at the near-cloudless sky. 'Lovely day for a swim,' he said. 'Come on, honey, up you get.'

He held out his hand to Lisa but she shook her head. 'I'm too drunk,' she said.

'Nah, you're fine. Come on.'

She waved her hands at him. 'Marcus, I'm drunk.'

Meyer's face hardened. 'Stand the fuck up.'

She frowned up at him, using a hand to shield her eyes against the sun. 'What's wrong?'

Meyer grabbed her arm and pulled her to her feet, then smacked his beer bottle across her face. She staggered back against the railing. 'Marcus?' she said, her eyes wide with disbelief.

'What the fuck, Marcus?' shouted Shepherd.

Alvarez disappeared below deck.

Meyer pointed a finger at Shepherd. 'Shut the fuck up!' he shouted. 'She's had this coming.'

Tears were welling in Lisa's eyes. She touched her lips with her fingertips and stared at the blood on them. 'What's wrong?' she asked. 'I don't understand.'

Lopez walked over to her. He stopped at the starboard-side chair and bent down to pick up a length of chain and a padlock.

'Marcus, honey, what's going on?' asked Lisa.

'You're going for a swim,' said Meyer. 'Now shut the fuck up.'

Lopez walked over to Lisa and slapped her so hard that she was knocked to the deck.

Shepherd took a step towards her but Meyer pointed a warning finger at his face and told him to stay where he was.

Lopez wound the chain around Lisa's left ankle and locked it tight with the padlock.

Lisa wiped her mouth with the back of her hand. 'Marcus, what was that for?' she said.

'You're a fucking grass,' said Meyer.

Alvarez appeared from below decks carrying a concrete block. He put it down next to Lisa, and Lopez used a second padlock to fasten the other end of the chain to it.

'You're an undercover cop,' said Meyer, 'working for the NCA. Everything you've ever said to me has been a lie, pretty much. And you're going to get what's coming to you.'

Lisa stared at the concrete block and realised what was going to happen. 'You can't do this to me,' she gasped.

Meyer grinned cruelly. 'I'm not going to do it,' he said. 'Jeff is.'

Shepherd's eyes widened. 'What?'

Meyer continued to stare at Lisa. 'Mind you, Jeff isn't Jeff. His name is Rich Campbell and he's been a bit of a bad lad.'

'Marcus, what are you playing at?' said Shepherd. 'Why tell her my name?'

Meyer turned to look at him. 'You've got to kill her now, haven't you? She knows who you are.'

'Marcus, please, stop,' said Lisa. Tears were running down her face and she pushed herself back against the hull.

'Shut up, bitch!' shouted Meyer. 'You're lucky I'm just

throwing you over the side and not letting my friends here cut you up first.'

'Marcus, listen to me,' said Lisa. 'Yes, I'm a cop. You're right. But they know I'm here with you. They know I'm on the boat. If I don't get back, they'll know what happened.'

'Really?' said Meyer. 'And when exactly did you tell them you were on the boat? Because I've been with you all the time and I've been monitoring your phone for weeks.' He waved his hands around. 'Call for help, you bitch. If you've got the cavalry ready to come to your rescue, now's the time to call them.' He looked port and then starboard. 'I don't see anyone, Lucy. Do you?' He glared at her. 'Except your name's not Lucy, is it? How do you want to die, bitch? Do you want to die as Lucy or Lisa?'

'Marcus, please . . .'

Meyer waved at Shepherd. 'Time to do your stuff,' he said.

'Are you serious?'

'You heard her. She's a cop. She knows who you are. If we don't off her, you're facing serious prison time. And the rest. She knows your real name.'

'Because you fucking told her!'

'This is no time to be splitting hairs,' said Meyer. He said something to Lopez in Spanish. Lopez pulled out a gun and pointed it at Shepherd's chest.

Meyer smiled at Shepherd and waved the bottle he was holding. 'I've just told him to shoot you if you don't push her over the side.'

'Yeah, I gathered that,' said Shepherd.

'It's time to step up,' said Meyer. 'You want to work with me, you need to prove yourself. And, don't forget, she was all sweetness and light with you for no other reason than she wanted to put you behind bars with me. She deserves it. No question.'

Shepherd nodded slowly. Lopez was moving backwards, away from Shepherd, putting plenty of space between them. It would take Shepherd two, maybe three, steps to reach the Colombian and he would have all the time in the world to pull the trigger. Alvarez was still standing by the concrete block, leering as if he was enjoying the conflict. Lisa was lying with her back against the hull, sobbing.

'Come on, Jeff. Just one push is all you need. The block will do the hard work.'

Shepherd walked towards Lisa. He stood over her and offered her his hand. 'Fuck off!' she said.

'Don't make this any harder than it has to be,' said Shepherd.

Meyer laughed. 'That's right, bitch,' he said. 'Let's get this over with.'

Shepherd bent down, put his hands under her shoulders and lifted her up. She was a dead weight and he had to hold her against the railing. Alvarez moved away to Shepherd's left and Lopez was now standing close to the port wheel.

'Please don't do this,' said Lisa.

Lopez spoke to Alvarez in Spanish and Alvarez picked up the concrete block.

'Come on, Jeff, time's a-wasting,' said Meyer.

Shepherd put his face close to Lisa's. 'Hold your breath,' he said quietly.

'Fuck you!' she shouted, her eyes blazing with hatred.

He stared at her, trying to show her that he was serious. 'Just do it,' he whispered. 'Hold your breath.'

She opened her mouth to curse at him, but then she closed it. He could see how scared she was.

'Just fucking do it, Jeff, or you can go over the side with her.' Shepherd looked over his shoulder. Meyer was glaring at him, breathing heavily. Lopez gestured with his gun. A large semi-automatic.

'I'll do it,' said Shepherd. 'She's a fucking grass and that's the end of it.' He turned to Lisa. Tears were running down her face now. 'Hold your breath,' he mouthed, then threw her over the side. The chain tied to her ankles rattled across the deck then it went tight against the block. Alvarez threw the block over the side after her.

Shepherd began counting in his head. One thousand and one.

According to the chart, the water was about thirty metres deep where they were. One thousand and two.

Shepherd turned to Lopez. The Colombian was staring wide-eyed at the spot where Lisa had gone into the water. The gun was pointing down at the deck, forgotten in his hand. One thousand and three.

Meyer peered over the side of the cat, his hands gripping the rail. Alvarez was standing next to him. 'Die, you fucking bitch!' shouted Meyer. One thousand and four.

Shepherd stepped back and to the side, then slashed the side of his hand against Lopez's throat. One thousand and five. Lopez staggered back and Shepherd moved quickly, grabbing the gun with his left hand and head-butting him on the nose. He felt the cartilage crack and blood splattered down the Colombian's face. One thousand and six.

Shepherd pulled the gun from the Colombian with his left hand, transferred it to his right and put two rounds in the man's chest. Lopez slumped to his knees, his mouth working soundlessly. One thousand and seven.

Meyer had jumped at the sound of the shots and turned to face Shepherd. He drew back his arm to throw the bottle he was holding. Shepherd shot him in the face. The back of Meyer's head exploded and he fell over the side, the bottle clattering to the deck. One thousand and eight.

Alvarez was raising his hands. Shepherd's mind raced. He

didn't have the time to take prisoners. But he couldn't afford to have Alvarez sailing away while he did what had to be done. One thousand and nine. He swung up the gun and shot Alvarez in the left leg. Alvarez screamed in pain and went down. One thousand and ten.

Shepherd threw the gun over the side and rushed to the diving equipment. He grabbed two sets of weight belts and wrapped them around his left arm. One thousand and eleven. He picked up an air cylinder with a regulator attached. It snagged on the restraining strap and he had to yank it hard to free it. One thousand and twelve.

He carried the tank to the edge of the boat, stepping over Alvarez who was now lying on the deck, bleeding heavily. One thousand and thirteen. He swung his leg over the railing, took a deep breath and jumped into the sea. One thousand and fourteen.

The water was warm and the change in temperature barely registered as he slid into the waves. One thousand and fifteen. The cylinder he was holding had a standard regular set – a main one and secondary spare one on a slightly longer hose. He pushed the main regulator to his mouth and bit down, then used his right hand to turn the knob at the top to allow the air out. At first nothing happened but after the third twist he was able to inhale and he began to breathe. One thousand and sixteen.

The weight belts and the weight of the tank overcame his natural buoyancy and he sank quickly. He looked around, breathing slowly and evenly. The visibility was good, and he had no trouble finding Lisa. She was about twenty feet below him, trying to swim up but held back by the block chained to her feet. One thousand and seventeen.

She was panicking and burning through the oxygen in her lungs and wouldn't last long at the rate she was moving. But at least she'd done as he'd said and was holding her breath: there were no bubbles escaping from her mouth and nose.

He tried kicking towards her but without fins it made barely any difference to his trajectory. One thousand and eighteen. One thousand and nineteen.

She had her back to him so she couldn't see him. She was thrashing around but nothing she did would make any difference, the concrete block was far too heavy.

His feet touched the sea bottom and he push himself towards her. One thousand and twenty. One thousand and twenty-one.

Lisa bent double and tried to pull the chain from her ankle but it was too tight. Bubbles started to trickle from between her lips.

Shepherd kicked harder. She was still some distance away and running out of time. One thousand and twenty-two. One thousand and twenty-three.

Lisa stopped trying to pull the chain off her leg and tried swimming again. She went up until the chain was tight and thrashed around as if she could claw her way to the surface.

Shepherd reached her and grabbed her leg. He pulled her down towards him. One hundred and twenty-four. Initially she continued to struggle but then she suddenly stopped and looked around. Her eyes widened in disbelief when she saw him. She bent at the waist and tried to grab him. He put the second stage regulator to her mouth and she bit it greedily. Her chest heaved as she sucked in the air. He held her by the shoulders and kept his face close to hers as she gradually relaxed. Her breathing became slow and regular, and the panic went from her eyes. He gave her the OK sign and she nodded.

Shepherd pointed at himself, then up at the surface, then mimed cutting, telling her that he had to go back to the boat

to get something to cut the chain. She nodded. He flashed
another OK sign, then untangled the weight belts from his
arm. Almost immediately he started to rise and he let the
regulator slip from between his lips. His natural buoyancy
carried him upwards and he kept his head up and breathed
out as he went, equalising the pressure in his lungs.

It took him only six or seven seconds to break through
the surface. He swam around to the stern and climbed the
steps on the port side. Alvarez had taken off his shirt and
used it as a tourniquet around his injured leg. 'Please help
me,' he said.

'You're on my list,' said Shepherd. He hurried below decks,
looking for a toolbox. He found one and pulled out a pair
of wire-cutters. He hurried back to the deck, grabbed another
weight belt and jumped over the side.

He sank quickly. Lisa had dropped to the sea floor and
was holding the air cylinder, plumes of bubbles trickling out
of the regulator.

Shepherd reached the bottom, then kicked himself towards
her. His chest was burning but he knew he had plenty of air
in his lungs. On a good day he could hold his breath for
close to two minutes, and even when he was exerting himself
he was easily able to go for a full minute. She saw him coming
and held out the primary regulator. He took it, slipped it
between his lips and began to breathe. She was much calmer
now, and gave him an enthusiastic thumbs-up.

He wrapped the weight belt around his waist and fastened
it, then went to work on the chain with the wire-cutters. It
took him several attempts but finally he sliced through one
of the links, close to her ankles. He dropped the wire-cutters,
took off his weight belt, then gave her an OK sign and pointed
to the surface. She nodded and he wrapped his arms around
her and the cylinder as they started to rise to the surface,

She looked into his eyes all the way and he saw a mixture of gratitude and confusion. A few seconds later, they broke through the surface.

They kept their regulators in their mouths as they swam around to the rear of the catamaran and climbed aboard. Lisa fell to her knees. Only then did she spit out her regulator. 'Thank you,' she said. 'Thank you, thank you, thank you.' She sat down and put her head into her hands.

'Are you okay?'

She nodded. Shepherd put the cylinder back in the rack, then helped Lisa to her feet. Lisa's mouth opened in horror when she saw Alvarez lying on the deck, his leg soaked in blood. 'You have to get me to a hospital,' Alvarez slurred.

'You'll be fine,' said Shepherd. He pointed at Lopez, who was on his back, his shirt-front a bloody mess, his eyes wide open and staring lifelessly up at the sky. 'Compared with him, you got off lightly.'

'What happened?' asked Lisa, her voice trembling.

'Don't ask.'

'Where's Marcus?' asked Lisa.

Shepherd jerked his thumb at the sea. 'He went for a swim.'

'I don't understand.' She bit down on her lower lip, like a frightened little girl.

'I had to move pretty quickly to get down to you,' said Shepherd. 'There was no time to play nice.'

'You shot them?'

'I didn't have much choice,' said Shepherd. 'You were running out of time.'

She forced a smile. 'Thank you,' she said. 'You saved my life.'

'As I was the one who pushed you in, it was the least I could do.' He nodded at the hatch leading below decks. 'Can you see if there's anything down there I can wear?' he said. 'I need a change of clothes.'

Lisa hurried over to him and hugged him. 'That's twice you've saved my life,' she said. 'I guess I belong to you now.'

She stood up on tiptoe and tried to kiss him, but he put his hands gently on her shoulders and eased her away. 'Lisa, we need to talk.'

It was almost eleven o'clock and Standing had moved his bike a dozen times when he saw Ali Hussain walk out of the office. He was several hundred yards away, parked close to a pizza-delivery restaurant. It was a good place to set up because there were always bikes parked outside, but the view of the office wasn't great, especially when people came out of the stairway and turned in the opposite direction.

As he watched, Hussain paused at the bottom of the stairs, giving Standing a clear view. It was definitely him. A second man came out, shorter and with a longer beard. Both men were wearing light-coloured *salwar kameez* and skullcaps, and had sandals on their feet. Standing started the engine and put the bike in gear.

Hussain and the man he was with walked to a grey Prius. The other man got into the driving seat and Hussain sat next to him. A few seconds later the Prius pulled away from the kerb and headed west. Standing glanced over his shoulder, checked the road was clear and headed after the Prius. He had the loaded Glock in the pocket of his Belstaff jacket, along with a roll of duct tape and a polythene bag.

Lisa helped Shepherd moor the catamaran to a buoy in the middle of the bay. They had taken Alvarez below deck and laid him on one of the beds. Lisa had fashioned a tourniquet from a length of rope and doused the wound with antiseptic.

He was begging for them to get him to hospital, but Shepherd knew if they did that the local police would be involved and life would become very complicated.

They had wrapped Lopez's body in a piece of tarpaulin and left it behind a sofa in the main cabin.

'I need you to stay below deck with Alvarez,' Shepherd told Lisa.

'What are you going to do?'

'Just do as I say,' he said sharply. 'I'll explain later.'

She opened her mouth to argue but could see from his face how serious he was so she pouted and did as she was told.

As she went below, Shepherd went to the stern, phoned Willoughby-Brown and brought him up to speed. 'So we've got two dead and one injured?' said Willoughby-Brown, when Shepherd had finished.

'I'm afraid so. There wasn't enough time to start cuffing people. Lisa was drowning and I had to get to her.'

'And the drugs are in the boat?'

'I haven't seen them personally but Meyer said they were packed into the hull.'

'How much?'

'He didn't say exactly but I reckon at least a ton. Maybe two.'

'Excellent. But the only live body we have is a Colombian?'

'Yes. The captain. His name's Alvarez. That's what Meyer said, but he might have been lying.'

'And what's the story with Lisa?'

'She's shaken up.'

'How much have you told her?'

'I've left it vague, but she knows that I know she's a cop.'

'You told her?'

'I pretty much had to. So what do we do now? I've got a dead body, a guy with a bullet in his leg, and I've no doubt Meyer's body will turn up eventually.'

'You're not injured?'

'I'm fine.'

'Okay, so how about this? I'll call up the DEA and hand it over to them. They've wanted Oscar Lopez for a long time. They'd have preferred alive to dead but beggars can't be choosers. And they'll want to try to turn this Alvarez. Plus they get to announce a huge drugs bust.'

'And Lisa?'

'She can stay there and help the DEA. I'll get the DEA to tell her that you were working under cover for them and I'll put you on the first plane out. Everybody wins.'

'But she's okay?'

'Okay in what way?'

'Job-wise.'

'She seems to be clean, if that's what you mean.'

'I just don't want her kicked out because of the way things went.'

'You have to admit she's been less than professional.'

'It was a tough job, especially for someone so young. And, in a way, she's responsible for the way it went down. If she hadn't been on the boat and Meyer hadn't wanted to kill her, we'd have had to arrange an arrest. With decent lawyers Meyer might have walked.'

'You're saying she deserves a commendation?'

'I'm saying she had a difficult job to do and she deserves respect for that.'

'I hear you,' said Willoughby-Brown. 'In the meantime, you stay put and I'll get the DEA to attend.'

'I'll be waiting for them.'

'What's the name of the boat?'

'*Plain Sailing*. Registered in the Cayman Islands. We're in the middle of the bay, pretty much. And tell them we'll need an ambulance for the captain.'

'The DEA can handle that. You're not going to be able to get a flight tonight, but we'll book you on tomorrow's. Looks like you get a free night in Paradise.'

'I'd rather be home, Jeremy.'

'With the au pair?'

Shepherd didn't respond, just ended the call.

The Prius was approaching a set of lights on green. The car was still heading west and Standing was a hundred yards behind. He accelerated to get closer but then a siren wailed behind him. He took a quick look in the mirror. A police BMW was overtaking, its lights flashing. He doubted it was him they were after, just plain bad luck. The vehicles ahead of him were pulling to the side.

The lights changed to amber and the Prius accelerated, getting through just as they went red. Standing cursed and pulled over to the side of the road. The police car overtook him, slowed as it went through the red light, then sped off down the road. The Prius had disappeared into the distance. Standing considered going through the red light and giving chase but a second siren kicked in behind him as another police car came speeding down the road. Standing had no choice other than to stay where he was. The second car roared by, sirens wailing and lights flashing.

A few seconds later the traffic lights turned green. Standing twisted the throttle and gave chase but five minutes later, with no sign of the Prius, it was clear that they had turned off somewhere. He headed back to his hotel. There was nothing more he could do tonight.

Two hours after Shepherd had spoken to Willoughby-Brown, a rib with four men on board drew up next to *Plain Sailing*. Lisa was still below deck, keeping an eye on Alvarez. Shepherd went to the stern and held up his arms so that they could see he wasn't a threat. The four men had a military look to them, broad shoulders, square jaws and short haircuts. Two were holding carbines on shoulder straps and aimed their weapons up at Shepherd. He smiled down at them. 'Hi, guys, I'm on your side,' he said. 'Jeff Taylor. Hopefully you're expecting me.'

The man at the front was a few years older than the rest and Shepherd figured he was in charge. Even sitting down it was obvious he was tall, and his forearms bulged at the sleeves of his polo shirt. He motioned for the men with guns to board and they hurried up the steps on the starboard hull. Shepherd kept his hands in the air until they had patted him down. Once they were sure he wasn't armed, the senior agent came on board and introduced himself. 'Mike Craig,' he said. 'I need a quick sit-rep from you and then I'm to get you back to your hotel until one of our head honchos gets here from Bogotá. There's a lot of buzz at the moment, obviously.'

Shepherd ran through what had happened. Craig's eyes widened when he described taking out Meyer and Lopez, then wounding Alvarez.

'You did that single-handed?' asked Craig.

'Yeah. But to be fair there was only the one gun. If everyone had been packing I might not have been so lucky.'

'Former special forces?'

'I've had a chequered past,' said Shepherd.

'So we've got Oscar Lopez down below, this Alvarez with a bullet in his leg, and Marcus Meyer out at sea somewhere?'

Shepherd nodded.

'And a ton of cocaine in the hulls?'

'That's what I was told.'

Craig grinned. 'Sounds like a good day's work.'

'And the credit's all yours,' said Shepherd. 'My boss explained that I have to be kept out of it, right?'

'That's what I was told. And I was told there's an under-cover cop involved?'

Shepherd nodded. 'Lisa Wilson. But she's been using the name Lucy Kemp. She's downstairs watching Alvarez. She can give you a full briefing on Meyer and what he's been up to for the past few months.'

'What is she? Scotland Yard?'

Shepherd shook his head. 'National Crime Agency. It's the British equivalent of the FBI.'

'I think my boss will want to handle her debriefing,' he said. 'He's on his way.' He gestured at the small boat. 'We'll take you back to your hotel now,' he said. 'And thanks again.'

Standing spent the day exercising in his room, and writing fictional entries in his anger diary for Dr Doyle. Although he was making everything up, he was surprised to discover that thinking about even fictional stressful events would make him angry, and working out how he would deal with them was actually helpful. It wasn't something he'd spent much time contemplating before. He knew he had a quick temper and had just accepted it. But as he wrote in the diary he realised that sometimes he was reacting too quickly and inappropriately, and that there were advantages to taking at least a few seconds to consider the repercussions of his actions. He had almost blown his career because of acting without thinking, and if he was going to stay in the SAS he had to change his ways. For the first time he could appreciate that Dr Doyle was helping him on that path.

Shepherd woke up at nine o'clock. He opened the blinds cover-ing the window that overlooked the terrace and discovered a young man with a military haircut sitting outside. He put on a towelling bathrobe and opened the door. 'Have you been there all night?' he asked.

'Yes, sir,' said the man, getting to his feet. He was in his mid-twenties, wearing a lightweight linen jacket over khaki trousers.

'No need for "sir",' said Shepherd. 'Do you mind telling me why?'

'Protection,' said the man.

'Protection from whom?'

'From anyone who might want to do you harm, sir.'

Shepherd could see the bulge under the man's left shoulder, showing that he was carrying a concealed weapon in a holster. 'I'm not under arrest or anything?'

The man laughed. 'Hell, no, sir. I was just told to babysit you until our boss gets here.' He grimaced. 'No offence.'

'No offence?'

'About the babysitting. That came out wrong.'

Shepherd grinned. 'No problem. I'm going to order breakfast. Do you want anything?'

'I'd better not, sir.'

'Coffee?'

The man nodded. 'Yeah, coffee would hit the spot.'

'You might as well have eggs as well,' said Shepherd. 'Babysitting can take it out of you.'

'Thank you, sir.' He waited until Shepherd had closed the door before sitting down again.

Shepherd picked up the phone and requested two full breakfasts, coffee and toast for two, then shaved and showered. He had just finished changing into a clean shirt and jeans when a waiter delivered the order.

Shepherd invited his bodyguard inside to eat but the man insisted on staying on the terrace. Shepherd smiled as he saw him wolf down his meal – he clearly hadn't eaten for a while.

Shepherd had just finished his breakfast when there was a knock at the door. He opened it to find a giant of a man on the terrace, well over six five and with a weight-lifter's build. He had wraparound sunglasses and took them off to reveal piercing blue eyes as he offered his hand, which was the size of a small shovel. 'Cliff Figg,' he said, shaking Shepherd's. He was wearing a large ring with a green stone. 'I run things in Colombia. I just wanted to swing by and thank you.'

Shepherd opened the door wider and Figg had to duck his head as he crossed the threshold. 'I thought you had something else in mind,' said Shepherd, as he closed the door. 'Putting a guard outside my room seemed a bit excessive.'

'That was for your protection,' said Figg. He dropped down onto one of the sofas, which creaked under his weight. 'For all we knew, Lopez might have had men with him and they'd be out for revenge. They can be vicious, the Colombians, and the last thing I'd want is for something to happen to you on my watch.'

'Then thank you for that,' said Shepherd. 'But I'm leaving on a flight this evening so I'll be out of your hair.' He sat down on a teak chair.

'And no one will even know you've been here,' said Figg. 'I sort of feel bad that you won't be getting any of the credit.'

Shepherd shrugged. 'The job's done, that's all that matters. How are things going with Alvarez? Is he talking?'

Figg nodded. 'Can't shut him up. With Lopez dead and the drugs confiscated, he knows he won't last ten minutes without our protection. He'll tell us everything he knows, but he's still a relatively small fish.'

'I'm sorry Lopez isn't able to talk.'

Figg chuckled. 'There's no way he'd have said a word to us. Between you and me, there are no tears being shed for Oscar Lopez. He's killed four of our people in Colombia and we're pretty sure he's been active in Miami. There's a lot of our guys who want to shake you by the hand.'

'Good to know,' said Shepherd.

'Is it right you weren't armed?'

'He had the gun, yeah.'

'You took a gun off Oscar Lopez and shot him with it?' He nodded appreciatively. 'That's quite an achievement.'

'He was distracted.'

Figg leaned over and patted Shepherd's knee. 'You Brits are always so modest,' he said. 'I bet you even apologised before you shot him, didn't you?'

Standing drove the bike back to Kilburn at just before ten o'clock that night. He was fairly sure that Hussain had been driven home in the Prius so, rather than sit outside the minicab office, he parked up just after the traffic lights where he had lost his quarry the previous night. A side-road offered a good view of the junction and he settled down to wait. The loaded Glock was in the pocket of his jacket, along with the roll of duct tape and the plastic bag.

The Virgin flight to London was getting ready to board so Shepherd phoned Katra and told her he was on his way back. 'You're definitely coming home?' she asked apprehensively, as if she feared he might change his mind.

'I hope so,' he said. 'The job here is all done so I'm hoping my boss will give me a few weeks off.'

'If he doesn't, I'll kill him.'

Shepherd laughed. 'I'll tell him that.'

'You're owed a lot of time off, Dan,' she said.

'I know, baby, and we'll have a proper holiday.'

'Where are you now?'

'Still in St Lucia.'

'Is that girl there? The one who sent you the texts?'

'She's with the police at the moment.'

'Has something happened?'

'There's an ongoing investigation here and she's helping with that.'

'And you won't be seeing her again?'

'I swear, baby. That job's done.'

'What about going there for a holiday instead of Florida Keys?'

'St Lucia?'

'Why not?'

'The weather will be better in the Keys. It rains here in the afternoon. And I'll be honest, the food isn't great .But I'll take you wherever you want to go,' he said.

'Love you,' said Katra.

'Love you too, baby.' Shepherd ended the call. He tapped the phone against his head as he watched the passengers queuing to board the plane. Truth be told, he didn't really want to return as a tourist to the island, not after what had happened. There was always the worry that the Colombians would be looking for Jeff Taylor, out for revenge. But if he'd said no, Katra would probably have wondered why he didn't want to take her. Sometimes dealing with family and friends was as difficult as dealing with targets, and while he always tried to tell the truth to his nearest and dearest, it wasn't always the best option. Hopefully he'd be able to persuade her to go to the Florida Keys instead – he'd certainly be more relaxed there, not constantly looking over his shoulder.

His second call was to Willoughby-Brown, but it went

straight to voicemail. 'It's me,' said Shepherd. 'I'm getting on the plane. Due back first thing tomorrow.' He ended the call and switched off his phone, picked up his bag and joined the boarding queue.

It was midnight when Standing saw Ali Hussain. He was in the passenger seat of a Prius but it was a different one from the evening before, and the driver was a young man in a denim shirt. This time the red light caught them, and as the car pulled up Standing was able to get a good view of the passenger. It was definitely Hussain. The lights changed to green and the Prius accelerated away. Standing turned into the main road and followed at a safe distance. The Prius made a right turn after a few hundred yards, then continued for almost a mile before turning left. Standing held back as it was clear they were almost at their destination. He was a good two hundred yards away from the Prius when it stopped outside a white-fronted semi-detached house. Hussain got out, waved goodbye to the driver and went inside.

Standing waited until the Prius had driven away before he parked the bike and walked to the house, keeping his helmet on. Most of the houses in the street had been converted into two flats, and where there had once been a single front door there were now two. The upper floor of the house Hussain had gone into was in darkness and there was a light on in a downstairs room. Standing assumed that he lived on the ground floor. All the curtains were drawn and there didn't seem to be any CCTV or security lights, so he went to the back.

There were glass panels in the kitchen door and he smiled to himself. He looked at his watch. He had plenty of time. The deepest stage of sleep usually occurred after about ninety minutes so that would be the best time to break in. He sat down with his back to the wall and practised slow breathing. He didn't like waiting, but he didn't hate it, either. It was just something that had to be done. The longest he'd ever been on a stakeout was in Syria when he had spent ten days in a hole in the ground with a sniper, on the trail of a jihadist from Birmingham who had left the UK to join ISIS. The jihadist had posted several beheading videos on his YouTube channel, and had personally set fire to a petrol-soaked cage containing three Syrian police officers. Unusually for foreign-born jihadists, he hadn't concealed his identity and had been identified by US drones. The CIA had passed the intel to MI5 and the spooks had handed it to the SAS. It turned out that the ten-day stakeout had been a waste of time – the jihadist was killed in a drone-strike on the other side of the country. That was the problem with intel: sometimes it was just plain wrong.

Standing had a good sense of time passing and he only checked his watch twice. Once at two thirty and again just before three o'clock. He got to his feet and shook his arms and legs to get his circulation moving, then went to the kitchen door. He took off his helmet and placed it on the ground, then pulled the roll of duct tape from his pocket and ripped off pieces, which he stuck to the glass panel closest to the lock. When most of the glass was covered, he hit it with his elbow. There was a dull crack but otherwise the tape had muffled the sound. Carefully he pulled away the tape and bits of glass with his gloved hands and placed them quietly in the rubbish bin at the side of the house.

The key was in the lock on the inside of the door and he reached inside and turned it. He twisted the handle but the door refused to open. He put his hand back inside and groped for a bolt. He found it, slid it back, and this time the door opened.

He picked up his helmet, stepped into the kitchen, shut the door behind him and stood for several minutes, breathing softly and listening. There was a shuddering rattle to his right and he tensed, then realised it was just the fridge. A tap dripped onto a plate, making a dull splattering sound. A dog barked in the distance. When he was sure he hadn't disturbed anyone, he tiptoed across the kitchen, placing his helmet on the counter as he went, and stopped in the hallway. There was an open door to the left leading to a small bathroom. Then another to the left and a third to the right. From the layout he guessed that one opened into a living room, the other into the bedroom. Standing hoped that Hussain lived alone, but if not, he would use the duct tape to take care of anyone else in the flat.

He moved silently down the hall and eased open the door to the right. It was a small living room with a cheap plastic sofa and two matching armchairs. There was a strong smell of cigarettes and an overflowing ashtray on a coffee-table.

That left just one bedroom. So no children, which made things easier, but there could still be a wife. He moved silently across to the door, turned the handle and slowly pushed it open a few inches. He heard snoring, a pig-like snort followed by a long, slow whistle. He listened carefully. Just one snorer. He pushed the door wide, stepped through it and closed it behind him. There was a strong smell of body odour and cigarette smoke.

The curtains were drawn but plenty of light leaked into the room from the streetlamp outside. Hussain was sleeping on his back in the middle of a double bed, a thin quilt over his body. The bed was against the wall, facing the door, so Standing was looking down at him. He found himself matching the man's breathing, slow and even. There was a wardrobe to the left, a dressing-table by the window and, next to it, a brass hookah pipe. Hussain had thrown his clothes over a wooden chair by the bed and placed his skullcap on the headboard.

He was alone so Standing knew he had all the time in the world. He moved silently across the carpet, put his gloved hand over Hussain's face and squeezed. After a few seconds the man's eyes opened. He stiffened, then tried to move, but Standing held him fast with his left hand and showed him the Glock in his right. 'If you make any noise I will shoot you. Blink if you understand.'

Hussain stopped struggling and blinked.

'Good man. Now I'm going to take my hand away from your mouth. If you make any sound, any sound at all, I will shoot you. Blink if you understand.'

Hussain blinked. There was no fear in his cold brown eyes, just hatred.

Standing kept the gun pointed at the man's nose as he slowly took his hand away.

Hussain opened his mouth to speak but Standing wagged a finger at him, telling him to keep quiet. 'You rape children, and then you kill them,' he said quietly. 'You are scum.'

Hussain shook his head. 'Sir, you are mistaken.' His breath was foul and his teeth were yellowing. From the look of them, they had never been cleaned.

'You recognise me?' asked Standing.

Hussain frowned. 'No, sir. Sir, I think you have the wrong person. This is a case of mistaken identity.'

'Look closely, Ali,' said Standing. 'Refresh your memory.'

Hussain shook his head again. But Standing could see from the look in his eyes that his denial was a lie. 'I came to your office. Remember?'

Hussain made a show of pretending to remember, and nodded. 'Ah, yes.'

'I asked for Ali Hussain, and you pretended he wasn't there.'

'Peter? You said your name was Peter?'

Standing smiled. 'See? You do remember. And not long after that, some men tried to warn me off. They said I should get out of town. A coincidence, do you think?'

Hussain's eyes narrowed as he struggled to get the measure of Standing and what it was he wanted.

'Not long after that I was warned off by a couple of heavies, who came at me with guns, Ali.' He waved the Glock in his face. 'This is one of them. Funny old world, huh?'

'What do you want?'

'I want to know why you're allowed to get away with raping and killing kids. Who protects you, Ali? The guys who came after me were whiter than white. So it's not ISIS or al-Qaeda who are watching your back, is it? So who is protecting you, Ali?'

Hussain said nothing.

'Open your mouth, Ali,' said Standing.

Hussain frowned, not understanding.

Standing gripped his face and squeezed, forcing Hussain's teeth apart. Hussain struggled as Standing tried to force the barrel into his mouth. 'Okay, okay!' he said.

'Okay what?' said Standing.

'I'll tell you.'

Standing let go of the man's face. 'Tell me what?'

'I work for MI5.'

'Bullshit.'

'It's true. I am a friend of this country. A good friend.'

Standing shook his head. 'I don't believe you.'

'It's true. Why would I lie about that?'

'Because I'm about to put a bullet in your brain. You'd do anything to save your miserable life.' He went to grip his face again and Hussain flinched.

'It's true, I swear! I work for MI5!'

'You're a spy, are you? Do you think I'm fucking stupid?'

Hussain nodded furiously. 'I work for them. I give them information.'

'Bollocks,' said Standing.

'It's true – may Allah strike me down if I'm lying.'

'Allah isn't the one who's going to be doing the striking,' said Standing. He back-handed Hussain, hard. 'If you work for MI5, who's your contact there?'

Hussain glared at him defiantly. 'His name is George.'

'That's all? Just George? Bollocks.' He raised his gloved hand again.

'That's the only name he gave me. It might not be his real name, I understand that. But I call him George.'

'And where do you meet this George? You pop around to MI5 for tea and cakes, do you?'

'There's a house, near Victoria station. When he wants to see me, I meet him there.'

'You just call him up, do you? You call up and ask for George at MI5 and he just pops around, does he?' He pointed a finger at Hussain's face. 'Maybe you abuse young girls together. Is that it? Is that what happens?'

'I send him a text,' said Hussain.

'You're lying.'

Hussain gestured with his chin. 'My phone's over there. Look for yourself.'

There was a Samsung phone on the bedside table and Standing picked it up. 'What's the password?'

Hussain told him the password and Standing tapped it in.

'Last time I saw him was four days ago,' said Hussain.

Standing checked the messages. There was one four days ago from Hussain to George: *I need a meeting tomorrow 9 a.m.*

And a reply from George: *Confirmed.*

Standing checked the calls log. George hadn't rung Hussain. 'So you never talk to him on the phone?'

'Sometimes.'

'He's happy to arrange a meeting on the basis of a text?'

Hussain frowned, not understanding the question.

'Does he call you? Do you call him?'

'Sometimes he calls me back.'

'And you always meet at the same place? This house in Victoria?'

Hussain nodded.

'Where is it?'

Hussain gave him the address.

Standing put duct tape across Hussain's mouth and tapped out a message for George: *I need a meeting tomorrow 9 a.m.*

He sat down on the end of the bed and waited. Five minutes later the phone rang. It was George. Standing gritted his teeth and let the call ring out. The phone stopped, and a few seconds later there was a beep to let him know a message had arrived. **Is there a problem?**

Standing sent another text. **That man has been near my house. I am staying with a friend. We must meet tomorrow.**

There was no reply, but about thirty seconds later the phone rang. It was George. Standing let it ring out again. It stopped but the caller didn't leave a message.

Standing stared at Hussain. 'Do you want me to shoot you, Ali?'

'Of course not.'

'Then I need you to do exactly as I say. I'm going to call this George back. You are going to say that you want to meet him tomorrow, at nine o'clock. At the house in Victoria. He will want to know what's wrong. You tell him that you saw me outside your house and that you are now staying with a friend. You don't want him to know where you are because you're scared. And tell him you have information for him, something important, but don't say what it is. You want to tell him in person. Do you understand?'

'Yes,' said Hussain.

'This George. Does he speak Urdu or whatever language it is you use?'

'We speak in English.'

'Yeah, well, you better had do. If I hear you say anything in another language I'll put a bullet in your head and I'll be off. If I even think you're tipping him off, you're dead. Understand?'

'I understand.'

'This is your one chance, Ali, and if I were you I'd grab it with both hands. You want a meeting tomorrow morning at the safe house. Nine o'clock. You saw me outside your house. And you have information for him. Understand?'

'Yes.'

'Tell him you couldn't answer the phone because your friend is here.'

Hussain nodded.

'You try to fuck me over and I'll shoot you, I swear.' Standing tapped him on the head with the barrel of the gun. 'Hold out your hands,' he said. Hussain did as he was told. Standing put the gun down on the bed, then bound the man's wrists with duct tape. He pulled him up into a sitting position, then picked up the phone and pressed the button to call George. As soon as the phone was answered, he held the phone close to Hussain's ear.

'My friend is here, I couldn't answer your call,' said Hussain.

Standing leaned closer, putting his ear near to the phone so that he could hear both sides of the conversation.

'Where are you?' asked the man. He sounded white, middle-class, educated. Almost certainly Oxford or Cambridge. Standing had run into more than his share of the type, usually out-of-their-depth officers.

Standing glared at Hussain and waggled the gun.

'With my friend,' said Hussain. 'I am safe here. That man was at my house.'

'Did he talk to you?'

Standing shook his head.

'No, I just saw him. So I left and now I am with my friend.'

'And why the meeting tomorrow?'

'I have information for you.'

'What sort of information?'

'You know what sort,' said Hussain.

'Something is about to happen?'

'Yes.'

There was a short pause before the man spoke again. 'Ali, is everything okay?'

Standing pointed the gun at Hussain's nose and nodded.

'Everything is fine,' said Hussain. 'I have to go now.'

Standing took the phone from him and slipped it into his pocket.

'So you believe me now?' asked Hussain.

Standing nodded. 'Yes.'

'So now you understand,' said Hussain. 'I am an asset.'

'Not to me you're not,' said Standing.

'That's what George always says. He says I am an asset.'

'What does he look like, this George?'

'Older than you. He is fifty, maybe. Shorter than you and fatter. He always smokes small cigars. The same size as cigarettes but they are cigars. So now you believe me? I work for MI5. I help this country.'

'Yes. I believe you.'

'So now you will let me go?' asked Hussain.

Standing shook his head. 'No.'

'You lied!' His eyes flashed with anger.

Standing shrugged carelessly. 'I didn't.'

'You said you wouldn't shoot me.' There were tears in his eyes, now. Tears of frustration.

'I'm not going to shoot you,' said Standing. 'I wouldn't waste a fucking bullet on the likes of you.'

'Why do you hate Muslims so much?'

'This isn't about you being a Muslim. It's about you being a child-rapist. It's about you murdering my sister.'

'Your sister?'

'Lexi Chapman. Your pal Faisal seduced her and passed her around and when she objected you gave her the heroin that killed her.' Hussain's eyes widened. 'Yes, I know everything,' said Standing.

'You killed Faisal?'

'The two of you killed my sister. Now it's payback time.'

'You can't kill me,' said Hussain, his voice trembling. 'I'm an asset. MI5 needs me. This country needs me.'

Standing put down the Glock, ripped off a piece of duct tape and slapped it across the man's mouth. 'I'm fed up with listening to you, to be honest.'

Hussain glared at Standing, his eyes filled with hatred now.

Standing took the plastic bag from his pocket and pulled it over Hussain's head, then used the duct tape to seal it around his neck. When he had finished he pushed Hussain back onto the bed, keeping hold of his bound hands. Hussain began to rock from side to side, but there was nothing he could do and his eyes widened with fear.

'How does it feel?' asked Standing. He put his face close to Hussain's. 'How does it feel, knowing you're going to die? And that the man watching you die hates you with a vengeance?' The duct tape around Hussain's mouth pulsed in and out with his desperate attempts to breathe. 'And the last thing you're going to hear is the name of the girl you killed. Lexi Chapman. You killed her and now I'm killing you.'

Hussain tried to lift his hands to claw at the bag but Standing held them in a vice-like grip. The inside of the bag began to mist with condensation and the pulsing became more frantic. Hussain's whole body shuddered and his head thrashed from side to side for a full thirty seconds. Then the struggles began to subside and eventually he lay still. Standing took off a glove and felt for a pulse under the duct tape around Hussain's neck. There was a faint beating, faint but there. He put his glove back on, wound more tape around the bag and waited another minute. The second time he checked there was no pulse.

He removed the tape from Hussain's wrists and put the gun into the dead man's hand, pressing the fingers against the butt, trigger and barrel, then wiped the butt roughly over the palm and fingers to trap skin cells in the gun's handle grips.

He put the scraps of duct tape in his pocket, along with the gun, took a towel from the bathroom, a black rubbish bag and his helmet from the kitchen, and left the house.

Shepherd walked out into the arrivals area at Gatwick airport, half expecting to find Willoughby-Brown waiting for him. Instead there was a large man with a shaved head in a grey suit, white shirt and a blue tie holding up an iPad with the name 'JEFF TAYLOR' on it. Shepherd frowned, wondering what was going on.

He switched on his phone and saw there was a text message from Willoughby-Brown. Short and to the point. **There will be a car waiting for you.**

Shepherd walked over to the man and nodded at the iPad. 'That's me.'

'The car's outside, sir,' said the driver.

'Where are we going?'

'Victoria.'

The driver had parked a BMW 3-Series in the short-term car park. Shepherd let him go ahead while he phoned Willoughby-Brown. 'I'm here, what's going on?'

'My contact wanted a meeting at short notice and he hasn't turned up.'

'Which contact?'

'Ali Hussain. The Muslim that Standing's after. Hussain phoned me to say that he'd seen Standing near his house and that he'd gone to stay with a friend. He wanted a meeting at the safe house we use. He also says he has intel on a forthcoming terrorist event. So there's a lot at stake.'

'What do you need me for?'

'I need you to organise his protection. Just get here as quickly as you can. I'm getting a bad feeling about this.'

Willoughby-Brown ended the call and Shepherd walked over to the car. The driver already had the engine running.

It was cold and damp, and even though Standing had brought a black rubbish bag and a towel to lie on, he was still chilled to the bone as he lay under the hedge at the back of the garden overlooking the house in Victoria where the man called George believed he was due to meet Ali Hussain at nine a.m.

He didn't have to look at his watch to know the time – it was eight thirty. He had been lying under the hedge for almost five hours. He knew that MI5 would be at the house well in advance, to make sure the premises were secure, so he had gone straight from Hussain's flat, parked his bike near the station and walked to the safe house. It was small, detached, with a tiny garden in front and a larger patch of grass surrounded by hedges at the rear.

Standing set up his observation point under the hedge at the right-hand corner, which gave him a view of the side of the house and the approach to it. He'd placed the towel inside the black bag to provide some insulation against the cold wet earth and had smeared dirt over his face. Then it was just a matter of waiting, and he was good at that. He practised Dr Doyle's deep breathing techniques as the minutes crawled by.

At seven o'clock three men got out of a dark saloon and let themselves into the house as the car drove off. They were wearing overcoats and suits, a far cry from the heavies that had tried to get him into the van. Brains rather than muscle. Lights went on in the rooms as they went through them one by one. Two of the men came out of the back door and stood in the garden. They were talking, giving the area only a cursory look. Standing had his exit strategy prepared if they did a walk-around of the perimeter – all he had to do was roll to the side and he would be in the neighbour's garden. As he watched the two men, lighters flared and he saw the red dots of lit cigarettes. Smokers.

At eight o'clock another car arrived and one man got out. He was in his fifties, wearing a dark overcoat with the collar turned up against the morning chill. He went to the front of the house and rang the bell. Standing heard the front door open and close. He shivered but blotted out the cold. He had long since discovered that if he concentrated on a specific area of his body he could make it warmer by force of will alone. He started with his feet and slowly worked his way up to his chest.

At a quarter to nine a blue BMW 3-Series pulled up in front of the house. A man got out. He didn't seem to be dressed for a cold London morning: he was wearing a light jacket and jeans and carrying a kitbag. Standing smiled to himself as he recognised Dan 'Spider' Shepherd. The Legend.

As Shepherd walked towards the front door of the detached house, a man in a Burberry trenchcoat stepped from the side of the building. Shepherd raised his hands to show that he wasn't armed. 'Shepherd,' he said. 'Willoughby-Brown's expecting me.'

The man was wearing a Bluetooth headset and said something into it, listened and nodded, then waved at Shepherd to approach the door.

There was a brass lion's head knocker and an electric doorbell. Shepherd pressed the bell twice. He heard footsteps and the door opened. It was Willoughby-Brown, wearing a dark overcoat that looked like made-to-measure cashmere. He also had a Bluetooth headset in his right ear. As Shepherd went inside, the guard went back to his position.

'What's going on, Jeremy?' asked Shepherd, as Willoughby-Brown closed the front door behind him. They were in a large hallway, with doors to left and right. At the top of the wooden staircase another man, in a raincoat, was watching them with cold eyes.

'Come through,' said Willoughby-Brown. 'The kettle's on.'

Shepherd followed him down the hallway to a kitchen that appeared to be stuck in the fifties, with old-fashioned units, a Formica-topped table and an electric oven that was spotlessly clean but streaked with rust. The floor was linoleum in a checked pattern that had worn through in places.

The kettle was boiling and there were two chipped mugs, each with a teabag in it. Willoughby-Brown poured in hot water and took a carton of milk from the fridge. He sniffed it warily before adding a splash to both mugs. 'There's sugar if you want it,' he said, pointing at a bag with a spoon sticking out of it.

'What is this place?' asked Shepherd, dropping his kitbag on the floor. 'A safe house?'

Willoughby-Brown nodded. 'Old-school,' he said. 'It was used for debriefings and interrogations right through the fifties and sixties. It's still on the books but very few people know about it. These days, I'm pretty much the only one who uses it.' He swirled the teabags in the mugs, fished them out and dropped them into the sink. He added two spoonfuls of sugar to his, stirred, sipped and grimaced. He nodded at the table. 'Take the weight off your feet.'

'I've been in a plane for getting on nine hours so I'll stand,' said Shepherd. 'Why am I here?'

Willoughby-Brown tapped his Bluetooth. 'Yes, go ahead,' he said, turning his back on Shepherd. He nodded as he listened, said, 'Yes,' a few more times, then ended the call and sat down. Shepherd leaned against the door frame. 'You don't want your tea?' asked Willoughby-Brown.

'I just want to know what's going on,' said Shepherd.

'As I told you on the phone, while you were away Standing went on the rampage. He attacked the MI5 team we sent to bring him in. One of our guys has lost a spleen. Another's knee is broken so badly he's going to need a replacement.'

'They were trying to pick him up, you said. With guns.'

'He'd already assaulted two of my men in Hyde Park so, yes, they were armed.'

'But you can see why that might provoke a response.'

'Are you serious?' spluttered Willoughby-Brown. 'He

attacks a group of your colleagues and you think he might have been provoked?'

Shepherd put up his hands in apology. 'I just wanted to get a feel for what's going on, that's all.'

'What's going on? I'll tell you what's going on. Former Sergeant Standing has gone rogue and he's put the fear of God into Ali Hussain.'

'Ali Hussain? Who's he?'

'He's one of our agents. Standing has been around to see him, which is one of the reasons we're here. Hussain wants our protection and he has intel about a forthcoming terrorist attack.'

'So, two birds with one stone? That's convenient.'

Willoughby-Brown's eyes narrowed. 'What do you mean?'

Shepherd shrugged. 'Nothing. Just commenting. So where is this Ali Hussain?'

Willoughby-Brown looked at his watch. 'He should be here any moment.'

'For a debriefing?'

'That, and protection. Standing was outside his house. Hussain's gone to stay with a friend and is on his way.'

'He spotted Standing? In the street?'

'You sound like you don't believe him.'

Shepherd wrinkled his nose. 'Standing should be good enough at surveillance not to show out,' he said. 'But maybe Hussain was being extra careful. So why didn't he come straight here?'

Willoughby-Brown sighed. 'I don't know. He called last night.'

'Why not just send your people around and pick him up straight away?'

'Because he doesn't want anyone to know that he talks to us, obviously,' said Willoughby-Brown, dismissively. 'If he suddenly gets into a car with two white men in dark suits, people are going to notice. Look, he's one of the best sources we've got. He's the real thing. He's like Father Christmas – he knows who's naughty and who's nice and is happy to share that information with us.'

'Happy? Because you pay him?'

Willoughby-Brown shook his head. 'He's a concerned citizen. He loves this country and despises those who want to create havoc here.'

Willoughby-Brown's phone rang and he tapped his Bluetooth headset. He listened, then cursed under his breath. 'When?' he asked. He screwed up his face as he heard the answer, then ended the call. 'Ali Hussain is dead,' he said. 'Somebody wrapped a plastic bag around his head last night.'

'Where?'

'His flat. He was probably killed not long after he made the call to me.' He stamped his foot, hard. 'That bastard Standing. I'll make sure he rots in jail for this.' His face was flushed and his nostrils flared as he paced up and down the kitchen. 'Fuck, fuck, fuck,' he said. He touched his Bluetooth headset again. 'Tell everyone to stand down. He's not coming. This has all been a waste of time.' He listened for a few seconds. 'Yes, back to the office. I'll have my car pick me up. Debriefing at two o'clock this afternoon. No, wait, make that four. I've got a two o'clock meeting.'

He ended the call and lit one of his small cigars. 'This is so fucked up.' He opened the kitchen door and walked outside.

Shepherd joined him. He nodded at the cigar. 'Health and safety? Can't smoke indoors?'

'It's a place of work,' he said, 'and the cleaners have been known to complain.' He blew smoke at the ground. 'Fuck,' he said. 'Isn't it amazing how quickly things can turn to shit?'

'So you think Standing killed this Hussain?'

Willoughby-Brown sneered at him. 'Of course. What – you think he suddenly decided to kill himself? Standing must have been there when he heard Hussain phone for help. Killed him before he could get to the safe house.'

'Hussain told you he was staying with a friend?'

'That's what he said.'

'How could Standing be at the friend's house?'

Willoughby-Brown's eyes narrowed. 'What are you getting at?'

'I'm just trying to make sense of all this,' Shepherd said. 'You never told me why Standing went after Hussain.'

'Who knows what's going through his head?'

'He hates Muslims, is that it? Killed them out in Syria and now wants to kill them here?' Shepherd watched Willoughby-Brown carefully to see how he would react. They both knew why Standing was after Hussain. But Willoughby-Brown didn't know that Shepherd had spoken to Standing, or that Shepherd knew exactly why Standing was on the rampage – knew and empathised.

Willoughby-Brown stared at his cigar, then took a long drag and blew smoke. He didn't answer the question.

The man who had met Shepherd came around the side of the house and spoke to Willoughby-Brown: 'We're heading off, sir,' he said. 'Are you okay to lock up or do you want me to do it?'

'I'll do it,' said Willoughby-Brown, and the man handed him a set of keys. A short while later they heard car doors open, slam shut and the vehicle drive off.

Willoughby-Brown concentrated on his cigar. 'He's no idea what he's done,' he said eventually. 'Hussain was one of the best sources of intel we had in north London. We're not going to be able to replace him.'

'I doubt that,' said Shepherd. 'There are plenty of Muslims who hate the jihadists as much as we do.'

'Ali Hussain was the gold standard. The best. Standing has no idea of the damage he's done.'

'Maybe he does,' said Shepherd. 'Maybe he just doesn't care.'

'The more you talk about him, the more it sounds to me as if you're on his side.'

'It's not about sides,' said Shepherd. 'But have you tried looking at it from Standing's point of view?'

Willoughby-Brown frowned as if he hadn't understood the question. He took another drag on his cigar.

'You haven't been honest with me from the start, have you, Jeremy?' said Shepherd. 'Did you think I wouldn't find out the real reason why Standing hates Hussain's guts? Why he wanted him dead?'

'Why don't you enlighten me, Daniel?' said Willoughby-Brown, quietly.

Shepherd gritted his teeth, knowing he had already said too much. But he hated the way Willoughby-Brown was trying to manipulate him. Trust was the most important commodity in undercover work and Shepherd no longer trusted Willoughby-Brown. He was fairly sure their relationship was now damaged beyond all repair, so he had nothing to lose by putting all his cards on the table. 'Okay,' he said. 'Maybe I should do just that.'

Standing breathed slowly and evenly as he watched the two men standing near the house. Shepherd wasn't happy about something – his body language alone told Standing that. He had no doubt that the man with the cigar was the one Hussain knew as George. That wouldn't be his real name, of course. MI5 officers never used their real names. But Standing was sure that the man Shepherd was talking to was responsible

for Lexi's death, and for that he would be held to account.
He reached down with his right hand and patted the Glock
in his pocket as if to reassure himself that it was still there.
It would soon be time to make his move.

Shepherd was becoming increasingly frustrated at the way
Willoughby-Brown seemed unwilling – or unable – to admit
he had been wrong in offering protection to Ali Hussain.
'You don't seem to understand why Standing did what he
did,' said Shepherd. 'Or are you just pretending not to understand in some pathetic attempt to justify what you did?'

Willoughby-Brown's face hardened. 'You're getting peril-
ously close to insubordination, Shepherd,' he said.

'Now it's "Shepherd", is it? What happened to "Daniel"?'

'I'd be very careful about what you say from now on,' said
Willoughby-Brown.

'Matt Standing killed the man responsible for the death
of his sister. She was raped and then they gave her a drug
overdose to keep her quiet. Yet you keep making it sound as
if he's on some sort of mindless rampage.'

'He's killed a prime source of intel on terrorist activities.'

'Why would he care about any intel he might or might
not have had? Hussain killed his sister. Don't you get that?'

'He put your colleagues in hospital, don't forget.'

'Because you sent them to bring him in. And they had guns,
remember? You shove a gun in the face of an SAS soldier and
he's going to react in the way he was trained to react.'

'You're not taking his side, surely.' Willoughby-Brown nodded
slowly. 'Or maybe you are. You've clearly spoken to him.'

Shepherd ignored the accusation. 'It was his sister, Jeremy.
They screwed her and then, when she threatened to go to
the cops, they gave her an overdose of heroin to silence her.
How the fuck could you protect a child-killer?'

'To be fair, Daniel, the girl injected the heroin herself. No one put a gun to her head.'

'And now I'm back to "Daniel"?' He shook his head in contempt. 'They gave her pure heroin. They knew she was a kid and wouldn't understand the difference. She injected it like she always did and a few minutes later she was dead. Ali Hussain knew what was going to happen. It was murder, Jeremy. They murdered her.'

'It's a grey area.'

'How's it a grey area? They gave her pure heroin knowing it would kill her. That's not a grey area. That's murder, pure and simple. And it's not the first time they've done it. I'm told it's happened before. Three times at least.'

Willoughby-Brown's eyes flashed. 'Who told you that? It was Standing, wasn't it? You went behind my back and spoke to him, didn't you?'

Shepherd pointed his finger at Willoughby-Brown's face. 'Don't try to put this on me,' he said. 'It isn't about me. It's about what you've done. You've been sheltering a child-abuser who kills his victims. He's killed at least four young girls, girls that he and his friends raped and abused. He should be behind bars, Jeremy. What the fuck are you doing protecting him?'

'You have no idea what you're talking about,' said Willoughby-Brown, avoiding Shepherd's angry stare.

'Really? Educate me.'

Willoughby-Brown blew smoke up at the overcast sky. 'Those terrorists you killed last month. How many lives did that save?'

'Who the fuck knows? It's hypothetical. But the death of Alexia Chapman is real. It happened. A young girl died. And before she died she was abused by God knows how many men. And you're protecting the guy who did it.'

'That day you and your team took down twenty-two jihadists and killed eight of them. You stopped a plot to kill God knows how many civilians with automatic weapons, and they were plotting explosions, too. You don't want to put a number on that, but I will. Hundreds would have died, Daniel. You saved hundreds of lives that day. Hundreds of men, women and children are alive today because of what you did.'

Shepherd frowned. 'So? What the fuck does that have to do with Alexia Chapman?' But as soon as the words left his mouth, he knew the answer to his own question. 'The intel came from Hussain?' he said.

'Exactly.'

Shepherd shook his head. 'No,' he said.

'Yes,' said Willoughby-Brown. 'He has been our source for the best part of three years. The intel he has given us has neutralised seven terrorist plots and resulted in us taking dozens of dangerous jihadists off the streets.'

'I don't believe this,' said Shepherd. 'You gave this guy a pass to abuse and kill young girls because he was grassing up his friends?'

'Not his friends. He hates fundamentalism as much as we do. He's on our side.'

'He's a fucking child-killer!' shouted Shepherd. 'What the fuck is wrong with you?'

'You're not looking at the big picture, Daniel. And I understand that. You're a foot-soldier in this war. I'm a general. We have different views of the battlefield.'

'You're saying the end justifies the means. That's what you're saying.'

'I'm saying that Hussain has given us rock-solid intel that has resulted in the neutralising of dozens of terrorists.'

'And murdered four girls. That we know about. Jeremy,

for all we know he might have done this dozens of times. How could you not prosecute him for what he did?'

'We needed his intel. Look, you're angry. I can see that.'

Shepherd sighed, but the noise turned into a low growl. 'You have no idea how angry I am.'

'And I understand that. Do you think I'm happy about what's happened? Of course I'm not. But I can see the bigger picture. If Hussain had been arrested two months ago and thrown into prison, those people you saved would be dead now.'

'You pulled the cops off, didn't you?'

'Not personally, no.'

'I know you weren't the messenger, but you sent people to warn them off. You killed the investigation.'

'And I told Hussain it had to stop.'

'And he ignored you, didn't he? He carried on abusing.'

'He promised me it wouldn't happen again.'

'Well, he lied to you.'

Willoughby-Brown sighed. 'It's all immaterial now, isn't it?'

'Yeah, he won't be doing it again, that's for sure. But that's no thanks to you. If Standing hadn't killed Hussain, he'd still be out there grooming and killing, under your protection. You gave him a Get Out of Jail Free card, and shame on you for that.'

'It's all about the greater good,' said Willoughby-Brown. 'Do you know how difficult it is to get good, reliable intel from the Muslim community? We can't send people in because they're too easily spotted. They have to be home-grown and, believe me, they're few and far between. You know as well as I do how many jihadists have come out of north-west London. Mohammed Emwazi, a.k.a. Jihadi John, lived in Maida Vale. The other three jihadists in the Beatles were all from Shepherd's Bush and White City. Those suicide bombers in

Tel Aviv? Asif Hanif was from Hounslow and Omar Khan Sharif had been a student at King's College. Half of all Islamic terrorism offences and attacks on UK soil over the last decade have been carried out by jihadists living in London. We need to keep a lid on the jihadists coming out of the London mosques, so the few assets we have, we have to protect.'

'Even when they kill children?'

'There's no proof that Hussain has killed anyone,' he said. 'The abuse, well, that's cultural. Where he's from, girls get married at twelve.'

'There's nothing cultural about giving drugs to underage girls and raping them,' said Shepherd. 'That's criminal. And you let him get away with murder, Jeremy. Shame on you for that.'

'I heard you the first time,' said Willoughby-Brown. 'Look, we're going around in circles. What's done is done.'

Shepherd opened his mouth to tell Willoughby-Brown what he thought of him, but knew there was no point. 'I'm going home,' he said.

'Probably best. Do you want me to arrange a car?' He flicked ash onto the grass.

Shepherd ignored the question and walked away. There was so much more he wanted to say, and part of him would happily have beaten Willoughby-Brown to a pulp. But he was already unsure whether or not he still had a job with MI5. If he assaulted his boss, his career would end there and then. Though that ship might already have sailed. He could feel the adrenalin coursing through his system but he forced himself to relax. He let himself into the kitchen, picked up his bag and went out of the front door. As he left, he pulled out his phone to order an Uber taxi.

Standing saw Shepherd walk into the house. The MI5 man stood smoking his cigar, then put his hand to his Bluetooth headset and began speaking. He turned so that his back was to Standing so he took the opportunity to crawl out from his hiding place. As he moved across the dew-spotted grass he pulled the Glock from his pocket. He walked quickly, his training shoes making almost no sound on the grass. He was breathing slowly and evenly, and felt totally calm, despite the enormity of what he was about to do.

The man flicked the last of his cigar away and it sparked through the air before landing on the lawn. He touched the Bluetooth headset to end his call, then turned to walk to the back door. He froze when he saw Standing coming towards him and instinctively put his hands in the air. Standing pointed the gun at his face and reached out with his left hand. The man flinched, expecting a blow, but Standing ripped the Bluetooth from his ear and threw it away.

The man regained his composure somewhat when he realised Standing wasn't going to hit him. 'You're Matt Standing?' He glared at him. 'Of course you are. Who else would you be?'

'And who the fuck are you?' asked Standing. 'I'm sure you're not really called George.'

'Jeremy Willoughby-Brown.'

'That's your real name?'

'Does it matter?'

Standing ignored the question. 'You're with G-Branch?'

Willoughby-Brown nodded. G-Branch was the MI5 department responsible for international terrorism and counter-espionage.

'And you thought Ali Hussain was an asset, did you?'

'He was. But now he's dead. Thanks to you.'

'News travels fast.'

Willoughby-Brown shrugged. 'We checked his flat, obviously.' He nodded at the gun. 'And now you're here to kill me?'

'My sister died,' said Standing. 'And you were protecting the men who killed her.'

'You pull that trigger and you'll bring a world of hurt down on yourself,' said Willoughby-Brown. 'You know that. Your life will be over.'

Standing kept the gun pointed at Willoughby-Brown's face. His finger tightened on the trigger as he considered his options. He wanted the man dead, more than anything. And the man deserved to die, no question. Because of him, Lexi had died. And other girls had died, too. All those deaths could be laid at the feet of Jeremy Willoughby-Brown, yet there was no way he would ever be punished by the system. So far as MI5 was concerned – and the government along with it – the end justified the means. Lexi and the other girls were collateral damage in the fight against terrorism.

'You kill me and you'll be hunted down. There'll be no hiding place for you,' said Willoughby-Brown, quietly.

'No one knows I'm here,' said Standing. 'I'll have an alibi. And there are no witnesses.' He shook the Glock. 'Hussain's prints and DNA are all over this gun. Your killing will go down as a jihadist hit.'

Willoughby-Brown's face tightened and he glared at Standing. 'Just get on with it, then.'

'I've got to count to ten first,' he said.

'You what?'

'I've got a therapist. She's helping me with my anger-management issues. She says if I'm angry I should count to ten.'

'Are you serious?'

'She knows what she's doing.' He lowered the gun slightly so that it was pointing at Willoughby-Brown's chest. He was a crack shot, but the bigger the target the better. 'One. Two. Three. Four.'

'You're taking the piss,' said Willoughby-Brown.

'Five. Six. Seven.'

'You're not going to shoot me. If you were you'd have done it already.'

'Eight. Nine. Ten.' Standing pulled the trigger twice in quick succession, a perfect double tap. Both rounds hit Willoughby-Brown in the heart and he slumped to the ground without a sound. Standing stood looking down at the dead man for several seconds. There was no doubt he felt better. He had no regrets. None at all. He dropped the gun on the grass next to the body and walked away. That was when he saw Spider Shepherd running towards him.

Shepherd's phone was telling him that his Uber driver was still five minutes away when he heard the two shots from the back garden. He knew immediately what had happened. He dropped his bag and ran at full pelt down the driveway and around the side of the house, just in time to see Standing toss a gun onto the grass. Willoughby-Brown was lying on his back, arms splayed.

Shepherd waited for Standing to walk up to him. Standing stopped about six feet away, his arms at his sides. 'You're leaving the gun?' asked Shepherd.

'It's got Hussain's prints on it.'

'That's your plan? The cops aren't going to buy that, not with Hussain already dead.'

'You'd be surprised,' said Standing. 'MI5 terrorist-fighter gets shot by jihadist. Jihadist commits suicide. This way the public gets a hero and a villain. It's a win-win situation. No one has to know that Willoughby-Brown was a facilitator of child abuse and murder. Hussain is shown to be an ISIS supporter who got what was coming to him. No one's going to ask why he put a plastic bag over his head. They'll just be glad there's one less terrorist around.'

'Except Hussain wasn't with ISIS. He was working with Five. He helped stop terrorist acts.'

'He raped my sister. And he killed her.'

Shepherd nodded. 'I know, Matt. And I'm sorry about that.'

'You've got kids?'

'A boy. He's in the army.'

'Chip off the old block?' Standing tilted his head to one side as he looked at Shepherd. 'And how would you feel if someone raped and killed your boy?'

'You know how I'd feel,' said Shepherd, flatly.

'And what would you do?'

'You know what I'd do. But that's hypothetical.'

'Really? Can you stand there and tell me you've never done something illegal because you knew it was the right thing to do?'

'This isn't about me, Matt.'

'Well, it sort of is because you're standing there as if you've got something in mind. What do you want, Spider? To take me in?'

'How many people have you killed, Matt?'

'In London? Or out in the Middle East? A lot, if that's what you're asking.'

'But we aren't at war with the men in London.'

'You might not be but I am. Yes, I killed Hussain. The bastard had it coming. Faisal Khan fell off the building, though I don't expect anyone will believe that. And, yes, I shot Willoughby-Brown and, given the same circumstances, I'd do it again. But no matter how many have died, it doesn't come close to making up for the death of my sister. Nothing I do is ever going to bring Lexi back, I know that. But that's not why I did it.' He held up his hands, ready to fight. 'Think you can take me, Spider?'

Shepherd smiled. 'Maybe.'

'You're a legend, I know, but you're fifteen years older than I am and you're not combat-ready. I am.'

'So we fight, is that it? Man to man?'

'If you try to stop me, yes. We'll fight, I'll win and I'll leave.'

'And then what? You spend the rest of your life on the run?'

Standing shook his head. 'I won't run. I'll go back to the Regiment, see if they'll have me. You can go to the cops and make your allegations.' He grinned. 'But I wonder how keen MI5 will be to have their dirty linen washed in public? Look at how Willoughby-Brown bent over backwards to keep the cops away from Hussain, a child-rapist and murderer. What did I do? I killed the men responsible for murdering a kid. Four kids. And one of those men was a high-ranking MI5 officer.' He shrugged. 'I reckon Five will be keen to have this swept under the carpet. I reckon they'd prefer that Willoughby-Brown died a hero. What do you think?'

Shepherd took a deep breath and exhaled slowly. Standing was right on many levels. Shepherd had taken revenge several times. And he had broken the law, for what he had seen as the greater good. Willoughby-Brown had been in the wrong protecting Hussain, though Shepherd understood the man's logic in doing so. And, yes, if anyone ever harmed Liam, Shepherd would lash out instinctively. That was what fathers did. They protected their kids.

'Spider? I'm waiting.'

'I'm sorry about your loss, Matt.' said Shepherd, quietly. 'More sorry than I can say.' He turned and walked away.

Two weeks later

'I have to say, Standing, you've really pulled yourself together,' said Colonel Davies, flicking through the report. 'The therapist in London says you did a magnificent job in overcoming your anger-management issues. And the Regiment's doctor says you're fit for active duty, both mentally and physically.' He tossed the file onto his desk and beamed up at him. 'Well done.'

'Thank you, sir.' Standing was at attention, staring at a spot on the wall behind the colonel's head.

'I have to say that the last time you were here I did have my doubts. But you've proved me wrong and I hope you'll continue to do so.'

'I'll do my best, sir.'

'You're an asset to the Regiment, Standing. A real asset. We need more men like you. I regard this as a new start. A brand new start. Keep your nose clean and we'll have your stripes back in a year or so.'

'Yes, sir.'

'And no more lapses. You keep that anger under control and you'll go far.' He looked at his watch. 'Right, get your gear together. We've got a troop heading out to Syria and you're going with them.'

'I'm looking forward to being back in action, sir,' said Standing,

'I bet you are,' said the colonel. 'Civilian life is all well and good, but it can be boring at the best of times.'

Standing tried not to smile as he turned on his heel and walked out of the room.